Charles Edwards Lester

The light and dark of the rebellion

Charles Edwards Lester

The light and dark of the rebellion

ISBN/EAN: 9783337207854

Printed in Europe, USA, Canada, Australia, Japan

Cover: Foto ©Andreas Hilbeck / pixelio.de

More available books at **www.hansebooks.com**

THE

LIGHT AND DARK

OF THE

REBELLION.

Forsan et hæc olim meminisse juvabit.—VIR.

PHILADELPHIA:

GEORGE W. CHILDS, 628 & 630 CHESTNUT ST.

1863.

STEREOTYPED BY L. JOHNSON & CO.
PHILADELPHIA.
PRINTED BY DEACON & PETERSON.

"IN giving the resolutions that earnest consideration which you request of me, I cannot overlook the fact that the meeting speak as 'Democrats.' Nor can I. with full respect for their known intelligence and the fairly presumed deliberation with which they prepared their resolutions, be permitted to suppose that this occurred by accident, or in any way other than that they preferred to designate themselves 'Democrats' rather than 'American citizens.' In this time of national peril I would have preferred to meet you upon a level one step higher than any party platform; because I am sure that from such more elevated position we could do better battle for the country we all love than we possibly can from those lower ones where, from the force of habit, the prejudices of the past, and selfish hopes of the future, we are sure to expend much of our ingenuity and strength in finding fault with and aiming blows at each other."— *Extract from President* LINCOLN's *letter to Hon.* ERASTUS CORNING *and others,* June 12, 1863.

CONTENTS.

Light and Dark of the Rebellion.

I

What Kind of a War This is.

THE first shot into Fort Sumter was the signal-gun of the greatest and the strangest war ever waged on earth.

That shot was thrown to the feet of Liberty *in defiance.* It was intended to inaugurate a life-or-death-struggle between Slavery and Freedom. It did its work; and the cannon which threw it will live longer in history than the torch of the wretch who burned the Ephesian Temple.

Again, and on a higher stage, the struggle was to come, to test the vital forces of Civilization and Barbarism,—of Progress and Retrogression,—of Order and Anarchy,—of Life or Death, for men and communities, for society and governments. Above all was it a final grapple between the Past whose dead had buried its own dead, and the Future which was to give life to all.

Something *like* this had been witnessed during the many thousand years of deadly strife the human race had been going through, in approaching Liberty as the road to God,— the shrine where all nations are yet to worship.

The records of human defeats, sufferings, and triumphs, show little more than the heroism of the true and the good in resisting the false and the bad.

7

It seems to be the will of Heaven that nations must work out their own salvation *as nations*. The final Court of Appeals, to which even the uneducated conscience points its indexing finger, will judge the individual, not the community.

When nations pass away, they never return. We survey their wrecks stranded on the shore of time, merely to read some commentaries on their history,—their rise and development, their decline and fall. But civilization, which means progression towards the just, the great, the safe and sublime, was the law God instituted for society.

Great thoughts never die. They go among the eternal archives of human hope and security, to which the treasures of successive ages are committed.

In the literature and arts of the ancients, we have most of the finest thoughts of the finest minds,—the chief records of the noblest deeds of the noblest men. And thus the torch of light is safely transmitted from age to age.

All its effulgence was shed over us from the hour our country was born. We have inherited all the earth could give us, with the fairest and broadest field for its use and development. The Creator had looked on us benignantly, as our fathers sailed for a new home beyond the sea, to find a resting-place for earth's children.

Thus high did Heaven seem to fix its purpose on North America,—thus high did our founders comprehend the fact.

Our history had been more wonderful than the dreams of Oriental fancy. All the images of wealth, prosperity, and power that had ever thrilled the brain-pulses of the most ideal disciple of Plato, vanished into thin air before the form of Young American Liberty, rising from this fresh continent, proclaiming to the race freedom, order, and happiness for all. No such treasure had before been committed to men. When he spread this festival, he asked all nations to come. Hardly a day went by, but some winged messenger came from the Old World, freighted with hearts that were weary, seeking a new roof-tree,—with muscles that were over-strained by the unpaid toil of Europe; but all ready to carry out the dreams of personal, manly, ennobling social life.

The best minds and the warmest hearts on the other side of the water understood America. They knew our history, and they burned with enthusiasm to mix their fortunes up with our earlier settlers.

They did; and even this tide of national disaster has hardly arrested their coming. They are arriving still, and they will yet find fertile soil and free institutions for their free possession, till at last all Europe and Asia will together rejoice in the triumph of the thoughts and desires of all the brave and humane men who constructed our system of civic life.

And thus we went on till 1860, pressing our free course to wealth without limit, to prosperity beyond our own comprehension, and to happiness so complete that we forgot the source of it all,—when we made the dreadful discovery, for the first time, that our career was arrested, for a while, if not forever. We were not going too *fast*; we were only on the wrong road. We were rushing madly from the sphere where our Maker had placed us, and he laid his great hand on his own work, when suddenly thirty millions of people, under one government, stood paralyzed on the brink of ruin.

We had allowed Slavery to become the law of the land. We had dethroned the Liberty we had boasted of, and enthroned the Dagon of Human Servitude in its place. We had prostituted to the basest purpose the great gift bestowed on us so lavishly; and in the merciless greed for gain, when we already had a thousand times more than we could use, we ran riot into every form of luxury and licentiousness which could tempt the appetite, exalt the pride, or inflame the ambition of our people.

Religion, with all its sublime traditions, and all its holy beckonings to the better life we could lead, had lost much of its

magic power over the great masses,—over the young and the
old, except the few who were mercifully removed from the
great whirlpool of the heated life we were living; the rest all
clutched like birds of prey for the nearest carrion; and we
jumped the life to come.

In the midst of our National Belshazzar-Feast, of pride,
voluptuousness, and enchantment, the shot at Fort Sumter fell
like a bolt of lightning. It struck the hearts of the revellers,
and we began to take our eyes from the dust and turn them
up to heaven.

By one wave of that wand which never waves twice to do
its work, the handwriting was written on all the walls, and the
Palace of our greatness was sinking to ashes. The Republic
was at stake. We had played, and we had lost.

We had attempted an impossibility. *We had tried to make
Liberty and Slavery live together in the same soil.*

While the free North was prospering, we had allowed the
enslaved to be immolated. While we could flourish under
the fragrant branches of Liberty's tree, we were manuring
the roots of the Upas, whose branches were spreading over
our Northern communities, our homes, our hearts. Its
subtle and deadly poison had already struck through the
veins and arteries, and approached the springs of life.

For a moment we were like a traveller arrested in the speed
of his journey, with a fevered pulse and difficult breathing.
The discovery did not come all at once; nor is it certain that
the nation has yet felt it deeply enough to be ready to recover. To Europe it looked like the beginning of our national end,—an irrevocable leap to ruin.

Was it death? or was it fever with delirium?

It was all!

The only question now, after two years of struggle, which
blot out all the puny strifes of other empires, is, whether
there is *a resurrection and a redeemed life for the great Republic of the world.*

II.

The Real Heroes of the War--The Rank and File in the Hospital.

FIVE days after the first Bull Run battle, I went through the improvised military hospitals of Washington. Since those dark days of terror and blood, I have not left the District of Columbia, except for one day.

During these twenty-two months, I have seen, I suppose, not less than forty thousand of our wounded, sick, and disabled soldiers,—at one time hardly less than five thousand being here from my own State (New York). Very few days have gone by in which I have not seen some of their sick or wounded "companions in arms" from nearly all the other loyal States.

But my object is by no means to depict, even if my pen could do it, any very considerable number of scenes of agony, terror, or death. *I shall not write a book of horrors;* one rather of cheerfulness, heroism, and hope. There is light even in a Military Hospital. I have wished to "let that light out," and have it illumine a million of hearts and homes, far away from the halls and chambers that have been consecrated by a sublimity of patriotism, affection, love of home, and unfaltering endurance. One ray of such sunshine is worth more to the bereaved than a whole tale of tragedy, or a night of gloom.

As I could not expand the space allotted to this volume, my difficulty has been in knowing rather what I could best leave out than best put in. I have known some cases I would have gladly introduced, each of which would more than fill a book like this. But I have endeavored to choose, from the wilderness of material, such scenes as would best illustrate the different phases of American character in the field and the hospital. In following this plan, I have preferred to take things somewhat at random; and, in sacrificing order in time and appropriateness of connection, I may have better succeeded (I trust) in bringing scenes more vividly to the mind of my reader.

Every case spoken of in this work I either witnessed my-self, or I derived the facts from sources which stamp them with entire authenticity.

The great Prince Eugene once said, "Anybody can be brave in battle under a good leader; but he alone is the real hero who can be brave when the battle is over."

The decisive conflicts of armies may be, and generally are, short; but their results last forever.

Those who lead embattled hosts and come home unscarred from the fields where whole battalions melted into the earth, and *corps d'armées* parted never to form in battle-line again, are crowned with the wreath which Victory loves to throw over the brows of its chieftains. Their names embellish the stately pages of history. Their examples live in the dreams of all young soldiers the nights before they leave home for their first campaigns. Monuments rise with their sculptured emblems, "to greet the sun in his coming." The sword or battle-axe they drew, or swung, was in the cause of home, country, and heroism. These monuments become Meccas of human devotion; and to them the men of after-times go, as to sacred shrines, to pay their tributes of admiration and gratitude. But, while these proud names make their undis-puted way down through the centuries, the great "rank and file," who won the field by their imperturbable coolness, the iron nerve that held steady when all was at stake,—hacked, hewn, battered, but immovable,—trusting in their leader,—

and at last slain,—these are forgotten. They are swept beyond the annals of history and the recollections of men.

Where are the innumerable hosts that followed the ensigns of the conquerors who founded the empires and dynasties of antiquity? Who has written their record? What monuments have preserved their deeds?

We know little on these subjects.

The Roman soldier, who left his wife on the banks of the Tiber, to carry the eagles of Italy to distant lands, was sure that his family would not be forgotten if he fell. If he lived, some part of the soil he helped to conquer became his own farm; and there, as a Roman military colonist, he remained as one of the pioneers of civilization, and a defender of "the Eternal Empire."

By modern nations it is now considered the duty of government to extend to the disabled soldier all its paternal aid. It is, however, only of recent date that the system of sanitary hospitals has been established, by which all the appliances of modern art should be brought into use to restore the health of the sick, bind up their wounds, and give back once more the shattered veteran to his home and his country.

England and France had been foremost in taking this grand step, to soften the asperities of war by the skill and humanity of science; and especially in the Crimea did the results place the whole world under obligation. With all the advantages of their experiments and demonstrations, our country was enabled to advance the sanitary military system by still further strides. In another portion of this volume I shall find space for some facts and illustrations on the matter, which I think legitimately appertain to the object I have in view.

2

III.

The Work of the Pen in this War.

A THOUSAND books will be written about this Rebellion. Let them all come: the world will need them. Let every scene worth remembering be recorded by each looker-on. Let each man tell how the battle which he saw raged,—how his comrades fought and fell,—how each battalion answered to the order, *Charge!*—how each regiment closed in solid column, and each division formed its last line of defence or attack. Let no well-authenticated fact be lost. For we must not forget—least of all should the men who hold the pen—that, while we are straining our vision with these strange sights, we become the sacred depositaries of materials from which the artists of a later age will mature their sublime and finished pictures.

But, fully as the incidents of the war have photographed themselves through the press, countless facts and scenes worthy of record may never get their place in history. We have been making history faster than all the pens could write it.

This conflict has had to pass in review before the honest face of the Daguerrean lens : thus it has, in a certain sense, been compelled to write its own annals. But what would otherwise, at best, be only a lifeless and meaningless mass of material, has with the magic touch of the pen been instantly made instinct with life and radiant with significance. The empire of the pen can never be broken. The long line of its masters shows no interregnum. In leaping some chasm in the Dark Ages, we find the light of one great author flashing from one side of the gulf, and the light of an earlier writer streaming in to meet it. We who are humbler members of the great Republic of Letters must look for no exemption from the great law: the lesser must yield to the greater. The working million cannot hope to be remembered as units. They toil, and think, and fight, and write, *as armies*. They weep and exult, they forge and produce; but they can have no place in far-off history. They march through the desert; but they must leave the glory of eternal remembrance to Moses, who leads them through.

Authors form no exception. There are only a few books of much value long after they are written. A thousand historians wrote about the Decline and Fall of the Roman Empire, during fourteen centuries, till Gibbon constructed from the bewildering mass his imperishable work. Away into oblivion that host of authors floated,—beyond the reach of all but the learned and the curious. But their labors were not lost. It was a long stretch of Time's river in its sluggish passages. But it bore on its bosom the slowly accumulating records of the centuries, and they poured their treasures into Gibbon's hands. He saved them forever.

IV.

Heroism in the Hospital.

* * * * THE surgeon said, "He can hardly live."

He laid the hand down softly, and left *this* patient, to pass through the ward.

It seemed to say that all that earth could do had been done, to save the life of the gallant young soldier. I followed the surgeon a few steps on the routine of duty. We stopped, and looked each other in the face. He knew I wanted to know the whole truth.

"Must this boy die?"

"There is a shadow of a chance. I will come again after midnight."

I went back, with a heavy heart, to the cot we had left, and, knowing something of hospitals and dying men, I sat down to wait and see what new symptoms would occur, with the full directions of the surgeon in any event.

The opiate, or whatever it may have been, which I had last administered, could not take effect at once; and, somewhat worn out with the day's labors, I sat down to think. To sleep, was out of the question; for I had become so deeply interested in this young man it seemed to me I could not give him up.

   *   *   *   *   *   *

It was nearly midnight. The gas had been turned off just enough to leave the light needed, and twilight was grateful to the sick-room; for in this vast chamber there were more than two hundred sick men. Now and then came a suppressed moan from one couch, or a low plaint of hopeless pain,—while at intervals thrilled from the high ceiling the shrill scream of agony. But all the while the full harvest-moon was pouring in all the lustrous sympathy and effulgence it could give, as it streamed over the marble pile called the Patent Office, the unfinished north wing of which had been dedicated to this house of suffering.

Almost noiselessly, the doors of this ward opened every few moments, for the gentle tread of the night nurses, who came, in their sleepless vigils, to see if in these hours they could render some service still to the stricken, the fallen, and yet *not* comfortless.

Leaving my young friend for a few moments, I walked through the north aisle; and it seemed to me—so perfect was the *régime* of the hospital, so grand were its architectural proportions—more like walking through some European cathedral by moonlight, than through a place for sick soldiers. The silence greater than speech, the suffering unexpressed, the heroism which did not utter one complaint, the complete-ness of the whole system of care and curative process, made one of those sights and scenes which I would not tear away from my memory if I could; for they have mingled themselves with associations that will link each month and year of time · to come with all the months and years gone before them.

*　　　*　　　*　　　*　　　*　　　*

I felt a strange interest in this young man, whom I had left in what I supposed was his last quiet slumber; and yet I knew he would wake once more before he died. I approached his cot again. He was still sleeping, and so tranquilly I felt a little alarmed lest he might never wake, till I touched his ⸱ pulse and found it still softly beating.

I let him sleep, and thought I would sit by his side till the surgeon came.—

I took a long, free breath, for I supposed it was all hope-lessly over. Then I thought of his strange history:—I knew it well.

He was born not far from Trenton Falls,—the youngest
son, among several brothers, of one of the brave tillers of that
hard soil.　He had seen his family grow up nobly and stur-
dily, under the discipline of a good religion and good government, and with a determination to defend both.　When his
country's troubles began, his first impulses thus found expression to his brothers:—"Let *me* go; for you are all married;
and if I fall, no matter."

He went.　He had followed the standard of the Republic
into every battle-field where the struggle carried him, till,
worn out, but not wounded, he was borne to this hospital in
Washington, a sick boy.　He seemed to have a charmed life,
for on several occasions his comrades had been shot dead or
wounded on either side; and when his last cartridge had done
execution, he carried off two of his wounded companions
from the field, bearing them and their muskets to the rear,—
if there were a rear in the flight from the Bull Run of July,
'61,—and nourished and watched and stood by these comrades
till they died, and then got the help of a farmer to carry them
with his cart, a whole day afterward, to be buried in a place
which he chose.

This boy's example had inspired that farmer with such
benevolence—if he were not inspired by patriotism already—
that he made honored graves for them; and the writer of this
work *knows* where their ashes rest.

When this was all over, the boy came back, as a kind of
rear-guard, of one, in the flight of the army of the Potomac,
and, having reached the city of Washington and reported
himself to his commander, fell senseless on Pennsylvania
Avenue.　He was taken to a neighboring house and well cared
for; and I saw him in the hospital of which I have spoken.

But this was only his life as a soldier.　There was another
and a deeper life than that.　The great loadstone that led him
away was the magnet of his nation.　Another loadstone held
his heart at home: it was the magnet of Love.

His wild and wayward history,—wild only with adventure and wayward only with romance, he seemed to me, as I looked upon his face, so calm, and chiselled into sculptured beauty, I thought, either he looked like an Apollino with his unstrung bow, or a nautilus, cast on the turbulent ocean, to be wafted to some unknown clime, or sink forever, on the floor of the deep sea, to find a coral sepulchre.

His dark eyelashes—bent up in such clear relief against their white ground—slowly and calmly began to *move*.

I sprang to my feet; for it seemed to me there was a chance yet.

The surgeon was long in coming; and yet I knew he would come. He *did*. His sharp and experienced eye, as he approached the cot, opened with surprise. Touching my shoulder, he said, with surprise,—

"He is still alive."

In an instant, taking the hand of the dying or dead boy,—I scarcely knew which,—a faint smile passed over the surgeon's face.

"I am not sure but he may come up yet. If he revives, there is one chance left for him, if it be but one in a thousand. But I will work for that chance, and see what it will come to. 'Here Art triumphs, if it triumphs at all.'"

The pulse seemed to be coming as he took the hand.

"It acts strangely; but I have seen two or three cases very much like it. Mind you, I do not think we can do much with this case; but you stay and watch, and I will come back in half an hour."

So, while he went through some other wards, I watched the patient. The last glimmer of life, which had given some light as this scene was being enacted, faded into what seemed to me the calmest repose of death.

But then, I thought, it is a strange sight, a heart filled with the earnest passions of youth, in the first hopes of life budding into their fruition beneath his own primeval forest-shades, where if there be an element that ever sanctified an early life it would have built a sanctuary—for the love he must have borne to the fair being for whom he had treasured up his boyhood's jewels, for whom he gave up every thing of the earth earthy, to rescue a Republic, and then go back after this episode of suffering to inaugurate the life of a citizen farmer on the bleak hills of New York:—if all this could not sustain him, what could?—

In former visits to him he had made me his confidant in regard to these matters. He seemed to be *haunted* with the idea that he would, after all, return to Utica, and once more see those he loved; and yet he also seemed to me like one whose days were numbered, and the surgeon had told me, after repeated counsels with his professional brethren, that it was next to impossible to save his life, and that I must not expect it.

All the while I clung to the belief that some vitality of faith, or love, or hope, or patriotism, or divine aid, would still send that boy back to the banks of the Mohawk.

I saw another nervous twitch around the temples. I felt his pulse. It was an indication of hope, or sudden death.

The surgeon came by again.

"That boy has wonderful vitality," he said, as he looked at his face. Whether it was purely my fancy, my hope, or a fact, I did not know, but twilight seemed to pass over his face.

"Yes, yes—I—I—wait—a moment. Oh, I shall not die!"

He opened his eyes calmly, and then a glow which I shall never forget suffused his cheek, and, lifting his emaciated hands for the first time in several weeks,—feebly, it is true, but they seemed to me strong,—he exclaimed, in a natural voice, "How floats the old flag now, boys?"

The transition from death to life seemed like enchantment. I could scarcely believe my senses. And yet I knew that if he ever rallied this would be the way.

I now feared that his excitement would carry him beyond his strength. I could not keep him from talking. I was bending over him to see if he would remember me. Looking me steadily in the eyes, his brows knit with perplexity for a few seconds, when with a smile of delight and surprise he said, "Yes! yes! It is you, Mr. L——. I am glad you stayed with me. I have been dreaming about you while I've been asleep; and I must have been asleep a great while. How long?"

I told him enough to let him understand how ill he had been,—how long,—and how weak he still was. He did not realize it. His eyes wandered down to his thin hands, white as alabaster, and through which the pale-blue thread-like veins wandered.

"Oh! Is it I?—so lean? I was not so when I fell sick."— And large tears rolled down his cheeks.

I implored him to be quiet and rest, and I promised him he should get better every day, and be able to go home in a short time. But he grew impatient the more I tried to soothe and restrain him.

He looked at me beseechingly, and asked, " Won't you let me talk a little? I *must* know something more, or it seems to me I shall go crazy. Please put your ear down to me: I won't speak loud,—I won't get excited."

I did.—" Have you got any letters for me?"

"Yes, but they are at my office. You shall have them to-morrow. They are all well at home."

"And Bella?"

"Yes."

"Oh, God be praised!"—

After a few moments of repose, he again opened his eyes wide.—

"I have been gone so long from the army! It seemed as though I never could get back when I got home. I got away; and I wandered, and wandered.—Oh, how tired I was! Where is McDowell?—*Is* General Scott dead? They said so.

Did they carry off Old Abe? How did he get back? Did the Rebels get into Washington that night? How long have I been sick? What place is this?—Oh, my head! my head!"

I was frightened. He had risen from the deep ocean into the sunlight for a brief hour, and now he seemed to be going down to come up no more. The tender chord of memory had given way. In a little while the surgeon came by, and I told him what had happened.

"I was afraid of that. But I think we can manage it. If he wakes again within two hours, give him this powder on his tongue, and a sip of the liquid. If he does not, wake him gently."

      *   *   *   *   *   *

And so that anxious night wore away. In the morning he woke bright and clear; and from that hour he began to get well. But for whole days his life was pulsating in its gossamer tenement, fluttering over the misty barriers of the spirit-world.

Bella's letters, received during his extreme illness, could now be read. They were among the noblest ever written by woman.

      *   *   *   *   *   *

"Our heart-prayers for you have been answered by our Father. We now wait only for your return. When we parted, it was not with repining: you had gone to the altar of your country in solemn and complete dedication. I too was prepared for the sacrifice. I expected it, although I knew how crushingly the blow would fall. But if you had not loved your country better than Bella, it would have broken her heart. I hope now in a few weeks you will be again by my side. When your health is once more restored, I will promise in advance, as you desire, not to try to keep you from rejoining your regiment; and if the stars have written that

Walter shall not be my husband, God has decreed that I shall die a widow never married."

* *. * * * *

He did return to the Mohawk Valley. He married Bella. He returned to the war; and on the eve of the great day of Antietam he heard that his son was born, and the hero-father *died* by the side of Hooker.—*Sic transit gloria mundi.*

V.

Mount Vernon in Other Days.

THE stream of Time, which sweeps almost every thing human to oblivion, passes without injury by the everlasting column of Washington's *fame*. Those convulsions which threaten the permanence of our Union, and sicken us with the strifes of parties and the gore of battle, only render more and more dear the name of the Father of the American Republic.

The nations of the Old World, as they lift their wearied and half-palsied arms to strike for Liberty, utter the name of Washington with veneration, gratitude, and love. Wherever the all-glowing sun lights up the homes of earth's children,— through all the continents and islands, along all the shores and rivers, on every green mountain's side, and down every blushing valley,—the old tell his history to the young, and all nations rise up and call him blessed.

All that belonged to him has become dear to mankind. The ground his feet pressed is sacred. The trees he planted with his own hand, the groves through which he walked at evening, still seem to breathe his name as they rustle their zephyr-music. Even the sparkling ripples of that majestic stream which flows on by Mount Vernon seem to utter intelligible words to the ear of the pilgrim who from that green lawn looks through the bending boughs by moonlight on the glistening waters.

It was a beautiful spring morning, many years ago, when we set out from Washington to visit for the first time this Mecca of Liberty. The balmy air wafted through the carriage-windows the fragrance of early flowers, just peeping out from the warm banks of the Potomac. The sun came calmly up over the old dome of the Capitol, and the mists rose from the bosom of the river to greet him, and then floated far away into the blue sky, as spirits go when they leave us for that bright land

"Where everlasting spring abides,
And never-withering flowers."

We could not say that there was a gay or glad heart among us : there would have been some, had we not been going to the Tomb of the Father of his country. But there was something so holy in the thought that we were approaching the spot where the greatest and purest of mankind rested from his heroism, that we felt mirth had no place in our feelings, and into that day levity could not enter.

But it was a cheerful ride, and an inspiring day. We do not remember that a cloud moved over our little party during the excursion; nor was our cheerfulness interrupted till we had reached the shrine of our pilgrimage and stood before the sarcophagus where the dust of Washington reposes.

No matter for our ride along the river, nor for its picturesque bends, or banks, or lawns, or woodlands. At every turn in the road we saw the calm waters of the silver stream, around which linger memories that are sanctified by all that is brave in chivalry and touching in patriotism.

A long ride through the oak forests brought us to the venerable mansion where Washington lived and died. At the porter's lodge we stopped to see the only living servant of the Patriot. She lived in the lodge, and still watched the gate.

She was fifteen years old when "the general" came back from the wars, covered with victory; and he remembered her well as he rode through the gate, and said, "Ah, my little Sylvia, the Britishers didn't hit me, after all : and they have all gone back to Old England, and I have come home to live and die on the estate :"—and young Sylvia seized "the general's" hand and wet it with her tears. She saw Washington die;

3

she saw him when he was dead : and when she spoke of him she looked up to heaven, and, pointing her hand away, said, " Well, if we ever go there we shall see him again."

We left this octogenarian keeper, and she said many a kind word to us as we went on slowly threading our way to the mansion,—through deep ravines from which only the upper sky was visible, and now emerging on eminences from which we hoped to get at least a glimpse of the mansion. But holier feelings filled up the interval.

We were passing over new ground, where, warm with life and radiant with beneficence, the form of the hero so often passed. Even the air seemed haunted by his presence: every step we took was an epic.

See the outlines of the great historical picture. Passing this same rugged avenue, first the *youth* George Washington, with his surveying-instruments, to measure off the vast wilderness of the West, the happy homes he was afterwards to offer his brothers made free:—young *Major* Washington, setting out to instruct them in the art of war, to prepare them to achieve their independence:—*Colonel* Washington, on his departure to repel foreign and savage invaders:—*the Representative*, passing to and from the Congress of the patriots:—the heroic *general*, coming at long intervals through that war of fraternal blood, and going forth again to the sanguinary struggles of the Revolution, where brave men staked *Liberty* in the desperate game with King, Lords, and Commons:—the Farmer, going out to and returning from his fields:—the *President*, on his way to administer the government of a people he had led through the exhausting perils of an all-but exterminating war:—and, last of all, the *citizen* Washington, who had scorned a crown, as too base a reward for his long services in the cause of human freedom—returning by the same road we were travelling, his great heart filled with longings for home.

The carriage rising an eminence gave us a glimpse of the

wall and observatory of *the Home of Washington*. We were not ashamed of a few tears which came unbidden to our eyes.

We reached the gate of the mansion. A *ruin*—an *old* ruin —stood before us. It was not a feudal castle, with deep trench once filled with water; nor draw-bridge, over which once clat-tered the hoofs of warriors' steeds; nor massive arch, under which bent the plume of knight; nor spacious court-yard, in which the spears of an heroic band flashed in the moonlight; nor vast banquet-hall, that rang to the clangor of Crusader or the merry shout of victorious warrior who had come from measuring lance with the Infidel, to tell his tale of adventure to the startled ear of Europe. There was no watch-word; no vesper-chime stealing softly on the evening air; no hollow chant nor monkish prayer in gloomy chapel; no moon-lit watch on the overlooking tower. No one of all these. It was grander, better, dearer, than all this heroic legend.

It was once the home of the Father of a great and glorious nation, whose eagle wings now stretch from the turbulent Atlantic—far away over rich valleys waving with corn and dotted with happy habitations, rugged mountains, wide rivers, and green prairies—to the golden shores of the Pacific, where Empire looks toward the purple East and has made the circuit of the globe.

It was a *ruin!* The master of the house had long since gone away to another country, and Time had left the mansion like

" Some banquet-hall deserted."

The master would never return.

The servants told us that the *present* master would *next* year repair the dwelling.

"Oh, no!" we would have said to him. "Leave the holy place as he left it. Ye cannot make us think he has come back; ye cannot make good his place. Let the spot where he lived and died be left. *Eternity* is his dwelling now. Let *Time* spread its ivy never-sere kindly over the mansion, and let not the winds blow harshly against it; for the great master is gone, and will return no more.   Ye cannot make the place what it once was."

They showed us the apartments which are thrown open to visitors.   We had letters; but we asked no privileges *there* which could not be accorded to all.   We saw the hall, the drawing room, the parlor, and the dining-room, with the richly sculptured mantel-piece which La Fayette gave him.

As we passed out under the open sky, they pointed out to us the chamber where Washington died.   We looked up to the windows.   They showed us the lemon-tree he planted, old, but green still,—and many plants in the conservatory, with long box alleys, and large squares, and page bushes, all planned and planted by his hand.

Down the green slope towards the river, not far from the bank, they showed us *Washington's Tomb*.   We reverently gathered there, and bowed in silence and gratitude.

As the sun was going down behind the old oaks, fringing the edges of the clouds with gold, we entered our boat, and sailed slowly by under the lengthening shadows of the sacred groves which cluster their foliage around *Mount Vernon*.

*   *   *   *   *   *

Those were better days than we have now.

VI.

Cloaked Foes—Croakers, and all other Secessionists.

No war ever began with greater unanimity than this. The mighty heart of the people leaped at a single bound, from its full but tranquil pulsations, into the wild and hurried beatings of a continental enthusiasm. From the bleak hill-sides of New England, from the shores of the ocean lakes of the North, from the undulating prairies of the distant West, from the crowded marts of commerce, and from ten thousand hamlets of peace and plenty, a million men came, rushing to avenge the insulted honor of the nation and plant once more on our outer battlements the fallen standard of the Republic.

The flow of that current was irresistible; every thing gave way to the tramp of the embattled hosts. It was no time for trifling, nor for triflers. The secret foe of the Union kept his own counsel. The men whose hearts were with the parricides of the Fatherland stood back from the on-rolling tide, and cursed the gathering tempest. But the horde of politicians, who had retired in sullen disappointment from the late Presidential election, with hearts all covered with gangrene, and pockets once filled, but now emptied of the rewards of corruption and crime,—many of these seized the first chance that invited to new scenes of robbery and peculation.

The politicians of all parties, en masse, adopted the war, and they have carried it on to this day. They, at least, have " made a good thing out of it," as they say.

But this greedy horde could not all be satisfied. There

were not green things enough for all the locusts; there were not lambs enough for the whole pack of wolves. They were not patriotic enough to fight anywhere except at an election; —they were too lazy to work, and they must eat. There were not commissions enough in the army, nor sinecures enough in civil life, for the more "decent" of this class; and finally, when the war had been inaugurated into a grand, solemn fact, and it rose up to the gaze of the world in all its stupendous proportions, black with treason, and smoking with blood unrighteously shed,—this unpaid, unbribed, un-washed locust-swarm seized the first occasion to disparage the administration, and to exaggerate the ill fortune and condemn the management of the war.

Every disappointed seeker for office began to "doubt how the thing would come out." Day by day he shook his head despairingly; and when he was finally told to "get out of the way, and be off" with himself, he swore, in the holy in-dignation of his soul, that "the generals were all fools, the Cabinet all rascals, and Old Abe a &c."

Then the *Secessionists* proper. Washington swarmed with them. They were never asleep. Well might a member of Mr. Davis's cabal, in writing to a friend there (the letter was intercepted), say, "The Lincolnites may rest assured we shall only *alarm* their capital. We do not want it. It is of more use to us in their hands. It answers all our pur-poses. Our friends are there, and they are doing their work." They were, and they found no lack of coadjutors or agents in any department: while their sympathizers were slyly gliding from *salon* to *salon* in every hotel where the best society held its *conversazzioni*.

So, too, was it in the private houses of the rich. Washing-ton had always been a Southern city. Now it was A SE-CESSION CAPITAL. Its society had always been of the Southern type. There were wealth, taste, pride, gallantry, beauty, pleasure, and somewhat of the *abandon* which we recognize the nearer we go to the tropics. Few of the rich families of the North came here, fewer still lived here. All the richest families of the South did both. Washington they looked upon as their *Northern home*. Here all the Foreign Embassies were established, and spasmodic efforts were made to have and hold a Republican court.

But over it all was spread the slime of Slavery. The population was made up of Foreign Ministers, Heads of Department, Members of Congress, Judges of the Supreme Court, old dowagers and wives of absent officers, poor clerks, "poor whites," shiftless and lazy negroes, and still poorer and lazier office-seekers.

Once rid of the atmosphere reeking with the slave-lash and the bowie-knife, which the politics and politicians of the South had infused into Washington, there came the first hope of society in the capital. It was the only capital of any nation without society. I need not say that by society I mean intercourse between that body of men and women who represent the highest culture and intelligence, the greatest refinement, delicacy, and blandishments of women, the loftiest standard of honor and chivalry in men, the fullest appreciation of learning, art, and beauty to which a nation has attained. To be society worthy of the name, such *réunions* must represent the best civilization of the people. In later days, such society has not been seen in Washington. Its palmy days passed away with the graceful *régime* of Ladies Washington, Madison, Hamilton, Sedgwick, Bingham, and that glorious company of superb women who lent the fascinations of wit, taste, and beauty to adorn the early days of the Republic.

But through the medium of such society as we have had, the view of practical secession has been industriously injected, and in all its subtlest forms. It has worn chameleon hues; it has borrowed, for the time, all the lights and shadows that lay within its reach.

In one coterie, severe criticisms were passed on generals at the head of their armies; and, with all the eagerness of cormorant birds snuffing the carrion from afar, they seized the first discouraging rumor floating on the idle wind, and blew the gentlest breeze into a tempest.

If a secession woman had a husband, or brother, or lover, who had been refused a commission in the army, *she* did not hesitate to predict "the final failure of the Yankee cause, and the ultimate triumph of the chivalric sons of the South," "*the dear, sunny South.*"

And thus indignant crinoline, which had flirted in vain for a lover by being patriotic, became secesh when sailing in disloyal waters.

In another circle, of men, or women, or both (all of the upper classes, so called), serious and downcast looks were seen, and to every new visitor the "deep and painful regret" was expressed "lest Mr. Lincoln might be going too far in making his arrests;" "and are they not arbitrary? And then to take *gentlemen* from their offices, and *even from their sleeping-chambers*, and convey them to a distant city, and plunge them into a foul prison, tenanted by felons and haunted by rats! And then think of General Butler! that vulgar Yankee! who published one of his tyrannical edicts, and placarded the insult on every corner of the Crescent City, to the ladies of New Orleans"——!

And yet these same "gentle angels" were at the time besieging President and Secretaries for a commission for ——, "a brave and gallant fellow, who had rendered such signal services to the Federal cause, and longed so earnestly to put the old flag back where it once waved so proudly."

This class of females have shown an alacrity and cleverness in their management in Washington which would have been tolerable at least in an honest cause. But they were completely outdone by the *artistes* of the secession drama. Some few, sprightly, sharp-witted, and—as the world goes—*charming* women, undertook the more difficult parts. They were in no hot haste to win. They were looking for the main chance,— to fail once or twice, perhaps, but *to win at last.*

Never did Paul Morphy move chess-men with more studied care; never did he conceal more completely every line of expression in his face; never did his heart palpitate with half the excitement, while making his decisive and finishing play.

These *women of the world* watched every expression in the eyes of their listeners, and measured every gesture they made before the men who, meeting them by design or accident, swelled the retinue of their impoverished but pretentious court.

Nothing but well-merited severity, visited at the right time and on the right heads, broke up this den of she-vipers that were striking their deadly fangs into the vitals of the Republic. There was squirming and hissing, but the *den* was finally broken up.

All these subtle agencies of secession worked harmoniously with bolder and more public demonstrations of disloyalty. In both Houses of Congress, men no better than South Carolina traitors (often not half so bad), and always more dangerous, unblushingly reviled the Union, laughed the Republic to scorn, and trod the holy traditions of our *common*-WEALTH into the dust.

These traitors were allowed to play the part of Catiline in open House,—in open Senate,—in the streets,—most of all, in that loud-mouthed, blatant talk which is deemed *eloquence* in bar-rooms, but bad manners in decent society, and treason anywhere.

And one of the chief themes of noisy discourse—*illegal arrests!* Why illegal? Is it illegal to arrest the murderer of a *man?* and is it not legal and just to seize and incarcerate the villain who is contemplating the wholesale murder of the friends of the nation,—the defenders of its Union,— the protectors of its peace, its nationality and life? Is violence to be the law? Is the wretch who brandishes the torch of the incendiary recklessly, and scatters fire, arrows, and death through peaceful and loyal communities, to go on in his dreadful mission unchecked, unmanacled, unchained?

If such men escape justice, where can good citizens look even for mercy?

If the *severity* of Mr. Lincoln is complained of by treason-hatchers or treason-mongers, how infinite must be the all-forgiving benevolence of that much-abused man!

No! no! a thousand times No! No blood rests on that troubled head.

VII.

Army Chaplains, and Old Mortality.

IT is supposed that every regiment has its chaplain. A large number of Congressional statutes have been enacted on this subject, for the regular army. By an act approved July 17th, 1862, the qualifications of chaplains in the army and volunteers are thus defined :—

"That no person shall be appointed a chaplain in the United States army who is not a regularly ordained minister of some religious denomination, and who does not present testimonials of his present good standing as such minister, with a recommendation for his appointment as an army chaplain, from some authorized ecclesiastical body, or not less than five accredited ministers belonging to said religious denomination."

His allowances are : one horse, two rations, and twelve hundred dollars a year, or somewhat over fifteen hundred dollars. He is governed by the laws of discipline, like all other officers.

Such are the provisions made for this important class. Their duties are perfectly well known. They are pastors of their regiments, which constitute their congregations. All their duties begin and end with their "charge." To fulfil their oath of office, they must do all in their power for the temporal and spiritual good of their members. Every Christian man knows what these duties are, and especially do soldiers.

To a faithful and conscientious clergyman, who delights in doing good, no better or broader field of activity or usefulness is needed or desired. To look after the well-being of a thousand men, exposed to an amount of danger, disease, and death fourfold, and sometimes a hundredfold, greater than they would be in the peaceful pursuits of civil life; to watch by the sick, or wounded, or dying soldier, with no bed but the ground; to win his respect and affection; to entertain him in his hours of weariness and pain; to write letters for him to his friends; to win the way to his brave heart, and inspire his soul with sublime aspirations for the better life to come; to administer to his parting spirit the infallible consolations of Christianity, secure a safe burial-place for the departed, and shed over the sepulchre all the solemn honors of Christian burial; and, finally, to send the whole record to his family;—such is the duty of an army chaplain. Nothing less was contemplated by Congress in creating the office, and God will accept nothing less from the minister, if He greets him on his advent to judgment with the words, "Well done, thou good and faithful servant." Of our twelve hundred chaplains, how many such have we?

This is a painful subject to discuss; for I know of nothing that would cost me a keener pang than to appear to attempt to speak lightly of the ministers of religion, much less of the faith of the "Holy Man of Nazareth." Nay, it is chiefly because I attach such infinite value to revealed religion, as the only hope of man on both sides of the tomb, that I am jealous of this cause.

Our Government has sent these spiritual pastors, teachers, fathers, and guides, and commissioned them to look after the good of upwards of a million of men; and a great Christian Republic expects them to do their duty. The common impression is that they do

I am sorry to dispel the illusion; but I must. We will first probe the sore, and then look for a remedy.

If we divide the army chaplains into five classes, we may more readily comprehend the case.

First. There are some men who, by means best known to

themselves, *stole* their way into the service. They were not only destitute of every qualification for the chaplaincy, but they were not fit to live in decent society. Of course, such appointments were obtained by unfair means. It is hoped that their numbers were few, and that most of them have been dismissed. But, as they were seldom seen by their regiments, they did little direct harm to their flocks. But they brought disgrace enough on the Government and their profession, by frequenting scenes of vice and pollution and indulging in the lowest forms of bestiality.

The *second* class was made up chiefly of men of faultless morals, perhaps, but who had no liking for the practical business of "saving souls," and least of all for the rough life of the camp. I have seen many such men, who in the longest conversations would neither make an allusion to the subject of the Christian religion nor recognize an allusion to it by others. Some of them had never gone any further in the clerical profession than to enter it; or if they had assumed pastoral relations, they had pocketed their salaries and walked through their parts. Against such chaplains no charges could be brought, for they seldom visited their regiments, except for an excursion of pleasure, to witness a dress parade and ride with the staff on a "grand review." They managed to keep their furloughs all right, and they lived as luxuriously as they could on good salaries. But if they ever thought of their regiments, thinned by battle or wasted by disease, the thought brought no serious twinge of conscience, nor was their *honor* wounded by skulking from a duty they had sworn to perform. This class is by no means a small one.

A *third* list embraces invalids and broken-down men, who, for the most part, were physically incompetent to the duties they proposed to undertake,—unsuccessful preachers, who, after years of failure, discovered at last, what everybody else always knew, that they never had "a call to preach." But the war broke out, and they must "join the army." Nobody

had any objection, and they went. Confirmed invalids, who
'had scrimped and eked out a lean kind of existence, now
louching down on family relations, trying to teach the clas-
sics in some academy, or wandering about, living on their
brethren in the ministry! Why, every kind-hearted person
would aid so worthy and "so good a man " to get so good a
place. It may seem all right; but in doing a kindness to one
man, an eternal wrong is done to the souls of a thousand.

The *fourth* is a higher, but still inefficient, class. They are
men who went to do good to their fellows and their country;
their hearts were in their work; their every word and deed
said to the bayoneted column marching to the field, "Where
you go I will go; your country shall be my country, and my
God shall be your God." Such men go with their regiments.
They enter at once into all their interests and feelings. They
make it their *sole business* to take care of the health, the comfort, the morals, the manners, the happiness, the very salvation, of their soldiers. They break down the first few days, or
weeks, or months of a campaign; they are furloughed, and
their regiments are left without any social or spiritual guide;
no prayer is said by the sick-bed; no word of consolation is
whispered in the ear of the dying, and the poor boy sinks into
a neglected soldier's grave.

The *fifth* and last class are model chaplains,—the only men
who are really qualified to fill the office, and whose usefulness,
in the highest sense of the word, cannot be overestimated.
No men in the army or the country are doing more good in
the great cause. Their qualifications are peculiar; so are
their duties.

They are sound, able-bodied men, who can endure the hardships of a campaign as well as any officer. They know what
they undertake, and they are not surprised when they find the
hard work coming. Such a man starts with his regiment,
and before one week is over he has won every heart in it.
The first man that is sick finds the chaplain at his side. All

bad language is laid aside in his hearing. All uncleanly habits are modified or abandoned. Better attention is given to the laws of health. More and better books and journals are got and read. A kinder and more humane feeling is inculcated among the men. Letters are more frequently written to friends. More money is sent home. Any thing lost is oftener found; any thing stolen is oftener returned.

Such a chaplain can call every man by name. He knows the history of every man, and every man honors and loves him. He makes him, in the best acceptation of the term, his "father confessor." It is needless to say that not a single man in such a regiment can escape the benign influence that emanates from the man of God. He can no more escape it than the lamb in the meadow, or the wild beast in the desert, can escape the sunlight. That sunlight illumines, softens, refines, purifies, strengthens. It shines all through the camp. *It reaches all the officers,* and, if they were good men before, they rejoice and become better; if they were bad, they keep silent and grow no worse. I have observed that officers of regiments which have such chaplains invariably hold the same language in speaking of them. They "do not know what they could do without their chaplains." They know how much easier it is to bring a regiment up to a high standard of discipline, and hold it there, with the aid of a devoted chaplain's example and ministrations. His influence is good, and only good, and that continually. Nothing can make up for its absence.*

---

* In citing a passage from one of Rev. Wm. H. Channing's Washington Discourses, I cannot help thanking that devoted minister again, in behalf of hundreds of the sick he has comforted.

"It has been the testimony of experienced surgeons, that never in a long life has it happened to them, amid such companies of wounded, to see so many cases of agonizing distress. Early that morning, and late that evening, was it my privilege, as one of the chaplains of the hospital, to minister to the wants of these fellow-beings. I could tell you of many, many scenes. I will single out but three; and I do it for no petty purpose of exciting superficial sympathies. I stood by the bedside and wrote a

Nor let it be supposed that among the rank and file the words of the Bible or the voice of prayer sound unfamiliar. I have seen whole regiments where the great majority were well-educated Christian young men. I should hazard little in saying that nine out of ten of our native-born soldiers are

---

parting letter, faintly dictated to me by a stalwart man, beyond the years of middle life,—one of the grandest styles of men that come from our common people. He had received three bullet-wounds, and, as if that was not enough, he had been shattered by a shell, and his life was fast giving out. Had he not been a Hercules he would have died a week before. And yet, agonizing as were the cramps that distorted his limbs, it was with a perfect serenity of expression, with entire self-command, that that man dictated to me what he knew well,—his parting words to his wife and children, whom he left only a few months ago, 'that they would unite in prayer for him to God; that he possibly might be restored, but his sufferings would end most probably in death.' The spirit of the Prince of Peace was there.

"And there was another case. He was a young man, a lately-married man, one whose home had not yet been blessed with children, who had left behind him a devoted wife and gone forth to serve his country. If you had seen him sleeping there and studied his features as he slumbered, the delicate chiselling of his countenance, and a sweetness in his look,—a latent inspiration,—you would have said he was a poet. Yet he was wounded mortally. As I asked him for his last words to his wife, he said, 'Tell her that I am wounded; tell her that I am here; but do not tell her how much I am injured, because it might be the source of too much pain.' There was something in the delicacy and dignity and consideration for that sweet friend whom he had left behind, which seemed to be overflowing with the spirit of the Prince of Peace.

"The last of these instances, which was perhaps more touching, is of a boy who had scarce seen sixteen summers. He was a model for a painter or a sculptor. He could scarcely speak at all, but managed, however, to utter these few words before he received the last offices of his religion (he was a Catholic): 'Would that I could write to my mother!' Thus, as the soul is passing away, how fondly it turns to the memory of a mother! After he was gone, we opened his papers. I found letters from that mother to him, testifying that this boy, all through these battles, month by month, had never forgotten her. Month by month, or quarter by quarter, as his pay came in, he sent it to her. It was my last sad duty yesterday afternoon to write a letter to that mother; but I could write in the confidence that the Prince of Peace was there, and with the perfect assurance that her beautiful, brave boy, whom she had sent forth with benedictions, would be restored to her in the eternal home, never to be separated again."

as well or better informed of the nature of religion, and the obligations it imposes, than the men they left at home. I am equally persuaded that, making fair allowance for increased exposure to rough influences, the removal of the restraints of civil life and the amenities of happy homes, they are better. They are certainly more moral and decent, and commit fewer excesses; for they have fewer opportunities to indulge in those lower vices which, either openly or secretly, are always eating away at the vitals even of what we call Christian communities.

There are, too, in our Xerxean host, tens of thousands of upright, conscientious, Christian men, who still remember the instructions of pious mothers and exemplary ministers of the gospel,—men who carry a little Bible or Testament in their knapsacks in all their marches. These were many of them parting gifts of mothers, wives, sisters, and loved ones; and many a soldier would sooner part with any other of his little possessions.

How wrong, how cruel, to cheat that soldier by giving him no chaplain, or something worse,—a bad one!

And then the whole body of commissioned officers have been educated in the Christian religion, and, Providence be praised, a generous portion of them are Christian men. They are all friends of virtue and morality *in the camp* at least, and always are ready to second a good chaplain in the execution of his mission.*

* * * * * *

I wish I had space in this book to give some account of

---

* The following extract is from the letter of a gentleman who describes what he saw:—

Standing by General Mitchel's bedside, he reached out his hand and took mine, and, looking up in my face, he said, "It is a blessed thing to have a Christian's hope in a time like this." An hour after, he beckoned me, and, feebly shaking my hand, said, "You must not stay any longer; go now, and come to me in the morning." Major Birch, who had been untiring in his attentions, entered, almost convulsed with grief. He had

what I have seen of the work of our chaplains in the hospitals since this war began. At several different periods, almost every one of the (from ten to forty) hospitals of the District sent out its dead every day. In each establishment provision was made for the services of army chaplains. While even here, under the immediate inspection of the Government, hundreds of men drooped and died, without seeing a chaplain's face, and thousands were tumbled into holes and trenches, without Christian burial,* still a faithful few

---

just taken down the last will and wishes of his beloved commander. He conducted the Rev. Mr. Strickland to the bedside of the general, and beckoned me to follow. I did not hear the words of the general as the Rev. Mr. Strickland stooped to speak to him; but I did hear him say, "Kneel down," and then ask Mr. Strickland to make a short prayer. How still he lay while that prayer went up to the throne of the God of battles! At its conclusion, as we rose, his eyes rested on me, and his hand was extended again. "You can do me no good," said he, faintly: "do not stay." His mind seemed perfectly clear and calm; but he was failing constantly.

Oh, it is a tearful sight to us all to see a father thus dying; dying in the same house with his two sons and they not know it,—not permitted to look upon his face,—not permitted to treasure his last words, his last look; that all these must be given to strangers. But they are too sick yet to bear the blow; it would shatter them; therefore they must be kept in ignorance till a coming hour. Seven P.M.—General Mitchel has breathed his last. He is gone from us. Our hopes that were placed on him must be lifted higher,—higher. With Victor Hugo, we must learn to say, "It is not generals or soldiers, but God, who must give us the victory in this war of the powers of darkness." General Mitchel had entire possession of his faculties till within an hour or two of his departure, when his reason seemed to wander. His last intelligent look was to the Rev. Mr. Strickland. Seeing him approach the bed, he looked up devoutly, and, lifting his hand, pointed upward twice. So passed he from among men.

* "SOLDIERS' FUNERALS.—There is no department of the army so well officered, as to numbers, as the *ministerial*. Chaplains abound throughout the army, but nowhere do they abound so plenteously as in this city. The smallest hospital has its chaplain, and some of the larger ones have as many as three. Notwithstanding this abundant supply, a large majority of the five thousand patriots who slumber near the Soldiers' Home have been consigned to mother earth with little more ceremony

never deserted their posts or flagged in their duty. I have known such men pass whole weeks among the sick and dying, —night and day,—remitting their toil only for a little food or sleep, till the strength of the strongest gave way. Oh, how often, when the lowly-uttered prayer was going up by the side of one dying man, have I seen other sufferers through the ward languidly turn their ears to listen to the words of holy consolation,—all sick, all suffering, all sorrowful, but all famishing "for the bread of life"! Such are the spots for prayer.

> "Oh, when the heart is full, when bitter thoughts
> Come crowding thickly up for utterance,
> And the poor common words of courtesy
> Are such a very mockery, how much
> The bursting heart may pour itself in prayer!"

---

than the coffining without the military ceremony to which they were entitled, and not even a chaplain to commit ' dust to dust.'

"If the chaplains of hospitals cannot find time, between drawing their pay and distributing 'soldiers' banners,' to attend the funerals of soldiers who die in hospitals, why may not one be stationed at the Soldiers' Home for this purpose?"— *Washington Chronicle.*

VIII.

L'Esprit de Corps—Eloquence in the Army.

FOND as are Americans of public speaking, and natural orators as most of them are, it has seemed to me very strange that we should have seen so little of it in our armies.

Appeals to the patriotism and the valor of soldiers, by their leaders, have, in all ages and with all people, been among the most potent agencies invoked for inspiring courage and inflaming enthusiasm. All the great generals of antiquity made passionate and eloquent addresses to their armies on the eve of battle. Their example has been followed by military leaders in all countries and all times, from the chief of a petty tribe of savage warriors to the great captain of an innumerable host.

It was under the electric influence of patriotic eloquence that our countless battalions were gathered and marched to the field; and some of our most brilliant successes in this war have followed such appeals. Fired by the zeal thus awakened, nearly all victories against fearful odds have everywhere been won. The fiery words of Peter the Hermit set all Europe in a blaze, and launched a million Crusaders on the shores of Asia.

Who has forgotten the thrilling scene which Scott describes of the sermon of the youthful Scotch chaplain, Mackelbriar, when the small but determined band of Covenanters halted, with their dripping swords, to withstand the next shock of Claverhouse's cavalry!*

---

* "The banner of the Reformation is spread abroad on the mountains in its first loveliness, and the gates of hell shall not prevail against it."

Returned prisoners tell us that, before going into battle, the rebel officers address their men in strains of fiery invective against the Federal Government, charging it with every crime, and depicting scenes, attending their march, of butchery and brutality horrible enough to make a savage shudder.

The voice of the skilful and impetuous orator is often as powerful in a bad cause as in a good one. Nothing more imposing can be found in Milton—that most eloquent of all writers—than the addresses of Satan to his scathed, defiant secession host. They exceed in sublimity of diction even the eloquence of the orators of heaven.

The effect of eloquence is not to be measured by the strength of the argument or the justice of the cause. Logic is bad, but competent hands can easily dispose of truth. Rhetoric deals only with conclusions. Conviction is its sole object. This is as often won by foul as by fair means.

This great lever of social power has been wielded with

"Well is he this day that shall barter his house for a helmet, and sell his garment for a sword, and cast in his lot with the children of the covenant, even to the fulfilling of the promise; and woe, woe unto him who for carnal ends and self-seeking shall withhold himself from the great work, for the curse shall abide with him, even the bitter curse of Meroz, because he came not to the help of the Lord against the mighty! Up, then, and be doing! The blood of martyrs, reeking upon scaffolds, is crying for vengeance! The bones of saints, which lie whitening in the highways, are pleading for retribution! The groans of innocent captives from desolate isles of the sea, and from the dungeons of the tyrant's high places, cry for deliverance! The prayers of persecuted Christians, sheltering themselves in dens and deserts from the sword of their persecutors, famished with hunger, starving with cold, lacking fire, food, shelter, and clothing, because they serve God rather than man, all are with you, pleading, watching, knocking, storming the gates of heaven in your behalf! Heaven itself shall fight for you, as the stars in their courses fought against Sisera! Then whoso will deserve immortal fame in this world, and eternal happiness in that which is to come, let them enter into God's service, and take arles at the hand of his servant,—a blessing, namely, upon him and his household and his children to the ninth generation, even the blessing of the promise, for ever and ever. Amen."—*Old Mortality.*

matchless ability and effect by Southern commanders. They
did not rely only upon "general orders" read to the troops.
Every officer threw a fresh firebrand into the centre of his
regiment before the order "March!" was given. The influence thus exerted by stirring speakers over ignorant and
deluded men acted like a spell of enchantment.

Union officers who were long detained as prisoners in the
South have told me that to this cause, in great part, could the
fanatical zeal of the Confederate army be attributed.

With us, nearly all this has been lacking; and we have
paid very dear for it. It has been a costly sin of *omission*.

In the beginning, this system was proposed by several of
our best officers, and it seemed likely to be carried out. But
it is said that it met with great disfavor from certain quarters, especially from officers in the regular service. In this
respect, as in some others, many of these officers were not so
completely qualified for the business of a great war as they
supposed. West Point had done for them all and perhaps
more than could any other military school.* But those who
had seen active service had generally had but a few men in
their commands; and those men were mostly foreigners, of
the lowest rank in society.

When the ARMY OF THE PEOPLE took the field, inferiority
of breeding or social position found no place. The rank and
file rose even above mediocrity; and many of the regiments
counted privates who in all but military knowledge and experience were not a whit behind the commanders of the regular
army.

It is worth inquiring how much may have been gained or
lost by the spirit which regular officers have manifested

---

* People who know nothing about West Point are in the habit of speaking disparagingly of our national military academy. But no foreign officer of distinction has taken any such view of the case. Their united
testimony—from Russia, Prussia, Austria, and France—places the system of military education at West Point on a par with, and some superior
to, the best military schools in the world.

towards citizen soldiers. I know that all men educated as a special and privileged class feel a pride in their profession. If they did not, they would disgrace it. Nor is it difficult to imagine that an officer of regulars may feel something of a twinge when "ranked" by a volunteer who was brought up to wield the goose of a tailor, or mix liquors behind a bar in the Bowery. But the least intelligent regular must not forget that some of Napoleon's greatest marshals were stable-boys and tapsters.

A noble attempt in the right direction was made by Colonel (now General) John Cochrane early in the war. At a review of his splendid regiment, the First United States Chasseurs, in the presence of the Secretary of War, he delivered an oration on the leading issues of the national contest worthy of his great reputation as a polished and powerful speaker. Short as was his address, he swept the whole field, and pressed his unanswerable argument home to the heart of each one of his thousand men. What had never before been thought of was brought up to full view; what had been obscure became clear; what had been doubtful was made certain; and the merits of the national cause, and the certainty of its final triumph, were the themes of the speaker's discourse and illumination. On one subject General Cochrane spoke with great boldness. His eye had pierced much further into the future than the policy of the administration or the popular vision had penetrated. He saw clearly then, what time has made so apparent, that *either slavery or the Union must die.**

---

* He says:—

* * * * * * * * *

"Soldiers, to what means shall we resort for our existence? This war is devoted not merely to victory and its mighty honors, not merely to the triumph which moves in glorious procession along our streets. But it is a war which moves towards the protection of our homes, the safety of our families, the continuation of our domestic altars, and the protection of our firesides. In such a war we are justified, are bound to resort to every

The issue had been made. The insurrectionists had made it. It came; and it was made and met. A *country* was at

---

force within our power. Having opened the port of Beaufort, we shall be able to export millions of cotton-bales, and from these we may supply the sinews of war. Do you say that we should not seize the cotton? No: you are clear upon that point. Suppose the munitions of war are within our reach: would we not be guilty of shameful neglect if we availed not ourselves of the opportunity to use them? Suppose the enemy's slaves were arrayed against you: would you, from any squeamishness, refrain from pointing against them the hostile gun and prostrating them in death? No: that is your object and purport; and if you would seize their property, open their ports, and even destroy their lives, I ask you whether you would not use their slaves? Whether you would not *arm their slaves* [great applause], *and carry them in battalions against their masters?* [Renewed and tumultuous applause.] *If necessary to save this Government, I would plunge their whole country, black and white, into one indiscriminate sea of blood,* so that we should in the end have a Government which would be the vicegerent of God. Let us have no more of this *dilletante* system, but let us work with a will and a purpose that cannot be mistaken. Let us not put aside from too great a delicacy of motives. Soldiers, you know no such reasoning as this. You have arms in your hands, and those arms are placed there for the purpose of exterminating an enemy unless he submits to law, order, and the Constitution. *If he will not submit, explode every thing that comes in your way. Set fire to the cotton. Explode the cotton. Take property wherever you may find it. Take the slave, and bestow him upon the non-slaveholder, if you please.* [Great applause.] *Do to them as they would do to us. Raise up a party of interest against the absent slaveholder, distract their counsels; and, if this should not be sufficient, take the slave by the hand, place a musket in it, and in God's name bid him strike for the liberty of the human race.* [Immense applause.]

*　　*　　*　　*　　*　　*　　*　　*　　*

"But, soldiers, to accomplish all this, not merely arms are necessary, not merely men to carry them, but that powerful and overwhelming spirit. which constitutes and makes us men,—that spirit which lifts us above the creeping things of the earth, and brings us near the Deity, in accomplishing his work on earth. Oh, then, let us not think that the 'battle is to the strong;' let us not merely depend on discipline and order, but, with that fervidness of soul which inspired our fathers at Bunker Hill and Saratoga and Yorktown, come forward and give effect to all that is valuable in the name of patriotism and honor and religion.

"Never—no, never—will you succeed until that spirit is once more

stake,—and a *whole* country. It was no trifle we had to contend for. It was not only an empire,—it was the hopes of *the world*. If we failed, where could the wet and tired dove of human hope find shelter with her good news?

We must have something to repose on,—something to hope in. Where can we go if we slip our anchor now?

Is there any thing else that is safe?

---

manifested and developed which actuated the soldiers of Cromwell, who, on the field, invoked the Lord their God to arise. So let it be with us. We must be at least one with Him in spirit. Let us, like Cromwell, invoke the Almighty's blessing, and, clothed with the panoply of patriotism and religion, strike for our homes and our country. [Immense cheering.] Let us,—oh, let us,—without reference to any differences of the past, keep our eyes steadfastly on the great object to be achieved,—the nationality and independence of this country, the salvation of civilization from the insults and assaults of barbarism; and then, but not till then, will you be worthy to be recognized as a distinguished portion of our great American army." [Long-continued cheering from the whole regiment.]

5

IX.

Statesmen and Events

MEN *strut* everywhere,—most of all in the *front* of em pires. *Real* statesmen keep themselves out of sight; *sham* statesmen always parade themselves.

"France ! ma belle France !"

But only now and then, and far between, Richelieu appears.

How many quack doctors have had ready-made prescriptions for our national and international troubles! Yes, remedies that would cure *any* complaint! They would do just as well for one disease as another. It might be a constipation of the bowels in a young gentleman two weeks old, or a collision of empires. Liver, kidney, lights, smelts, sweet-breads or kingdoms,—"all the same, sir: only three dollars a dozen."

This trash abounds everywhere. Most of all does this rubbish collect around the halls of statesmanship in this country, where everybody knows every thing.

Every great statesman keeps a man to sweep all such rubbish out of his chamber. *Everybody knows every thing!*

How true this is in our blessed and abused country! A French gentleman said a good thing the other day.

" Why, monsieur! your citizens all know so much, I wonder if they allow your President to know any *thing.*"

" Monsieur, they don't give him a chance."

" Oui, monsieur. But how the devil does your President *do* any thing?"

" I'll tell you, monsieur. Our President does his duty. He is clothed by the Constitution with just as much authority as he needs to execute the laws."

"But, monsieur, you make no limit, then, to his authority. You have one great tyrant."

"No, sir! That is your European way of doing business. We find our house in flames, and our babes in bed! They must be saved, and we do it at any and all hazards. Our Government was made for our people, and our protector must take care of them. That protector *must* have, and *does* have, all the power he needs for the work. You talk about *provost-marshalship*, and call it despotic. You are right: it is. God uses it. He is the Provost-Marshal of the Universe. But he assumes no extremer prerogative in any case than the Chief of the New York Fire Department, who blows up one building to save a city.

"Power *must* be put forth. Somebody must have it. Joan of Arc might not have stood a very good chance of an election if she had gone to the polls. But this did not stop her from having her name known forever as the Maid of Orleans. So with your emperor. He found France floating helplessly in the surging sea of a social Deluge. He laid his strong arm on the helm and brought the ship to! The 1st of December, France was worthless. The next day she became an empire. The *coup d'état* fell like a bolt from heaven. But you are proud of your nation's history from that memorable 2d of December."

"Yes, oh, yes, monsieur. But you violate all your traditional constitution."

"No, sir; not for a second! In France I know you have no constitution. You may get up one every few years, but with the first *émeute* in Paris down it goes, and you scream out, from the Hotel de Ville, 'Vive la République!' and when your Lamartine republic has had its day, a day sanctified by the best blood of Paris and illuminated by the sunlight and the starlight of the finest genius of your noble country,—after all, you have to come to the centre, the home of all Frenchmen and all men,—confidence in the government, *faith in power.*

"You have had to do that often in Paris; and Paris is France, and France *now* is Napoleon. Let him slip, let him blunder,—one mistake, one divorce of Josephine, one more silly attempt to conquer the unconquerable Russians,—and you will find in your transient ruins some dead honors to sleep on.

"But, my dear sir, do me one favor. Don't, please don't tell me that we have not made provision for all *our* troubles. In France you have to do *any* thing to get out of a scrape. Our *constitution* does not die. We need no *coups d'état.* These difficulties are all provided for. Our President has all the executive authority of the nation vested in himself. When he fails in his duty, then, and not till then, we have a revolution."

"But you have one very great revolution now."

"Sir, here you make a mistake. It is *not* a revolution. It is only an *insurrection.* It is simply a family quarrel, in which your nation has not yet been invited to intervene or interfere. We have some linen (that needs washing, to be sure) which we intend to put through a straight, clear-starch process; and we should like to get over our little domestic affairs, if we can, without being troubled."

"Well, but Governor Seymour tells me that the President takes too much authority on him."

"Well, sir, I think Governor Seymour has made a very great mistake."

"But do you not think Governor Seymour was elected by your New York people?"

"Undoubtedly."

"Well, he is the law?"

"No! the man is not yet born who is the *law* for America. We keep *legislators* to make our laws."

"Well, what shall his Excellency Governor Seymour do?"

"Just what I think he is determined to do."

" What is that?"

" Stand by the flag, the Government, the war, till the last enemy is put under our feet."

" If he does not do that?"

" Then let him look out for breakers!"

" What you say? Breakers?"

" I mean this. If Governor Seymour tries to turn this tide against the war or the Government, he will be swept away like shavings in the wind."

" Well, then, you think your good and great Government will be permanent?"

" No, sir,—*eternal!* The world seems to have nothing to do with itself just now but to look after our affairs. I have sometimes thought that it was 'love's labor lost.' But it is quite possible you may have work enough at home to occupy you."

" Why? We are very quiet in Europe, particularly in France."

" You are just now. But within my time I have seen several revolutions in France. In 1830 you exiled Charles X., the first gentleman in your country, when you should have hanged his ministers. In '48 you sent a mob of women, gathered from the purlieus of Paris and drunk with rum, to drive Louis Philippe, the prince of your own choice, from his bed at Versailles; and you set him afloat in a fishing-smack on the British Channel. Again, you chose Lamartine, and turned your backs on him. Again, Cavaignac; but you did not like his soldierly conduct. Then you elected Louis Napoleon,—for which I forgive you. It is the best thing you have ever done since the time you allowed the despotisms of Europe to chain up your eagle on the rock of St. Helena."

" Yes; he was our Prometheus."

" Well said. You will not complain that you have a master *now?*"

" O, vive Napoleon!"

" Very well. So I say. He is the only Frenchman who can rule France."

" You—you—monsieur—what do you with your *constitution?*"

" We abide by it. It answers all our purposes. It has not yet been violated in a letter, least of all in its spirit."

" Do you expect to endure?"

" We do. Not a shadow of trouble on that score flits over the heart of a well-informed citizen; not a tremor of hesitation has yet chilled the pulse of our fighting people. This is only the first episode in our history, of which your annals are so full, in which a nation wakes up to look after itself."

" I know France has had some very severe revolutions."

" How long did it take for France to bring the coronet of Burgundy to Paris? How long for England to subjugate Wales or Ireland? how long to bring Scotland to her throne? How long will it take to keep kingdoms together, if you preach and predict the untimely death of this republic?"

" Well, I think, if you can keep up now, you will do almost an *impossibility.*"

" Well, sir, I think we can do it, with or without the sympathy of European Governments. If we have that sympathy, we shall be glad. If not, we will try and shift for ourselves."

" What do you mean by the word *shift?*"

" I mean we will try to manage so that we shall take care of ourselves."

" Oui, monsieur! Now I understand. You think you can get on without any help from Europe?"

" I do, most emphatically; and, if we could not, it is very doubtful if you could give it to us. You will have your hands full at home."

X.

A Hero Soldier neither in the Rank nor File.

WHEN the martial and patriotic fires began to blaze along the hill-tops of Western New York, and our young men were rushing by tens of thousands to join the national standard, one brave fellow who seized the torch with the wildest enthusiasm, and worked hardest in the cause, found it impossible to get his name enrolled with the company of his own town, —Bloomfield.

All his companions passed examination. When the surgeon came to B. F. Surby, he found that he had a *stiff knee*, caused by the kick of a horse while he was a boy; and he was rejected.

He could run as fast, mount a horse as quick, play as good a game of ball, and shoot as well as any one of his comrades, —better, it was acknowledged, than most. He was athletic, lithe, hard, spry, and made for action and daring. He was twenty-five years old, and all ready to fight. But, with all this, he could not go; he was, however, determined to go, and no surgeon or recruiting-officer could stop him.

When the company marched to Canandaigua, he went with them to join the regiment. He put in his pocket all the money he could scrape together, and paid his own way as long as it lasted; and, when it gave out, partly by the help of his companions and partly by cking out in mother-wit what he lacked in cash, he reached the head-quarters of General King, where, his name not appearing on the roll, he was asked to give an account of himself.

What follows is in his own words, as I took them down

while he lay wounded in the Douglas Hospital last December. The incidents are well known to many officers and soldiers in the *corps* in which he served. But the peculiarly *naïve* manner in which he told the story, the total lack of all ostentation or egotism, and, above all, his perfect self-control and even cheerfulness under the pain of a severe wound in the left leg, and a compound fracture in the arm, which he was waiting for the surgeon to amputate, made it one of the most interesting cases I have seen.

"Once beyond the Potomac, I'd be blazed if I wouldn't have a chance. So I tried the old Bloomfield game over; but it was no go: I could not put on the uniform of a soldier; I could not have a gun to kill rebels. But I was bound to fetch it, some way or other. I finally got my case before General King, and he got an officer of his staff to take me as his orderly: so I had my way at last, and once in the army (if I did get in at the back door) I could go along, and ride a good horse into the bargain. That finished the *stiff knee* business, which had bothered the Bloomfield surgeon. So I thanked the stars for my good luck, and waited for the first battle.

"This was in a reconnoissance in force towards Orange Court-House, where we had some nice amusement,—just enough to stir up the blood of green Western New York boys.

"But nothing very serious happened till the battle of South Mountain, which began to look like war as I had read of it in the histories of great generals. Of course you know all about that battle.

 * * * * * *

"But then came some bad luck. I'd been thinking all the time it was too good to last. The officer I was serving got sick after the battle of Cedar Mountain, and had to come on to Washington. Of course I had to come too; and here I remained waiting on him several weeks. In the mean time I lost all chance to be in the battles of Gainesville and Bull Run.

"When my commander got better, but not well enough to take the field, he sent me over to look after his horses, and, knowing my anxiety to be with the brigade, he gave me permission to join it, and the use of his horse.

"I lost no time in doing that. I got in the staff again, and began to feel at home. General King had fallen sick, and was succeeded by General Hatch. We were in the splendid battle of South Mountain, where I had *one of the great days*, worth more than all my life before. Oh, how glorious the old flag looked every time the smoke rolled off and we saw her still streaming!

"In the heat of this bloody engagement, when our men were fighting *just right*, the general was wounded, and, being near him at the moment, I had the sad satisfaction of helping to carry him from the field."

"But," I inquired, "as you seem to have been where the shot flew thick, had you not met with any mishap so far?"

"Nary a scratch,—nor the captain's horse."

"Well, what came next?"

"The grand and blood-red field of Antietam, all of which I saw; and I never expect to see a better one;—nor do I want to. That was no boys' play."

At this point Doctor Pinco, the accomplished surgeon of the hospital, came up to see how his "hero-patient" was getting along. After examining his leg, he pronounced it doing well enough. "That will give you no more trouble. But I am inclined to think I shall have to take this arm off."

"You are welcome to it, doctor. I think it has done me about all the good it ever will."

"Well, I will see you again during the day." And, at a hint from the doctor, I rose and walked with him down the ward, looking through his clear, experienced eyes at many interesting cases under his surgical treatment. Like all men of true science, and especially all masters of the healing art, he looked after his half a thousand suffering patients with the tenderest solicitude. But he seemed to regard Surby with a peculiar interest.

"He is a real hero," he said. "I must take that arm off in the morning; and I wish you would come up. He will mind it no more than the sting of a mosquito. He is always cheerful,—always happy."

*   *   *   *   *   *

"Well, now for Antietam," I said, as I once more took a chair by his side.

"General Doubleday took command of us there, in place of the wounded General Hatch. In forming his division the night before the battle, while the general and his staff were riding along through the lines, a rebel battery opened on us with shot and shell. A soldier was standing about two rods in front of me. A small shell took his head clean off, and struck my horse in the side, just behind my leg, cutting the girths, and *exploding inside the horse*. I only remember the fire flew pretty thick, and, after in some way getting up into the air higher than I was before, I next found myself on the ground among some of the pieces of the horse.

"The first thought was, 'There goes the captain's horse, and I'm left to foot it!' A somewhat sudden falling back took place, and I started. 'But, by Jove, I won't lose that saddle!' and back I put to get it. While I was working away as fast as I could, the general rode by, and, seeing what I was doing, sung out,—

"'Quit that, fool, if you care any thing about your life!' and, as I found it rather difficult to untangle the saddle, I concluded to leave with what traps I had, and return after dark. I did; but it was too late.

"I felt bad. 'What *will* the captain say? I've lost his horse and saddle, and God knows what. Well, I'll see what I can do; I haven't lost my small arms, at any rate; and perhaps I can manage to get another horse before the battle opens in the morning.'"

"Not hurt yourself?"

"Nary a bruise. But I was pretty well spattered up with blood, I remember. So that night, after looking round, and not getting my eye on a horse, I lay down under a fence near our right wing, and thought I would take a nap. But I cared more for a good horse than a good sleep. As luck would have it, I heard, pretty soon, some horses coming down pretty fast. They had evidently broken loose. I sprung for the first one, and missed him. The next was a few rods behind. 'Now,' says I to myself, 'is your last chance;' and it was, for there were only two. I struck for him, and caught him by the bridle-rein. It was light enough to see, and I soon found out I had got a good horse for the captain. I brought him up to the fence and lay down, being pretty well satisfied that what further running that animal did that night he would have to do with me on his back."

"Whom did the horse belong to?"

"He belonged to me."

"Where had he come from?"

"Upon my soul, I forgot to inquire."

"The next morning all was astir, for a battle which had yet no name. But everybody was well enough satisfied that a great fight was coming. It was plain as sunrise that McClellan meant to fight, and that every man in the great army of the Potomac knew it, and was ready to do his duty.

"There was a different feeling among the men and officers the night before, and that morning, from what I had seen before any other battle. Each man knew that defeat that day involved the fall of Washington. But not a doubt of McClellan's generalship or our success entered the mind of a single soldier. So completely had the commander-in-chief won the hearts of every *corps*, that the whole army and he were *one man* at Antietam. Many troops were there to fight under him for the first time; but the moment they rubbed against Mac's old campaigners they melted right in, and the whole body was one army.

*　　*　　*　　*　　*　　*

"So passed that wonderful day. When I hitched up at night, and got my blanket off the saddle-bow and unrolled it to go to sleep, I found two Minie balls snugly imbedded near the centre of the hard roll.—'Thank you, gentlemen: you fired a shade too low.' So I came off safe enough there, and, when I *did* think of it, I made up my mind I was not born to be shot."

"Your new horse behaved well?"

"Finely, and I got very much attached to him. But, poor fellow! I had to kill him to save myself. I was fond of riding about inside our lines, and sometimes beyond them. I knew it was rather a risky business; but I did it, part of the time as a volunteer scout, and at other times on my own hook, and was not sorry for it, for I now and then got information which may have been worth something.

"I generally managed to get along without any particular trouble, and with many a good run managed to get home safe. But one night I got into a scrape.

"I knew that two or three mounted men were near the enemy's picket-lines, and, thinking it might pay, I started about midnight, and rode in a circuitous way to get near enough to reconnoitre from a quarter where I should not be suspected. I saw a very fine horse tied up to a tree, and I wanted that horse. I came very near succeeding. But I was suddenly notified by a ball whistling by my head that I was discovered. I put out, and, finding my horse, put spurs to. Whistle, whizz, whizz, whistle, the balls flew by. It was a close pursuit, and a hard, long run. I passed our lines safe. But it was too much. My horse never was worth much after that. I felt bad about it, for the poor fellow had saved my life more than once. But I had taken good care of him, and, after all, what did it matter? It was all in the cruise.

"Finally, the army was before Fredericksburg. During a part of that fight we were troubled by the enemy's sharp-shooters.

They were picking off our officers and best artillerists, from a very long range. I saw how the thing was working, and I managed to get into an old deserted house (in which Washington is said to have spent some time when young) which could stand a pretty heavy shot.

"I had a splendid rifle, and plenty of ammunition. It was a fine cover, and I used it to some advantage. A large open window looked out just in the direction I wanted, and as fast as I loaded I slyly took a look out, picked my man, and blazed away. I did not stay at the window any unnecessary length of time, for generally a bullet came whistling through the hole a second or two after my flash.

"Heavier shot at last began to strike; and then, after I had fired, I slid round behind a solid stone chimney standing near the centre of the house. I kept this up for a considerable time, till an accident happened.

"As I was approaching the window for another fire, a shell came through the side of the house, and burst about three feet over my head. Down I went, of course, and began to survey the damage. One piece had struck my left arm, making a compound fracture below the elbow; another piece had struck my left leg, just above the knee.

"I thought now, as I had done a pretty good day's work, I would contrive in some way to haul off for repairs and get among my friends. Some of the men at a battery not far off had heard the shell explode in the house where they knew I was firing, and, discovering me, carried me off to the hospital quarters, where after a while my arm was tinkered up in a hurry, my leg was dressed, and I lay down and ate my supper, for I was as hungry as a wolf.

"'Well, old boy,' said I to myself, 'you have had your way: you determined to come to the war, and you did. Now look at yourself, and see how you like it.'

"I *did* look at myself. I didn't look very handsome, it's

true; but I looked well enough for all practical purposes,—
and I *felt* still better.

"Being of no particular use down at Falmouth, they sent
me up here, where I arrived the other day. The doctor down
at Fredericksburg botched my fractures, and, between jolting
about and one thing and another, I must have the arm taken
off now; but, as my leg is nearly well, I shall be about again,
almost as good as new, in a few days."

The next morning, after inhaling ether, he was taken into
the amputating-room, when Dr. Pinco performed one of his
beautiful operations. The arm was taken off three or four
inches below the elbow, and dressed, when Surby was returned
to his cot. The attendants said he was not out of bed over
five minutes.

Of course he got on finely, and in a few days he was
walking around town to return the calls of friends who had
visited him in the hospital.

But what was he to do now? His name did not appear on
the rolls of the army; he had never been mustered into the
service; in fact, the Government knew no such man as *a
soldier.* Generals King, Hatch, and Doubleday, and a large
number of officers besides, knew him, but only as *a volunteer
independent scout.* They knew the deeds of valor, and the
difficult and important services, he had performed,—services
which if rendered by a private regularly mustered into the
army would have early given him a commission. Now he
was to leave the hospital, with one arm the less, no money in
his pocket, and only the shoddiest style of clothes on his
back, to get to his home the best way he could.

He was certainly in a most anomalous position. But he
had friends enough,—more than he needed; for he could
make his own way.

Some of his former commanders caused the facts to be
made known to the War Department; and every thing that
was right and proper was done, and with a promptness, fair-

ness, and despatch which had seldom, if ever, characterized that Department before its present administration. Surby was at once mustered into his regiment, to take effect from the day his company marched out of their native Bloomfield. This gave him pay for the whole time, allowance for clothing he had never drawn, one hundred dollars bounty money, a new patent arm that looks just like its mate, an honorable discharge from the army of the United States, and an annual pension of ninety-six dollars for life. Here's a chance for some bonnie lassie to win *the handsome scout of the Potomac.**

---

* In a letter dated Washington, March 22, 1863, he says :—

"C. Edwards Lester, Esq.

"Dear Sir:—I have finally conquered. I am now an *enlisted* man. Through the kindness of Generals King and Doubleday, and (my) Captain Dennis, I have been mustered into the United States service, to date from December 26, 1861. Too much praise cannot be given to Captain Dennis for his untiring efforts in my behalf, in procuring an order from the Secretary of War to have me mustered into the service and receive my pay, bounty, and pension. I wish, also, to mention Surgeon Pinco as one of my warmest friends, with Major Breck, who has taken a great interest in my case. The kindness of General Doubleday and staff will never be forgotten. I hope always to prove myself worthy of their esteem. I feel that I have done my duty to my country, and some little good to the cause for which we are shedding our blood.

"Yours, faithfully,

"B. F. Surby,
"Douglas Hospital."

XI.

Our Foreign Relations,—such as they are,—such as they may be.

SOMETIMES it is as true with nations as with individuals that an age is crowded into an hour,—that the flash of a sabre may do in a second what a whole generation has waited for,—that exhausted patience among men and governments may assume the prerogatives of the Almighty, and let the bolt and the flash come together. But beware where the bolt strikes.

This has had a full application in our recent experience at home. We found our enemies had become those of our own household. They attempted to break up our Government, to overthrow our Union, to destroy our prosperity, and wind up our history as a first-class Power. The Government of the United States had never deviated from the accomplishment of its legitimate objects. It was made for all, and it had protected all. No State could claim that it had been wronged in *any* measure, without instantly having its wrong adjusted by the supreme legislative, judicial, or executive power.

And thus, without any infraction of law or any invasion of prerogative, one section of the country was arrayed in hostility against the other; and suddenly we found ourselves threatened with the choice of two evils,—a struggle to the death, if necessary, against dismemberment, if not indeed against total destruction, or to submit tamely to inevitable ruin.

This was a new spectacle for the nations of Europe to look on; and, as might be expected, it gave them a good chance for showing how truly they had rejoiced in our prosperity or how glad they would be in our misfortune.

Russia,—by all odds the grandest of all European structures,—without waiting an hour for consultation with other
Powers, sent back her assurances of sympathy with us in
our efforts to frustrate this treasonable attempt to break up
a free and prosperous Government, which had proved so
powerful and beneficent a shield for the protection of all ·
its people.

Russia is the natural ally of the United States. She has a
vast territory, and all her people look to her for protection.
She has, during a thousand years, been slowly but surely
emerging from Asiatic barbarism into the light and strength
of modern civilization. She has, moreover, done what few
other nations have done: she has carried the masses of her
people along with her as fast as she has travelled herself.

Oriental in her origin, she has maintained a patriarchal
government. If it has ever been a despotism in form, it
was manifestly the only machinery strong enough to govern,
protect, and bless all her people.

She undertook a work far more difficult than Rome had to
do. She had to aggregate, harmonize, and blend together the
great nomadic tribes of the East. When from the affluent social systems of Asia, bursting with crowded populations, they
drifted westward on her now European territories, Russia was
submerged by wild, strange, and savage races. She had the
most stupendous task given to her which any nation has ever
had to perform. Contending with difficulties which had never
before been encountered, she has at last presented to the
world the wonderful spectacle of a mighty empire made up
of countless dissevered and warring communities, all ferocious,
all untamed, all nomadic, all speaking different tongues, and
representing all the religious superstitions of the East, but
now all blended in a homogeneous social and political system,
which has not only eclipsed, in the culture of its upper classes,
the refinement of European courts, and matched them in the
arts of war and peace, but has boldly struck the shackles of

slavery from the limbs of as many million men as now make up the population of all our free States.*

---

* A THOUSAND YEARS.

A thousand years, through storm and fire,
  With varying fate, the work has grown,
Till Alexander crowns the spire
  Where Rurik laid the corner-stone.

The chieftain's sword that could not rust,
  But bright in constant battle grew,
Raised to the world a throne august,—
  A nation grander than he knew.

Nor he alone; but those who have,
  Through faith or deed, an equal part,—
The subtle brain of Yaroslav,
  Vladimir's arm, and Nikon's heart,—

The later hands that built so well
  The work sublime which these began,
And up from base to pinnacle
  Wrought out the Empire's mighty plan,—

All these to-day are crown'd anew,
  And rule in splendor where they trod,
While Russia's children throng to view
  Her holy cradle, Novgorod,—

From Volga's banks, from Dwina's side,
  From pine-clad Ural, dark and long,
Or where the foaming Terek's tide
  Leaps down from Kasbek, bright with song,

From Altai's chain of mountain-cones,
  Mongolian deserts far and free,
And lands that bind, through changing zones,
  The Eastern and the Western Sea.

To every race she gives a home,
  And creeds and laws enjoy her shade,
Till far beyond the dreams of Rome
  Her Cæsar's mandate is obey'd.

She blends the virtues they impart,
  And holds within her life combined
The patient faith of Asia's heart,
  The force of Europe's restless mind.

That involuntary servitude should be abolished by the most despotic of nations, with the applause of the world, and the day of emancipation (March 3, 1863) be ushered in by chimes of gratitude and thanksgiving from every church-spire in the Russian Empire, while the great Republic of the world still binds the fetters upon four million slaves, will hereafter read strangely in history.

But a wiser and broader statesmanship than ours guides the destinies of Russia.

It was from such a nation that the earliest words of sympathy and confidence came when our first domestic troubles began; and it will not be forgotten hereafter by the Ameri-

> She bids the nomad's wandering cease
> She binds the wild marauder fast;
> Her ploughshares turn to homes of peace
> The battle-fields of ages past.
>
> And, nobler far, she dares to know
> Her future's task,—nor knows in vain,
> But strikes at once the generous blow
> That makes her millions men again!
>
> So, firmer based, her power expands,
> Nor yet has seen its crowning hour,
> Still teaching to the struggling lands
> That Peace the offspring is of Power.
>
> Build up the storied bronze, to tell
> The steps whereby this height she trod,—
> The thousand years that chronicle
> The toil of Man, the help of God!
>
> And may the thousand years to come—
> The future ages, wise and free—
> Still see her flag and hear her drum
> Across the world, from sea to sea,—
>
> Still find, a symbol stern and grand,
> Her ancient eagle's strength unshorn,
> One head to watch the western land
> And one to guard the land of morn!
>
> BAYARD TAYLOR.

NOVGOROD, RUSSIA, Sept. 20, 1862.

can people when this tempest has swept by us. We see new storms gathering over Europe, and our aid may be invoked against Russia, and invoked in vain. Statesmen know that, while individuals may forgive, nations never do.

* * * * * *

HOW HAS ENGLAND LOOKED ON THIS CONTEST?

Strange enough has been the course she has taken. She will hardly be able hereafter to explain it to others: it is doubtful if she can do it now even to herself.

England lives in America to-day, and is dying at home.

England is clinging to her sepulchres,—and she may well do it; for the places where her great ones repose are the greenest spots on her island.

We Americans cheated ourselves most egregiously when we thought England—once the head of the slave-trade, and only a few years ago the front of the abolitionism of the world—would turn her slavery-hating back on the only organized band of slavery propagandism on the earth!

Poor fools we! Just as though the *British aristocracy* (the true name for the *British Government*) meant any thing but interference and trouble for us when her Grace the Duchess of Sutherland chaperoned the gifted Harriet Beecher Stowe through the court of her Majesty, simply because Mrs. Stowe, by writing a great dramatic novel against slavery, could be made a cat's-paw to pull the chestnuts of the British aristocracy out of the fire!

Yes, abolitionism suited the purposes of the British aristocracy just *then;* and lords and ladies swarmed at negro-emancipation gatherings at Exeter Hall. On all such occasions three standing jokes were played off, to the infinite amusement of dukes and duchesses,—duchesses more particularly.

First, there *must* be a live American negro,—the blacker the better, sometimes; but they generally got one as *little* black as possible, and an octoroon threw them into the highest state of subdued frenzy admissible in the upper classes. The aforesaid negro must have escaped from the indescribable horrors and barbarities of slavery in the Southern States,—gashed, manacled (if he showed the manacles, so much the better),—a sample of American barbarism, and a burning shame on the otherwise fair cheek of the goddess of American Liberty.

"Oh, yes," said my lord Brougham; "nothing stands in your way now but negro slavery. Abolish that, and every heart in England is with you."

Secondly, at these Exeter Hall meetings they *must* have a live American abolitionist,—once a slaveholder who had emancipated his slaves. Here they found their man in the noble Judge Birney, as in the *first* they found a splendid specimen of a runaway octoroon in Frederick Douglas, Esq.,—the black Douglas,—and who, by-the-by, made a better speech by far than any aristocrat in England.

Thirdly, and last of all, some ecclesiastic gentleman bestowed upon the proceedings the benediction.

This would have been well enough,—certainly so far as the benediction was concerned,—had not future events proved beyond a doubt that, at the very moment these curious things were occurring, the whole *prestige* of the British empire was invoked to sanctify and adorn a spirit of hostility to the Government of the United States, and that the solemnities of our holy religion were also invoked in the same cause.

But to my unpractised eye it looked at the time very much as later events have shown it,—a thorough hatred of America by the ruling classes of England.

At one time Lord Brougham presided; again, O'Connell; and again, the venerable Thomas Clarkson: they even got his Royal Highness Prince Albert to do it once, on a somewhat narrower scale,—where even tender young duchesses could attend with impunity (the American negro always being present, like Tom Thumb in Barnum's chief amusements), and, being fortified with a supply of highly-perfumed kerchiefs, the young duchesses managed generally to live it through and revive after reaching the open air!

These farces were played off all through the British Islands; and the poor British people—who, from long habit, I suppose, go where "their betters" go, when allowed to—joined in the movement, and "*American* anti-slavery societies" were everywhere established. Even chambermaids and factory-girls contributed to raise a fund to send " English missionaries" over here " to enlighten the *North* about the duty of the *South* to abolish slavery."

Some of these scenes were sufficiently vulgar; but they were sometimes got up, in some respects, in fine taste. One occasion I recall with the highest pleasure, which, although ostensibly an anti-slavery dinner, was limited chiefly in its company to the literary men of London.

Among the good things of that evening was a short poem written for the occasion by Wm. Beattie, M.D., the gifted and well-known author of "Scotland Illustrated," &c. I do not know if it has been published. I remember two or three of the stanzas. It is an address from " England's Poets to the Poets of America."

Your Garrison has fann'd the flame,
    Child, Chapman, Pierpont, caught the fire,
And, roused at Freedom's hallow'd name,
    Hark! Bryant, Whittier, strike the lyre;

While here hearts myriad trumpet-toned,
    Montgomery, Cowper, Campbell, Moore,
To Freedom's glorious cause respond,
    In sounds which thrill through every core.

Their voice has conjured up a power
    No fears can daunt, no foes arrest,
Which gathers strength with every hour
    And strikes a chord in every breast,—

A power that soon in every land—
    On Europe's shore, on ocean's flood—

Shall smite the oppressors of mankind
And blast the traffickers in blood.

Oh, where should Freedom's hope abide,
    Save in the bosoms of the free?
Where should the wretched negro hide,
    Save in the shade of Freedom's tree?

Oh, by those songs your children sing,
    The lays that soothe your winter fires,
The hopes, the hearths, to which you cling,
    The sacred ashes of your sires,—

By all the joys that crown the free,—
    Love, honor, fame, the hope of Heaven,—
Wake in your might, that earth may see
    God's gifts have not been vainly given.

Bards of Freedom's favor'd land,
    Strike at last your loftiest key,
Peal the watchword through the land,
    Shout till every slave be free.

Long has he drain'd the bitter cup,
    Long borne the burden, clank'd the chain;
But now the strength of Europe's up,—
    A strength that ne'er shall sleep again.

If I should be challenged on the exactness or accuracy of my statements here, I wish to say that I saw many or most of the things I speak of, and am prepared to give the proofs if challenged; but the English journalism of that summer of 1840 (eighteen hundred forty) will save me the trouble for the present. All England was ablaze about American slavery and its abolition.

It was a noble enthusiasm among the people; but it was (anybody could see through it, for it was the veriest gauze) all an aristocratic sham. It did not mean any thing for human freedom. It meant hostility to the United States. *It was got up by British politicians.* Sir Robert Peel and the Duke of Wellington had no part or parcel in it, unless it were through sheer courtesy to the men of their class.

This English crusade against the United States was got up by the British aristocracy in sheer animosity against our Government,—not so much, perhaps, against our people, chiefly because they cared nothing about them. It was our *system of government they hated*, because it was a standing, growing, and luminous reproof of the blighting and degrading system of England, which starves the masses of her people in order that the privileged few may die of surfeit.

"Blackwood's Magazine," an authority not likely to be charged with hostility towards the British oligarchy, nor with favoritism towards our republic, said, in speaking on this same subject in the same year (1840),—

"It were well if some ingenious optician could invent an instrument which would remedy the defects of that long-sighted benevolence which sweeps the field for distant objects of compassion, while it is blind as a bat to the misery around its own doors."

Well said! I saw and felt it all when I went through the streets and lanes and cellars of Manchester, where fifty thousand blanched skeleton men, women, and children were, slowly or rapidly, dying of starvation. In that city, also, vast anti-slavery meetings were got up to induce the North to put down slavery in the South. These assemblages were invariably under the auspices of the aristocracy, and they were held where the police were stationed at the doorways to drive off the famishing, lest their plaint of hunger might salute the ears of their bloated task-masters.

There was no lack of cotton in Manchester then. There was something worse than that. It was the same old complaint you will find in any part of England,—the poor over-worked and under-fed to make the rich richer and the poor poorer.

I went up to Paisley, where more than half the population were being fed from soup-kettles,—and pretty poor soup at that. There, too, the abolition of American slavery seemed to be the only thing which drew forth the sympathies or reached the charity of the aristocratic classes.

So everywhere in England it was, "that long-sighted benevolence, sweeping the distant horizon for objects of compassion, but blind as a bat to the misery at the door."

It was not so in 1840 alone. I have been in England several times since, but I never saw a good year for the poor of that oppressive empire.

To show that this was all the poorest of shams, and that England owes us no good will, let us step from 1840 to 1863.

We see all things the same in England to this day, except in the "negro business." Here all is changed. British sympathy is now shifted from the slave and lavished on his master,—from "moral pocket-handkerchiefs and religious fine-tooth combs" to the overseer's lash and the unleashed blood-hound,—from the maintenance of free institutions to their overthrow,—from civilization to barbarism,—from liberty to bondage.

In 1840, Mr. Stephenson, our Virginia slave-breeding Ambassador near the Court of St. James, became so odious that no chance to snub or insult him was lost by the British Government.

Now, Mr. Adams, holding that same post, and embellishing it with all the great and noble qualities of illuminated talents and Christian philanthropy, is treated with far more neglect and far less cordiality by the same class which despised Stephenson and fêted Harriet Beecher Stowe.

Then England complained of our remissness or shirking in not doing our share towards putting down the slave-trade. Now all her sympathies are with the supporters of slavery itself, which is the only support of slavery on the earth; and her ship-yards and arsenals are taxed to their utmost to build fleets of the strongest and swiftest steam pirates to help the slave-driving Confederacy sweep our peaceful commerce from the sea and once more inaugurate the traffic in flesh and blood.

7

The British Government knew, when the Alabama's keel was laid, that she was to become a pirate; and our minister protested against it in vain. Three hundred of the rich merchants of England, in broad daylight, boasted of their purpose, and have exulted over its successful execution. The British Government gave the earliest and heartiest encouragement to the rebellion, by recognizing it as a belligerent power the moment its task-masters reached London. It allowed all the materials and munitions of war the rebels called for to be furnished, and it has, from the first hour, given to the rebellion all the aid and comfort it dared to furnish our enemies in their atrocious attempt to immolate liberty and enthrone slavery in the Western world!*

---

* It has amazed those who are familiar with Lord John Russell's public history that he should have trifled so heartlessly with the great issues of civilization and free government at stake in this rebellion. This shuffling has cost him the confidence of the great middle class in England and the respect of the world. If the following letter addressed to him may seem to be unlike letters usually written to titled men, I consider it quite respectful enough to the man who has struck hands with pirates and become pimp to the propagandists of negro slavery. Although written nearly two years ago, I see no occasion for retracting a syllable or cancelling a word.

MY LORD:—We have a habit you are not much accustomed to,—of straight talk and honest dealing: so you need not be amazed if we speak very plainly in this despatch.

You have all your life been a place-seeker or a place-holder. To get power and money, you have always turned your back on your friends and let your Reform measures go to the dogs. Whenever you have been an "out," and any American question came up, you were a warm advocate of our Republic. When you were an "in," you changed your tone. When Liberty was at stake in a foreign nation, or at home, you have been its noisiest champion,—if an "out." If an "in," you have done your best to crush it, in Ireland, Hungary, Italy, Spain, and Poland. It was with a pang that you saw even old Greece become free. For half a century, if an "out," you have brawled for Freedom and Free Governments; if an "in," you have resorted to the very last trick to keep there. You have, if an "out," always paraded your friendship for the United States, and virulently assailed any Tory or Conservative ministry. "In" again, you first veered, then hesitated, then tacked, and then attacked us, our Government,

No jurist will pretend to say that in all this she has not violated the spirit, if not the letter, of her own laws of neu-

---

and all American things. You know our Republic has never had any fair play from any ministry except the Tories or Conservatives. All Americans involuntarily say of British politicians of your stripe, "Save us from our friends, and we will take care of our enemies." But you have reserved the meanest and most bare-faced tergiversation of your public life till you were pressing the verge of your mortal existence. After pointing a thousand times with exultation to our great and prosperous nation, and deploring the two wars England waged against us, you are now gloating over the prospect (as you deem it) of our speedy disruption and downfall. After hobnobbing with every abolitionist and fêting every run-away American negro who managed to reach England, and imploring Britons no longer to use slave-grown cotton and sugar, you now take sides with the "nigger-driving" secessionists of the rebel States, who are trying to break down freedom in America and extend the area of that accursed institution and sanctify the revival of the African slave-trade. You are threatening war against the United States unless we will surrender two intercepted traitors on their way to your abolition arms and sympathies, the chiefest emissaries which the slavery you have always pretended to hate could send to your shores.

O JOHN RUSSELL! how unworthy is all this of the descendant of your great ancestor, who sealed with his blood on the scaffold his life-long devotion to the cause of justice and human freedom! Why must you, just as you are ending your career, rob your proud name of that ancient halo which has gathered around it, by expending your last efforts in trying to blot out Free Government, for which the founder of your race so nobly died, and perpetuating on our virgin soil African slavery, which the world is clamoring to see blotted out?

My lord, do you plead that the necessity of slave-grown cotton calls for so dastardly a betrayal by yourself of all the *souvenirs* of your life? and will you, to accomplish this purpose, trample on all the canons of international law and become public robbers and go and steal this cotton? If you attempt it, will you succeed? How much cotton would you get before your ministry went down?—before you lost a market for your commerce with twenty-three million freemen?—before our breadstuffs, which are now keeping the wolf away from British doors, would reach your shores?—before bread-riots would occur throughout the British Islands which would make you turn pale?—before all seas would swarm with our privateers,—now twentyfold more numerous than in 1812, when you found them too fleet and too strong for you?—before you encountered, in addition to two millions of our native soldiers and sailors, half a million of adopted citi-

trality, and the laws of nations. No intelligent man will deny that by these acts she has prolonged and inflamed this accursed war. No man in his senses supposes for a moment that England would have ventured on such a course of hostility and inhumanity at any other period of our history since the Peace of 1815.

No other thoughts can suggest themselves to impartial men now, while we are going through a domestic trouble,—a *great* trouble, which has filled every true heart in America or else-

---

zens,—able-bodied men, *formerly British subjects*, and burning to avenge the wrongs of centuries inflicted on their devoted island?

My lord, do you plead that the exigencies of statesmanship demand that you should turn the arms of the earth against you? Do you suppose that NAPOLEON would lose such a chance for avenging Waterloo? or Russia for taking Constantinople? or all despotisms for crushing your supremacy? or all the peoples of Europe for crushing monarchy?

It would seem that England should be willing, at least, to let us manage our domestic affairs, since she has incurred a quarter of her national debt in interfering with them;—that she should not now take to her arms "the foul corpse of African slavery on our soil," when it cost her *five hundred million dollars* to get rid of it in her own territories! Should not the Founder of Modern Liberty be glad to see how prosperously the brood of her young eagles had founded an empire-home in the New World's forests, and not writhe, and chafe, and bark at and hawk at our nest, till she could come here and tear it to pieces?

The time had gone by, we hoped, when England, our *own mother*, would try to become *our step-mother!* Why could she not have been proud in the pride of her daughter, and let her wear the jewels she had herself so nobly won? And yet malicious people say that England acts like some old dame, who, after parting with the title to a daughter's estate, feels that she has still some *reserved right* left to interfere in what no longer concerns her, and casts now and then an envious glance at beauty yet unshrivelled and conquests forever beyond her reach.

Can it be, my lord, that such unworthy feelings as these can now enter your heart as an English statesman? We cannot believe it. Can you desire to put one more great trouble on the heart of your beloved, widowed queen? We cannot believe it.

My lord, you should be engaged in doing some good to the people of your own empire, rather than in trying to hurt a great, a kindred, and a friendly nation. After attempting so long to be a statesman, do not finish by being only a ministerial bully.

where with a sadness which has dragged us "down to the depths of the earth."

That England should choose such a moment of our national adversity, such as she has so often passed through, of *vindicating the supremacy of government to save civilization,*—a moment when she saw what she fondly deemed a fatal blow · levelled at our prosperity, if not our very existence,—such a moment to join our foes to make our destruction sure!

Thank God! she was the only nation that contemplated with satisfaction our impending doom! Thank God! she will never live to see it! We have been punished for our national sins already, till the blood has burst from every pore; and the cup of trembling may be pressed still harder to our lips hereafter. But we shall not *die.* In the Doomsday-Book of Nations many a leaf must be turned after England's record has been passed, before ours can be reached. *Nations never die in the morning of life.* They are *chastised* in their youth that they may grow up in wisdom and right-eousness. But when they have grown hoary in crime, and chastisement will no longer end in reformation, they must go to their graves, unwept, unrepented, unforgiven.

*　　　*　　　*　　　*　　　*　　　*

It is always pleasant to turn away from the contemplation of British unfriendliness to our Government, and, crossing that narrow channel, greet the sight of the vine-clad hills of France. Once on that genial soil, the American feels at home. He may not speak its language, he may not understand its simplest expressions; but he feels among friends. France may be growing restive under the reign of Louis Philippe, and the fever of an approaching revolution may be felt in the heated air; or that great nation may have grown wild in the delicious delirium of a Lamartine republic; the *coup d'état* of the 2d of December may have just fallen; or he may find all France calm, prosperous, and happy under the strong but beneficent sway of the Emperor of her choice.

It is still France to the American.   So true is that saying of Rousseau, "It is possible to love friends better than
kindred."

This sentiment is nothing new in our times.   Under all forms
of government and at all periods of our political existence,
the two nations have been friends.   This friendship has been
broken up by no war; it has been disturbed by no revolution.   Nor is it at all likely to be.   The reasons are plain.
Under no possible circumstances can France love England;
under no possible circumstances can England like France.
France did not willingly resign her empire in North America;
and the moment our Declaration of Independence was made
she became our national ally, and helped us to wrest the
Thirteen Colonies from the grasp of her ancient foe.   She
again, for a miserable pittance, sold us the vast territory of
Louisiana,—*first* to strengthen our Government, and *second*
to keep it out of the hands of England.   It is safe to say that
if we had not held the mouth of the Mississippi we should
have had a very different history.

But this is by no means all we owe to France.   We are indebted far more to her efforts for the civilization of America
than we are even to her friendship since we became a people.

A glance or two at the past will make this clear.

Most of the continent lying within the limits of the forty-
ninth and twenty-ninth parallels of latitude belonged originally
to France; and all along its great shores and rivers she set up
the light-houses of civilization.   She explored all the great
lines of communication which the trade and commerce of the
continent follow to-day.

Beginning with the mouth of the great river St. Lawrence, she
penetrated the unknown bosom of North America.   Arrested
only for a day before Niagara,—that eternal miracle of the
physical creation,—the explorers pushed on over inland seas,
till, without the stars to guide them, they would have been
hopelessly lost on the waving prairies of the Far West.

Those early explorers were the Jesuit missionaries of France. They were the first pathfinders of our empire; they first carried the torch of Christianity and science into those unexplored regions.

Two centuries have gone by; but their monuments still remain. They can be traced from Arcadia to St. Anthony's Falls. The magic shores of Champlain and Lake George still hold the echoes of the shouts of the chivalry of France. They planted the *fleur de lis*, and it grows there still. The names of Montcalm and Champlain still ring among those mountains; and among the few stricken descendants of Indian tribes who still haunt those neighborhoods these names are household words.

The French left their language among the children of the forest, and it is preserved. The Iroquois still remember with tenderness and love the souvenirs left them by the humanity, the science, the genius and superb manners of the Jesuit fathers and the brave cavaliers of the age of Louis XIV.

Sailing up the other great continental river from the Gulf of Mexico, the French explorers reached the westernmost point their St. Lawrence brothers had made, till they met and held council on one of those anticlinal ridges where, if a drop of water be spilt on a sharp edge, half of it finds its way to the ocean through the St. Lawrence, the other goes to mingle with the warm Gulf Stream.

And so everywhere we follow the path of these explorers we find evidences of the efforts of the French to introduce civilization. They founded cities; they established missions; they explored regions utterly unknown; and they left in their writings imperishable monuments to their fame.

France came to America to give light, knowledge, science, religion, liberty. For no other purpose did she ever set foot on this continent.

England never came but for robbery, conquest, or to establish negro slavery. She never tried to civilize the American

Indian.   She never helped establish a colony on this continent, unless it may have been to reward a court favorite with
a monopoly or to make sinecures for her nobility.

New England owes her no thanks; for it was settled by
the Puritans, after she had hunted them out of her kingdom
like wild beasts.   Miles Standish, Roger Williams, Lord Baltimore, William Penn, Oglethorpe:—what did the British
Government ever do for any of these men, or their colonies?

True, England was ready enough to claim such colonies
as her *property*, and such colonists as her *subjects*, as soon as
they were important enough to tempt her cupidity.   But
what help did the British Government ever give these colonies?   It was claimed in the House of Commons, during the
debate on the Stamp Act, that we had been planted by its
care and nurtured by its protection.   "Planted by your care?"
exclaimed the indignant Colonel Barré.   "No! your oppres-
sions planted them in America.   Nourished by your indulgence?   They grew up by your neglect."

But, leaving all those old wrongs in oblivion, and for-
getting even the insults which followed them in later years,
a new generation had come up, prepared to look with
friendly eyes on what was once called in America *our fatherland*.   The two nations seemed to be coming together and
clasping hands in a lasting alliance.   A cable was laid on the
floor of the ocean that rolled between us; and *once*, at least, it
sent a message of amity, and it was heartily responded to.
Here the amity seemed to end.   The cable could go no further.
Was it ominous?   It seems up-hill work to lay another, particularly with both termini on British soil!   Yes! to flash by
submarine lightning new aid and comfort to the murderers of
our republic,—advising them that a new steam war-pirate for
their service has just passed the grain-ship Griswold in the
Mersey, the one to destroy the commerce and the lives of
loyal American citizens, the other freighted with bread to
save the lives of the starving operatives of Lancashire!

Most English statesmen seem to be laboring just now under a strange infatuation. They appear to forget from what sources this nation sprung, and the elements of strength and endurance we have aggregated in our progress; that we are not *one* people, but *all* peoples, since all have mingled to aggregate one republic; that these new combinations have resulted in a new form of national existence; *that none of us propose to surrender this system of political life;* that any other system must, at least for a long time to come, be an impossibility here; and that it is the fixed and unalterable determination of the great body of the American people to maintain their institutions forever.

If in taking this course we are to encounter the opposition of other nations, we are prepared to do it. We have done nothing to provoke it, as far as we know, nor is it likely that we shall. We wish to avoid it, if we can. But it would be going too far to say that we would purchase immunity from foreign intervention at any price whatever.

XII.

The Issue as the South made it:—Independence or Subjugation.

FROM the first hour of this Rebellion, its leaders have declared that there was only one issue to be tried:—*Independence* or *Subjugation*. They have never admitted the possibility of the suppression of the revolt through the triumph of the national arms. The overthrow and capture of their armies— the very worst thing they thought could ever happen—we supposed would end the struggle. They thought differently; and they still declare that they adhere to the ground they first took:—if they fail in achieving their separation and independence, they expect nothing but extermination.

Therefore they must prepare for it, for it will come: they have pretty nearly ruined themselves already; we can finish the work. If there must be a final sacrifice, it will not be the Union.

They have held up their subjugation as a bugbear to excite the sympathy or horror of the world,—like an arrested felon who declares that, if the officers of justice do not let him go, he will take his own life: as though anybody cared how soon he did it. It is a matter of no sort of consequence to mankind, how quick traitors die; but it is of some importance that, like Judas Iscariot, they should make way with themselves, and thus save honest people the expense of their conviction and hanging.

No! the world in 1863 can richly afford to dispense with the further services in the cause of humanity of all men and all communities whose sole business consists in sustaining slavery and the slave-trade, or any other man-degrading and Heaven-insulting system of iniquity. The death of tyrants is the resurrection of Freedom.

If the truth were all told, it is now plain enough that during the first year of the war we carried it on with a fatal degree of humanity. Mr. Lincoln had said, "Nobody is hurt;" and it seemed likely, under that system, that nobody would be,—except two or three hundred thousand of our youthful soldiers. They have left their bones to bleach on the fields of their valor, or they have been carried out dead from the hospitals, or they have gone home with broken-down constitutions or crippled for life.

The most stringent orders were given not to interfere with slavery or the slaves under any circumstances; not to destroy rebel property, but to protect it: and many a soldier has been shot down by the rebels while he was protecting the property of armed insurgents. Things had gone so far that slaves who passed our lines were ordered to be sent back; they could not be employed even in the most menial offices of the camp; while the idea of drafting them into the army sent a chill of horror through the veins of all "conservative men." Generals who attempted it, or proclaimed the slaves of all rebels in conquered territory *free*, were either severely reprimanded or relieved of their commands.

The idea of prosecuting a war with any great success on this system would have been simply ridiculous, had it not been suicidal. Tens of thousands of our best troops were kept up to their waists at work in water and mud, under a tropical sun, with gangs of negroes eating army rations and looking on the brutal immolation of the army itself.

The first blow levelled at this silly, shilly-shally way of waging an aggressive war, came from the sturdy hand of that earnest, clear-headed man, General Benjamin Franklin Butler. On the 25th of May, some fugitives from Hampton made their way to Fortress Monroe, and under a flag of truce—the then usual style—were claimed as fugitives from service under and by virtue of the Fugitive Slave Act. General Butler looked at the case as coming within the provisions of military law, and decided that, under the peculiar circumstances, he considered the fugitives *contraband of war*. *This* was the first time that term had been applied to escaped slaves. It was then inscribed on the charter of their freedom.

It was, too, the first gleam of good sense and military judgment on this subject which had flashed through the war.

From that hour the Revolution began to move. The Rebellion began to grow weak; the Union, to grow strong.

The Rebellion was assailed in its weak point: we had to undermine the castle which could not be carried by storm.

XIII.

The Mission of the Masonic Fraternity in this War.

THE beneficent influence of this great and humane institution, which has constituted a body-guard for humanity as it has travelled down to us from the ancient ages, has never been so widely or so deeply felt at any period as during the ragings of this unfraternal, and consequently unmasonic, war.

Masonry has never had a motto dearer to the hearts of its brothers than "PEACE ON EARTH, GOOD WILL TO MEN." It loves justice and country, and can draw the sword for both. It has done it in this war and in other wars. But it put forth herculean efforts to avert this trouble. Correspondence, appeals, counsel, invocation,—ALL were tried before the rupture came. Conventions met, North and South, East and West; everywhere the patriotic, the true, the brave, and the unselfish communed together; and at one time we believed that our great fraternity of more than a quarter of a million men could arrest the tide of Disunion and quell the storm of political madness and sectional hate. But the storm was too loud, the night too dark. We were on the breakers!—we struck! among the saddest hearts in the country, the very saddest beat in our bosoms.

But we were not alone. The gloom that clouded our spirits cast its shadow over every nation. The Old World sent back its cheering messages and hailed us in our sufferings. Wherever the news of our national disasters was heard in foreign countries, it called forth expressions of sympathy from uncounted thousands of our brothers, whom we never saw, and never shall see till the Grand Architect finally calls us all to sit together in his own Temple, each to receive the reward of his work.

Masonic incidents of the war could be multiplied without number. I shall give but few.

Let me say to those who know this brotherhood only by popular report or external signs and emblems, that its great object is *the elevation and happiness of our fellow-men,*—all brothers, because all children of the same beneficent and almighty Father who bids us walk together in unity and love on the earth till we meet again in another life, higher, purer, and better than this.

It should not seem strange that the members of such a commonwealth, on whose encampments no sun ever goes down and in whose canopy the stars shine forever,—a commonwealth that is limited to no clime and hemmed in by no mountains or oceans,—whose citizens, without regard to language or sect, always meet on common ground and greet each other as kindred, ready to put one's life in the other's stead,—all aspiring to the noblest life we can live,—it should not seem strange that a different tie should bind us together than binds other men.

Many and many a time, in scenes of carnage which have marked the prosecution of this war, has the widow's son found help.

In one of the frequent collisions which occurred between Stuart's cavalry and our own near the Blue Ridge, free-masonry shone out in all the glory of humanity with which it was delivered to us by the ancient founders of our institutions. Then American character came out, in its *oriflamme* of heroism, to prove that we have a country, and that the old banner must be kept floating. Floating! Yes! The next man that hauls down that flag, *"shoot him on the spot!"* General Dix never uttered better words than these.

    *   *   *   *   *   *

But that the true, earnest-hearted love of our brothers should die in the depth of all our home-troubles,—that hu-

manity should for once grow pale before the skeleton form
of terror,—we never thought of that. But you know, brothers
mine, that we love humanity no less—that our fellow-men are
no less dear to us—even if they have not come within the
charmed circle of our common love. Many of them are our
brothers who will be; for our great fraternity must, sooner
or later, embrace all the true and faithful who dwell in all
climes, who speak all languages, who love humanity as the
nearest approach to God.

Yes! one day, my brothers, we shall all come together. In
our common home we shall all meet. No good being can in-
terrupt our calm contemplations We shall, as true men and
real brothers, come together at last!

And what a meeting will that be! No wanderer lost,—
a family complete in heaven!

*　　*　　*　　*　　*　　*

Oh, what a gathering! From our first grand master to
our present honored one,—an unbroken chain of nobly-de-
scended successors, who have ever given us "light from the
East," and consolation in all the sufferings and trials of our
humble but sanctified brotherhood, as it has done its good and
heroic work, down through the dim and doubtful ages.

That will be the day of our triumph! We can expect to see
what we *believe* in now,—one brotherhood that God loves and
pardons, and one brotherhood which tried on earth to make a
brotherhood in heaven. We live in the eternal sunshine of
hope. To us all the present belongs, and that "present is all
flashing with the purple light of love." We have faith in our
truth to each other,—in our national love; we believe in the life
that now is, and a still stronger faith we hold in the better life
to come. Yes! this faith holds us up when we are sinking. It
sustains us in desponding hours, when we begin to doubt even
if the earth goes round the sun,—when the last fragment of
Galileo's world is crumbling at our very feet. Yes! then we
say, "Thy will be done!"

XIV.

The Real Dignity of Citizenship—Robert J. Walker.

AFTER Paul had been carried into the castle of Jerusalem, from whose steps he had addressed a blood-thirsty mob of his countrymen, the chief captain of the castle ordered him to be examined by scourging. As they were binding him with thongs, he "said unto the centurion that stood by, Is it lawful for you to scourge a man that is a Roman, and uncondemned? When the centurion heard that, he went and told the chief captain, saying, Take heed what thou doest, for this man is a Roman. Then the chief captain came, and said unto him, Tell me, art thou a Roman? He said, Yea. And the chief captain answered, With a great sum obtained I this freedom. And Paul said, *But I was free born.*"

Citizenship meant something in those best days of the Roman Empire. Valor, justice, and loyalty to the constitution of Rome had for centuries imparted a dignity to citizenship which commanded the admiration and respect of the world. In a distant province and on another continent, far from the capital of the Cæsars, Paul had only to announce those magic words, "I am a Roman citizen: I appeal unto Cæsar;" and his person at once became sacred.

"Thou appealest unto Cæsar, unto Cæsar shalt thou go."

Men made Rome,—not the *gods*.

In no nation has citizenship been surrounded with greater security and glory than in the republic of Washington. He has been to the commonwealth of the Potomac more than Romulus was to the republic of the Tiber. That commonwealth must be preserved, as was its great prototype. Rome never dealt daintily with traitors. She never had but one in her Senate, and he "fled like a lated ghost that snuffs the morning air" the instant his treason was discovered. Our Senate-House swarmed with traitors, and they were allowed, with unpardonable impunity, to blaspheme the Union even in the presence of its most sacred altars.

But, while these degenerate scoffers at a common nationality were maturing their conspiracy for its overthrow, another and a vast company of loyal and great citizens were preparing for its defence, and at the first signal of danger they came crowding around the ark of the Constitution with a higher and completer dedication.

Among them all, there was none purer or greater than the man whose eloquence and patriotic exertions had successfully defeated in Mississippi and the whole Southwest the first onset against the Union, thirty years before. Youthful then, but not so vigorous as this rebellion found him, he has brought to the aid of the country all the vigor and might of his genius and all the prestige of his mature and enviable fame. In all the attributes which make up the chancellor of the exchequer, the advocate and jurist, the patriot and the statesman, his fame is full. No man in private life has brought to the support of Mr. Chase, in his grand and successful measures of finance, such powerful arguments and lucid illustrations. His papers on this subject have been read by all the bankers and statesmen of America and Europe.

Those, however, who have not enjoyed a familiar acquaintance with Mr. Walker cannot be expected fully to appreciate his intellectual character and acquisitions.*

---

* I shall never cease to consider myself fortunate in having formed the acquaintance of Governor Walker at an early period of life. The first cessation of my academic studies I seized with avidity for a journey to the Southwest. What I supposed would be a visit of a few days to the delightful city of Natchez, in 1834, ended in a protracted delay, solely for the purpose of profiting by the instruction of Governor Walker in the

The intellect of Robert J. Walker presents a rare combination of qualities seldom found united in the same individual. It is at once practical and profound, active and strong, inventive and laborious, bold and cautious. The basis of this peculiar mental organization is to be found in the perfection of those fundamental faculties which contribute to the extent and accuracy of knowledge as well as to its practical and logical use. Mr. Walker is gifted with extraordinary powers of observation, and with a memory of the most tenacious character. His imagination, although subordinate to the judgment, is sufficiently powerful to give character to his whole intellect; but it is chiefly observable in the boundless resources which it places at his disposal in any emergency requiring the exercise of that faculty.

Few men who have travelled so little have seen so much or derived equal profit from their personal observations. Mr. Walker is by no means unacquainted with the observations of others; yet the most valuable information he possesses, and that which he uses to the best effect, he has acquired in his own personal experience, confined chiefly to his native country. No American is more thoroughly acquainted with the United States, their physical features, their public improvements, and their boundless resources of all kinds. His knowledge on all these subjects is not general and indistinct, but is surprisingly accurate and minute. Indeed, there is, in all the operations of Mr. Walker's mind, whether merely passive and receptive or active and creative, such an intensity that every impression made upon it, either by observation or reflection, constitutes a vivid picture, distinct and perfect in its outlines, and ever ready to appear at his command to instruct and delight his friends.

---

principles of law and public economy. For what little I may have written or done that has been or may become of any service to my fellow-men, I shall always be grateful to him as my wisest and best master. Above, I have ventured on an analysis of his philosophical genius.

In argument or investigation, the movements of Mr. Walker's mind are so quick and active, its resources so unbounded, and the results of its action often so unexpected and surprising, that no ordinary effort will suffice to follow its subtle processes or to understand the principle which controls them. With an equal prospect of success one might undertake to analyze . the rays of reflected light which emanate from a superbly-polished diamond, and which, in their intensely pure and perfect brilliancy, change with every motion of the gem and with every shade of color in the surrounding objects. Mr. Walker's mind seems to be just such a source of intellectual radiance.

Nothing enters it that is not transformed by its magic power into shapes of usefulness and beauty. Its internal action is intensified by his peculiar bodily constitution,—by the transparency of the physical medium through which it observes, and by the delicacy and perfection of the organization in which it resides. No intellect was ever so little influenced by the mortal framework which enclosed it. The moods and conditions which affect so powerfully the minds of other men are utterly devoid of any influence over the soul of Mr. Walker. Under all circumstances, objects present themselves to his mind in their usual forms and colors, and are given out again in new and extraordinary combinations.

Perhaps the most remarkable trait in the mental character of Mr. Walker is the fertility of his inventive or projective genius when applied to political, social, or economical subjects. This is nothing less than the true creative faculty, though it be exercised exclusively in practical affairs. It is the imagination applied to the most useful and important of all work,—the poetic inspiration made to perform its noble office in the homely departments of ordinary life. No one can fully appreciate this quality in Mr. Walker's mind who has not witnessed the wonderful wealth of inventions which he pours out in profusion on all occasions when called upon to present measures

for some great and pressing emergency. The single suggestion which may be finally adopted, though selected with infinite judgment, gives no adequate idea of his intellectual resources. It is necessary to know and estimate the ideas which
have been set aside and rejected, in order to understand fully
the character and value of that which is retained. It is his
habit to empty his fertile brain of its thoughts on any such
subject, and then to choose the one which seems most suitable
to the end required. Like some great magician, he pours out
a multitude of gems, all sparkling and brilliant, and calls on
you to select the one which most pleases your fancy, or he
exercises the same choice for himself; and, like the true magician, his store seems inexhaustible.

Most observers would characterize Mr. Walker's mind as
being pre-eminently inductive; and perhaps he himself would
regard this as the true appreciation of his intellect. Certainly
no man was ever more studious of details, or sustained his
theories by a stronger array of facts. But I cannot help
thinking that the deductive faculty, after all, is the predomi-
nant one in his mind. This alone will explain the quickness
and fertility of his inventive genius. Either through the facts
by some intense activity of generalization, or by an intuitive
faculty apparently independent of facts, he seems to see at a
glance the great general truths which rule the economical and
political world. He is infinitely laborious and indefatigable
in marshalling the facts and testing his generalizations by
them, explaining every apparent exception, and modifying
the expression of general truths so as to comprehend the infinite number of particulars which only seem to conflict with
each other. Never satisfied until the subject of investigation
is utterly exhausted, he pursues it, with untiring patience and
ardor, into all its minutiæ and collateral ramifications. He
follows every thread of philosophical connection to the last
extremity, and having satisfied his most unsparing critic,—him-

self,—he pronounces the result with confidence of full conviction and with the certainty of absolute demonstration.

In the true sense of the term, Mr. Walker is a genuine lover of philosophical truth and a sincere seeker of it. Such is the analysis of the mind of this extraordinary man, as I have read it for many years.

XV.

The United States Sanitary Commission*—How it started, what it intended to do, and how it has been done.

SOME brief account of the Commission should come into this book, for three good and satisfactory reasons. *First,* the country knows very little about the matter. It has gone along too quietly to jostle itself into notoriety, and it has been too busy with its great work to cultivate ostentation. Thank God that science never takes one step backward,—that humanity never retrogrades! *Second,* the objects of this Commission should be more fully known to our people. Blood and carnage have ruled the hour: the people of this nation and other nations have stood gazing in blank amazement at this wild drama, with no time to think of any thing

---

* When the suggestion of a General National Sanitary Commission was presented to the President, he authorized it *at once,* and clothed the Commission with all necessary authority. It was too convincing to need arguments, and too plain to need illustration. This prompt response was one of the most striking proofs that the wisest action of a really free nation comes from the heart of its people. The President not only acted quickly, but wisely. The men he appointed commanded the confidence of the country; and they command it in a still higher measure to-day:—

The Rev. Henry W. Bellows, D.D., New York; Prof. A. D. Bache, LL.D., Washington; George W. Cullum, U. S. A., Washington; Alexander E. Shiras, U. S. A., Washington; Robert C. Wood, M.D., U. S. A., Washington; William H. Van Buren, M.D., New York; Wolcott Gibbs, M.D., New York; Samuel G. Howe, M.D., Boston; Cornelius R. Agnew, M.D., New York; Elisha Harris, M.D., New York; J. S. Newberry, M.D., Cleveland; George T. Strong, New York; Horace Binney, Jr., Philadelphia; The Right Rev. Thos. M. Clark, D.D., Providence. Rhode Island; The Hon. Joseph Holt, Kentucky; R. W. Burnett, Cincinnati; The Hon. Mark Skinner, Chicago; Frederick Law Olmsted, New York.

but the great strife itself. *Third, this Commission has moved sanitary science ahead.*

It is too early yet to determine the boundaries of its conquests. But it is safe to say that it has inaugurated in its own field a far better system than had ever existed before in any country. It has come up from what Lord Bacon so well denominated the source of all power,—the bosom of the people.

One evening, as nearly as I can learn, Rev. Dr. Bellows, and some other gentlemen, in a pleasant *réunion* in a private room in New York, discussed a plan which, under the sanction of their great names and through the indefatigable labors of these pioneers ever since, has resulted in the formation and superstructure of one of the most beneficent and glorious institutions in the world.

The founders did not contemplate in the beginning the achievement of impossibilities. They undertook to do what should be done,—what it was right to do,—what was needed; and they did it at the right time. It has been a practical working machine. Its objects were to make modern sanitary science become the handmaid of the rifled cannon; to cure by the matchless agencies of humanity and learning as fast as gun-makers could mangle; to save all unnecessary loss of health or life; to improvise means of rescue and recovery; to improvise hospitals on the battle-field; to send the disciples, and sometimes the apostles, of the laboratory, the scalpel, and the kitchen, to every camp, and, through the smoke of embattled hosts, to bring away in Good-Samaritan arms the wounded, the helpless, and the dying; to lead the van and press the rear of every *corps;* to advise about the location of camps, the best *régime* for an army's diet and clothing, the personal habits of soldiers, and the proper cooking of their food:—in a word, how the patriot soldier may, with all the appliances of science and humanity, be able to do his full duty to his country before he falls in her cause or returns with honors to his home.

Such were the objects of the Sanitary Commission; and these objects they have quietly and successfully accomplished even beyond their best hopes. Some illustrations are needed to show these points more specifically. Let the Commission speak for itself.

FIRST. ITS ORGANIZATION AND DUTIES.

In their first report to the Secretary of War (December 9, 1861), the Commission says:—

"SIR:—By direction of the Sanitary Commission, I respectfully submit the following report of its operations since its appointment by you, on the 9th of June, 1861, pursuant to the recommendation of the Acting Surgeon-General, under date of May 22. 1861.

"By your order appointing the Commission, it was vested with no legal authority, and with no power beyond that of 'inquiry and advice in respect of the sanitary interests of the United States forces.' It was directed especially 'to inquire into the principles and practices connected with the inspection of recruits and enlisted men, the sanitary condition of the volunteers, to the means of preserving and restoring the health and of securing the general comfort and efficiency of troops, to the proper provision of cooks, nurses, and hospitals, and to other subjects of like nature.'

"The Commission has from the first fully recognized the fact that its office was purely auxiliary and advisory, and that it was created solely to give what voluntary aid it could to the Department and the Medical Bureau in meeting the pressure of a great and unexpected demand on their resources."

In a circular (October 22, 1862) for general information, they more minutely unfold their objects. These are stated to be to—

"1. Maintain constant inspection of camps for the dissemination of intelligence regarding the prevention of sickness.

"2. Maintain the preparation and distribution of short but thorough medical and sanitary papers for the guidance of medical and other officers.

"3. Relieve the wounded on battle-fields, by supplying them with condensed food, stimulants, and means of preserving life, as at the battle of Antietam, when twenty thousand dollars were expended in a few days.

"4. Keep a corps of experts in constant circulation in all our hospitals, reporting defects, correcting evils, and doing their utmost to alleviate the radical sources of suffering.

"5. Maintain the machinery for collecting and distributing the supplies furnished by the homes of the land,—a business of great labor, expense, and wide agencies.

"6. Afford special relief at our various 'homes' for sick and wounded men who are *in transitu* from camps and hospitals.

"7. Make the general wants and condition of sick and wounded men a constant study, and strive, by influences on Government, on Congress, and the public, to secure such new laws, or general orders, or *to make such a public opinion* as will induce constant improvement in their condition."

And still further :—

"The plan of the Relief Service of the Sanitary Commission is—

"1. To secure, as far as practicable, reserves of hospital and ambulance supplies, in order to be prepared to act with efficiency in emergencies.

"2. To cover in its work, as far as practicable, the whole field of the war, dispensing supplies wherever most needed, to all in the service of the Union, without preference of State, arm, or rank, army or navy, volunteer or regular.

"3. To study the whole field, by means of carefully selected and trained medical inspectors, in order to determine where supplies are most needed, and to watch against their misuse.

"4. While administering to all pressing needs of the suffering, to carefully avoid relieving the officials in charge in any unnecessary degree from their responsibility, but to do all that is possible to secure his full rights to the soldier unable to help himself.

"5. To cordially co-operate, as far as practicable, with the hospital service of the Government, endeavoring to supplement, never to supplant it."

SECOND. THE NECESSITY FOR THE ESTABLISHMENT OF THE SANITARY COMMISSION, AND WHAT IT HAS DONE.

"A large percentage of the disease and weakness of our armies up to this time (in other words, the waste of many millions of our national resources) has been due to the inexperience of medical and military officers alike as to the peculiar dangers and exposures that surround the soldier in camp and on the march, and which render the money the nation has expended in putting him into the field a far more precarious investment than it would be were he kept under strict subjection to sanitary laws. The liability of soldiers to disease should be far less than it is. It would be so were they required to observe the laws of health. They and their officers, and the people and the Government, have thus far too generally overlooked those laws. But the last twelve months have taught the army and the people the immense importance of sanitary science in war.

"Our school has been costly, but it has already taught us much. For the last three months, thousands and thousands of wan and wasted forms brought North by railroad and on hospital-transports, stricken by no rebel bullet, but by far deadlier enemies of the nation,—malarial fever and camp-dysentery,—have been impressing on the people the lesson the Sanitary Commission has been endeavoring to teach ever since the war began,—viz.: that our soldiers were in far greater danger from disease than from the violence of their enemies, and that we lose ten men uselessly by preventable disease, for every man destroyed by the enemy."

The dreadful battle of Fair Oaks gave the Commission a full opportunity to test its usefulness and efficiency. In a letter from Mr. Olmsted, Secretary to the Commission, dated "Sanitary Commission Floating Hospital, Tender 'Wilson Small,' White House, June 10, 1862," he says,—

"During the week since the engagement of Fair Oaks, more than *four thousand* have passed through our hands, —half this number having been taken away on the transports of the Commission. Scarcely the slightest provision had been made for them, except on these transports; and when they were not at the landing, the weight of care for the sustenance and comforting of the poor wretches sent in from the field by railroad, during the time they necessarily remained here, fell almost wholly on those of the Commission's agents who were not at the time detailed to either of the transports. Messrs. —— and —— were among these; and the protracted severity of the labor which they willingly undertook would have been possible only under the influence of the belief that lives depended on the last exertion of their energies, strained to the utmost, and that with men to whom the saving of life became a passion."

It was utterly out of the power of the medical staff of the army to meet so frightful an emergency; and had it not been for the timely provisions of the Commission, Heaven alone knows how few of those four thousand men would have been saved!

Again, July 4, 1862, in speaking of the operations of

the members and agents of the Commission on James River
during and after that Iliad week of heroism on the Pennin-
sula:—

"Thousands of brave men are now lying, without sufficient
shelter, food, or attendance, in the camps and depots on James
River. Very many of them are destined to perish, who could
have been preserved by a blanket, a suit of hospital clothing,
and a few days' allowance of proper diet and stimulants instead
of their ordinary rations. The Commission has saved hundreds,
if not thousands, of men since this campaign began, by supplying these inexpensive wants. A very few dollars provides
what can save a soldier's life, worth in mere money value
hundreds of dollars to the army and to the community. At
this time, of all others, the country cannot afford to waste the
lives of men trained by a year's experience, and made veterans
by the terrible week of continuous battle through which they
have just triumphantly passed.

"The transport-service of the Commission is also rendering
indispensable aid to the country in bringing North men who
would have perished if left in the malarious hospitals of Virginia, but who are enabled, after a short sojourn in a healthy
northern climate, to rejoin their regiments. More than ten
thousand sick and wounded men have thus been transported
to the North by the Commission, with special attention to
their care and comfort, up to this date. By thorough system,
complete ventilation, attention to all sanitary conditions, and a
liberal supply of comforts and appliances which Government
does not yet provide, it is believed that these 'floating hospitals' have been made superior to those heretofore employed
in the service of any country.

"This is but a part of the work on which the Commission
is engaged. But it is at this moment by far the most pressing.
Its magnitude is appalling, in view of the multitude of those
to whom the question whether help from the people shall reach
them to-day or to-morrow is a question of life or death, and

in view, also, of the moral certainty that a few days will increase that number by thousands. For the sake of this work,
the Commission has thought it right to contract its other
operations for the present and concentrate its resources mainly
on the relief of the sick and wounded on the Peninsula.

"It may be said that Government should do all this without
help from private charity. Were this true, the default of
Government would not excuse us in leaving our soldiers to
perish without an effort to save them. But it is only partially
true. While active operations are in progress, and especially
at the close of great battles, the prompt and thorough relief
and treatment of the sick and wounded require an amount of
force, in men, material, and transportation, which no Government has heretofore been able to keep permanently attached to
its medical department. At such times volunteer aid from
without is indispensable to prevent the most fearful suffering
and waste of life, however faithful and untiring the medical
staff may be. Such aid must be regularly organized in order
to be economical and efficient; and the Commission, with its
large corps of officers and agents on the ground, experienced
in their duties and in confidential communication with the
military authorities, seems the best organization through which
the sympathy and affection of the people can reach and relieve
the people's army."

The following letter to George T. Strong, Treasurer of the
Commission, from Dr. C. R. Agnew, one of its eminent medical
council, written from the Peninsula, July 1, 1862, gives a
graphic account of scenes he witnessed:—

"MY DEAR MR. STRONG:—I wish you could have been with
me at White House during my late visit, to see how much is
being done by our agents there to alleviate the sufferings of
the sick and wounded soldiers. I have seen a good deal of
suffering among our volunteers, and observed the marvellous
variety and energy of the beneficence bestowed by the patri-

otic and philanthropic in camp, in hospital, and on transports
for the sick; but nothing has ever impressed me so deeply as
this. Perhaps I can better illustrate my meaning by sketching
a few of the daily labors of the agents of the Commission as
I saw them. The sick and wounded were usually sent down
from the front by rail,—a distance of about twenty miles,—
over a rough road, and in the common freight-cars. A train
generally arrived at White House at nine P.M., and another at
two A.M. In order to prepare for the reception of the sick
and wounded, Mr. Olmsted, with Drs. Jenkins and Ware, had
pitched by the side of the railway, at White House, a large
number of tents, to shelter and feed the convalescent. These
tents were their only shelter while waiting to be shipped.
Among them was one used as a kitchen and workroom or
pantry by the ladies in our service, who prepared beef-tea,
milk-punch, and other food and comforts, in anticipation of
the arrival of the trains. By the terminus of the railway the
large Commission steamboat *Knickerbocker* lay in the Pamunkey, in readiness for the reception of four hundred and fifty patients, provided with comfortable beds and a corps of devoted
surgeons, dressers, nurses, and litter-bearers. Just outside of
this vessel lay the *Elizabeth*, a steam barge loaded with the hospital stores of the Commission, and in charge of a store-keeper,
always ready to issue supplies. As soon as a train arrived, the
moderately sick were selected and placed in the tents near the
railroad and fed, those more ill were carried to the upper saloon
of the *Knickerbocker*, while the seriously ill or badly wounded
were placed in the lower saloon and immediately served by
the surgeons and dressers. During the three nights that I
observed the working of the system, about seven hundred sick
and wounded were provided with quarters, and ministered to
in all their wants with a tender solicitude and skill that excited my deepest admiration. To see Drs. Ware and Jenkins,
lantern in hand, passing through the trains, selecting the sick
with reference to their necessities, and the ladies following to

assuage the thirst, or arouse, by judiciously administered stimulants, the failing strength of the brave and uncomplaining sufferers, was a spectacle of the most touching character. If you had experienced the debilitating influence of the Pamunkey climate, you would be filled with wonder at the mere physical endurance of our corps, who certainly could not have been sustained in the performance of duties involving labor by day and through sleepless nights, without the most philanthropic devotion and the highest sense of Christian duty.

" At Savage's Station, too, the Commission had a valuable depot, where comfort and assistance was dispensed to the sick when changing from the ambulances to the cars. I wish I could do justice to the subject of my hasty narrative, or in any due measure convey to your mind the impressions left on mine in observing, even casually, the operations in the care of the sick at these two points.

" When we remember what was done by the same noble band of laborers after the battles of Williamsburg and Fair Oaks in ministering to the wants of *thousands of wounded*, I am sure nothing but feelings of gratitude and thankfulness of the most heartfelt kind can arise.

" Yours, sincerely,

"C. R. AGNEW.

"July 1, 1862."

Hardly had the smoke curled off from the battle-grounds of the red Peninsula, before the seared and blasted field of Bull Run was again to shake under the tread of two hundred thousand soldiers, and old graves were to open for another uncounted host.

During that long day of slaughter, while all Washington was listening to the distant, but distinct, roar of artillery which reverberated heavily over the Capitol, the corps of the Sanitary Commission were at their work. Messengers were flying backward and forward, over the land, up and down the river, to and from the battle-field, and the telegraph-wires were quivering unceasingly with the restless flashings of the lightning.

The awful history of that tragedy was read in the rapid procession of several hundred one-, two-, and four-horse ambulances, which passed down towards Long Bridge, to return freighted with the wounded, the mangled, and the dying.

But meanwhile the Sanitary Commission was doing its work of sublime mercy.

But the fiend of Rebellion, more fiendish than ever, had not yet exhausted his malice. The rebel leader had from the beginning promised his deluded followers with the possession of the national capital, and, once more almost in sight of its domes and towers the infuriated horde, flushed with victory, were pressing on, determined to win the prize.

Once more the gifted but rebel "Lord of Arlington" looked off wistfully upon his home-mansion, rising among the venerable trees of his old ancestral estate, where he had spent his happiest and noblest days.

But the doors of Arlington House had been closed on him forever. Nor could the chief of the Southern Rebellion make good his promise to his desperate myriads. The city which Washington founded was not to be trod by a foreign or domestic foe. *Its* soil was indeed *sacred!*

*　　*　　*　　*　　*　　*

Both armies had crossed the Potomac, and again they were to measure their strength. The field of Antietam was to be lost or won. Leaving to the historian of the war a description of the lurid carnival which Death held over those devoted plains on that carnage-day, let us follow the Sanitary Commission on its gentle, angel-protected path.

*　　*　　*　　*　　*　　*

When night fell on the awful field of Antietam, the stars shone down on ten thousand of our wounded men. Thousands had been carried to the rear of each corps, as the fight went on; thousands of the disabled or wounded had been trampled into the earth by the march of advancing columns; but from the mingled masses of dying and dead horses and men the lacerated and bleeding were borne away by the hands or in the arms of their comrades to places of transient repose, where, at least after some hours, they might have a cup of water held to their lips.

The battle had raged over an area much larger than the island of Manhattan, and every rod and rood of that ground was covered with the wounded and the slain.

The agents of the Sanitary Commission were early on the field of Antietam,—although they had hardly rested from the wasting toils of the slaughters of Virginia, and the hardly less prostrating fatigues of forty hospitals in the District of Columbia, then containing nearly twenty thousand suffering soldiers. Not only were the agents of the Commission there; the ablest surgeons, members of the Commission itself, were on the scene, and gave themselves to the work, night and day, till, from sheer exhaustion, they laid themselves down fainting by the sides of their bleeding patients,—rebels and loyalists: no distinction was made.

For the next few days, around the neighborhood of Antietam the clock did not strike an hour whose history was not crowded with scenes to which the genius of pen or pencil could impart no more grand or touching delineations.

*   *   *   *   *   *

Says Rev. Dr. Bellows of Antietam,—

"Our independent means of transportation often enable us to reach the wounded with stores in advance of all Government or other supplies. The first *two* days are more important than the next ten to the saving of life and the relief of misery.

"At the recent battle-ground we were able to be present in advance *two days of all supplies* (beyond the small amount in the nearly empty storehouse of the army medical purveyor), with twenty-five wagon-loads of stimulants, condensed food, medicines, and conveniences. Within a week we despatched successfully, by teams, to the scene of battle, from Washington alone, 28,763 pieces dry-goods, shirts, towels, bed-ticks, pillows, &c., 30 barrels bandages, old linen, &c., 3188 pounds farina, &c., 2620 pounds condensed milk, 5050 pounds beef-stock and canned meats, 3000 bottles wine and cordials, and several tons of lemons and other fruit, crackers, tea, sugar, rubber cloth, tin cups, and hospital conveniences."

From the indomitable Dr. Agnew, on the field, as he saw it:—

"I left Dunning's wagon—in fact, all the two-horse wagons and ambulances of our train—constantly going, and carrying relief to thousands of wounded.

"The wounded were mainly clustered about barns, occupying the barn-yards, and floors, and stables, having plenty of good straw, well broken by the power threshing-machine. I saw fifteen hundred wounded men lying upon the straw about two barns, within sight of each other! Indeed, there is not a barn, or farm-house, or store, or church, or school-house, between Boonsborough, Keedysville, and Sharpsburg, and the latter and Smoketown, that is not gorged with wounded,—rebel and Union. Even the corn-cribs, and in many instances the cow-stable, and in one place the mangers, were filled. Several thousands lie in the open air upon straw, and all are receiving the kind services of the farmers' families and the surgeons.

"I hope I never shall forget the evidences everywhere manifested of the unselfish and devoted heroism of our surgeons, regular and volunteer, in the care of both Federal and rebel wounded. Wherever I went, I encountered surgeons and chaplains who had given themselves no rest in view of the overwhelming claims of suffering humanity.

* * * * * *

"We have been ahead of every one, and at least two days ahead of the supplies of the Medical Bureau,—the latter fact

due to its want of independent transportation. A single item
will show the value of our supplies. We have given out over
thirty pounds of chloroform within three days after the battle.
The medical authorities had not one-hundredth part of what
was needed, and in many places important operations were
necessarily neglected and life lost. *Our chloroform saved at
least fifty lives, and saved several hundred from the pain of
severe operations.* The want of chloroform was the most
serious deficiency in the regular medical supplies, and, as the
result, amputations which should have been primary will now
be secondary or impossible. (The mortality from secondary
amputations is very much greater than from primary.)"

But I must stop here, by saying that the Sanitary Commission has not confined its exertions to the Potomac and its
adjacent neighborhoods.

It is a national institution. *It moves with the war.*
Wherever our armies march, or sail, or battle for the Republic, from the Atlantic coast up all its bays and rivers, around
the Florida capes, along all the coasts of the purple South,
from the Rio Grande to the mouth of the Mississippi, and
floating with our gunboats over its ample bosom, from the
yellow waters of the Missouri down towards the summer-land,
—everywhere our flag is carried in this crusade for the Republic, the Sanitary Commission is just as present and efficient
there as it has been on our bloody fields of the Potomac. No
organization for a similar purpose established on the earth ever
covered so broad a field; no association ever existed which carried its purposes into effect so soon. No one ever commanded
so completely the confidence of the world; no one ever achieved
so much with such small means. No one has combined in so
large and so wide a measure the highest efforts and the most
earnest congratulations of so many gifted and glorious men.

But, while its direct object has been, and will be, limited
to the practical business of saving men's lives, its mission will
not be confined even within so vast a field. It must overleap

all such boundaries. HUMANITY, EDUCATED BY SCIENCE, AND GUIDED BY THE DIVINE INSPIRATIONS OF CHRISTIANITY, IS YET TO MAKE THE CONQUEST OF THE EARTH.

The United States Sanitary Commission has been the good genius of this bad war. Its Eddystone Light has flashed its hopeful rays all over the angry surges that have been dashing around it. It could not, like THE GREAT MASTER, say, "Peace, be still!" but it could set the signal of humanity and hope, and come to the rescue when there was no one else to save.*

This work it has nobly done; it is doing it still.†

---

* SICK SOLDIERS.—The number of soldiers registered on the books of the Sanitary Commission as having entered hospitals since November 1, 1862, and up to April 1, 1863,—five months,—is as follows:—

Central office at Washington	68,000
Louisville	60,000
Philadelphia	7,000
New York	6,000

Total...............141,000

† To enumerate the services of the Commission in detail would far transcend the limits of this work; and yet I cannot dismiss the subject without saying one or two things more.

1. THE MEANS OF RELIEF ADMINISTERED TO SOLDIERS THE VERY INSTANT THEY NEED HELP.—The department of Special Relief, which has been under the charge of Mr. F. N. Knapp, has done a great deal by way of *help at the moment it was needed.* More than one hundred thousand soldiers going to the war or returning from it have come within the range of Mr. Knapp's kind intervention. His "Soldiers' Homes," "Rests," "Reliefs," and all sorts of stopping-places, have been multiplied all over the country, just as far as the army has gone and just as fast as they were needed. The provisions Mr. Knapp has made do not include only something to eat and drink,—not merely roast beef and coffee,—but a comfortable bed for the tired soldier, where he can repose after his campaign and get strength to go on his way. It means any clothing he may need, any little luxury he may desire, so that when the train backs in to take him home he may, *with his full pay,* got for him without a penny discount, and a *through* ticket, take his seat in a car at Washington and get out of that same car at Chicago.

2. TO SAVE SOLDIERS FROM IMPOSITION, EXPENSE, AND DELAY.—How mercilessly our poor comrades are sacrificed when they leave the camp!

To fight for the flag while they are in the ranks is the religion of the true soldier. To go home when he is honorably discharged is his next thought; —and he wants to go home *quick*. No car can go fast enough. Mr. Knapp's arrangements suit these cases exactly.

Then these little cities of refuge are at all the grand junctions of our continental system of intercommunication. These are literally "The Homes of the War." The wounded or sick soldier comes: a surgeon is ready; nurses and attendants—men and women—come. They are all welcomed and all cared for as they would be in a father's house. More than sixty thousand human beings now live to rise up and call that man blessed; and then the grand reservation is left to him still:—"Inasmuch as ye did it unto one of the least of my disciples, ye did it unto me."*

---

* I have heard of no general officer who has not expressed his hearty approval of the whole management of the Commission, nor one who did not feel that the good done by the Commission was incalculable. Major-General Rosecrans, in his distant and difficult field, has had ample means of knowing what the Commission has done.

While he highly appreciates and does not undervalue the charities which have been lavished on the army, experience has demonstrated the importance of system and impartiality, as well as judgment and economy, in the forwarding and distribution of these supplies. In all these respects he declares the United States Sanitary Commission stands unrivalled.

Its organization, experience, and large facilities for the work are such that the General does not hesitate to recommend, in the most urgent manner, all those who desire to send sanitary supplies to confide them to the care of this Commission; inasmuch as they will thus insure the supplies reaching their destination without wastage or expense of agents or transportation, and their being distributed in a judicious manner without disorder or interference with the regulations and usages of the service. This Commission acts in full concert with the Medical Department of the Army, and enjoys its confidence.

XVI.

The Duty of the Republic to its Fallen Heroes.

"Cœlumque aspicit et dulcis moriens reminiscitur Argos."—VIRG.

"Such honors Ilion to her hero paid,
And peaceful slept the mighty Hector's shade.
 * * * * * *
Here let me grow to earth! since Hector lies
On the bare beach deprived of obsequies.
Oh, give me Hector! to my eyes restore
His corse, and take the gifts! I ask no more.
 * * * * * *
The best, the bravest of my sons are slain.
 * * * * *
For him through hostile camps I bend my way.
 * * * * *
Lo! to thy prayer restored, thy breathless son.
 * * * * *
Steeped in their blood, and in the dust outspread,
Nine days neglected, lay exposed the dead."—ILIAD.

THE first duty of a Government is to protect the life of the soldier; the second is to give him honorable burial when he has fought his last battle. This duty has been recognized by all nations, and it has been considered imperative. No nation so barbarous as to neglect the ashes of its patriots,—no family so divested of social affection as not to desire to recover the earthly relics of one of their number who died away from home.

That mysterious chain which binds the heart of the survivor to the dust of the departed is now binding the hearts of an innumerable company of our people to the graves of our fallen soldiers. To recover the ashes of the loved one is the first thought that occurs; and the uncertainty of the spot where the body is reposing intensifies the grief. Promiscuous burial the human soul abhors.

This feeling is natural, and it cannot be repressed. Virgil has beautifully expressed it in the line we have quoted above. With his back to the earth and his eyes on heaven, the dying soldier thinks of his beloved home. It is generally among the very last wishes of those dying among strangers, that they could die at home.

Our fancies will visit the red fields of valor which have been sanctified by the baptism of patriotic blood; they will haunt the halls of our hospitals, filled with the suffering, and steal into the countless chambers of the bereaved, where Rachels are " weeping for their children, and will not be comforted, because they are not."

The duties of Governments to their fallen soldiers apply with peculiar force to the soldiers and families of republics. Our grand army of a million men is a fair, full, and honorable representation of the great body of the people. There are whole regiments and brigades where there is not a man who did not leave home and kindred for the war,—kindred who watch with tenderness and apprehension the news of every battle, and whose affection spreads its drooping wings over the camp where the soldier sleeps. How many of our rank and file would not have Christian burial if they died at home, and some plain stone, at least, *in memoriam*, placed to mark the last couch of the sleeper? How many of our army, fallen already, have not left friends who would part with some treasure to recover the bodies of those they loved, or at least to know the spot of sepulture?

Hundreds of instances—yes, thousands—are known of attempts, often fruitless, to find, identify, mark, the spot, or make inquiries about the graves. The Western battle-fields alone have grouped a million stricken hearts around those suddenly-created sepulchres of the brave. Our officers and soldiers put forth their last heroic exertions, in every skirmish and in every fight, to bring off our dead, or bury them on the field, preserving their identity as far as the horrible exigencies of war will allow.

But this was not enough; and the Sanitary Commission early undertook to obtain information by which "the place of burial of the volunteers who have been killed in battle, or who have died in hospitals, may be established. They have also elaborated a system of records for those dying in hospitals, and of indications of their burial-place, by which their bodies may be identified; which has received approval, and been ordered to be carried out, blanks and tablets for the purpose being furnished to each regimental quartermaster."

This plan was warmly embraced by Congress and the Soldiers' Relief Associations, and it was in the main adopted, and has been carried out as far as it seemed possible.

One thing more was needed. Besides having cemeteries, larger or smaller, wherever our soldiers have fallen, we should have a great national cemetery for soldiers near Washington, where all our brave men who fall in the service in this neighborhood, or who can be brought here, may have honorable graves. Each State could have a space allotted for its own citizens; and this City of the Dead should be embellished by emblems of art and beauty, which exalt and refine civilized life. The cost of this war for one hundred minutes would munificently accomplish this.*

---

* Soldiers who die in the camp of General Hooker are given a suitable burial. In all cases the bodies are enclosed in good pine coffins, obtained from the Quartermaster's Department, and the interment is made with the ceremonies due the rank of the deceased.

XVII.

How to end the War by the Arts of Peace— Eli Thayer's Plan.

BACON said that the worst thing in national or international war was the decline of the arts of peace; and by their decline he measured the approaches of nations to barbarism. And yet the student of Bacon very well knows that he was not "a peace man." He indeed regarded peace as the normal condition of society, as health is the normal condition of the human body. But he claimed no exemption for Governments and communities from the law of purgation and blood-letting. He held that when a nation could not come out triumphantly from a war of defence, that nation either had never had any vitality, or she had lost it; and, further, that a nation which could not go successfully through a long, devastating, and merciless civil war to vindicate its constitution, its laws, and all the elements of its nationality, suppressing rebellion against its sovereign power and crushing its enemies under its feet, and then settling back to its wonted repose, stronger than ever,—he regarded such a nation's doom as sealed.

And all history was with him,—all history has been with him to this day. His own England proved it. In her earlier epochs the Britons had only once proved themselves strong enough to resist the shock of foreign invaders. Rome alone was unable to subdue Britain; and nothing but the untimely death of Cæsar saved that island from becoming a helpless colony of Rome. The Saxons, the Danes, and the Normans all came and conquered, and the race of the Angli gradually faded away.

But from the Norman conquest grew up gradually, though surely, a great nationality, which we now call England. That nationality grew up by war, and war only. The arts of peace had little to do with the consolidation of England as she stood in 1815. By war, William of Normandy extended his kingdom through a large part of England. By war his successors. conquered and annexed the Principality of Wales. By war, and a war of centuries only, was the Emerald Island brought under the yoke and kept there. By war—unrelenting and unprovoked—was Scotland annexed to the hated crown of the Plantagenets. By one of the most ferocious and bloody civil wars that had then been known was England able to consolidate her own Government, maintain her central authority, and hold even her old rebellious subjects loyal to her throne. She extorted loyalty from all the peoples she conquered; and she did it at the mouth of the cannon and the point of the bayonet. Who ever heard of England settling a rebellion by *compromise?* The day she did it would have been hung in black: from that hour her decline and fall would have dated. She would have parted with the prestige of union, entirety, wholeness, invincibility.

And yet England does not hesitate now to advise us to deliberately cut our empire into pieces,—to halve it with rebels,—to compound the most stupendous felony of all the ages,—to treat for peace with a lawless band of murderers holding the knife at the throat of a common mother! In giving this advice, her impudence is not even graced with the counsel of the fox who recommended all foxes thereafter to give up the silly fashion of wearing tails. England has not yet lost hers,—although she may hereafter find out that the steel-traps are laid in the dangerous path she seems determined to follow.

America take England's advice about this insurrection! Just as soon would we have taken her advice about putting down the Whiskey Rebellion. We prefer to follow her example rather than her counsel,—*shoot it down.*

*   *   *   *   *   *

But, while no great insurrection against sovereign authority was ever successfully and permanently suppressed *by arms alone*, there are other agencies which can be invoked that in our case would prove omnipotent. Let us go back to Greece. The rock of Athens, and the few vales and mountains which stretch away from that light-house of ancient civilization, went through centuries of home-struggles before she consolidated her people and her power and became the leader of the nations. Then began her conquests, *chiefly through colonization*, which made her the queen of the commerce and the arts of the world. Wherever her colonists settled, they subdued surrounding communities through the arts of peace, resorting to force only for the first settlement of her people, and afterwards only for self-protection.

So was it with Rome, and on a far grander scale. Her policy was conquest, through two agencies which she never dissevered. She never suppressed an insurrection by force of arms alone. She always confiscated the lands of the disloyal as fast as she got military possession, and gave them to her own true citizens, who settled on them, and defended them *by arms*, in the name and by the authority of Rome. In this manner it happened that she so consolidated her power in the Peninsula that her union of the Italian states, tribes, and peoples remained unshaken and unthreatened for nearly a thousand years. If a word of treason was uttered by a disappointed politician, he went to exile, or he was hurled from the Tarpeian rock. If a planter attempted to excite insubordination on the distant plains of Lombardy, a cohort of Roman soldiers sent him in chains to Cæsar, and his estate was cut up the next day into a hundred homes for the exempt veterans of the army.

Whenever and wherever the rights of a Roman citizen were interfered with, in Europe, Africa, or Asia, an armed expedition went at once to avenge the insult, and, after summary justice had been dealt out, a portion of the expedition remained and *settled on the lands of the enemies of the republic*, and another Roman colony was born. *Rome fought to save, and not to destroy, civilization.* Once only, in her life of twelve hundred years as a nation, did she conquer only to exterminate. Carthage and Rome could not both be supreme. in the Mediterranean; but several centuries had to witness the rivalry before the verdict of supremacy was awarded. Roman statesmen cared nothing for Africa; for her nomadic tribes were not worth conquering, and, with the exception of Egypt, her soil could not support a colony. But Carthage had harassed and worried, and at one time nearly conquered, Rome; and it became necessary to blot her out. *The war was carried into Africa;* and the future history of the Carthaginian Empire was all summed up in that memorable bulletin of Scipio,—

"Carthago est delenda."

An approach to this was seen some centuries later, when the army of Aurelian turned their backs upon the smouldering ashes of Zenobia's capital.

Elsewhere, the arts of peace kept pace with the tread of the Roman legions. From Alexandria to the Golden Horn, from the Danube to the Guadalquivir, from the borders of Scotland to the plains of India, wherever the Roman Eagle unfurled his wings of conquest the armed colonists of the great republic of antiquity put the spade and the plough to work. Those colonists carried with them all the implements of the highest civilization of that age and all the ages that had gone before it. It was, therefore, an easy matter for Rome to save all she gained. She took no step backward till she stopped colonizing other lands.

So, for several hundred years, Rome sat securely on her Tiber-washed throne, in the midst of a thousand strong and flourishing colonies scattered all through the known world, like stars in a solar system,—all owning allegiance to the federal authority, all prosperous in each other's prosperity, all basking in the same beneficent sunlight, and all sharing the same almighty protection.

In this manner and in this way alone did Rome suppress rebellion, extend her empire, and consolidate the strongest and the best government in existence. It was never a despotism but for a day; and with the close of that day Tarquin was driven into exile. Rome had but one traitor; but the scorching satire of Cicero sent him skulking from the Senate-House, and when he had left the Capitol his power to breed treason died.

Thus the Eternal City—the nursing-mother of a hundred million colonists, with their descendants—held her seat of empire, the giant guardian of the human race.

The history of the Roman system of conquest by colonization served as the model for England in the extension of her power and the spread of her empire. All the foreign possessions England ever got she obtained by conquest and aggression; all she has ever held she has held by colonization.

It has hitherto been unnecessary for us to make any aggression on the territory of other states; and it will doubtless continue so for a long time to come. We have by fair treaty purchased all the Indian titles which we hold. We bought Florida of Spain, and Louisiana of France, and California of Mexico. Texas became ours first by peaceful colonization, next by a treaty of annexation as between two sovereign states.

*   *   *   *   *   *

Now the question comes home to us in the midst of this greatest of all known rebellions, how shall we put an end to the war, and, after vindicating the sovereign authority of the Federal Government, settle all doubts about the right and the ability of intelligent men to have, administer, defend, and perpetuate free institutions, and settle those doubts forever?

European statesmen do not believe that a vast empire like

ours can exist any longer as a simple republic. They have no faith in the durability of any government which does not sustain and is not sustained by an aristocratic class. They hold that one or two of the three standard props of strong governments must be resorted to. *First*, there must be a privileged class, who shall control the wealth and honors of the state. and the politics of the country. This condition is imperative. *Second*, there must be an established Church, whether it be represented by a priest of Isis or an Archbishop of Canterbury. This, more or less, controls the consciences of the people. This may in a dire emergency be given up, as in France, where all Christian sects are treated *professedly* on an equality. But the *Third :* there must be a monarch,—an emperor, a king, a prince,—a throne for the aristocracy to sustain, and a throne to sustain the aristocracy. These are regarded in all European countries, *by everybody except the slave-masses and the few illuminated and humane thinkers,* as the essential elements of enduring power and the only foundations on which civil institutions can permanently stand.

But this is only a formula of the past. So did the founders of this republic regard it. They believed in a Church without a Pope,—equal rights and privileges without an aristocracy,—an empire without a king. They constructed a state on this idea, and for three-quarters of a century that state stood firm, "growing," in Webster's fine words, "stronger and stronger every day in the affections of the great body of the American people, and commanding more and more the admiration and respect of the world."

These men made no mistake in their philosophy of government. Their theory has not only worked as well as any other state theory ever did, but it has been patent to the obtusest observer at home and abroad that their system was the only one which could be made to work in our society. Their theory may not have been a good one as applied to the colonies founded in this hemisphere by the bastard Latin races. They have proved for two centuries that they could flourish only under a monarchical *régime*. The moment Mexico, and the whole horde of Spanish and Portuguese colonies from Louisiana to Patagonia, achieved what they pompously denominated their "independence," they began to go to decay,—and with chances ten to one better than our early settlers had for the acquisition of wealth and the spread of commerce. Only two or three of the score were saved. Portugal saved Brazil by monarchy, and we saved Texas by colonization.

It was all a difference of races, religion, and education.

Let Napoleon have Mexico, if he can get it. As she is and has been, she has ceased to be of any value to herself or anybody else. Somebody must take care of poor Mexico. She has had patriots and statesmen, and she has them still. Her people are almost as brave as they are proud. But she is rolling feverishly on her bed of helplessness and sorrow,—while that bed is made in more than regal splendor; for it rests upon an empire of silver and gold.

    *   *   *   *   *   *

The only mistake our fathers made in making our Government was in not annihilating slavery on the spot, so that they might go reverently as they did, and boldly as they *might*, into the very "Holy of the Holies" of the Temple of Freedom, to offer themselves once for all time and all nations a sacrifice for human liberty.

Oh, if they had only done it, and completed their work, and presented their offering "without spot, or wrinkle, or any such thing"!

They foresaw every thing but this, that they were unwittingly bequeathing to their descendants a terrible legacy:— of contending with a myriad of full-grown, envenomed serpents, all sprung from the infant viper which they could so easily have strangled.

But, with all our vain regrets over the only thing they left undone, let us devoutly thank God for all their noble achievements, and address ourselves manfully to the solemn business before us. That slavery would grow and spread they did not dream, much less that it would grow strong enough to coil its slimy folds around the heart of the Republic. They emancipated their slaves, and they did not doubt their descendants would follow their example.

No, honored fathers! we venerate and love you still. You had to go through a crusade of seven years. Our crusade will be shorter than that.

    *   *   *   *   *   *

If, then, the Union is to be saved at any and all hazards, why shall we leave unemployed one of those strong agencies of civilization which other nations have had to call into action, when they had to consolidate their governments, or die?

ELI THAYER has been ringing the true policy into the adder-ears of our legislators for a long time,—*almost unheeded.* That I might not misrepresent in the slightest degree his whole scheme, I requested him to give me the brief of it in his own handwriting; and here it is. It effectually disposes of the two questions that have made all the trouble,—THE SLAVERY QUESTION AND THE NEGRO QUESTION.

"WASHINGTON, D.C., February, 1863.

"DEAR SIR:—

"In accordance with your request, I send you herewith the principal features of the plan for the reconstruction and restoration of the rebel States.

"The agency which I propose to employ is ORGANIZED FREE LABOR, a power for the first time used in the settlement of the Kansas controversy, and afterwards in the establishment of the free-labor colony in Western Virginia.

"Having for the last ten years advocated this agency as the readiest and best means of eradicating slavery from this continent, I am happy now to assure you that a majority of the Cabinet, two-thirds of both Houses of Congress, and the people of the loyal States, without distinction of party, have now come to entertain the same views with myself.

"That this agency is perfectly well adapted to the reconstruction and restoration of the rebel States, will become apparent by considering that *one* of *three* methods must be made use of in crushing the rebellion and restoring peace.

" I. By the military force we may annihilate the white race of the South : making a desert, we may call it peace.

" II. By such force we may subjugate them; but it will require at least half a million of men to keep them in subjection.

"III. The third method is to secure the reconstruction, restoration, and permanent loyalty of the rebel States, by placing therein, as permanent residents, a sufficient number of loyal free-labor men from the Northern States and from Europe to hold the political and military power, with the will of such loyal elements as may by this means be developed.

"The first of these methods is too abhorrent to the sentiments of humanity to find an advocate.

" The second method would be worse than the establishment of a Southern Confederacy; because a standing army of half a million of men, if it did not convert the republic into a military despotism, would be equally fatal to its existence by soon devouring the property of the whole country.

"The only practical solution, therefore, of the rebellion, which promises future peace and prosperity to the country, is the infusion into the rebel States of a sufficient number of loyal people to reconstruct their governments and to bind them indissolubly to the Union.

" The advantages of this method are—

" 1st. It is easily accomplished.

"2d. It is the best political economy.

"3d. It solves both the Slavery and the Negro question.

"4th. It will do more than to repair the damages of the war.

"I. It is easily accomplished. If the rebel States were opened to this immigration from the North and from Europe by the proper confiscation and distribution by State laws of the landed estates of rebels, one million of men would be furnished annually for the reconstruction of the rebel States. In the loyal States alone there are now more than forty thousand men ready to join the proposed expedition to the single State of Florida and to reside there permanently.

"In these Northern States, at the present time, wages are high and the entire population is able to find employment, while in several of the European States the encouragement of labor was never less than at present. Therefore, if such is the ready response of the people of the North, now well employed, what might we not expect if the call were made upon all nations of Europe for emigration?

"II. It is the best political economy. This method creates at once a base-line of productive industry, ever expanding, and ever strengthening itself by expansion. It is a thorough sifting process, retaining all the loyal elements and removing all others. By this method of conquering we will hold the conquered country by an *army of producers;* by any other method we could only hold it by an *army of consumers.* By this method the rebel States would soon be able to bear a portion of the burden of our debts and taxation; by any other method they would constantly increase these burdens.

"III. This method solves the Slavery question, by making all the States *practically* as well as theoretically free by the very process of reconstruction. It also solves the Negro question, by furnishing to those sections where the negro now is, and where his labor is the most profitable, a class of employers whose enterprise, energy, and thrift will enable them to profit by the labor of the negro after paying a fair compensation for his services. In this way the entire colored race, not only of the South, but of the North as well, will have an

11

opportunity to vindicate their manhood and their claim to equal rights under the most favorable circumstances.

" The labor of the negro is needed *in this country*, and should be properly encouraged. It is a poor policy for a new and sparsely-settled country to export its laborers, and a policy not much better to withhold from them their wages. The true policy for us is to encourage, promote, and strengthen labor by all just and proper inducements and rewards.

" *The labor of a country is its wealth.*

" But this is not all. The negroes of the Northern and Middle States would in this way be induced to migrate to the Gulf States, where they would enjoy a congenial climate and where their labor would command the highest wages.

" IV. This method will do more than to repair the damages of the war, by establishing a higher grade of civilization. If by thus ending the war the human race attains to a higher position on this continent, that higher position is cheaply secured, at whatever sacrifice.

" The triumph of free labor, encouraged by suitable rewards, and the eradication of the last relic of tyranny in the republic, will be secured by this method of reconstructing Southern society and Southern governments.

" This method implies and secures a greater population in the Southern States than they have ever had,—a more productive population, also, because stimulated by freedom and all its attendant agencies. In this way we shall have, at the close of this war,—

" 1st. A greater population than ever before.

" 2d. A homogeneous population, inspired by a common policy.

" 3d. A more productive population, because each will labor for his own interests.

" 4th. Security against all future disaffection and rebellion ; and, from all these causes, higher prosperity, greater national strength, and attainments in civilization above all yet known to men.

"I have thus given you what may properly be termed only an abstract of the plan. I might have shown that this work is all to be accomplished in accordance with STATE RIGHTS and by State laws. It *ought*, therefore, to find favor in Southern latitudes.

"Very truly, yours,

"ELI THAYER.

"C. EDWARDS LESTER, ESQ.,
"WASHINGTON, D.C."

This is conclusive. It might have gone further, and swept away the few remaining cobwebs that still hang dangling over the eyes of the bewildered devotees of African colonization yet among us. One quotation from a very able writer in the "Daily Chronicle" (Washington) sets the matter at rest:—

"All schemes of colonization, therefore, whether of white men or black, which involve penetration beyond the reach of existing communications or far removed from the firm basis of existing establishments, are false in conception and principle, and must be fatal in practice,—not less false or fatal, however, than those more frequent schemes of founding colonies on unhealthy coasts, where there is no back-country or accessible interior population to support them, under specious pretences of great commercial prospects and a future eclipsing the prosperity of Havana, New York, and Boston.

"The sad history of the attempts of the French at Tehuantepec, the English at Vera Paz, the Belgians at Santo Thomas, the English on the coast of Honduras, the French again at Cape Gracias, the Prussians on the Mosquito shore and in Costa Rica, and the still earlier efforts of the Scotch at Darien,—attempts of individuals, companies, and Governments, and all of them abject and disastrous failures,—we say, the history of these should warn us against similar futile efforts in the future. We have been personal witnesses of the sufferings of deluded emigrants under the tropics, the ignorance and infatuation of whose leaders rose to the magnitude and took the shape of crime, and as such should have met with exemplary punishment."

*　　*　　*　　*　　*　　*

The merits of Mr. Thayer's plan were presented, January 9, 1863, in a report of the Committee on Military Affairs, prepared by Hon. Mr. Buffinton. Its brevity and great ability render it desirable to give it the largest possible circulation :—

"Recognizing the importance of whatever measure may tend to the defeat of the unprovoked and iniquitous rebellion against the Government, your committee have given to this resolution and the enterprise it contemplates careful consideration. To lay the foundations of a free and Christian state is at all times a work of honor, in which the statesman may take a patriotic pride; but to firmly plant such foundations upon the ruins of a malignant rebellion, and thus organize order out of chaos and transform treason into loyalty, in a time like this, to an American Congress becomes no less than an imperious duty.

"Florida, in territory, is one of the largest States in the Union, containing thirty-eight million acres of land, of which broad domain twenty-one million acres are still unsold Government lands, subject to entry under the liberal provisions of the Homestead Law. Much of the other seventeen million acres is in the present possession of undisguised and active rebels, and may at once be put upon the market under the righteous requirements of the Confiscation and Tax Laws.

"Her peninsular position, and the Gulf Stream running down her entire eastern coast, commands for Florida an equability of climate that makes residence within her borders desirable, and secures advantages to the agriculturist not to be met with elsewhere through all the extent of our territory.

"For the growth and exportation of naval stores and the leading articles of commerce she offers unexcelled facilities: indeed, with her longer season and surer exemption from frost, she has a decided advantage over Louisiana even in the cultivation of the sugar-cane, and has probably a larger district than any other State fitted for the growth of long-staple cotton, and is, indeed, the only State where may be successfully grown the Cuba tobacco.

"While all the great staples of the southern temperate zone flourish throughout Florida, in her southern and eastern sections may be cultivated in their luxuriance the fruits and plants of the tropics.

"Large tracts of live-oak and yellow pine, of almost price-less value to our navy, abound in Florida, and whose posses-sion for such use would be warranted at almost any cost.

"By position Florida commands the Gulf. To economize time, and save to the rich and growing commerce of Mobile and New Orleans. Texas and our Pacific coast, the perils of the voyage around her sunken keys, the national Government, previous to the rebellion, by generous donation of public lands, secured the building of a railroad across her territory from the Atlantic to the Gulf.

"Considerations growing out of each and all of these facts, thus briefly alluded to in the investigation which the subject has prompted, have pressed themselves upon your committee, and, we doubt not, will suggest themselves as of weighty im-portance to every member of the House.

"But your committee would beg leave to suggest other con-siderations connected with this proposition of even more present importance. Through the fears and threatenings of a reign of terror, Florida has been driven into open rebellion against the Government and Union, scores of her loyal citizens brutally murdered, and hundreds driven into exile or at the point of the bayonet forced into the rebel ranks. Her loyal citizens in exile are importuning the Government for protection, that they may return to their desolated possessions and rebuild their once beautiful homes and throw the old flag again to the breeze. Twenty thousand resolute loyal men placed upon the soil with guns in their hands will be sufficient protection for these loyal men and themselves, and Florida will at once return to her old allegiance and to the prompt and honorable discharge of all the duties of a loyal State. To erect the pillars of a free and loyal commonwealth upon such ruins is certainly a work that must command the homage of every patriotic heart; but more than this, even, is promised by this enterprise: it offers a refuge for the thousands of freed men pressing our lines,—a place at once ready, cheaply reached, and where they may find, with equitable remuneration, abundance of employment in labors with which they are familiar and in a climate admirably adapted to their wants, and, under the fostering care of friendly legislation and friendly institutions, rapidly progress into a higher and more useful individual and social position.

"And while so much of good is to be secured, and adapting its usefulness so happily to the special needs of this very time, your committee are glad to be able to remind the House that the enterprise has also an economic phase. The loyal armed occupation of Florida relieves the navy of thirteen hundred miles of blockade, at an expense of twelve thousand dollars per day,—not only relieves the national treasury of this large daily expenditure, but, what is by no means of less importance, gives these numerous vessels liberty for service elsewhere."

XVIII.

The Night of the Battle of Ball's Bluff.

It was a gloomy night in Washington. One of the unexpected and heart-chilling disasters which befell our arms in the early history of the war had that day happened at Ball's Bluff (October 21, 1861). Our forces had been routed and slaughtered, and the gallant Colonel Baker, who had left the Senate-chamber to lead his splendid California Regiment to the war, had fallen, dying instantly, pierced at the same second by seven bullets. This was a *national* loss. His place in the army, in the Senate, in the hearts of the people of California and Oregon, in the admiration of his companions-in-arms in Mexico, and in the realms of eloquence, would remain vacant. No man living was invested with all these rare and great attributes in so eminent a degree. The apparently well-founded suspicion that he had fallen a victim to the foulest treason subsequently mingled the intensest indignation with inconsolable grief for his cruel and untimely death.

It was late in the evening when the news reached Willard's; but a large crowd was still there, among whom, as always, were many well-known public men. In those days secession was more popular in Washington than it has since been or is likely ever to become again. Not only was some slimy spy lurking within earshot of every man worth tracking, but there were scores of strong sympathizers with the rebellion, who caught with avidity the first rumor of disaster to the national arms.

These abettors and agents of Davis wore the mask as closely

as they could; and, although the *habitués* of the capital could
tell them at a glance, and, by an instinct of loyalty nearly infallible, know when one of them entered the room, yet on
some occasions the sudden announcement of bad news for our
cause threw them from their guard and the gleam of fiendish
delight flashed from their faces.

"Baker was killed at Ball's Bluff this afternoon."

Never did news transform men's countenances quicker.
One class received it with blank amazement and horror; the
other, with demoniac exultation.

Words fell which neither party could restrain; and the
blood of the coolest began to boil when they heard the murdered Baker's name insulted.   A movement was made which
bolder men than traitors would not have attempted to resist.
The villains started, by a common impulse, for the two doorways, or that mosaic pavement would have worn another color
within ten seconds.   A minute later, the place was cleansed;
the unclean spirits had gone out!—all but one, perhaps.

A very red-faced, stalwart man, who had stood by and seen
all that had been going on without saying a word, finally
remarked, with a pretty determined air, that "as for himself
he didn't care much about the fight.   He lived on the Lower
Mississippi, and the people down his way could take care of
themselves.   As long as they owned the Mississippi, the
d—d Abolitionists could make all the muss they pleased.   We
hold the Gulf of Mexico, and the Northwest, and the Yankees may be d—d."

A very tall, lean, awkward, bony-looking man sidled quietly
up to the Mississippian, and, putting his nose, by a stoop, quite
close to his face, said, in unmistakable *far*-Western trough,—

"Look here, stranger," and gently emphasizing his remark by taking the stranger's left ear between his thumb and
finger; "now, yu may not know it, but I live in Minnesoty,
and we make that Mississippi water you call yourn, and we
kalkilate to use it some."

The stranger's hand moved pretty quick for a side-pocket, but not *quite* quick enough. I saw a movement, I heard a blow, and the blood spattered surrounders slightly. In less time than such enterprises' usually require, the stranger had fallen heavily on the marble floor, striking his head against an iron column, and remaining in a condition which rendered it desirable to have his friends look after him, if he had any.

The Western gentleman was congratulated,—when he apologized, "I didn't want to hurt the feller, and I didn't care about his bowie-knife going through me, nother. But the tarnal traitor must let the old country alone, and *partickilarly* that big river. We want to use that *thar*, out West."

*   *   *   *   *   *

Baker's body was brought across the Potomac the evening he fell. It rested all day, and then by ambulance was conveyed to Washington, and carried through the same hospitable doorway of his friend Colonel Webb from whose steps I had parted with him as he mounted his horse and gave us his warm, earnest hand only two or three mornings before! Oh, how radiant was his face! how athletic and symmetrical his form! how unsullied his ambition! how pure his devotion to God and country!

"God spare *his* life, at least!" we said, as we saw him disappear around the corner! *This* prayer Heaven could not grant.

*   *   *   *   *   *

The following day, when the last preparations for the tomb had been made, we went to gaze once more, and forever, on what of earth remained of the form which so lately enshrined the noble spirit.

> "Then mournfully the parting bugle bid
> Its farewell o'er the grave."

*   *   *   *   *   *

California claimed her hero and statesman, and his ashes now repose on the calm shore of that ocean which washes the western base of the empire for whose glory he lived and died.

His body lies in Lone Mountain Cemetery, near the city of San Francisco, and over it will rise one of the most superb monuments which the genius of Art has ever erected in honor of human greatness.

California has committed this magnificent work to Horatio Stone. I have tried to give an exact description of the models and drawings, which I studied with some care.*

---

* MONUMENT TO GENERAL BAKER.

This monument, designed to be constructed of white marble, in the general form of the triumphal arch. Ionic order of architecture, to be thirty feet in height ; and, as shown by the drawings of each of the four views, to be embellished by two hundred and fifty figures, in processions, grouped compositions, series of single statues, and armorial supporters,—besides the colossal statue of Baker, which is designed to be eight feet high.

The estimated cost of the work is one hundred thousand dollars.

The Designs for the Monument to Edward Dickinson Baker, late U. S. Senator for Oregon, and Colonel of U. S. Volunteers for California.

The comprehensive motive of this design has been to commemorate, through an elevated expression of sculptural language, the genius, patriotism, statesmanship, and valor of the eminent citizen whose memory it is intended to honor, as manifested in the chief public relations and actions of his career which entitle his memory to such historical honors; and the endeavor has been to make the sculptural reading (through single statues, groups, processions, and symbols) at once so comprehensive and definite as to obviate the necessity of inscribing in letters, little more than the name of the original of the statue, upon the walls of the structure.

The method pursued, as the designs will show, is to represent, upon the walls of the base of the structure, symbolic compositions and figures, in alto-relief, embodying the attributes, principles, and affections which at once inspire and are developed and protected by enlightened and valorous patriotism, and to make them appropriately expressive as to the life of the citizen representative, and the nation he serves. To represent upon and before the walls of the superstructure: first, in front, the statue of the citizen whose story is to be recorded; second, upon the end plane of the wall, at the left of the statue, to represent the civil service of Baker, in a bas-relief of the U. S. Senate; third, upon the end plane of the wall, at the right of the statue, to represent the heroic service of Baker, in a bas-relief battle-scene; fourth, on the rear, standing, against the centre of the wall, in a position corresponding with the statue in front, and over the entrance to the vault, the cinereal vase, upon which is represented, in a series of

In the closing paragraph of the last speech of Baker in the Senate, provoked by the insulting words of the Catiline whom

---

groups, the chief lesson of immortality and glory,—namely, the women at the sepulchre,—and two other groups presenting votive wreaths to the Angel of Fame; and finally, upon the frieze of the structure, to represent the last honors to the hero, in the martial funeral procession.

Execution of the Plan, in detail.

The general form of the triumphal arch has been chosen for the structure, in view of its heroic associations, as well as its adaptation to the requirements of the sculptural illustrations; all of which are designed to be wrought in white statuary marble, from the same quarry and of the same quality as the whole mass of the structure.

The *Ground-Plan* of the base, with a projection from the centre of each side of the parallel walls, making the form of a cross, furnishes sixteen planes to receive the illustrative symbols and statues, and is so constructed in order to secure, from the angles of projection, variety and force of expression to the general mass, as well as the statues and groups, by the shadows they will throw upon them. The projection of the base in front also provides a pedestal for the statue, that in the rear the same for the vase of Immortality. A niche is cut in the walls of the superstructure behind each of these, to form a shadow for their relief. The projections of the base beneath the bas-relief of the Senate and of the battle are designed as proper supports to these compositions, and to furnish special planes for the armorial representations of Oregon and California.

Sculptural Story, in detail. Front View, No. 1.

The statue of the subject of the story, being the central object of regard, the initial letter of the sculptural biography, demands the embodiment and expression of all that it may be made to convey of the individuality and life of the original, with reference to his claims of commemoration, independently of associated records and symbols,—a requirement which the endeavor has been to fulfil, and with satisfactory success, in the modelled study of the statue, from which the imperfect outline is sketched.

The mantle and scroll will, through all ages, proclaim the civil eminence of him whom they shall represent, in sculpture, to have clothed and endowed.

The plumed hat, and the sword lying near, will declare the added function and dignity of martial leader.

The next question, Where was the public service rendered? is answered by the symbols of the nation, wrought upon the base of the statue, namely, the U. S. shield and eagle. In this composition the eagle holds in his

for a few days longer Heaven had condemned our patience to
tolerate as a Senator of the United States, Colonel Baker,
rising in his place, said,—

---

talons the Union angle of the flag, which sweeps entirely around the U. S.
shield and those of all the States, which stand behind and rest against the
national shield, and thus indicate their subordinate and protected relation.

On either side, as supporters of the national shield, are wrought the
ever-burning lamps of national affection, one of them twined with the oak,
the other with the laurel wreath. These are also representative of the
affection that will continue to cherish the memory of national defenders.

Regarding the diffusion of light to be, if not the chief function of Freedom, his first duty, I have placed a torch in the talons of his eagle-herald.

Upon the side plane of the base of the statue, at the left, stands the
figure of Justice; upon the right, that of Liberty,—the comprehensive prin-
ples defended by him whose statue stands above.

Upon the planes of the base of the structure, at the left and right of the
last-named figures, are those representing comprehensively Patriotism
and Valor, or the civic and heroic functions or divinities. They are each
defending the symbol of the Union,—the fasces,—and by their action indicating that the subject of the commemorative honors has merited the oak
and the laurel wreaths.

Side View, to the left of Front No. 2.

Beneath the bas-relief of the U. S. Senate is wrought the arms of Oregon, the State represented by the Senator. Upon the planes of the base
comprehended in this view are wrought the figures of History, Poetry,
Eloquence, and Justice, some of the teachers, inspirers, and conservators
of civilization. Poetry and Eloquence are here in the action of contesting
for the supremacy of their influence upon the exertions of the senatorial
orator. In this series, History, in the act of recording, stands as the first
teacher; Poetry, the awakener of emotional life and of aspiration to civil
excellence; Eloquence, the inspirer of efficient use of developed spiritual
power; and Justice, as the embodied achievement.

Side View, to the right of Front No. 3.

Beneath the bas-relief of the battle-scene, which represents the hero
leading a charge, is wrought the arms of California, the State he represented
as military leader. Some modification has been made in this, to harmonize
it with the composition of forms and lines around it, and because it appeared to me proper to bring the miner out of his reduced proportions on
the field of the scutcheon, and to make him, as the representative of
Labor, a companion of Wisdom and her fellow-supporter of the shield. But

"There will be some graves reeking with blood, watered by the tears of affection. There will be some privation. There will be some loss of luxury. There will be somewhat more need of labor to procure the necessaries of life. When that is

should this modification prove unsatisfactory, it can be restored to the accepted composition.

Upon the planes of the base, presented to view on either side of the California arms, is continued the series of statues which began with History and ended with Justice on the reverse view of the base. They are Liberty, Science, Religion, and Immortality, or the Angel of Spiritual Victory. In other words, they are placed in the order in which they are supposed to represent the successive stages of the progress of civilization up to its crowning development. They are at once the divine inspirers of heroism, and the most precious possessions of man, which heroism is called upon to defend. In this series Liberty is giving a torch to the eagle-herald, for the reason stated in another place. For obvious reasons, the discoverer of the electrical telegraph is made to personate Science.

Rear View, No. 4.

The vase of sentiment has wrought upon its front a group illustrating the chief lesson of immortality,—the women at the sepulchre,—conveying the idea, "He is not here; he is risen." Upon either side are groups of mourners bearing wreaths of honor and affection, and of angels of victory receiving them, and indicating the glorification of the hero.

In the plane of the base, below the vase, is the door opening into the burial-vault. Upon the panel of the door is wrought the fasces and shield of the United States, and upon these are suspended the symbols and honors of civil and heroic service, namely, the scroll and the sword, with the oak and laurel wreaths. Upon the door-jambs, on either side, stand the ever-burning lamps of affection; here their stems are twined with the flowers, indicative of the affection of grief.

Upon the side planes of this projection of the base are the figures of Immortality and History.

The planes of the base of the structure, on either side of the door, are left vacant for inscriptions.

No. 5.   The Frieze-procession.

The martial funeral procession starts over the battle-scene; in that section the flag is borne drooped and draped. In the section of the front, the caparisoned horse is led; in the section over the scene in the Senate, the bier is borne. In the section over the vault the procession stands at "rest on arms," while the chaplain is in the action of prayer.

12

said, all is said. If we have the country,—the whole country,—the Union, the Constitution, free government, with these
will return all the blessings of well-ordered civilization. The
path of the country will be a career of greatness and of glory
such as our fathers, in the olden time, foresaw in the dim
visions of years yet to come, and such as would have been
ours to-day, had it not been for the treason for which the
Senator too often seeks to apologize."

XIX.

Soldiers' Relief Associations.

No records preserved on the earth can ever tell what good these associations have done. All their work has had to be done in a hurry. Of course much of it has been imperfectly done. But it will always be true that some hundreds of thousands of brave men have known of the generosity of their absent friends, and their sympathy with their loved ones, in the tented field.

I do not think that any of their efforts were wasted, even though the offerings may never have reached their destinations. In the tempest of so wild a revolution some wrecks were sure to take place. But the soldier's friend always had the will, and in any event the will was taken for the deed. To *remember* an absent friend, is the first impulse of a true heart. "To know that we are remembered, is a genuine consolation." Above all is it so when the boy, sleeping in the mud or snow, in Virginia, wakes from dreams of home, with its crackling hickory fire and its laughing faces around it, and is told that a box has come for him, filled with all the home-things which made his life happy before he woke from the delusion of childhood that "the world was without a foe." Perhaps the case is fairly enough stated in the following which was written last autumn. Says the Washington "Chronicle:"—

" We have been favored with a copy of a letter on this subject (Relief for Soldiers), addressed to the citizens of New York, by Mr. C. Edwards Lester ; and the following extracts come home to the feelings of our people. Mr. L. says—[ED.]

" For a while after the war began, the number of sick and

wounded soldiers was comparatively so small that few suffered neglect, except from the incomplete provisions of the sanitary department of the Government. These defects were, however, remedied with all possible despatch. But it was impossible thus suddenly to cover so broad a field. But the utmost energies of the Government were put forth, and the Sanitary Commission was no sooner appointed than they, or their duly constituted deputies and agents, visited every military camp and hospital in the country, everywhere organizing a sanitary *régime*, which has been acknowledged to be the most perfect any army, great or small, has had in the world.

"After relieving all immediate wants of the sick and wounded, special attention was given to the preservation of the health of the army,—the whole system of diet, clothing, habits, safeguards against climatic exposures in marching, and every thing appertaining to the life of the camp. Never was an army so generously provided nor so carefully looked after. Appeals were made to the country, and contributions of every comfort, and even luxury, were forwarded in quantities almost incredible. The wisest and most efficient inspection and distribution of all these contributions were made throughout the whole army. It is thus estimated by the best-informed persons, officers and surgeons, and soldiers themselves, that not less than fifty thousand lives were saved.

"But no such system can ever be devised which covers the whole ground and works with perfection. There is always a large margin left for individual charity and personal exertion, and this margin must be filled. Soldiers' relief associations were early formed at Washington, composed of civilians from every State, who went vigorously to work. All the hospitals in and around the capital were frequently visited, and whatever was required for the comfort of the inmates was procured to the extent of our ability. Generous donations were sent our association from New York, which fortunately consisted last fall in clothing and other things appropriate for winter, and last spring in what was so imperatively called for by the exhausting heat of Washington.

"But all that has been received was but a drop in the bucket, compared with what is now being demanded. Then our sick and disabled soldiers were numbered only by scores and hundreds. Now they are counted by thousands. I know you will respond to this call. The great State of New York has had, and will have through the war, more of her sons in the field and hospitals than any of her sister States, and she must not flag now in her duty; nor will she. Her great heart is pierced with sorrow, and many a sister, wife, and mother will not be comforted, because their loved ones are not. But it is much easier to hear that the brave boy fell on the field, dying gloriously under his country's flag, than to learn, when too late, that he lingered perhaps for weeks, fading slowly away in a hospital, with no kind hand to wipe the death-damps from his brow as he was going to his Father's mansion in heaven. Oh! who would not rather die at his own home, and go to sleep under the wide-spread tree beneath whose younger branches he played in his innocent and unclouded boyhood?

"I have not time nor disposition to depict the scenes I have witnessed in the military hospitals of Washington. The young man, with his right arm amputated, with no friend to write a letter to his home, even to let his kindred know that he is alive, and where he is,—how his eye brightens as some old neighbor approaches his cot to do for him what the Good Samaritans of the world all do to relieve the sick, the suffering, and the dying! Painful as it always is to recall scenes of grief and desolation, I must allude to one which, among many others, fell under my own observation in the hospital which, as a member of the New York Soldiers' Relief Association, I was specially charged to visit.

"Among the many noble and patriotic sons of Erin who early enlisted, was one who left a wife with two young children. His regiment joined the army of the Potomac, and he sent his monthly pay to his home. His children sickened and died. I need not depict the gloom or solitude of the little apartment which the young mother returned to from the graves of her babes, while her beloved husband was on a distant battle-field.

" On that field he was severely wounded in the foot, and sent on to a Washington hospital. The surgeon delayed amputation until it was evident that it could alone save his life. The chaplain sent at once to the soldier's wife, telling her to hasten to Washington if she wished to see her husband alive.

" She was poor; but she did not hesitate. She pawned her little household goods, and arrived before the amputation. When it took place, she saw it had been delayed till it was too late. The worms had already taken possession of what was so soon to be their inheritance. They were crawling around where the scalpel struck. Either through carelessness or horror, the surgeon inflicted a slight wound in the end of his forefinger. The brave soldier soon died; but that loving wife stood by his couch steadily to the last. When all was over, and she had seen him decently laid in his tomb, she returned to what was once her home, but no longer a home for her, for her children and their sire were all dead. Inflammation began in the surgeon's finger. He delayed the necessary remedy until it was too late also in his own case. The virus from the soldier's dead foot had spread through the surgeon's system. He reached his home and died !

"Such are the scenes we witness, with others far more shocking, and many not less strange. Think ye our associates have not had enough to do, with all the aid which the men and women of New York can give us ? In a word, our Washington Associations endeavor to do to our disabled soldiers what you would do for them if they were suffering in your own neighborhood.

" Will you, then, come forward and help us ?

" These are not the least effective means by which this unholy war can be soon brought to a close, and the dove of peace unfolds its wings over a redeemed and consolidated republic.

"I have seen great good done by our Soldiers' Relief Associations. The mere fact of their existence was a boon to the soldier: it was a fraternal response from Washington to the firesides of the East, the North, and the West; and I am sure that the clerks of Washington have done their full duty in these tender and generous services. But I am yet of the opinion that the contributions for the army which are sent to the United States Sanitary Commission are far more wisely bestowed than they have been or can be in any other way. I am sorry to say that so much unnecessary waste, delay, and expense are incurred by adopting any other mode.*

---

* In speaking of this matter, the Sanitary Commission use the following language, chiefly to introduce an unpublished letter of General Washington:—

"It is hardly just to let this report go forth to the public without a more distinct reference to the deep and earnest, resolute and abiding spirit of patriotism in the women of the country of which the Commission daily receives more tangible evidence than can be conveyed in words. From a backwoods neighborhood, for instance, comes a box containing contributions of bedclothing and wearing-apparel from sixty women and children, the invoice running thus: *One pair of stockings from the widow Barber; one quilt, two bottles currant wine, one cheese, Mrs. Barber; two pillow-cases and one pair stockings, Jane Barber; one pair stockings and one handkerchief, Lucy Barber; one pair mittens and Robinson Crusoe, Jedediah Barber;'* and then follows the list of contributions of another family. A few devout words only are commonly added to such a list, but they imply that the donors are ready to give all they possess if it shall be needed to maintain the inheritance of our fathers. Blankets worn in the Revolution, and others taken in the last war with England, heirloom linen, with great-grandmothers' hand-marks, and many family treasures, are sent as free-will offerings, with simple prayers that they may contribute to the comfort of some defender of liberty. To the same end, the first ladies of the land, if any are entitled to that appellation, have, without cessation, during all the hot summer, been engaged daily in dry, hard, plodding work, sorting, marking, packing goods, and carrying on extended and tedious accounts and correspondence with the precision, accuracy, and

regularity of trained merchants.   In all there is little of romantic enthusiasm, but much, and, as the months pass, more and more, of deep-
seated, abiding, self-sacrificing resolution.   It seems as if the women were
just now beginning to feel how much they love their country; and the
inquiry, 'How can we best do something for the army?' is coming from
every quarter,—from the border slave States as well as the free.   That it is
important that this desire should be gratified, and with judicious economy
directed where it will most truly aid, however slightly, the strength and
comfort of our soldiers, there can be no question.   Although our volunteers are, as compared with the soldiers of other armies, generously paid,
few large armies of modern times have been as little influenced by mercenary motives.   The gifts which, especially when sick and wounded, the
men have sent to them from the women at home, can but have an ennobling influence upon them; and the aid given in this manner to the army
must create, in all those from whom it proceeds, an interest in and sympathy with the army and with its objects which will prepare them constantly for greater sacrifices and more resolute devotion to the Government, should it be needed.   How well Washington understood this, the following letter, written by his own hand at a time when he must have been
overloaded with business of the grandest importance, gives evidence.   It
has never before been published.

" Copy of a Letter from General Washington to Mrs. Bache (Daughter of
Franklin).

"HEAD-QUARTERS IN BERGEN, N. J., 14th of July, 1780.
"MADAM :—I have received with much pleasure—but not till last night—
your favor of the 4th, specifying the amount of the subscriptions already
collected for the use of the American soldiery.

"This fresh mark of the patriotism of the ladies entitles them to the
highest applause of their country.   It is impossible for the army not to
feel a superior gratitude on such an instance of goodness.   If I am happy
in having the concurrence of the ladies, I would propose the purchasing
of coarse linen, to be made into shirts, with the whole amount of their
subscription.   A shirt extraordinary to the soldier will be of more service
to him than any other thing that could be procured him; while it is not
intended to, nor shall, exclude him from the usual supply which he draws
from the public.

"This appears to me to be the best mode for its application, provided it
is approved of by the ladies.   I am happy to find you have been good
enough to give us a claim on your endeavors to complete the execution of
the design.   An example so laudable will certainly be nurtured, and must
be productive of a favorable issue in the bosoms of the fair, in the sister
States.

"Let me congratulate our benefactors on the arrival of the French fleet off the harbor of Newport on the afternoon of the 10th. It is this moment announced, but without any particulars, as an interchange of signals had only taken place.

"I pray the ladies of your family to receive, with my compliments, my liveliest thanks for the interest they take in my favor.

"With the most perfect respect and esteem,

"I have the honor to be, madam,

"Your obedient and humble servant,

"GEORGE WASHINGTON."

XX.

The Dark in the White House.

"WILLIE LINCOLN is dead!" Everybody in Washington knew Willie, and everybody was sad. Sad,—for it seemed hard for the noble and brilliant boy to be taken away so early, while the sun was just gilding the eastern mountains without a single cloud, and he could look down the sweet valley and see so far into the future.

Sad for her who held him as one of the jewels of her home-coronet, dearer than all the insignia of this world's rank. That coronet was broken. It might still dazzle and grace, but it could never be the same coronet again.

Sad for the master of the Executive Mansion. There was weight enough pressing on that tired brain,—sorrow enough pressing on that great heart. With the burden of a mighty republic on his shoulders,—a republic betrayed and wounded in the house of its friends,—a republic that had cost so much and become so dear to its own true children, and in whose prosperity the hopes of all men "who waited for the consola-tion" of the nations were bound up,—a republic for whose safety and triumph God, angels, and all good men would eternally hold him responsible,—it seemed to us all, when we heard the news of the boy's death, that even Heaven's own sweet fountain of mercy had dried up.

*   *   *   *   *   *

It was a wild winter night; but I desired once more to see how far the process of Willie's embalmment had gone; and, as Dr. Brown wished to make one more visit to the President's House that night, I took his arm at a late hour, and we walked up together. The wind howled desolately; angry gusts struck us at every corner; tempest-clouds were careering high up in the heavens. The dead leaves of the last half-peaceful year, as they flew cuttingly against our cheeks, seemed to have come out of their still graves to join in the dreadful revelry of the Death of the Republic of Washington on the very anniversary of his birth; for it was the eve of the 22d of February,—the night in which he was born.

"Is it not among the strangest of things that this event should have happened?"

"No, doctor: I do not so regard it. You remember some very striking events that have happened in connection with the building we are approaching?—The White House has not been any more exempt from trouble than the other dwellings of America. Poor General Harrison entered it as a prince goes into his palace to rule a great people: in one month he was borne from it to his grave.

"He who shall be with us and all loyal men hereafter an unmentioned name, the occupant of this house by accident, and, administering the government without honor, left none to regret his retirement, turned parricide, and now rots in a traitor's grave.

"General Taylor, fresh from the fields of his fame as a patriot warrior, came here only to pass a few months of excited and troubled life and then surrender to the only enemy to whom he ever yielded.

"Fillmore, who also was summoned here by the act of God, after acquitting himself most manfully and honorably of all his duties, had scarcely vacated this mansion before he was called on to entomb the wife of his youth and the mother of his children, of whom the one he loved best soon after went to the same repose. He descended from this high place to become the chief mourner; and his ovation was a funeral at Buffalo.

"So, too, with his successor, who left the new-made grave

of his only son in Concord—killed in an instant—to be in-augurated at the Capitol and enter as a mourner this stately mansion.

"Yes! how true it is! 'Uneasy lies the head which wears a crown.'"

*   *   *   *   *   *

"Yes, gentlemen," said Edward, the chief doorkeeper: "it is all still in the house now."

We entered the Green Room.

Willie lay in his coffin. The lid was off. He was clothed in his soldier's dress.

Willie had been embalmed by Dr. Charles D. Brown, who uses only the process of Professor Sucquet, of Paris,—a process by which nearly all illustrious Frenchmen who have died within our times have been embalmed.

To those who are not fully informed of the process of Sucquet, it may be added that no arsenic or other poisonous chemicals are used, but an infusion is made of a fluid without mutilation or removal of any portion of the body. In a few hours the body begins to grow hard and marble-like; and this change continues till petrifaction is complete,—when the body becomes a statue, and changes no more for ages. It was by this beautiful and only process known to men of science worthy of the name, that the body of William Wallace Lincoln was perfectly prepared for its final resting-place in the home of his happy childhood.

* * * * One look more at the calm face, which still wore its wonted expression of hope and cheerfulness, and we left him to his repose. * * * *

The coming storm was clouding the heavens with a deeper mourning, and its wild howlings wrapped "the Home of the Presidents" in sadness and gloom. "God heal the broken hearts left there!"

XXI.

The Life of an Army Paymaster for a Day.

ITS adventures and experiences make up some of the striking episodes of military life. I thought I could not do better by my reader than to give here, just as I got it, the following passages from an actual day of paymaster-life, furnished me by Major J. LEDYARD HODGE, one of the most accomplished paymasters of the army.

The entire authenticity of the record is certain, and the raciness of the recital will speak for itself.

"Early in the autumn of 1861, I was directed to pay a regiment of volunteers near Washington. The payment, for some reasons best known to those through whom my order came, was to be made immediately; and the sum of seventy-five thousand dollars was handed to me at the same time as the order.

"It was then in the days when 'greenbacks' were unknown, and the money I received was good, solid gold and silver, fresh from the Mint.

"Being at that time a paymaster of about three weeks, standing, and as unaccustomed to the possession of seventy-five thousand dollars as a midshipman to the society of admirals, I felt no small responsibility for the safe custody of the treasure, and considerable anxiety as to the proper disbursement of the money, to be correct in my payments to the soldiers and watchful for the security of my bondsmen.

"The rolls were given me about two o'clock in the afternoon; and, aided by my equally inexperienced clerk, I worked at them faithfully all that evening and late into the night.

13

"My first determination was to remain on guard over the money till morning, with a loaded revolver in my hand, and the doors of the house all locked up to the third story, in which I roomed. However, I compromised with my conscience by throwing myself down for a nap alongside the chest, the doors locked, the light burning, and the revolver within reach.

"Many a time since then have I slept soundly with twice and three times the amount I then had, in a wooden chest, with a whole division around me, recruited from the miscellaneous characters that roam the streets of our big cities, and I alone in a canvas tent, with only a single sentry outside, whose bayonet might be the very instrument to pry open my box or silence my resistance.

"But that night, in a secure house, in the midst of a guarded city, my rest was any thing but sound. If I slept, it was to dream of robbers carrying off the chest; if I remained awake, I fancied every sound of the night was the attempted breaking open of a window or door.

"Morning at last was gladly welcomed, with a most determined resolution that before another night I would convert as much as possible of my precious metals into soldiers' receipts, which, however valuable they might be to me, would hardly tempt any one else to appropriate them.

"The pay-rolls were shockingly imperfect; for the regiment was a new one, and the officers, if possible, less acquainted with their duties in making the rolls than I in paying on them. I would have liked to remain in town a day, to examine and compare the rolls more carefully, and obtain from more experienced officers information and advice on the hundred questions concerning pay, always necessary to be determined when a regiment is paid off, and more especially when that regiment is receiving its first payment after entering service.

"It is then that all the hard questions have to be met and

determined,—that the date of commencement of pay for every man of the whole thousand has to be settled, and a calculation of odd days made for every payment,—that the fond illusions caused by representations of the recruiting officers have to be dispelled, and the privates made to understand that they are not all to receive the pay and allowances of a 'major-general commanding a separate army in the field,' double rations included,—that officers discover that they do not draw pay from the date they agreed to take commissions as colonels and majors, but only from the time the United States agreed to receive them as such,—that it is clearly demonstrated to the assembled company that it is not entitled to three captains and six lieutenants,—and a thousand other points, equally difficult to explain satisfactorily to those whose pecuniary expectations are blasted by such explanation.

"Deliver me from ever again making the first payment to a volunteer regiment just raised, and not at all disciplined ! I would rather, at any time, take four which had been paid two or three times, and to whom there was only the regular even two months' pay coming,—where every man knows exactly what he is entitled to, and steps up in his turn and rakes off the table his twenty-six dollars with the satisfaction of one who feels he has fairly earned it.

"All these innumerable questions were proposed and decided during my three weeks' acquaintance with the laws and usages of the Pay Department; and let me here tell any unfortunate innocent brethren who think it such a nice thing to be a paymaster, that the common or unwritten law of England, composed of customs that have existed from time immemorial, and which said customs can only be settled by some three thousand volumes of decisions and reports, is plain and simple to the unwritten or common law of the Pay Department of the United States Army.

"Fortunately for me, perhaps, I was at that time in comparative ignorance of what was to happen to me. I knew I had my rolls very incompletely made up, but the regiment must be paid at once: it might move any hour, and the orders were imperative. So I trusted to having all my amendments and corrections made when I reached the ground.

"I had already discovered one great principle, which I recommend as of much importance to all paymasters; and that was, that you can always obtain from the company and mustering officers of a regiment any imaginable certificate of muster, or other instrument in writing, whereby their payment will be facilitated or the amount to be paid increased.

"I once had a set of rolls to pay where the mustering officer certified that he and all his men were duly enlisted and sworn into the military service of the United States to assist in suppressing the rebellion on the 1st day of February, 1861,—two months before Fort Sumter was attacked. I called his attention to this little discrepancy; but he insisted that they were ready and willing to enter service then, and he didn't see why they should not be paid from that time. I can't say 'I saw it' in that light. I have often thought I would require some officer, before paying him, to certify that he had entered the service on the 4th of July, 1776, and been continuously on duty ever since, and was entitled to longevity rations accordingly. I have not the slightest doubt he would have unhesitatingly given the required certificate.

"But to return to my trip. Trusting to luck, and unbounded certifying and affidavits, to cover up all defects, both of the rolls and the payments thereon, I started on a bright Wednesday morning for the camp of the regiment. A four-horse ambulance, furnished by the quartermaster, contained 'Cæsar and his fortunes,' which consisted of the specie-chest and contents, an overcoat, a revolver, and a haversack with cooked rations for two days, and 'whiskey for five.'

"The escort was composed of my clerk and the driver,—not as powerful a guard as the two gunboats and regiment of infantry that escorted a party of paymasters up the Tennessee River to protect them from any polite attentions on the part of John Morgan, but sufficient, as I *then* thought, for all the dangers I was likely to meet. I changed my mind before I got back.

"As I said, it was in the beginning of September, 1861,. when the confused mass of men driven back to Arlington Heights from the defeat of Bull Run was just beginning, under the organization of General McClellan, to bud out into the afterwards celebrated 'Army of the Potomac,'—at the time when the rebels held Miner's and Munson's Hills, and their flag could be seen from the top of the Capitol, while their pickets scoured the country within four miles of Washington.

"A few nights before, a brigade of troops had been marched over the Chain Bridge to protect its farther end, and were then engaged in building the two forts that cover the approaches by the Leesburg turnpike. It was one of these regiments that I was sent to pay.

"We went along beautifully by the river road, and laughed at the enemy's cavalry and guerrillas, till we reached the bridge. There on the hill frowned a heavy battery behind an earthwork. At the end of the bridge two brass howitzers promised a full allowance of grape and canister to all unauthorized travellers, while the flooring of the bridge itself taken up for several yards would have made it very inconvenient for cavalry to charge over on a gallop.

"While the flooring was being relaid, I inquired the reason of this extra precaution, with a brigade on the other side guarding the approaches, and was comforted by the reply that the rebel cavalry thought nothing of cutting in behind our men and picking up stragglers and plunder close down on the river, and that the night before they had appeared about half a mile above on the opposite bank and fired at our pickets.

13*

"The brigade was about two miles out on the other side, and could be reached only by a road cut through the woods by the troops, and barely wide enough for a wagon.

"Pleasant prospect, I thought; but it was broad daylight, and there was plenty of company,—commissary-wagons with provisions, stragglers hunting their regiments, officers who had been in town on leave and without it, sutlers' wagons, and country-people.

"As soon as the bridge was made passable, we all poured over. Every thing went on as straight as could be: we didn't lose the road but once, and then found ourselves in the camp of a New York regiment, who were intensely disgusted when they found a paymaster had strayed in among them by mistake, with no intention of favoring them. We nearly upset half a dozen times (which is nothing uncommon in roads only three days old, with all the stumps of the trees yet standing), and were detained half an hour while our team, added to the six horses of a Parrott gun, hauled the gun and its limber out of the creek, where it had stalled in fording. But in due course of time we reached the camp.

"The arrival had been expected. Good news, like evil, travels fast, and no sooner did the ambulance commence mounting the hill where the fort was being built and the regiment was encamped, than the peculiar welcome always extended to a paymaster commenced. Every man in sight shouts, 'Paymaster! Paymaster!' as loud as he can bawl, and then immediately dodges behind a tent, or wagon, or any thing that will conceal him, as if he expected to be shot at the next second.

"I drove directly to the colonel's quarters, had a tent pitched alongside as an office, borrowed the necessary camp tables and chairs, gave out the company rolls to be receipted, and invited the field and staff officers in the mean time to step up and be paid. This invitation they were by no means slow to accept, and in a short time their pockets were considerably heavier, and their hearts, I suppose, proportionably lighter.

"When these few payments were made, the company rolls not being yet signed, there succeeded an interval which could only be properly filled by all hands then present, the chaplain included, taking a drink,—first with the colonel in honor of my arrival, and next with me, that I might soon call again.

"I, of course, made due inquiries as to the military situation, and found that we held, or were considered to hold, a very strong position on the hill where we were then standing, with a beautiful line of retreat over this interesting road I had just traversed, and secure communication, especially at night, with our base of operations the other side of the Potomac, by means of the unfloored Chain Bridge. Our outside pickets were about a mile out to the front, and beyond them the enemy were reported in strong force at Dranesville, about five miles off, and their pickets and mounted patrols came down every night and rode along within a hundred yards of our sentries, who had orders not to fire on them, as we were by no means anxious to bring on a skirmish, even, till the two forts were completed.

"By the time we had gone through the manœuvre above mentioned, which, as I said, had to be twice repeated to secure a thorough knowledge of it, and I had acquired this information of the military position of affairs, the first company appeared with its rolls. The regiment had been at work in the trenches of the fort, except two companies out on picket, and the men had just 'laid down the shovel and the hoe' and fallen in with great alacrity for payment.

"The usual practice is to give out the rolls to be signed by the men, and then bring them back to the paymaster, who calls out the names of the men whose signatures he finds on the returned rolls, and hands them their money as they step up in answer. An officer of the company stands by the pay-table, to see that the proper man comes up when his name is called, and that no personating of sick and absent soldiers is attempted. When the officers choose to play the rascal (and, I am sorry to say, this is often the case), the United States Treasury is apt to suffer; and many a dead man has drawn pay, and numerous John Smiths have been mustered, their receipts duly given, and the money handed out by the unsuspecting paymaster, the captain gravely standing by and allowing the representative of the man of straw to pocket the sum, which is soon afterwards divided, in the proportion of about twenty dollars to the honorable officer and six dollars to the honest soldier.

"Every one that has been in any way connected with our army has, I suppose, seen a regiment paid off. The scramble among the various companies to get their rolls signed first and returned (as they are taken up in the order in which so returned), the overwhelming politeness of the sutler to the paymaster,—how he offers to supply tables, chairs, whiskey, cigars, and all other refreshments for his use, and finally suggests the propriety of his establishing himself at the pay-table in order the more securely to collect his little accounts,—how disgusted he is if the paymaster does not see it in that light (and no honest paymaster will), and goes off and establishes himself as near as possible, where he hails every man as he passes off from receiving his money, and, by alternate coaxing and threatening, induces him to pay what he, the sutler, says he owes.

"Then the long line of men, drawn up in single file in alphabetical order; the quaint expressions as they come up in turn (for every man considers himself bound to say something when he receives his money); the yells and shouts if some dissatisfied grumbler stops to question and argue about how much is due him, and delays the whole line, whose eyes are fixed on the pleasant prospect ahead, and heads perpetually twisted to count the number before them. Every now and then some particularly fractious individual undertakes to make an extra row, and is marched off by the guard till he cools down; while a general settlement of all debts is going on over the neighborhood, accompanied by the usual disputes and differences of calculations that always attend such closings of accounts.

"In this manner I paid out money steadily all that afternoon till after sundown, and by that time had completed. every thing, except the two companies on picket, who would not be relieved till the next morning, and one other company, whose muster-rolls were so hopelessly incorrect and imperfect that there was no remedy but to make them out entirely fresh. The captain of the company accordingly went to work, while I, at the invitation of the field-officer of the day, who was a major of the regiment I was paying, rode out to accompany him in his rounds of the pickets.

"We went about a mile, and then rode along our line. They were stationed in the edge of a wood, with open fields in front, and about a hundred yards from a country road, over which the enemy's mounted patrols deliberately trotted every night. Our boys thought it very hard they couldn't take a resting shot now and then, on bright moonlight nights, at these impudent vedettes; but the orders were imperative: so they watched them pass by in silence.

At the time we visited the picket-line, however, it was all quiet enough; not a sign of an enemy to be seen, unless it were two or three thin columns of smoke going straight up in the motionless air and apparently about a mile off. The pickets said they were from the camp-fires of one of the rebel outposts. I took their word for it,—didn't think there was any use of making a personal examination: so we rode back to camp.

"Soon after our return, supper was announced, and I joined a mess of some six officers at the usual bill of fare of an officers' mess,—cold meat, hot coffee, crackers, and a bottle of whiskey. It was as pleasant and well-enjoyed a meal, though, as I ever had. Every one was in high spirits: the war had just opened; no one thought of the terrible losses ahead; and the scenery, the bright moonlight night, the breathing of the fresh pure air, the songs of the soldiers in the adjoining camp, —every thing went to make a cheerful, pleasant hour. In less than forty-eight hours the brightest of that party lay dead in that very tent, killed in a picket-skirmish; and the swamps of the Chickahominy and the fields of Gaines's Mill and Antietam have left but two more of the six who laughed and chatted around that camp-table.

"After supper we strolled up to the unfinished fort, and from its parapets, with a full moon in a cloudless sky, we saw as beautiful a panorama as any lover of nature could desire. Away off beyond us could be tracked the course of the river, its stream looking like silver in the light; below, a line of camp-fires traced the encampments of the Union troops down along the heights in front of Washington, till lost in the distance; and in front a solitary sparkle in the whole expanse of country seen from that elevation told of the danger and enemy to be looked for out of that darkness and uncertainty.

"Camp-life is one of early hours: the maxim of 'early to bed and early to rise' is carried out there better than in any other place I know of, not excepting the best-regulated nurseries. My hotel was my ambulance; and I have since been well satisfied with much worse accommodations than that second story of a four-horse ambulance, with an overcoat and blanket for covering. I had my clerk alongside, the specie-box underneath, and a sentry at each end of the wagon: so I felt pretty secure, and slept 'like a top,' except every now and then when a sudden jerk made every thing rattle.

"For some time I was too sleepy to find out the cause of this unaccountable proceeding. Finally an extra shake roused me sufficiently to investigate matters,—when I found that the horses were fastened to the pole of the ambulance, and their movements disturbed our slumbers. This was soon remedied; and again we were all quiet, when the clear ring of a musket-shot sounded as it were close at hand. It is wonderful how sound is heard of a clear, calm night. That shot was from a sentry a mile off. The rebel patrols, as usual, were taking their nightly rounds down the road. The moon brought them out sharp and clear against the background of trees behind them. The men of the scout were hardened by past immunity, and they rode along laughing and joking.

"Just as they came to the turn of the road where it led away from our line, one of them, in reply to a remark from a comrade, said, 'D——n the Yankees! Who cares for them?' It was too much for our sentry, who from the edge of the woods on our side had been watching them. A sharp report, the singing of a Minié bullet, and one of the horsemen reeled in his saddle, was caught by his friends, and the party dashed off; while the word of alarm passed down the line of our pickets for miles, and the guards turned out with full expectation of seeing a rebel column, only to swear at the unlucky sentry and wish him in the guard-house, where he found himself early next morning as a reward for shooting a rebel contrary to orders.

"We were out early enough next morning, and at work making up the defective company's new rolls. I expected to be through and off for town by eleven o'clock. But I reckoned without my host. It was ten o'clock before the two companies on picket came in: then they had to sign their rolls; and in the mean time I paid the company whose rolls had just been prepared. I had finished that job, and was commencing the other two, when an orderly came up at full speed.

"'Where's Colonel——?' He was standing in the tent at the time.

"'Here is a note from General ——, sir. I was told to deliver it as quickly as possible.'

"The note was short and simple enough. It read as follows:—

"'The enemy are said to be advancing from Dranesville.

Move with your regiment out to the turnpike, and await orders there. Immediate.'

"The next minute the long roll was beat, and every thing changed as by magic. I turned round a minute to gather up papers and money and tumble them indiscriminately into the box. By the time I had finished, the companies were forming. The men rushed in from the trenches of the fort in their shirt-sleeves, caught their muskets from the stack, and took their places, without waiting for coat, blanket, or haversack.

"They cheered and shouted and danced. One would have thought they were going to a frolic.

"Ten months afterwards I saw that same regiment (what was left of it) fall in on the morning of the battle of Malvern Hills. There was no cheering, no dancing, no laughing. The men's faces were set and solemn; they looked round carefully to see that nothing was left, that their blankets were well slung, their canteens full, their cartridge-boxes handy. Those men who danced and cheered would probably have run away had they met an enemy that day. *At Malvern Hills they fought like devils.*

"In ten minutes the regiment was off. I offered my services as an aid to the colonel, borrowed a horse, and started, leaving my box in charge of my clerk and the camp-guard, knowing it was useless to try and get it back over the river then.

"We went over the same route I had come out,—down the hill over the branch, up through the long cut and newly-made road on the other side (how I blessed that cut that evening!) and out to the turnpike. Here an order was received to move out the pike to support the troops who had gone ahead of us; and, looking back, we could see a long line of troops coming up by the river road on the other side, while the occasional flash of a brass gun in the sunlight told of howitzers and Napoleon guns in plentiful supply.

"Every one expected there would be a fight, of course. Troops were moving; orderlies were rushing round, hunting up the persons for whom they had despatches; aides-de-camp, and spare officers generally, rode by, looking as important and solemn as if General McClellan had just sent for each of them personally to obtain their views and advice.

"In the mean time the regiment had halted, and the men, somewhat fatigued by their rapid march, did not seem so enthusiastic as at first. Those who had left their coats behind complained of being chilly; and all regretted their haversacks.

"Suddenly a rumor ran down the line that it was all a hoax; that a company of rebel cavalry had scared one of our patrols, who had rushed in and reported all Johnston's army advancing; that our cavalry had been out to Dranesville, and reported nothing there but some violent secesh women and *pigs*, the latter of which they took possession of, not thinking the former worth that trouble.

"Sure enough, in a few minutes the order came to return to camp. I have heard of that celebrated army that swore terribly in Flanders. If it beat the portion of the army of the Potomac that was out on this excursion, it was a remarkable body of men. Such an outpouring of oaths, such a variety of expressions, all centred on one object,—the man or men who gave the alarm,—was never before heard. He was the best-cursed man in the country. I will answer for one regiment, each individual of its thousand members did nothing else but swear at him from the time the regiment started back till it reached camp, broke ranks, and dispersed for a late dinner.

"I was not in a saintlike frame of mind myself. I had two companies to pay; it was after three o'clock, considerably; the roads and woods would be full of stragglers from the different regiments who had been out that day; there was a gradual clouding over of the sky, and the moon would not rise till after nine. Altogether, I did not admire my ride home that night at all.

14

"However, I hurried through my payments, made short work of the various complainants and questioners who at the end of the paying off of a regiment always come up with their special cases for explanation and settlement, hardly waited to say good-bye to or take a farewell drink with the officers who had treated me so kindly, and by five o'clock I was rattling down the hill, with as firm a determination of being within the corporate limits of the city of Georgetown before dark as a man could well have.

"Down we went to the branch, and through it, and had just started up the cut that led up the hill on the other side, when I saw at the farther end, on the top of the hill, the white top of an army-wagon thrown out in relief against the already fast-darkening sky.

"'Hold on, driver: two wagons can't pass in this road. We must haul to one side and wait till that fellow gets by.'

"So we pulled out and waited. Down came the wagon, with wheels locked and teamster swearing as usual; but after it came another, and another, and another; and so the line kept on, till upwards of forty had passed. It was a commissary train, with a supply of rations for the whole brigade. For over one hour did that train keep us waiting at the foot of that cut. Job himself would have lost patience; as for me, I was so mad I couldn't even swear. However, it passed at last.

"But now it was dark, and we had to go over this wild road cut through the woods. Every man we met would know the ambulance and what it contained, and I pretty much considered my throat as cut already.

"Innocent people may wonder what I was afraid of, so far within the lines of our own army, and within a mile of camps where whole brigades of men were posted. Not of the rebels, surely? No, indeed; I felt safe enough on that point. But there was a certain class of people, called *stragglers and camp-followers*, with respect to whose company on a dark night and in a lonely place we may well use the petition of the

Litany, and exclaim, 'Good Lord, deliver us.' They would think no more of robbery and murder than of eating their dinner; and a paymaster with a chest of money was a chance not to be neglected.

"I took the seat alongside the driver, with a revolver in my hand, put my clerk behind to protect the rear, made a mental promise to shoot the first man that touched the horses' heads, and told the driver to 'make time.'

"How I watched as we went up that hill! Every stump of a tree was a man crouching by the road; every cricket that chirruped was the cocking of a musket; every bush that rustled was a person moving in the undergrowth. Twice we met a couple of soldiers going to camp, and each time I expected to see the horses' heads seized, and was surprised when they passed by as a matter of course.

"Didn't I feel relieved when we came out of that dark, uncertain road on to the turnpike? and wasn't a load lifted off my breast when I answered the challenge of the sentry at the head of the Chain Bridge, showed my pass, crossed the bridge, and felt the ambulance rattling along at a fast trot over the river road to Georgetown? I slept well that night. And so ended my first trip as a paymaster."

XXII.

The Immolation and Redemption of the African Race.

NATIONS pay dear for Liberty. Civilization—the sole object of free government—crystallizes slow. But, once firmly established, it resists the untiring "course of all-impairing Time."

The true civilization, in perfection, is yet to come. The world has been filled with false civilizations; and history shows that they have not vitality enough to preserve nations from decadence.

It has been just as plainly proved that where slavery existed it either destroyed civilization or was destroyed by it. The two never could live together. China and Japan are the only two ancient Asiatic nations that have preserved their early civilization, or even their existence. *Slavery never existed among them.*

So in Europe: slavery destroyed every European nation that maintained it. Greece, Rome, the empire of the Othman,—where are they? But slavery never existed among the Magyars or Slavonic nations; nor have they ever been subjugated, much less destroyed. Hungary is a vast and illuminated nation, and is advancing in civilization; while Russia has removed the last encumbrance to her progress by emancipating twenty million serfs, and is now moving on to complete civilization faster than any other people. The Swiss *never* breathed the tainted air of slavery; her people have always been free, and in civilization they have lagged behind those of no other country.

At an early period England and France abolished villanage, and followed in the wake of Italy, which was the first of the nations to give revival to letters, commerce, and arts.

So we find that just in proportion as nations emancipated themselves from the thraldom of a system of forced or involuntary labor, just in that proportion they advanced in knowledge, wealth, and the elements of endurance. A careful survey of truthful history would establish this as a fixed and clearly-determined law for the, physical and moral progress and development of states. Nations may grow strong, or rather formidable, for 'a while, under the sceptre of a tyrant and the slave-lash of an oligarchy. But such strength is weakness: it does not last. It is against all the ordinances of God that it should.

This is pre-eminently true in our age, when daylight is dawning upon all peoples. Darkness has lost its power. Universal light is now asserting its dominion. No power can contend against it. Darkness must give way.

So far as my argument on the subject of slavery in the United States or elsewhere is concerned, it matters not whether the reader accept or not the code of revealed religion which I offer as authority; for profane history coincides with it perfectly. There is no sort of conflict between the two. The plagues that wasted the vitals of dead nations are just as legibly inscribed on their tombs, for their readers, as they were on the pages of prophecy before the events took place. God alone writes history before it happens. Both records are so clear that he who runs may read; and the wise and good man who reads either will run to rescue his country from the curse which God has chained to the chariot-wheels even of the mightiest empires which dare to make war on the eternal principles of justice which support his empire.

Go where we will, from the Pillars of Hercules to the gates of the Oriental morning,—

> "Rude fragments now
> Lie scatter'd where the shapely column stood.
> Their palaces are dust."

Journey through the home of the Saracens,—a race of scholars and warriors,—

*   *   *   *   *   *

"Dead Petra in her hill-tomb sleeps;
Her stones of emptiness remain;
Around her sculptured mystery sweeps
The lonely waste of Edom's plain.

*   *   *   *   *   *

"Unchanged the awful lithograph
Of power and glory undertrod,—
Of nations scatter'd like the chaff
Blown from the threshing-floor of God."

*   *   *   *   *   *

Let us calculate *the debt which America owes to Africa*. We can reach something like an approximation to the number of Africans or Africano-Americans who have lived and *died* on our soil. We do not propose to enumerate any considerable portion of the wrongs we have inflicted on that people,—how many we stole from their homes,—how many perished in the passage,—how many cruelties and indignities they and their descendants have suffered, and are suffering to this hour. That were a work for which any created being would find himself unequal. It will be found to occupy no inconsiderable space in the records of the last tribunal before which the human race will be cited to appear.

We will therefore determine, as accurately as we can, how many lives Africa has offered up for this nation. But first let us glance at the origin of slavery in the United States. We borrow a striking passage from the classic and powerful pen of Senator Sumner, who has probably investigated the whole African question, in all its relations, more profoundly than any other man living,—certainly more so than any other American. In one of his orations he draws the following picturesque and startling contrast :—

"In the winter of 1620, the Mayflower landed its precious cargo at Plymouth Rock. This small band, cheered by the valedictory prayers of the Puritan pastor, John Robinson, braved sea and wilderness for the sake of liberty. In this inspiration our Commonwealth began. That same year another cargo, of another character, was landed at Jamestown, in Virginia. It was nineteen slaves,—the first that ever touched and darkened our soil. Never in history was greater contrast. There was the Mayflower, filled with men,—intelligent, conscientious, prayerful,—all braced to hardy industry, who, before landing, united in a written compact by which they constituted themselves a 'civil body politic,' bound 'to frame just and equal laws.' And there was the slave-ship, with its fetters, its chains, its bludgeons, and its whips, with its wretched victims,—forerunners of the long agony of the slave-trade,—and with its wretched tyrants, rude, ignorant, and profane,

> 'who had learn'd their only prayers
> From curses,'   *   *   *   *   *

and who carried in their hold the barbarous slavery *whose single object is to compel labor without wages*, which no just and equal laws can sanction.

"Thus in the same year began two mighty influences; and these two influences still prevail far and wide throughout the country. But they have met at last in final grapple; and you and I are partakers in this holy conflict. The question is simply between the Mayflower and the slave-ship."

Beginning with the first importation of Africans in 1620 (nineteen), we find their increase till 1790, slave and free, amounting to 757,363. From 1790 (first census) to 1860 (eighth census), slave and free, 4,441,730. It is and will always remain impossible to determine the number of the African race whose ashes sleep in our soil; but, applying the ratio of increase from 1790 to 1860 to the period undetermined, it is easy to approximate the number. My most careful estimate renders it certain that the number of persons of

African descent who have died in our country cannot fall short of eight millions and a half, or nearly twice as many as are now living.

Thus we roll up the figures to thirteen millions, living and dead, each one of whom has felt the blighting curse of slavery,—more or less of the miseries and degradation which are its legitimate and inevitable consequences!

This is the immolation; and it is the most appalling and stupendous in the annals of the human race. Leaving out all the barbarities attending the capture and ocean-transportation, the brutal atrocities the stolen Africans suffered by a system of merciless task-labor under the lash, the maiming and torture of nerve and muscle, with the endless category of physical suffering, still each one of the mighty host of Africano-Americans—an army of *thirteen millions*, bond and free, living and dead—appears in solemn judgment against his individual oppressor and against the whole nation. The one has perpetrated the murder, and the Government has stood by and consented unto his death, and held the garments of those that slew him.

What are the counts in this terrible indictment?

1. *The annihilation of home,* whose charities are just as dear to the lower as to the higher classes of beings. Torn from their continental homes and transplanted to a new world, they should at least have had a chance to strike their roots into a stranger soil. But cupidity, accident, or caprice tore the plant up by the roots, and, with comparatively few exceptions, subjected it to a new and trying process of acclimation.

2. *The annihilation of marriage.* This sacrilegious blow at the first, the holiest, and the dearest of all God's institutions struck the race. It cast the deadliest blight which can fall on man. It made more bastards in America than ever lived elsewhere under heaven.

3. *The annihilation of light.* This means the impious inauguration of heathenism in the very garden of God. No

home, no wife or children he can call his own! Can a higher insult be offered to a man made in the divine image and for whom the Son of man died? Oh, how incomparably blessed in the contrast was the Thracian slave dragged to Rome to make, in the arena, a holiday for the slaveholders of the Eternal City! He left at least a home, wife, children.

> "I see before me the gladiator lie:
> He leans upon his hand; his manly brow
> Consents to death, but conquers agony.
>   *   *   *   *   His eyes
> Were with his heart, and that was far away:
> He reck'd not of the life he lost, nor prize,—
> But where his rude hut by the Danube lay.
> *There* were his young barbarians, all at play,—
> There was their Dacian mother,—he, their sire,
> Butcher'd to make a Roman holiday!
> All this rush'd with his blood: shall he expire,
> And unavenged? Arise! ye gods, and glut your ire!"

I am fully aware that a fallacy will be alleged against this argument,—that a demurrer will be entered against each and every count in the general indictment. It will be said,—

1st. That through slavery and the slave-trade alone have any portion of the African race been introduced to the light and blessings of civilization. This is a mean and blasphemous subterfuge. Just as though any such idea ever mixed itself up with the thoughts of the slave-vampires of the African coast! Just as though the century-protracted efforts of the Saracens to overthrow the religion of Christ were worthy of praise because they brought Christendom to its feet, in the vindication of Christianity! As soon should the sight of the fair-haired Angli boys brought to Rome and sold as slaves, and thus become the occasion of the introduction of the gospel into Britain, have justified the kidnappers who did the nefarious work! As soon plead pardon for the traitor of all the ages for selling the Man of sorrows, because "when he bowed his head on the cross he dragged the pillars of Satan's kingdom to the dust."

2d. They have risen far higher here in the scale of physical comfort. This I deny. They have not, *as a community*, enjoyed as much physical comfort as the wild beast in his lair, or the cattle on a thousand hills. By no means has their animal condition approached that of the native African tribes.

I fully believe—yea, I certainly know, and I believe and know it more profoundly than any slaughterer of men—that the wrath of man shall be made to praise God, while the remainder thereof he will restrain. But let no man, who has ever been a willing party to the awful crime we are speaking of, come forward now, while daylight is breaking over Africa, and claim any participation in the glory which is coming. For this dawn such men never longed; they never contemplated that rising sun with any exultation.

And yet how nobly has Africa earned the boon of civilized life ! She has from the earliest ages been the slave of the nations. All men who had ships went to her coasts and sailed up her great rivers to steal her children. The Egyptians lashed them to their toil, in the valley of the Nile. The Phœnicians, the Carthaginians, and the Arabs stole them from the Mediterranean coast. The Portuguese, the Spanish, the Dutch, the English, kidnapped them by the hundred thousand on the coast of the Atlantic ; and, last of all,—as late as within the memory of men now living,—the African slave-trade constituted the most profitable branch of the commerce of New England.

The blessed light of civilization which had irradiated every other continent never illuminated Africa. Great empires had been founded on the African coasts,—the arts that exalt and embellish life had been carried and cultured there by the Pharaohs, the Alexanders, the Hannibals,—the Arab, the Saracen, the Moor, and the Briton ; but it was not for the poor African. Light, which came to all others, came not to him. Every empire ever founded in Africa was cemented by the blood of her helpless people. But the day of her emancipation has come.

She has waited for it over three thousand years. God has accepted the sacrifice. The indications of Providence are too plain to be mistaken. No unknown portion of the globe has been so thoroughly explored during the present century. No nation has ever been so ready to receive Christianity and the arts of peace. No one can more readily be brought into the family of nations. No country ever had so many missionaries ready to carry to a benighted continent commerce, agriculture, manufactures, education, and the light of everlasting truths.

All hail, then, Niobe of the nations!

"Behold, I have taken out of thine hand the cup of trembling; . . . thou shalt no more drink it again."

"Behold, I will lift up mine hand to the Gentiles, and set up my standard to the people; and they shall bring thy sons in their arms, and thy daughters shall be carried upon their shoulders."

"Ye shall be redeemed without money."

"Thou shalt forget the shame of thy youth, and shalt not remember the reproach of thy widowhood any more. For thy Maker is thine husband, . . . and thy Redeemer the Holy One of Israel."

" O thou afflicted, tossed with tempest, and not comforted, behold, I will lay thy stones with fair colors, and lay thy foundations with sapphires. And I will make thy windows of agates, and thy gates of carbuncles, and all thy borders of pleasant stones. And all thy children shall be taught of the Lord; and great shall be the peace of thy children. . . . Thou shalt be far from oppression; for thou shalt not fear: and from terror; for it shall not come near thee."

"Behold, they shall surely gather together, but not by me: whosoever shall gather together against thee shall fall for thy sake."

"For I will tread them in mine anger, and trample them in my fury; and their blood shall be sprinkled upon my garments, and I will stain all my raiment. For the day of vengeance is in mine heart, and the year of my redeemed is come."

"Ethiopia shall soon stretch out her hands unto God."

"I the Lord have spoken it."*

---

* "And we may see in all this that law of compensation which God vouchsafes the wronged and suffering for all their woes and suffering. After being afflicted by nigh three centuries of servitude, God calls chosen men of this race from all the lands of their thraldom, men laden with gifts, —intelligence and piety,—to the grand and noble mission which they only can fulfil,—even to plant colonies, establish churches, found missions, and lay the foundations of universities along the shores and beside the banks of the great rivers of Africa, so that the grandeur and dignity of their duties may neutralize all the long, sad memories of their servitude and sorrows."—*Crummell's Future of Africa,* p. 127.

XXIII.

Office-Holders as they are, and how they should be.

OUR republic has a great many sins to answer for that she never committed. The republic *per se* has always been right. It is unfortunately true that her children have too often been wrong.

"Your *system* of government," said Guizot to me, on a certain occasion, "is perfect as an ideal. It is only necessary to have you live up to it."

"Yes; but you may pass the same criticism on the Nazarene Faith. Christianity is a perfect system:—its members are often *imperfect*. And yet you do not doubt that it will yet conquer the world."

It is very plain that the last two generations have taken very little pains to understand the government of the United States. Not one voter in a hundred ever read the Constitution; not one in a thousand ever felt how much that Constitution was worth. We are *beginning* to learn it now. It will take some time to read the lesson. *We must go through the fire.* We attach most value to those possessions which we came dearly by. From the first altars went up a pure flame of patriotic devotion. There was very little *sham* in those days. All through our early history was the clear ring of the hammer of the real blacksmith; and that ring can be heard yet.

Here is our curse. Our old blacksmiths are dead, and most of their nephews and grandchildren have been made brigadier-generals. God save us!

But he must do it by fire. Let the storm come: the true

metal can stand the alembic test. We have had amalgams enough,—*quantum ad sufficit*. Let us have a pure and good nation hereafter, or none. With this spirit, and in this spirit only, can we safely and surely render back to God (when we die) the sacred heritage we got from our fathers.

Now to one point. Who is a good soldier? Who can help his country now? *More* shoulder-straps can never get us out of our trouble. Heads and hearts alone can save us. Neither will be wanting, for the exigency invokes both, and both will be forthcoming. So grand a nation must not—cannot—perish.

How wrong we were to allow ourselves to get into this enormous trouble! how wrongly we went to work to cure it!

From sheer thoughtlessness, the brave men of the nation rushed to the rescue. Brave men saw only a breach in our walls: they must fill it.

But every selfish man, every politician, every trickster and trifler, saw a chance to "make a spec" out of it, and every Governor of a State and every secretary was besieged night and day for a commission :—"my son," or "nephew," or "a particular friend of mine," "must be looked after." No matter for the old country!—no matter for the flag!—no matter for the sanctified souvenirs of our origin, nor the holy dead of the olden time. My son, or nephew, or friend, "must have a commission."

What came of all this? Whole cohorts, rank and file, were led to indiscriminate slaughter by incompetent officers! The nation has worn mourning over this.

Further: not less than a thousand or two of these shoulder-decked gentlemen are gazetted as *deserters* to-day. If the private does this, he is punished by military law; and the penalty is an instant and ignominious death.

Shoulder-straps escape death,—and they are not often enough cashiered; nor has one of them been shot or hanged yet. Talk about Mr. Lincoln's severity! He has been breathing the "gales of Araby the Blest" over this rebellion, instead

of burying its aiders and abettors in a common sepulchre.
Mercy! Lincoln has shown enough for the most merciful
Hemp is the only quality he has lacked. It must be confessed
he is a poor headsman.

The great lack of the war has been the want of heroic
dedication to the country. With this dedication, we are in-
vincible; without it, we are lost!

I must say that, highly as I respect, esteem, and admire
the true fighting officer of this contest, I would still rather
be the admirer and historian of the rank and file.

The Government of this country belongs to its people, and
this people will take care of it. If all goes well, it is all well.
If things go wrong, stand from under. A general who cannot
win must give way to a man who can. An administration that
cannot crowd the war to a triumphant and glorious termina-
tion must give way to the people.

XXIV.

Scenes and Sayings in the Hospital.

THE scenes of the war which have brought out the finest heroism of the American character have been in the hospitals.

My distant readers will have heard or *known* more or less of the sanitary *régime* of the army,—by which I mean the way to get a soldier into good health again, through the agency of the best skill known to the healing art.

We have had to improvise hundreds of hospitals. It is only in our principal cities that we have had instant facilities to accommodate completely the sick and wounded. Thus, after the principal battles in the neighborhood of Washington, of Bull Run, Ball's Bluff, Winchester, and Antietam, we have had men brought in in long trains of ambulances by the hundred, of a morning, in every stage of suffering which attends fractured limbs and gunshot- and shell-, sabre- and bayonet-wounds, in literally thousands of forms.

By an act of the President, which met with the entire approval of those who knew the circumstances, most of the churches in Washington and Georgetown were taken possession of for the sufferers; and I am quite sure that when we saw the poor fellows carried in and laid down before these altars of God, it was the universal feeling that it was no desecration of the temples that had been consecrated to the worship of our Father in heaven.

It was with a melancholy and yet with a coveted pleasure that we looked upon such scenes. When a groan escaped from a suffering man, it was an exception to the rule; for not one in a hundred made a complaint; and there was infinite relief and satisfaction in seeing the surgeons proceed to their humane but exhausting labors.

In going to my accustomed place of worship, and finding that where every seat had been, a suffering soldier lay, and seeing no priest at the altar, it seemed to me that in the best days of a primitive Christianity no temple had ever been consecrated to holier purposes. The ministers of Christ had descended from the altar to carry their sublime precepts into practice, and, like Good Samaritans, were pouring oil into the wounds of the suffering.

The complete dedication of the Washington clergy of all denominations to this sublime work afforded to many thousand sick and wounded men the most touching and effective illustrations they had ever witnessed of the beneficent spirit of the religion of the Captain of their salvation. I have seen the fruit of such ministrations of kindness and benevolence,—the stalwart man who lay helpless as a child, stripped of all the pride of his strength,—a man who but a few hours before would have treated any allusion to the retributions of another life with levity or a sneer,—now softened by suffering and won by sympathy, greeting with cheerfulness the reading of any of the words of the Savior, and conversing with freedom about his own soul.

But here, as elsewhere, the easier and more felicitous triumphs of divine truth are made with the young.

*　　　*　　　*　　　*　　　*　　　*

The following touching scene, which was witnessed in a hospital at Memphis, can be relied upon as authentic :—

"We came to the body of a non-commissioned officer,—a fine, large man,—who during the last few hours had become insane. The bone of his thigh was shattered by a ball, so high up that amputation could not be performed : so nothing was offered him but to lie there and die,—watching the terrible hues of mortification come upon his limb, feeling the horrible poison steal up towards his vitals, grasping and deadening new tissues each hour. It proved too fearful for even the strong man, who to his physicians had uttered no cry or complaint; and his mind fled for relief to insanity. As we approached, he fixed a pair of cold, despairing eyes upon us, and exclaimed, pointing back over his shoulder, 'Do you see him, —Old Death, there,—sitting on the head-board and laughing? A grim army joker, in truth. The other night I felt a cold touch, and it woke me. The moon flung in a bar of light, and I saw Old Death feeling of my wound. The icy touch numbed it; and the next time I woke, his hand was closer to my body. So it goes; and he will soon be pulling on my heart-chords.' The maniac then stopped, as if for the purpose of reflecting, and during our stay would part of the time be musing, part laughing, occasionally breaking out with the exclamation, 'I plead to him that they would be lonely at the old home. A wife and child are pleasanter than a tomb.'

"And so we left him,—the utter corruption, the rottenness of the tomb, and the vitality of a great man, joined in one being, grappling upon the hospital-bed. Life, with the full, strong pulse of thirty years, had marshalled its forces, been defeated, and was retreating upon its citadel, pursued by the decay-growth of a few days. The arteries would soon, stung by the poison-tide, stagnate and block up the gates of the heart. His name was C. P. Dunster, from Illinois, I believe; but the regiment he belonged to I have forgotten."

———

A noble young fellow in one of the hospitals had been injured by the passage of a shell near his head. He scarcely thought of it at the time. But shortly after, a solid shot carried his left arm away. He was well treated on the field, and sent on to Washington for recovery. Here the effect of

the concussion of that screaming shell began to show itself
on the brain. He became delirious.

Watching by him one night, I took down some strange
ravings:—"No! I won't go home till the Union is safe. I
had rather die here by the roots of this tree, and dig my
own grave, than have any croaker in Wisconsin say that I
let the old flag drop. Not I! Bring it out! Let me see
it once more! I'm ready for the last charge! I don't care
how strong they are! I only want one more chance at the
rebels." And, lifting himself in bed, he plunged forward. I
caught him, and laid him down. A quiver went through his
body, and the pulse stopped!—

> "He slept his last sleep,—he had fought his last battle :
> No sound could awake him to glory again."

Another youthful soldier, slowly coming up from what he
called "that Chickahominy fever."—

"Don't you ever get disheartened?"

"Yes,—once in a while, about *myself*, while I am alone here
after midnight. It seems so long before daylight. I never
was sick before. But disheartened about our great cause?
Never! If I live, I shall stand by the flag. Why shouldn't
I do it as well as any other man? But if *all our army* sinks
into the earth, the cause is just as safe as ever. God cannot
afford to let this country go down."

Another still, in the same ward:—

A vigorous man, with both legs off, but doing well. "God
is always right, and we are generally wrong. * * * We are
not ready yet for restoration. We are not ready yet for the
redemption which I am sure is coming. * * * I went with
the Breckinridge party in the last election, for I thought they
would stand by the Union as it was when Clay and Webster

died. But I was awfully mistaken. *They never wanted to remain with us.* They embraced the first plausible pretext for separation. The leaders of this rebellion deliberately cheated and deceived us. General Butler, who presided over their convention, was among the first to discover that he and all the old Northern Democrats had been duped,—cruelly, foully, meanly *duped.* * * * When we National Democrats looked about and found out just where we were standing and where the country was falling, we were confronted with the cause, the occasion, and the pretext of all this treason and all this trouble. * * * The South saw no use in the Union except as an instrument for the protection and spread of slavery. Mankind had taken a very different view. We considered liberty the rule, and slavery the exception. The world, as a human family, had got tired of servitude. It was supposed that America was too large, too free, for any thing but freedom. * * * We had to come to the conclusion that it wouldn't pay to keep slavery up any longer; and I believe this is the feeling generally in the Army of the Potomac. * * * So far as I am concerned, slavery must hereafter take care of itself."

     *   *   *   *   *   *

The battle of Williamsburg was over,—the rebels driven from the field, the war-storm hushed, and the sad duty of burying our dead and caring for our wounded remained to be performed.

Groping our way through the darkness, we came upon the body of a pale, slender, beardless boy, a member of Company I, 37th Regiment, New York Volunteers,—one of hundreds who left their beautiful hill-girt homes in Cattaraugus county to battle for their country's integrity. We raised him up; he was not dead, but badly wounded.

On carrying him to our improvised hospital, the surgeon pronounced his wound mortal. No sigh nor groan escaped his lips; although, from the nature of the wound, he suffered greatly. As firm and brave as but a few hours before, when he met the enemy, he now met the great conqueror, Death.

When told he must soon die, and asked if he desired to send any message to his family, his mild blue eye lit up with unnatural fire; and, after a moment's pause, as if recalling his departing senses, he exclaimed,—

"Tell them I died fighting for the Stars and Stripes." These were his last words; and in a few moments LAFAYETTE MORROW, the boy-hero, was at rest.*

*   *   *   *   *   *

During the desperate fight at Williamsburg, while the color-company of the 57th New York went rushing through the blood and over the bodies of the dying and dead to take the place of a New Jersey regiment which had fallen back half slaughtered, one gallant fellow, who had been carried to the rear, was seen leaning against a tree, swinging one bleeding arm, while the other hung shattered and dangling by his side, screaming out, in his wild death-agony, "There goes the old flag! Hold her up, boys, forever!" And he fell, a senseless, gory mass, at the roots of the tree.

In returning from the field from which the rebels had been driven, two men from the same regiment left the ranks to look after the dead soldier. They dug his grave where he lay; and long before now "the oak hath shot his roots abroad and pierced his mould."

---

* This fact is related to me by one of the noblest young assistant surgeons in the army.

XXV

The Doom of the Rebellion.

How is it to end?

As all the other great wrongs of the world have ended,—not in blood merely; for men spill that freer than water over trifles,—but by *exterminating the power and the works of the wrong-doer*, and, if necessary, the wrong-doer himself.

This does not mean half as much as GOD means when HE has traitors to deal with. History, the sacred chronicler from the grave, is Heaven's secretary. Open his books, and see how the Ruler of nations treats bad leaders of communities and empires.

What became of a polluted world when its Maker could find no place in his great heart to screen or hold its bad people any longer?

He drowned them!

What became of his own *chosen* people, for whom he had wrought miracles by land and water, to whom he had committed his holy tabernacle,—the evidence of his divine presence by night and day in the everlasting flame, that never ceased to burn over the altar of his holy temple, telling that the Protector of Israel was there,—his chosen people, on whom HE had lavished the wealth of his kingdom, and to whom he at last gave the most precious gem in his diadem, his "eternally begotten and well-beloved Son"? Read the fate of that chosen people wherever the winds of heaven sweep, and, innumerable although they be, they are among the nations only the chaff on the summer threshing-floor.

What became of the Egyptian tyrant after he rejected the

counsels of the great Hebrew statesman and set himself up against Moses' "proclamation of emancipation"?

Drowning again.

What became of Sodom and Gomorrah? Brimstone and fire.

What became of Babylon and Nineveh, Tyre and Sidon, and all the great empires and states of antiquity? Any Sunday-school scholar can answer these questions. They did *wrong*; they *persisted* in wrong; they insulted God and ground his helpless ones into the dust. They were foretold their fate; they met it, and wound up their history, falling charred corpses into their sepulchres; and future Layards and Champollions have busied themselves in digging away with Birmingham picks and spades, to heave up from the ashes of ages some few remains of these triflers with "the divine humanity."

Modern history shows the same story; for God is just as much the Governor of all the earth to-day as he was before the Cæsars. No new dispensation has been granted to nations. It is graven among the pandects of eternity that "the nation that will not serve me shall perish."

Heaven's code never changes. The decisions of that court of final appeals are never reversed.

Charles I. of England did not understand this philosophy. His ignorance cost him his head from the window of Palace Hall.

Louis XVI. did not understand it; and his head rolled from the guillotine in Paris.

So have a whole regal mob of the oppressors of mankind, sooner or later, from Tarquin to Louis, been sent to their doom by the swift judgment of Heaven.

Modern nations have followed the same road as ancient empires wherever they have violated the great laws of civic prosperity and endurance. They have gone to ruin over the same beaten track where the dead dynasties of the past had left their bones.

No statesman will pretend, be he saint or sinner, that a man or a nation can contend against the Almighty and prosper. Justice and freedom are the fundamental statutes of God's system of jurisprudence. Neither men nor nations are exempt. These laws never change; and, thank God, we strike solid bottom when we are dealing with Him !

*   *   *   *   *   *

Whatever may have been the pretexts of this rebellion, every man who is not wilfully blind saw its immediate object in the beginning. But, separation once effected, was not the ultimate design equally clear?—*the establishment and consolidation of a colossal meridional empire*, stretching from the free States of this union towards the south, absorbing Mexico and Central America, Cuba, and all the islands of the surrounding archipelago, and appropriating all the South American states east of the Andes?

This empire was to *rest on African slavery* as its basis, and its wealth and power were to spring from a complete monopoly of cotton and the principal tropical products of the world.

Nor would the ultimate achievement have been beyond the regions of probability, had the leaders been allowed to break away from their allegiance and "go in peace."

They contemplated nothing impossible in the gradual absorption of these vast territories, partly by arms and partly by treaties of annexation. They would have been only re-establishing African slavery where it had but recently been abolished, more by the shock of revolution than as a reform in the gradual progress of society. They would have encountered no unconquerable obstacles in the re-establishment of domestic slavery. Slavery is congenial to the tastes of the Spanish and Portuguese nations, and in full harmony with the lower civilization which exists among their bastard American descendants.

Besides, they would have readily found an ally in Cuba, which, on fair terms, would gladly have joined this gigantic Power, and, asserting her independence, as all the other

Spanish-American states had done, sprung to the alliance to assert her freedom and save her half a million of slaves.

Stepping on the South American continent, this new Power would have trodden triumphantly over a score of torn and shattered republics, on its march to Brazil, where it would have found a cordial ally and partner in that vast but youthful empire.

Thus the only slaveholders and the only slave-empires of the earth would have met and reared a structure which might once more have arrested for an age the progress of mankind, if indeed it had not overwhelmed civilization.

Something far less strange than this would be had long been history. The civilization of ages was overthrown, and to all appearances the world's march was arrested for a thousand years. The combination of barbaric forces has often proved for the time too mighty for civilization. Even Christ's temples have been overthrown in a hundred nations, and thirty generations, embracing uncounted hundreds of millions, have ever since been groping in heathen darkness around their ruins. Although the mighty stream of human progress, *as a volume*, moves steadily on, yet some of its vast eddies move backward before their waters can once more mingle in the general current.

Such a concentration of all the elements of barbaric power, with all the irresistible appliances of modern inventions, could, by the forced labor of the enslaved and dependent classes, rear a structure against which not only the puny shafts of refined nations would strike in vain, but which would overshadow all other states and rule for a while sovereign of the ascendant.

No meaner vision than this rested on the eyes of the projectors of the Southern rebellion. The only difficult step in the accomplishment of this stupendous scheme was the *first* one,—secession from the Government of the United States. This was to prove an impossibility. All the rest would have

followed at half the cost in blood and treasure which the
South has already expended. The total enslavement of the
depressed classes, and the creation of a powerful oligarchy of
coadjutors, would have rapidly crystallized all the incoherent
elements of society throughout all those semi-barbarous and
revolution-devastated countries. Order would have sprung
from chaos, but it would have been the order which reigns in
the dungeons of the tyrant; wealth would have been multiplied by magic, but it would have been the fruit of involuntary and hopeless toil. But such did not happen to be the will
of Heaven. This virgin continent was not destined to so horrible a prostitution. The clock of Time was not to go back
again a thousand years.

*   *   *   *   *   *

All this seemed as transparent to thinking men then as now.
At the hazard of some imputation of a vanity I should not
wish to entertain, I will here print two short letters which I
addressed to Jefferson Davis towards the close of 1861, just
after he had sent in his message to the rebel Congress :—

"TO THE CHIEF OF THE SOUTHERN REBELLION.

"WASHINGTON CITY, December 7, 1861.

"SIR :—After having fled from the gates of the Capitol of
the republic, you still abuse the patience of mankind by
maintaining, at a safe distance, the semblance of a power you
do not possess, and issue proclamations and messages in solemn
burlesque of all the forms of civilized and free Governments.

"Your last state paper, although the worst of all your political compositions, is entitled to some notice, even at the hands
of VANITY FAIR, chiefly on the ground that it is the object
of this journal to amuse itself with the folly of the wise and
the wisdom of fools.

"After a careful reading of your message, we have not been
able to detect the motive of its composition. It reads more
like the nerveless plaint of a sick and disheartened traitor

than the clear and logical utterance of a conscientious and sagacious statesman.

"It is mainly made up of exaggerated accounts of Confederate victories, of baseless accusations against the Government of the United States and the humanity of its citizens and soldiers, and an equal mixture of defiance of and sycophancy to foreign states, with repeated appeals to the providence of the Almighty for aid in your Catiline conspiracy, and a gross libel upon his Holy Truth.

"Some few illustrations will suffice for our present purpose.

"You say, 'The condition of the treasury will doubtless be a subject of anxious inquiry.' We did not before know that you had a treasury. You must long ago have expended all the money you stole, and, although in possession of several mints, the world understands that you coin your currency with the printing-press. You say, 'The Government is enabled to borrow money *without interest.*' Then you are luckier than any empire we have heard from. You propose to make your treasury notes a legal tender for debts due 'corporations and individuals,' and think this will 'enlarge the field of their circulation.' This will succeed for a while,— *at the point of the bayonet.* You see a strong point in the convertibility of your 'treasury notes into Confederate stock at the pleasure of the holder, bearing eight per cent.' Mr. President, 'this reminds us of a little story,' as our excellent Rail-Splitter so often good-humoredly says.

"A certain shiftless husband was always trading dogs, and kept a ravenous kennel of them on hand. When the family were on the verge of starvation, he got rid of all except Boace, a very large Newfoundlander. Finally, at the urgent entreaties of his good and patient wife, he started off with Boace for a market. At nightfall he came back in high glee, and announced to his wife that he had sold Boace. The little woman was transported. 'How much did you get for him, dearee?' 'Fifty dollars,' responded this prince of financiers, with exultation. 'Oh, goodee! goodee! now we can have something to eat, and Jane can have a new frock! Oh, dear me! where is the money?' 'Oh, my dear, I sold Boace for fifty dollars, but I took it in two pups at twenty-five dollars apiece.' We shouldn't wonder if the holders of your treasury notes would prefer to keep old Boace! Such finance is worthy of the unblushing defender of Mississippi repudiation. You know, Mr. Davis, that not one of those bonds will ever be paid except in cats and dogs. Remember that Governments can trifle with the *liberties* of people much longer than they can with their *pockets*.

"You declare that 'the very efforts he [your adversary] makes to isolate and invade us, must exhaust his means, whilst they serve to complete the circle and diversify the productions of our industrial system.' Pretty small circle! You despise the labor of free men. Slavery never did and never can make a diversified industrial system. Such a system cannot live without foreign commerce; and yours is cut off, and cannot be restored until you return to your allegiance. In spite of all you say to the contrary, the merchants and journals of New Orleans (your great port) say that not three ships have entered or left that port for months together; and the only evidence that your seaports are not sown with salt is that the grass is growing in their streets.

"Mr. Davis, you ought to have known how terrible a work you undertook when you so coolly plotted the overthrow of this beneficent Government! If you had been either a sailor, a soldier, or a statesman, you would sooner have cut off your own right arm than have lifted its puny and shrivelled muscles to make war against the best and the strongest Government on the face of the earth.

"It would have been in better taste if you had said nothing about the barbarities of the war. You began them, and you have practised them all. You have turned whole districts into deserts, and driven thousands of Union men from their homes.

You have massacred their owners, you have stolen their goods and confiscated their estates. They and their sons have been dragged into your armies and compelled to fight against the republic of their fathers. So far from the course of justice having been interfered with in the free States, law never was more perfectly administered nor justice more fairly dealt out. The whole structure of civil life has stood unshaken and undisturbed. *At the South you know that law, justice, and equity have been utterly subverted and overthrown!* Everybody here is safe except traitors; in the South a Union man is a doomed man until the flag of the Union once more floats over his dwelling.

"We knew you were no better lawyer than statesman. But we thought you would hardly risk the satire of every jurist in the world by such a display of your ignorance of international law. You can have read little of the works of English jurists, and, if possible, heard less. We leave your opinions on this subject to the tender mercies of the law advisers of the crown.

"For the present we leave you with a few words. It would be a deep insult to many true and great men at the South to assume that you took the helm by their willing consent. You had this advantage,—your presumption made you first in the field, and what you lacked in personal merit or public favor you made up in audacity. You stood nearest the magazine, and you held the match. Others stood aside for your candle to go out. Any desperate man could have done the same thing with the same success. There was nothing original in this mode of doing business. Many a bad man, of not half your parts, has played the same trick with better grace.

"All through your heated, restless life, you have had but one object in view,—one goal to win: to make other men think better of you than you thought of yourself. Your chief misfortune consists in your having tried a job you are not equal to. Samson was far luckier; for when he threw his gigantic arms around the columns of the temple of the Philistines, he dragged the whole structure to the dust. The name of the wretch who burned the dome of Ephesus lived longer in history than his who raised it. But remember that Actæon was torn to pieces by his own hounds. To-day you inspire more terror in the midnight chambers of the South than McClellan. Look to your own hounds. When the vengeance which fate has laid up for you, like all other traitors, lights upon your head, the ministers of justice will come from your own household. The men you have deceived will sit in judgment when your day of reckoning comes. Yours."

No. 2.

"WASHINGTON, December 21, 1861.

"JEFFERSON DAVIS, ESQ. :—

"If your Postmaster-General has overcome 'the formidable difficulties' you spoke of 'in carrying the Confederate mails,' you will doubtless before now have received my first letter. Another epistle may reach you before your own hounds are unleashed.

"I shall look at some of the promises you made to the South when you inaugurated a subtle conspiracy which has since grown into the proportions of a great rebellion. Like many a reckless plotter of mischief, you have evoked more elements of trouble than you can manage. While you were raising, as you thought, only a storm of wind and fury which would grow calm at the bidding of any smart demagogue, you found a wild tempest roaring above your head, and ÆOLUS alone could command the winds back to their caves. You have more than once, since you made this discovery, said 'you had no conception the thing would ever go so far.' This is true. Nor have you now any idea how far it *will* go. Your eyes are only partly opened; you still 'see men as trees walking;'—but your eyesight will improve hereafter every day. What did you promise the South if she would break away from her allegiance? Independence, sovereignty,

and instantaneous recognition by the great foreign Powers
Your agents went to Europe, and, with no usher but a cotton-
bale reeking with the sweat of lashed and unpaid negro
labor, they tried to force their way into the palaces of empe-
rors and kings. They were repulsed; but they still cringed
and fawned for recognition, till they were spurned with cold
contempt from every royal ante-chamber in Europe. On the
very night that the Ambassador of the United States was the
guest of the Lord Mayor at Guildhall, with her majesty's
Ministers at his side, your court-ejected, nigger-driving en-
voys found more congenial company taking pot-luck in the
greasy tap-room of Fishmongers' Hall. You have always
insulted and hated England, because she wanted Mississippi
to pay her honest debts. Now you crawl to that monarchy
only to be kicked away as the whining chief of an unsuccessful rebellion,—as the champion of a peculiar institution
England hates, and the tawny self-crowned King of Cotton,
which she no longer wants. Did you read YANCEY's letter?

"You were luckier with your 'ambassadors' (as you
acknowledge them to have been) than with your emissaries.
MASON, SLIDELL & Co. spared you the further mortification
of more fawning, more cringing, more crawling, and more im-
pertinence, as the supple suppliants of kings, by changing
their voyage to Fort Warren, in sight of Bunker Hill, over
which you were to crack your slave-lash as the roll of your
bondsmen was called.

"You wished to be emancipated from the North, to which
you had so long paid tribute. You wanted to cut off all intercourse with us. We helped you in your glorious work. You
no longer pay tribute on Lynn shoes: you can't get them;
and you go bare-foot, black, white, and mixed. No more
tribute on Boston ice: you drink tepid water in dog-days.
No tax on Ohio bacon,—it is worth thirty cents a pound; on
Illinois flour,—it costs forty dollars a barrel; on Orange County
butter,—it brings fifty cents a pound. Your circulating

medium must be below par, or these commodities must be
growing very scarce.

" You were to cover all seas with your pirates. How many
letters of marque have been called for? You were to open
the slave-trade. How near have you come to winding up
slavery itself? Children laugh at the silly dog that lost the
meat and the shadow too! You would not sell your pew in
a Washington church, for you would need it the next Sunday after taking the Federal capital! What would you take
for it now? You made Montgomery your first seat of government, and you congratulated Georgia on her great destiny.
You skinned that neighborhood, and quit for Richmond.
Virginia was in turn congratulated. You skinned the mother
of Presidents and scraped her to the bone,—and again started
with your locust bands for Nashville, which will participate
in like congratulations and share a similar fate. By this
time the capitals and States where you hold your locust
court must have recalled, with empty stomachs and shrivelled
purses, the Spanish proverb, ' Save me from my friends, and
I will take care of my enemies.'

" You sunk what few ships you had at the mouth of
Charleston harbor, to keep us from getting in. We took the
hint, and are sinking a fleet of old whalers, to keep you from
ever getting *out*. We do not wish to burn your cities, but
we will exile them from the commercial world; we will blot
their very names from the maps of the navigator. We will
open new ports, and build free cities. Thither will flock the
fleets of all nations, and your slaves shall be our servants.
You were to send your cotton direct to Europe, and pay no
commissions to Yankees. We shall save you the trouble; for
we shall take the commissions and the cotton too!

" JEFF DAVIS! what have you done? Once you stood
fair among your fellows; your nation put a soldier's sword
into your hand: you have thrust it into the bosom of your
mother. You were respected, beloved, and even admired.

The South was prosperous, happy, and secure. Now she is bankrupt, miserable, and in peril. She is bound on Procrustes' bed, and the sword of Damocles is flashing over her head.

"The *cordon de guerre*, which has been steadily spinning for you by the hand of SCOTT from the distaff of Destiny, is now, under the steady nerve and clear gaze of young McCLELLAN, slowly but surely tightening its coils around you. The ocean is too small even for the furtive flight of your ambassadors; the continent has no desert or cave where you or your traitor conspirators can hide. Your sea-ports will become Antwerps,—your capitals a by-way, so that no man pass through them; your homes will be left desolate; you will be buried among the ruins of your peculiar institution, on which the world already sees written the doom

> 'Of nations scatter'd like the chaff
> Blown from the threshing-floor of God.'

And you have caused it all.

> 'Since him miscall'd the Morning Star,
> Nor man nor fiend hath fallen as far.'

"Yours."

The only commentary I shall add to these epistles is taken from a portion of a prominent editorial which appeared in the Richmond "Enquirer," the beginning of March, 1863, fifteen months after the foregoing letters were written :—

"THE THIRD STAGE OF THE WAR.

" We have fairly entered upon the third stage indicated by the President in his message, namely, that of a war for subjugation and extermination. The people of this Confederacy, isolated and shut up from all the world, have now to encounter the most horrible and demoniac effort for the assassination of a whole race that history has yet recorded, or, we believe, will ever have to record till history grows gray. For it is not every century, it is not every *æon*, that shows the world a Yankee nation. Yes, the Confederate people has now at last to strip for battle. It is a people that must this time very literally conquer or die.

"No doubt it would be agreeable to believe that this last stage of the war will be soon over, and must end in the speedy destruction of our intending murderers. But look round the map of the Confederacy, and judge if we can soothe ourselves with this belief. In the very heart of the country our gallant sentinel of the Mississippi—heroic little Vicksburg—has sustained indeed and baffled two tremendous sieges; but a third time her citizens see pouring in around them from the North and from the West enormous masses of the beleaguering foe; iron floating batteries again crowd down upon her; and even as you read these words two hundred heavy guns may be thundering upon her defences, a hundred thousand men may be pressing to the storm of her ramparts. Again she will drive them off, perhaps, and remain the famous maiden city of this hemisphere, the bulwark of the West. So be it! But the vision we see on the Mississippi does not look very like exhaustion or despair on the part of the foe just yet.

"And, again, look to the mouth of the mighty river. New Orleans is not a maiden city, alas! The base rag that has so often been rent and trampled before Richmond and before Vicksburg flies from all the towers of that deflowered city. Hordes of hungry Yankees, armed to the teeth, sit in the shade of her orange-groves and station negro guards over the mansions of her noblest citizens. All her best and fairest have to lament every day that their goodly city had not been laid in ashes before it became a haunt of obscene creatures. No sign of relaxation there! And, but a short way off, Mobile, by the shores of her spacious bay, keeps diligent watch and ward, expecting in the light of each morning sun to see the thrice-accursed Stars and Stripes gleaming through the smoke of a bombarding squadron. All along the Gulf, and round the coast of Florida, this omnipresent enemy who is said to have just been playing his last card is shutting up every river and planting his guns on every strong place. Savannah, shut in from the sea by Fort Pulaski, in the hands of the same inveterate Yankee, listens for the first boom of. the artillery that is to level her walls with her sandy soil; and Charleston, grimly calm, but with beating heart, stands waiting the onset of the great armada. Those few acres of old Oyster Point, it seems, already swept and devastated by conflagrations, are to be the object and the prize of the most potent armament by far that American waters have ever seen. This very moment, it may be, the black Monitor batteries are steaming between Sumter and Moultrie. No signs of relaxation, or of discouragement and despair, in the enemy here! Pass further, and you will find the whole coast, from Charleston to Norfolk, and every river to the head of tide-water, and every creek and sound formed by the sea-islands, swarming with their gunboats and transports, ready to pour in masses of troops wherever there is a chance of plunder, bridge-burning, and general havoc.

"From Norfolk all around Chesapeake and Potomac we are guarded by gunboats, and no living thing (save skulking smugglers) suffered to enter or go out. On the Rappahannock two hundred thousand men wait for a drying wind to move 'on to Richmond' once more, led by a genuine apostle of extermination. . . . And Northwestern Virginia is desolated by Milroy and his men; and Kentucky and the half of Tennessee, the richest and fairest lands of all the West, are entirely in the clutch of the enemy, while the rivers bring them up fleets of transports, and Rosecrans, with another large army, threatens to sweep all opposition from his path, and join the other brigands who are crowding upon Vicksburg.

"Where in all this wide circuit does the invasion seem

to be fainting or giving ground?   All round the border and in the very heart of the Confederacy the foot of the enemy is planted and his felon flag flies; and it means subjugation and extermination.   It is indeed the third stage of the war, and, we believe, the last; but the struggle will be desperate. If it be the 'last card,' it is one on which the stake is' life or death, honor or shame: either our name and nation will be extinguished in a night of blood and horror, or else a new sovereignty—the newest, fairest, proudest—will take her seat among the Powers of the earth, with the applause of man and the blessings of Heaven."

.

XXVI.

Kind Words to Africano-Americans.

FELLOW-MEN :—

The day you have waited for so long has at last come.

You are all free now,—or you soon will be. Your charter has been duly signed by the President of the United States, and that deed is ratified in heaven.

God is always on the right side : he is the everlasting friend of freedom.

Being free, your earthly salvation is put into your own hands. While you had a master, he gave you bread, clothing, and shelter, such as they were. In escaping the lash, you must provide these things for yourselves. You have always claimed you could do it, and your friends believe you can. What is still better, you have through generations proved you could not only support yourselves, but your masters too.

Now, laying all theories aside, and coming down to practical business, think what questions are before you. But first let me tell you what is not before you.

1. You need not give yourselves any trouble about the great question of your freedom. It is a *moral* fact. It will be an *actual material* fact sooner by far than you can prepare for it. Remember that when the song of freedom is once sung its notes will vibrate forever. Slavery is mortal, and must die; Liberty is eternal.

2. Give yourselves no solicitude about the prejudice against your color; for that prejudice does not exist in pure and generous hearts in such a form or to such an extent as materially to interfere with your prosperity and future elevation.

Let your minds rather be directed to the means you should employ for accomplishing the destiny which is now within your reach.

First. Get work as soon as you can,—any thing that is honorable,—and begin to lay up money.—If you are idle, you will be despised as vagabonds; if you contract bad habits, you will have no friends; if you commit crime, you will be punished without mercy. In no Northern community can you expect to escape punishment when you do wrong. The color of the white man may save *him*, no matter how black his crime or loathsome his bestiality. But if you once put that bitter cup to your lips you will have to drain it to the last dregs. Here your friends cannot save you. You must beware in time, and escape the danger.

The law was made for you as well as for white men, and in your case it will be sternly enforced. Few voices will be heard pleading in your behalf, on the ground that you have been a slave. On the contrary, you will find—what does not often happen—that all the *bad* as well as all the *good* will be arrayed against you. If you do not keep a sharp look-out, you will find that freedom, although a holy, is often a dangerous, gift. A great poet says, "Lord of himself,—that heritage of woe."

YOU MUST GET KNOWLEDGE.—Other things being equal, your progress and elevation will depend entirely upon the amount of your intelligence. *Ignorance* is one of the principal curses of slavery. In Heaven's name, rid yourselves of it as quickly as possible.

FIRST OF ALL, LEARN TO READ, and teach your wives and children. Do it nights and Sundays, if you can find no other time. And when this is done you will, indeed, find yourselves in a new world. You don't know how much good it would do you all. Ignorance cannot help you or anybody else. Ignorance is dark ; knowledge is light. Do not think you have done much till you can read that glorious book

which our Father sent down to us from heaven. It is his
voice. It speaks to you. You must learn to read it. But,
whatever you may neglect for yourselves, don't, oh, don't let
your children grow up in ignorance; for they would still be
under the curse of slavery. Get as near to the school-house
and a Sunday-school as you can. There will hereafter be no
law in the South punishing anybody that teaches you to read.
All good people will help you, and you will find it not only
very easy, after a little while, but very delightful. Then,
and then only, will you know what freedom is worth.

You must forget and forgive all the wrongs you have suffered. "If you forgive not, neither shall you be forgiven."
This is God's rule; and you must obey it if you would have
his blessing. I know how hard it will sometimes come to
forgive those who have sold your wives and children and
heaped on your heads wrong upon wrong. But you must do
it. Christ did it to his murderers. "Vengeance is mine, saith
the Lord."

All your friends are proud to hear that you have behaved
so well wherever you have been instantly set free. The foes
of emancipation predicted that you would be guilty of every
crime. But of the tens of thousands who have suddenly
passed into freedom, no record of crime yet appears against
you. We can now point to your example and justify ourselves for all the confidence we have had in you.

So too are we happy and grateful to learn that the three
millions and a half of your race who still clank the chain
are meekly and patiently waiting for the day of their liberation. God grant that they may wait patiently still! While
he is doing the work, do not stand in his way. Show to the
world that you were worthy to be free. The more you prove
this, the quicker the fetters will fall. Let it be God's act.
He will hasten it in its time.

From the beginning of the war till now, you have been compelled to look on, idle spectators of this great struggle; and

you know the reason why. The war was not begun by the North, nor was it carried on by the North for the sake of destroying slavery. It was begun by the slaveholders to destroy the Union, extend slavery, and open the slave-trade. The North went into it to preserve the Union; and when we found that slavery would destroy the republic unless slavery should be wiped out itself, then Mr. Lincoln declared freedom to all the slaves of all the enemies of the Union.

Now it has come to this, that this great war is between slavery and freedom. *It has become a war for you.* Now you can come into the fight, and take the field, and help work out your own salvation. And you must do it; for remember that "he who would be free, himself must strike the blow." If you will not help yourselves, whom are you to look to?

Yes, you must not hang back. Enlist in the army the first chance you get. If you are not as ready and willing to spill your blood for your own freedom as white men are to do it for you, then you will prove, what your masters have always said, that you are not fit nor worthy to be free. You are not asked to take a life, or use or destroy any property, except as soldiers, under the command of your officers. In all this you are doing but your duty as men and citizens of a great and glorious country.

You will not forget that mankind respect nothing so much as valor. To fight gallantly in a good cause will win for you and your race more honor and respect than you can win in any other way. By showing that you are good soldiers, you will do more towards your own progress and elevation than all your friends could do for you in a century.

In this way, and in this way only, can you repay the debt of gratitude which you owe to your deliverers. Every brave deed you do, the higher your fidelity to your flag, the more complete your subordination and discipline, the higher you and your race will stand, not only with your commanders and with the whole country, but with all nations.

Never before have Africans had such a chance! In the name, then, of your nearly five millions in the United States, of more than half as many in South America and the West India islands, and of the uncounted tens of millions on the continent of Africa, we call on you to shoulder the musket! and let your valor and martial achievements work the long-delayed redemption of a mighty people.

Another consideration, which is likely to be of grave magnitude hereafter, should not be left out of sight now. It is EMIGRATION,—NOT COLONIZATION MERELY. It has been a Sisyphus work for us to try to found colonies in Africa while we held millions of slaves at home and offered no inducement to emigrate except either to be made free at the price of expatriation, or to receive the poor boon of escaping the blighting influence of prejudice against color, at the cost of a life-long exile among barbarians of a darker skin, and no knowledge of civilization or the living God.

Few of your race went to Africa on these hard terms; and I am glad of it.

17*

XXVII.

African Troops—The Future Armies of the Republic.

THOSE who have declaimed loudest against the employment of negro troops have shown a lamentable amount of ignorance, and an equally lamentable lack of common sense. They know as little of the military history and martial qualities of the African race as they did of their own duties as commanders.

All distinguished generals of modern times who have had opportunities to use negro soldiers have uniformly applauded their subordination, bravery, and powers of endurance. Washington solicited the military services of negroes in the Revolution, and rewarded them. Jackson did the same in the War of 1812. Under both those great captains the negro troops fought so well that they received unstinted praise.

Bancroft, in speaking of the battle of Bunker Hill (vol. vii. p. 421, History of United States), says,—

"Nor should history forget to record that as in the army at Cambridge, so also in this gallant band, the free negroes of the colony had their representatives. For the right of free negroes to bear arms in the public defence was at that day as little disputed in New England as their other rights. They took their places, not in a separate corps, but in the ranks with the white men; and their names may be read on the pension-rolls of the country side by side with those of other soldiers of the Revolution."

In the Memoir of Major Samuel Lawrence (by Rev. Dr Lothrop, pp. 8, 9) the following passage occurs :—

"At one time he commanded a company whose rank and

file were all negroes, of whose courage, military discipline, and fidelity he always spoke with respect. On one occasion, being out reconnoitring with this company, he got so far in advance of his command that he was surrounded and on the point of being made prisoner by the enemy. The men, soon discovering his peril, rushed to his rescue, and fought with the most determined bravery till that rescue was effectually secured."

When the Committee of Conference on the condition of the army agreed that negro soldiers should be rejected altogether, Washington, on the 31st of December, 1775, wrote from Cambridge to the President of Congress as follows :—

" It has been represented to me that the free negroes who have served in this army are very much dissatisfied at being discarded. As it is to be apprehended that they may seek employ in the ministerial army, I have presumed to depart from the resolution respecting them, and have given license for their being enlisted. If this is disapproved of by Congress, I will put a stop to it."—*Sparks's Life of Washington*, vol. iii. pp. 218, 219.

Congress sustained Washington in disregarding the resolution.

The secret journals of Congress (vol. i. pp. 107, 110), March 29, 1779, show that the States of South Carolina and Georgia were " recommended to raise immediately three thousand able-bodied negroes. That every negro who shall well and faithfully serve as a soldier to the end of the present war, and shall then return his arms, *be emancipated* and receive the sum of fifty dollars."

Washington, Hamilton, Greene, Lincoln, and Lawrence, warmly approved of the measure. In 1783 the General Assembly of Virginia passed "An act directing the emancipation of certain slaves who have served as soldiers in this war."

We next give an extract from an act of the " *State of Rhode*

Island and Providence Plantations, in General Assembly," February session, 1778 :—" Whereas, for the preservation of the rights and liberties of the United States, it is necessary that the *whole powers of Government should be exerted* in recruiting the Continental battalions; and whereas his Excellency General Washington hath enclosed to this State a proposal, made to him by Brigadier-General Varnum, to enlist into the two battalions, raising by this State, such slaves as should be willing to enter into the service; and whereas history affords us frequent precedents of the *wisest*, the *freest* and *bravest* nations having liberated their slaves and enlisted them as soldiers to fight in defence of their country; and, also, whereas the enemy, with a great force, have taken possession of the capital and a great part of this State, and this State is obliged to raise a very considerable number of troops for its own immediate defence, whereby it is in a manner rendered impossible for this State to furnish recruits for the said two battalions without adopting the said measure so recommended;

" *It is Voted and Resolved*, That every able-bodied *negro*, *mulatto*, or *Indian* man-slave in this State may enlist into either of the said two battalions, to serve during the continuance of the present war with Great Britain; that every slave so enlisting shall be entitled to and receive all the bounties, wages, and encouragements allowed by the Continental Congress to any soldier enlisting into their service.

" *It is further Voted and Resolved*, That every slave so enlisting shall, upon his passing muster before Colonel Christopher Green, be immediately discharged from the service of his master or mistress, and be absolutely FREE, as though he had never been encumbered with any kind of servitude or slavery."

The negroes enlisted under this act were the men who immortalized themselves at Red Bank.

Arnold, in his "History of Rhode Island," vol. ii. pp. 427, 428, describing the "battle of Rhode Island," fought August

29, 1778, says, "A third time the enemy, with desperate courage and increased strength, attempted to assail the redoubt, and would have carried it, but for the timely aid of two Continental battalions despatched by Sullivan to support his almost exhausted troops. It was in repelling these furious onsets that the newly-raised *black regiment*, under Colonel Green, distinguished itself by deeds of desperate valor. Posted behind a thicket in the valley, they three times drove back the Hessians, who charged repeatedly down the hill to dislodge them."

Negroes have always been favorites* in our navy, and their names always entered on the ships' books without distinction. Commodore Chauncey thus speaks:—

"I regret that you are not pleased with the men sent you by Messrs. Champlin and Forrest, for, to my knowledge, a part of them are not surpassed by any seamen we have in the

---

* "In referring to Mr. Wickliffe's remarks against Generals Butler and Hunter, he (Mr. Dunn) pointed to the fact that General Jackson employed colored soldiers in the defence of New Orleans and complimented them upon their gallantry and good order. Kentuckians were in that battle with black men. Commodore Perry fought his battles on Lake Erie with the help of black men; and black men, too, fought in the Revolutionary War. Commodores Stringham and Woodhull severally testify to the valuable services of the blacks in the navy, saying they are as brave as any who ever stood at the guns. They fought before Vicksburg, and elsewhere.

"The rebels employ them wherever they can. When they cannot get them willingly, they force them, as they did at Yorktown, to take the front rank of danger. Why not now not only educate them to the use of arms, but prepare them to hold the Southern country wrested from rebels? He did not want the white man to go down and perish there. The negro population, armed, can hold the traitors in subjection. The gentleman from Kentucky was apprehensive if arms were placed in the hands of blacks that they would commit great barbarities. 'What,' he asked,—replying to that remark,—'had become of the Christian teachings which were said to prevail in the South?' He said that General Meigs had informed him additional numbers of blacks were required to man the ships, this class of persons having proved highly valuable in the naval service."

fleet; and I have yet to learn that the color of the skin, or the cut and trimmings of the coat, can affect a man's qualifications or usefulness. I have nearly fifty blacks on board of this ship, and many of them are among my best men."

In October, 1814, the State of New York passed an act to authorize the raising of two regiments of men of color.

The following proclamation and address of General Andrew Jackson covers the whole ground :—

"HEAD-QUARTERS, 7TH MILITARY DISTRICT.
" MOBILE, September 21, 1814.

"To THE FREE COLORED INHABITANTS OF LOUISIANA.

"Through a mistaken policy, you have heretofore been deprived of a participation in the glorious struggle for national rights in which our country is engaged. This no longer shall exist.

"As sons of freedom, you are now called upon to defend our most inestimable blessing. As Americans, your country looks with confidence to her adopted children for a valorous support, as a faithful return for the advantages enjoyed under her mild and equitable government. As fathers, husbands, and brothers, you are summoned to rally around the standard of the eagle, to defend all which is dear in existence.

"Your country, although calling for your exertions, does not wish you to engage in her cause without amply remunerating you for the services rendered. Your intelligent minds are not to be led away by false representations. Your love of honor would cause you to despise the man who should attempt to deceive you. In the sincerity of a soldier and the language of truth I address you.

"To every noble-hearted, generous freeman of color, volunteering to serve during the present contest with Great Britain, and no longer, there will be paid the same bounty in money and lands now received by the white soldiers of the United States,—viz.: one hundred and twenty-four dollars in money, and one hundred and sixty acres of land. The non-commissioned officers and privates will also be entitled to the same monthly pay and daily rations, and clothes, furnished to any American soldier.

"On enrolling yourselves in companies, the major-general commanding will select officers for your government from your white fellow-citizens. Your non-commissioned officers will be appointed from among yourselves.

"Due regard will be paid to the feelings of freemen and soldiers. You will not, by being associated with white men in the same corps, be exposed to improper comparisons or unjust sarcasm. As a distinct, independent battalion or regiment, pursuing the path of glory, you will, undivided, receive the applause and gratitude of your countrymen.

"To assure you of the sincerity of my intentions, and my anxiety to engage your invaluable services to our country, I have communicated my wishes to the Governor of Louisiana, who is fully informed as to the manner of enrolment and will give you every necessary information on the subject of this address. "ANDREW JACKSON,
Major-General commanding."
Niles's Register, vol. vii. p. 205.

At the close of a review of the white and colored troops in New Orleans, on Sunday, December 18, 1814, General Jackson's address to the troops was read by Edward Livingston, one of his aids, and the following is the portion addressed

"TO THE MEN OF COLOR.—Soldiers! From the shores of Mobile I collected you to arms,—I invited you to share in the perils and to divide the glory of your white countrymen. I expected much from you; for I was not uninformed of those qualities which must render you so formidable to an invading foe. I knew that you could endure hunger and thirst and all the hardships of war. I knew that you loved the land of your nativity, and that, like ourselves, you had to defend all

that is most dear to man. But you surpass my hopes. I
have found in you, united to these qualities, that noble enthusiasm which impels to great deeds.

"Soldiers! The President of the United States shall be
informed of your conduct on the present occasion; and the
voice of the representatives of the American nation shall
applaud your valor, as your general now praises your ardor.
The enemy is near. His sails cover the lakes. But the brave
are united; and if he finds us contending among ourselves,
it will be for the prize of valor, and fame, its noble reward."—
Niles's Register, vol. vii. pp. 345, 346.*

But the course of events has pretty effectually changed
public opinion on the subject. From Major-General Hunter's
department,† and from other quarters, the official reports of the

---

* For many of the foregoing data I am indebted to Mr. George Liver-
more's recent and valuable work, entitled "An Historical Research respecting the Opinions of the Founders of the Republic on Negroes as Slaves, as
Citizens, and as Soldiers."

† In a letter from General Hunter, written from South Carolina, Feb.
11, 1863, to a friend, he says,—

"Finding that the able-bodied negroes did not enter the military service
as rapidly as could be wished, I have resolved, and so ordered, that all
who are not regularly employed in the Quartermaster's Department, or as
officers' servants, shall be drafted. In this course I am sustained by the
views of all the more intelligent among them.·

    *   *   *   *   *   *   *   *

"In drafting them I was actuated by several motives,—the controlling
one being that I regarded their service as a military necessity if this war
is to be ended in a triumph of the Union arms. Subordinate to this consideration, I regard the strict discipline of military life as the best school
in which this people can be gradually lifted toward our higher civilization;
and their enrolment in the negro brigade will have the further good effect
of rendering mere servile insurrection, unrestrained by the laws and usages
of war, less likely. If any further argument were needed to justify my
course, it would be found in my deep conviction that freedom (like all
other blessings) can never be justly appreciated except by men who have
been taught the sacrifices which are its price. In this course, let me add,
I expect to be sustained by all the intelligent and practically-minded
friends of the enfranchised bondman."

services of negro regiments in the field are highly satisfactory. The superiority of African troops has been completely demonstrated in several important respects.

1. They have nothing to fear from those Southern diseases which prove so fatal to Northern men.

2. They can endure greater hardships and exposures, in. camp, on the march, and on the field of action.

3. They are more readily reduced to camp-discipline, and, from life-long habits of unquestioning obedience, are by no means likely to be guilty of insubordination; while desertion—especially in slave-districts—will be almost unknown.

Finally, they fight not only for freedom and all the blessings it brings, but to escape the ignominious and dreadful death they must endure if they once more fall into the hands of their revengeful task-masters.

But other considerations, of the gravest magnitude, must enter into the general estimate.

Whenever or however this war may end, nobody supposes it will leave us without a military and naval force strong enough to protect ourselves against insurrection at home and aggression or insult from abroad.

Our standing army will ultimately be made up chiefly of emancipated negroes; so will our navy; and they will in time make such a military and maritime force as never has been seen.

Since the days of slavery are numbered in the rebel States, where the institution falls with the fall of the rebellion, and in the border States, where the people, under an enlightened policy, are abolishing it themselves, it will require a vast armed force to enable the Government to carry out such mighty changes as will necessarily attend the reconstruction of Southern society.

For this stupendous work the negroes will be the reliable instruments of the Government in vindicating the strength, the honor, and the glory of the republic. Another heavy

18

force will be required in rebuilding the overthrown structures
and repairing the waste places of war's desolations.

It is not improbable, too, that another vast army may be
needed to build the Pacific Railroad, ship-canals, and other
great works of protection and defence.*

---

* In speaking on the subject of defence for the Northern frontier, Senator
Arnold, of Rhode Island, used the following striking language :—

"He said, It is the duty of the statesman not only to crush the rebellion,
but to cement the Union. This canal will revive the idea of *national
unity,*—the grand idea which has inspired the vast and sublime efforts of
the people to restore the national unity. This canal will be an east-and-
west Mississippi. He spoke of the unqualified devotion of the West to the
Union. There were rebels in the West, and elsewhere, who are seeking to
alienate the West from the East. To this traitorous band was addressed
the proclamation of the rebel General Bragg. How the West responds, the
rebels learned from the mouths of her cannon at Murfreesborough. The soldiers of the East and the West, fighting together on many a glorious and
sanguinary field, will with their blood cement a union and a nationality
so strong and deep that no sectional appeal can ever shake the loyalty of
the glorious band of loyal States. The West will regard as traitors alike
those who suggest a peace with any portion of the Mississippi in rebel
hands, and those who suggest a Union with patriotic, brave, New England
left out.

"The Northern frontier must be defended ; and this canal is the cheapest
and best means of defending it. While the Atlantic shore is protected
from any foreign enemy by three thousand miles of ocean, by forts and fortifications from Maine to Florida, by a navy which has cost hundreds of millions, the Northern frontier, not less important, is entirely defenceless, and
within easy cannon-range for hundreds of miles of a foreign territory.

"The Northwest cheerfully pays her proportion for the defence of the
Atlantic, and will pay further large appropriations now required. But we
ask, in justice, that the Northern frontier should be secured.

"He then read a memorial of ex-President Fillmore and others, showing
the exposed condition of Lake Erie, and showed that the lakes by the
Canadian canals were accessible to British gunboats, and the lake cities
and commerce were exposed to destruction. This canal will enable us to
place our gunboats on the lakes. He read a letter from Admiral Porter,
showing that we had now afloat more than fifty gunboats which could pass
from the ocean to the lakes by this canal.

"He then presented the importance—fiscal, commercial, and agricultural—of the interests thus seeking protection.

And he would be both a short-sighted and sanguine optimist who should leave out of the horoscope of the next few years the contingencies, if not the probabilities, of a collision with Great Britain. That struggle is as inevitable as this rebellion was. All the issues have been gathering, and the result must come. No mortal power can protract it forever. We must be prepared for it, so that it can at no time take us by surprise. This is now the feeling among all parties and sections throughout the country. This feeling will not change. Nations never forgive wrongs or insults. Ours must and will be avenged. The African race emancipated will hereafter constitute the great body-guard of the Union.

"Fifty-eight million bushels of breadstuffs were shipped from Chicago alone during the past year. The commerce of the lakes was at least four hundred millions per annum. *Corn*, since cotton had committed *felo de se*, was now *king*, and kept the peace between Europe and America. This enlarged canal is the cheapest mode of defending the lakes. The whole cost of the canal was only thirteen million dollars. This will turn the Mississippi into the lakes, and unite forever the East and the West. Every dollar thus expended in defence cheapens transportation.

"The capacity of the proposed Illinois Canal will be twelve times that of the Erie Canal. The largest steamers which navigate the Mississippi will steam directly to Lake Michigan. These grand results cost only thirteen millions. It will rapidly pay for itself, and is then to leave a grand national free highway. It will add to the taxable property of the Union as much, or more, than the Erie Canal has done. It will give stability to our Government, and add to the national wealth. It will increase both our ability to borrow money and to pay it."

XXVIII.

The Convalescent Camp of the Fourth Ohio.

SOME fortunate accidents first made me acquainted with this noble regiment and its accomplished surgeon.

There is something very strange and curious about this regiment. It entered the field with floating banners; it waited under arms a long time for a fight; it was well drilled, well officered, and well prepared for a fight; and yet fight it had none. It is altogether one of the most singular features of the war.

I will give its history as I received it from the surgeon of the regiment itself, as contained in his own official reports to his superior officers.

First in a letter to Colonel John S. Mason, dated near Newport News, Va., Aug. 24, 1862. He says,—

"SURGEON'S OFFICE, 4TH REGT. O. V. I.
"CAMP NEAR NEWPORT NEWS, VA., August 24, 1862.

"SIR :—I have the honor to represent the following facts connected with the sanitary condition of the regiment which you command,—viz. :

"1st. Of ten companies, numbering nine hundred and nine enlisted men, there are not to exceed three hundred (300) in good physical condition, present for duty.

"2. During the three months ending June 30, the regiment reported a daily average of seven hundred and forty (740) enlisted men present for duty.

"3. The marked depression of the strength of the regiment is due to the prevalence of a prostrating diarrhœa, which attacked alike the officers and men of the command on or about the 10th of July, and while occupying a camp near Harrison's Landing, Va.

"4. During the continuance of this endemic, there occurred more than six hundred cases (without being associated with a single death, from whatever cause); and, although its violence has now materially abated, its victims are still haunted with leanness, great muscular prostration, and remarkably feeble digestion.

" In view of the foregoing facts, it becomes my duty to recommend and to urge, so far as may be warrantable, that this regiment be allowed to remain in camp for a period of not less than thirty days, as being necessary to restore to their accustomed vigor and efficiency the men who since June, 1861, have been constantly engaged in the most active campaigning, both summer and winter.

" The regiment having been recruited in Central Ohio, it is suggested that their early recuperation will be facilitated by locating their encampment not materially south of Washington City.

" Very respectfully, your obedient servant,

" H. M. McAbee,

"*Surgeon 4th Regt. O. V. I.*

" To Col. John S. Mason, com'g 4th Regt. O. V. I."

On the 10th Sept. 1862, the following letter was written:—

"Near Fort Gaines, D.C., Sept. 10, 1862.

" Sir:—I have the honor to represent that of the six hundred and thirty-five men belonging to your regiment, now in camp, there are but one hundred and eighty-five able to do military duty.

" The enfeebled condition of those unfit for duty is due to the severe and unmanageable disease of the stomach and bowels by which the men were attacked while at Harrison's Landing, Va., and which has induced such impairment of the nutritive functions as can only be repaired by the most careful and

18*

well-directed dietetic and general regimen, steadily sustained for weeks, and such as is absolutely impracticable in the field.

"Indeed, it is a serious question whether the majority of those now ordered to duty are not in great danger of early and permanent disability by being taken into the field ere they are fully restored.

"The sequel which is so much to be dreaded in case the men are now overtaxed and exposed is typhoid fever, which when superadded to such a condition will in a large number of cases result in death, or at best in a complete wreck of health.

"Your obedient servant,

"H. M. McABEE,

"*Surgeon 4th Regt. O. V. I.*

"To Col. JOHN S. MASON, com'g 4th Regt. O. V. I."

And as late as the 8th of November, 1862, the following was sent to the Governor of Ohio:—

"NEAR FORT GAINES, D.C., Nov. 8, 1862.

"HON. SIR:—On behalf of one of the best regiments that Ohio has sent into the field, which is yet strong numerically, but rendered non-effective by disease, I beg leave to address you.

*   *   *   *   *   *

"There are of the regiment in this camp one hundred and forty (140) invalids.   There are at Harper's Ferry three hundred and fifty (350) non-effective men belonging to it.   And there are with the corps to which we belong, in the field, for duty, but *one hundred and twenty* (120).   The remnant— almost two hundred (200)—are scattered in hospitals.

"You ask, why are so many sick? I answer, the regiment has been in active campaign since June, 1861. During all of last winter it was in the field, often compelled to bivouac amid snow and ice.

"Coming out of such a winter campaign in the mountain country of Western Virginia, and while yet enervated by repeated forced marches, which measured miles by hundreds, it was suddenly hurled, with the speed of steam, at midsummer, from an elevation of two thousand feet to tide-level, and into the almost torrid climate of Harrison's Landing, Va.

"When we landed there, July 2, 1862, we had more than eight hundred (800) enlisted men present for duty; and at the expiration of three weeks we reported less than *three hundred* for duty, though we had buried but a single man from disease. We lost, meantime, one in battle, and had eight or ten wounded.

"A desperate form of diarrhœa attacked the entire camp, officers and men. From this disease, now chronic in the great majority of the entire regiment, the men will not recover so as to be fit for field-service this winter.

"They could do garrison-duty, but really ought to do nothing but rest. *Men cannot endure such campaigning, year after year, without respite.*

"The question is simply this,—viz.: Whether these devoted men shall be killed outright during the coming winter, without any compensating element of service to the country, or whether they shall be restored to vigor, by appropriate care, to take part in the spring and summer campaigns of 1863.

"Very respectfully, your obedient servant,
"H. M. McABEE,
"*Surgeon 4th Regt. O. V. I.*

"To his Excellency DAVID TOD,
"*Governor of Ohio.*"

Thanksgiving-day—a Yankee festival—the friends of the Ohio Fourth had fixed on for giving a banquet in the camp. Oh, how gladly the morning broke! How fresh and bracing was the air! How deep-blue was the sky! "Yes, Mr. Chase is to be there, and Miss Chase, and our members; and we shall have such a good home-time. You must come."

It was a nice ride; for who that has sweltered in Washington would not always be glad to get away from its mud or dust, and spring into the higher atmosphere of the surrounding hills that begirt the city as they rise up towards the Heights of Georgetown?

We seemed to be in the wild, wide, free country. Not *all* the green leaves were gone. Some few of the hardier shrubs still held their foliage. But the shrivelled leaves falling now and then from the old oaks told us that winter had sent its first blast.

We took the longest road to get there; for there was no hurry. Autumn was come: all its eloquent language, all its soberness and thoughtfulness, were around us. The last birds of summer were getting ready to go to their Southern homes, and we saw them, mated, plumed for leaving, sitting side by side on the top boughs, having the last chat with old companions, and then gliding off through the clear air to try their fortunes in lands they had never seen, but seeking what they were sure to find,—their Paradise,—a perpetual summer. Let no cruel shot divide the happy couple! Let such music never be stilled!

*   *   *   *   *   *

A turn in the road brought us to the crown of a beautiful hill, near Fort Gaines, where four hundred men from a single regiment were encamped in their picturesque Sibley-tent village, waiting to get well enough to take the field again, or to—die!

Mr. Chase was not there: he could not be. Somebody else made a speech.

When a word was said about home, it struck a chord which vibrated joyously, but still painfully, through every heart. They said, " Let us go home while we are unable to take the field. Let us recruit there. We will give up our pay; we will come back again: we have every thing here the Government or our friends could do; but let us go home to get well." I could not help assuring them that the President, the Secretary of War, the Surgeon-General, and all Congress would do it.

All made their word good. Many of the men were sent back to their own State. Homes by the hundred were made brighter during the howlings of winter storms; but I have heard that since the spring brooks have begun to murmur again, these restored and reinvigorated veterans are preparing to return to plant the insulted ensign of a protecting and endeared republic once more on the last battlement of this accursed rebellion.

XXIX.

The Proclamation of Emancipation.

IT was among the grandest acts in history. It will have more influence over the fortunes of the human race than any act of any other ruler of nations. Scarcely had a short month gone by before it was known to every sitter in the Valley of the Shadow of Death, and it shook the policy of every Government in Europe.

Those who sneered at it as a pompous *brutem fulminæ* forgot that *slavery never was restored where it had by supreme authority once been proclaimed abolished!* Liberty takes no such steps backward. Slavery had been abolished by proclamation in St. Domingo. It was the attempt to reinstate it that whelmed that island in blood. Anywhere else it will have the same effect.

Lord Russell ridiculed it because it was levelled only at "slavery over territory beyond Mr. Lincoln's control, while all the States and districts held by Federal arms were exempt." This would be a very flimsy objection even if it were true; but it is not true. His lordship forgets that "the Proclamation" *was purely a war measure.* Humane and sublime as the results may and will be, it was not done as an act of humanity. Its sole immediate object was like that of any other war measure,—to weaken the enemies of the country and strengthen its friends. In this light, of course, the measure was adopted for and intended to apply only to districts in rebellion. It was to take effect there at the cannon's mouth. Slave-labor there was a strong prop of the revolt. It either raised bread and meat on the plantations, or it did the heavy work of the camp. An able-bodied slave had, from the hour the rebellion began, been as necessary, and often as efficient, as a white soldier in the field. This gave the South half a million extra soldiers.

It would have been no "war measure" to proclaim slavery abolished in the districts which were loyal; for our friends there would thus not only have been punished for their loyalty, but deprived of the very slave-labor aid to strengthen them in fighting our enemies which the Proclamation was intended to rob the rebels of. And, besides, everybody of any sense knew that this Proclamation was not a mere isolated act. It was part and parcel of the imperatively necessary policy of an administration which was charged with the tremendous responsibility of rescuing the republic from an imminent and appalling danger. Universal emancipation of the African race in the United States was embraced in the plan; for the rebellion had made it inevitable.

Several preparatory measures had already passed. The Fugitive-Slave Act had been abolished, slavery itself abolished in the District of Columbia, compensation for slaves voluntarily emancipated proposed, and other measures propitious to the final result.

It was, moreover, entirely unnecessary to touch slavery in the hands of loyal men, for it was perfectly well known that all loyal States and districts would accept the offer of compensation for emancipation, rather than run the terrible risk of losing their slaves, their money, and perhaps, above all, the Federal protection for themselves, their homes and families.

In all such districts immediate or gradual emancipation was sure to come.

Having thus disposed of this captious and pointless objection, let us briefly inquire what were the immediate and what will be the ultimate results of Mr. Lincoln's Proclamation.

As a war measure, *it was the first effectual blow levelled at the heart of the rebellion.* It shook the structure to the centre.

It was the last thing the slave-oligarchy had thought of; it came upon them like the trump of doom.

It annihilated all hope of intervention by the Powers of Europe in behalf of the slaveholding rebellion. This they acknowledged themselves. They saw what was clear enough even to the blind,—that the first throne in Europe which took sides with slavery in America against freedom and free government would crumble to ashes in the earthquake of a revolution. This banished all idea of the recognition of Jeff Davis's oligarchy from the brain of every Minister in Europe.

The Proclamation was hailed with enthusiasm by all the uncompromising friends of the Union; and all intelligent men saw that, hastily as the verdict had been rendered sanctioning the act, the approval was the solemn voice of the nation, and *the ratification of the deed sounded the death-knell of African slavery.* It was the sudden beginning of a swift end.

Students of history! let memory go gleaning over all the fields of the past: you find not an instance recurring in which freedom once proclaimed by the sovereign power as the law of a State ever saw slavery live again. Some systems of wrong once sent to their graves have no resurrection.

But these results were only the first steps in the tread of the earthquake. That earthquake had shaken the world. It startled Cuba; its undulations heaved under Brazil.

Some events are understood just about as well before as after they happen. On the subject of African slavery the voice and example of no nation could be so potential as America's. When slavery was declared abolished in the United States, it meant that it had received its death-wound at the same hour in every other land. If negro slavery fell dead before our altars where liberty was born, it would carry all like systems with it to a common sepulchre.

This Proclamation cut a dead weight from our body politic. Sound and sensible men felt in every nerve of sensation a new, electric shock. East, West, North, South,—everywhere the vital stream of regenerating fire flowed through the nation. To the East it was a tribute to the dignity of free labor. To the North it promised to roll a new burden of commerce along all her lakes, rivers, and canals, created by the augmentation of well-directed industry. To the South it offered to save her from herself. The foul corpse of Slavery was unlashed from the fair form of Liberty and abandoned to sink forever.

This Proclamation gave us what we had in the beginning, and what we had lost,—the commanding post of honor and progress,—the van of the nations.

Finally, it cut the Gordian knot of the abolition of slavery in America, and secured the establishment of civilization in Africa.

For the first time we can speak intelligently and rationally of this great work which has been reserved for our emancipated republic to do.

19

XXX.

Contempt for Labor the Characteristic only of Slaveholders.

An oligarchy lives upon forced labor; and therefore labor is by an oligarchy always despised. Where labor can be wrung from unwilling muscles, either by the lash or any other appliance of despotic power, the laborer is held in contempt.

All this holds true of any one of the countless systems of oppression which have disgraced human society. It is true in India, where the work is all done by the slave caste. It was true in Greece, where the Helots were lashed to their toil. It is true in England, where a cessation from hard labor instantly pays the penalty,—*starvation*.

Such a system brutalizes its subjects. It shuts out light and the possibility of knowledge. It is stationary, and precludes progress. It is degrading; for it nurtures nothing but the lower passions. It therefore makes the slave the personifier of those qualities only which excite contempt. Labor is their sole business; and therefore labor is despised. In our country slaves are black: hence the prejudice against color. In the Orient the Cashmere is supremely fair and beautiful. But Cashmere slaves, being used only as instruments of barbaric taste or lust, are admired for their color, while their occupation and condition are the objects of tyrannical disgust. Where higher sentiments spring up, the slave is made free ; when the last vestige of degradation is supposed to be blotted out, the emancipated mistress becomes the admired and respected sultana.

Association does it all. An indelicately-dressed bawd is at

once arrested by any well-regulated police if she appears in the streets. But the same woman may dress with still greater indelicacy as a danseuse at the opera-house, and if she is beautiful, or dances well, bouquets are showered at her feet, and the applause rises in equal ratio to the indecency of the costume and performance. The beauty or voluptuousness of African women has been the chief source of all amalgamation. Beauty and emancipation remove prejudice against color in a remarkably small space of time. Nothing but *to be free* inspires respect.

Born and "raised" under the blighting influence of any slave-system, the master and the mistress are infected : contact alone breeds contamination. Man cannot take live coals into his bosom and not be burned.

Ungrateful as it is to make either the admission or the allegation, truth compels it : to grow up the irresponsible mistress of slaves casts a mildew over the female heart. It precludes the highest culture in woman ; for its short-comings are a constant source of irritation,—while the not unfrequent acts of deception and wrong-doing stir the baser passions into malignity.

This all springs from the system of slavery. No slave-mistress can entirely escape it. With noble and gifted spirits the influence is far less unpropitious. But this is only saying that noble spirits are strong enough to resist shocks which weaker ones cannot withstand,—that the *spiritual* soars above the *material*.

But, although the conquest may not be complete, except by heroic perseverance, yet under these unfavorable surroundings the few may reach a far higher character than they ever would have attained had they

> "through the cool sequestered vale of life
> Pursued the noiseless tenor of their way."

These are the few exceptions to the otherwise inflexible rule. The silver beams of a few stars may penetrate the mists : their brilliancy is only the more entrancing. The bounding blood of youth may be too pure and vigorous to be contaminated by the malaria : the youth is the more joyous and beautiful. The blinded bird may find its way to a friendly covert in the driftings of the storm, but the eagle alone escapes the tempest by soaring above it.

The dreadful truth remains : African slavery has a direct and inevitable tendency to degrade woman at the South.

A thousand illustrations have occurred since this war began. Wherever our officers or soldiers have paced the streets of cities, from Baltimore to New Orleans, or been seen in cars, hotels, or steamboats, they have been the objects of special indignity from well-dressed *ladies* who had been educated under the barbarous *régime* of slavery. Their conduct has often been characterized by a vulgarity and fiendish malignity which indicated the total loss of all the graces, or even decencies, which are supposed in well-bred society to belong inseparably to the gentler sex.

XXXI.

In the Valley of the Shenandoah.

ONE evening, falling in with a really brave and noble officer of the rebel army, who had been paroled in Washington as one of our prisoners taken in one of the night-skirmishes of the Shenandoah valley, I learned an incident well worth relating.

A squadron of two hundred of Stuart's Cavalry had surprised seventeen of our mounted pickets, who were completely surrounded, and, of course, ordered to surrender.

"Sir," said our lieutenant, "such is the fate of war," and, offering his sword, turned his horse to his command and gave the order,—

"Boys, empty sixteen saddles."

One flash from sixteen carbines obeyed. Dashing on the rebel captain and seizing him by the collar, he dragged him away, dangling at his horse's flanks.

"Follow, men!"

They did; and, riddled though their clothes were with bullets, they all escaped.

After the first mile had been made, the lieutenant checked up, and asked his prisoner, the captain, if he would prefer any other mode of riding.

Of course he did. As good luck would have it, the rebel's horse was loyal to his master, and he had in the *mêlée* followed him. One of our men seized his bridle-rein; and thus, as the rebel captain struck on his feet, his own horse whinneyed to his master's call.

"Now, captain, you must feel at home, I suppose, you are mounted again."

It was a strange coincidence. The rebel was sent to the Old Capitol Prison some days later, and among the courtesies shown to him there he found the identical copy of Xenophon's Cyropædia which he and his captor had both read, as class-mates, in Yale College, ten years before.

The captain considered this a clear case of Yankee chivalry and civilization. I do not blame him for his opinion.

*   *   *   *   *   *

Sergeant Mouser, Co. H, 4th Ohio Vols., left Delaware University in his Senior year to enlist. He made a brilliant speech at a flag-presentation before leaving his native village, —Marion, Ohio,—before an immense assemblage gathered to witness the departure of the first troops under the three months' call. He re-enlisted for three years, and became one of the most promising officers in his regiment.

On one occasion, being on picket-duty under the command of a lieutenant, information was received of the arrival of a body of rebel cavalry in a neighborhood about ten miles distant from his post, their evident intention being to collect some fine herds of fat cattle that were being grazed on the *glades* of the Alleghanies. He obtained permission to go, asking only for a single soldier and the guide who had brought the information, and engaged to drive in the cattle during the night. On reaching the house of the farmer who had charge of the cattle, just after dark, he saw through the window a party of rebel soldiers at supper; and, instantly dismounting, he rushed alone into the house, and, drawing his pistol, commanded, "Keep your seats, gentlemen. Finish your supper. You are my prisoners." And, calling from the door, he again commanded, "Sergeant, station your guards around the house. Throw out twenty horsemen as pickets. Send me an orderly, and report to me in person as soon as your orders are executed."

The party at supper sat in amazement, while he coolly secured the carbines that stood in the corner.

Outside, the soldier, who had been previously instructed,

gave his orders in a tone sufficiently loud to be heard within, and, with the guide, who led the sergeant's horse, according to previous instructions, galloped about the house in every direction, to give the impression of a considerable body of soldiers. Presently the guide appeared at the door, without entering, as "orderly;" and Sergeant Mouser took a seat at the table with his prisoners and ate a hearty supper. After this was over, he took the three rebel soldiers and the farmer into the loft of the house, and had some boards brought, with which he nailed up the door and window. He then shut up the landlady and cooks in the kitchen, securing the windows and door in the same manner. The soldier stood guard, while the guide started for a couple of trusty mountaineers some two miles distant, with whose assistance he drove off sixty head of fine fat cattle, the property of a rebel officer who resided near Winchester, Virginia.

About two o'clock at night, Sergeant Mouser and the soldier started for camp, and, overtaking the drove of cattle, arrived with them in safety early in the morning.

While his regiment was stationed at Romney, Virginia, he was attacked with fever, and sent to the hospital at Cumberland, Maryland, where he was placed on a bunk from which a dead soldier had been taken only the day before.

He grew worse; and his captain, who was strongly attached to him, obtained permission to go and minister to his wants, when he expressed his fears that the circumstance of being placed on the couch of the dead soldier was seriously affecting him, and desired to be removed. He was then taken to a private boarding-house, by the permission of Henry Salter, surgeon in charge, whose kindness is a noble exception to the *many cases of indifference manifested by many army surgeons.* But it was too late. The fever had already taken too deep a hold on his constitution. His friends having been telegraphed for, his father arrived in time to see him die; and his last words were, "Oh that I might have died in battle! But not my will—thine, O Lord, be done."

He was a pious professor of the Christian religion, and died triumphant in the faith. Rev. G. W. Burns, of Cumberland, accompanied the father, with the remains of the brave sergeant, to his home in Ohio.

   *   *   *   *   *   *

The more I have seen of this war, and the more I read of others, the more fully am I persuaded that the deeper a man's religious convictions become, the sublimer will rise his heroism. Macaulay well said, "Many a man has sneered at the Puritans; but no man ever did it who had had occasion to meet them in the halls of debate, or to cross swords with them on the field of battle."

XXXII.

A Well-Known New York Boy.

THE 9th N. Y. State Militia, 83d Volunteers, went to the war eight hundred strong. On their first muster after the first bloody field of Fredericksburg, they numbered *one hundred*. Many of the bravest and best young men in New York were in the ranks of this regiment. Among others, some of my readers will remember Henry Osgood, as a tall, athletic, handsome, and accomplished young man, living in 24th Street. Filled with patriotic fire, he started with his musket, and was with his regiment in all its fights, distinguishing himself by his gallantry and daring. At Fredericksburg he was wounded, —but slightly, as was supposed. He so represented it to his friends. Growing worse, however, he was sent with his wounded comrades—of his company only two being left—to the Lincoln Hospital in Washington. He wrote often to his home, concealing, if he knew, his real danger. His surgeon must have known from the beginning that the wound was mortal. But the soldier "preferred to suffer alone, without making those who loved him suffer unnecessarily;" and thus he continued his correspondence up to within a few hours of his death. His last letters were as cheerful as his first. They were all glowing with the sunlight of cheerfulness and hope; for his coming had always dispelled every shadow of sadness, and gloom could not live where he was.

I have seen many such cases, where young soldiers who knew they must soon die refused even to let any correct account of their state go to their friends. It was a far more admirable sight to witness such examples of magnanimous

self-forgetfulness, in the indescribable tortures of wounds and
amputations, than to look on any deed of courage on the
field.   In nearly all such instances, the fire of pure patriotism seemed to blot out all other considerations.   I have seen
that high sentiment rise into the full glow of an all-absorbing
passion, and leave its impress on the face after the heart
had stopped beating.   "My country! my country! I wish
I could do something more for thee before I die!"

I have seen many who had seldom thought about their own
death—boys who had left homes of luxury, fondled by
sisters' caresses and mothers' love—brought from the battle-
field and laid down in a hospital to die.   When the fading
twilight of a joyous youth was going into the deep eclipse
of Death's shadow, as it moved out, with unrelenting sternness,
from the unknown Land, those who *had* thought of the
last hour, so sure to come, and grown familiar with what cannot
be seen till we reach it,—who had been introduced to the
far-off Future till their Father's House became *their home,*
—such boys, and the thoughtless ones, all had one solicitude alike:—"Land where my fathers died,—save her, O
God!" * * *

* * * Young Osgood was buried at the Soldiers' Home.
In recovering his body, they had to open seven coffins before
they found the sacred dust of the loved one; and on the
coffin was inscribed another name!   Oh, to gather the ashes
of a stranger when the breaking heart can be healed only
after the last act of affection has been done to the departed!
I speak of soldiers' burials elsewhere.

XXXIII.

Border-State Men and Border-State Loyalty.

THIS great struggle to save the life of our nation has had to encounter obstacles hard to overcome, and prejudices almost insurmountable. The calm judgment of the thinking and patriotic head and heart of the North was all the time at work in concert with the corresponding class of men in the border States.

We at the North stood far enough away from the mine to feel safe whenever the explosion might come. Our border-State brothers had not so easy a time. To us it was only the howl of a tempest which could not reach us; with them it was the precipitation of doom at their very hearth-stones.

The serenity of the Northern millions was unbroken. We slept calm; we waked free from all care except the national trouble.*

---

* In his strong and eloquent speech in the Senate-House, before the National League, Tuesday evening, March 31, Mr. Carrington, U. S. District Attorney, remarked, "I love my native State with a pure and a holy love. When I stand upon her sacred soil, the very air around me is redolent with the sweet and solemn memories of the past. There lie en-'tombed the bones of my ancestors, and there lingers in helpless age and poverty my *beau-idéal* of human perfection and the dearest object of my heart's affection. Oh, I have a motive and cue to passion which our brethren of the North can never feel. They fight for their Government, their country, and their flag. We fight for the same Government, country, and flag, in which we have a common interest with them: in addition to this, we fight for our homes and firesides, and the green graves of our forefathers. For my own part, all I regret is that the time I have spent in the court-house was not spent upon the field of battle. But in this matter I have deferred to the judgment of my friends, who seem to think that my voice is stronger than my arm."

They suffered with *another* trouble. They loved our country as well, and many of them better than we. But what could they do? No voice or pen can tell. They could not gird the national armor on to go out to fight for our cause; for the first step they took from their threshold would be to the grave.

The "iron mask" was put on the face of every man who lived south of "Mason and Dixon's Line." He *could* speak; but his utterances would be smothered, *perhaps*,—nay, to a dead certainty. For Genius, which is contraband sometimes even in civilized nations, could have no chance to illuminate the ill-guided, misjudging, and deluded South.

The South,—*as a South,—as a whole, is gone*. This South has died of Negrophobia. This complaint has been charged on New England,—the real eagle's nest of the republic. But it is a great mistake. New England never had it; the North never had it. The North has put forth its best efforts to save the South from rushing on to and into her own ruin.

Who ever heard of such a noble offering as was made to the South, when a million of Northern men tried to put Fillmore again in the chair, when not a national tongue wagged against the effort? At that hour the South, as "a South," deserted us!

Let us go on. They asked for Pierce : we gave him to them. Again, they asked for Buchanan. By hard work and doubtful scratches, this poor emasculated traitor got in. And the result we all know. Buchanan! a man, or a *thing*,—who, after doing what harm he could to his country, tried in vain to hurt us abroad, where even the statesmanship of our enemies discovered in advance that he was either a puling fool in power, or a very Benedict Arnold (without his genius), to work what ruin he could, in leaving an office he had disgraced by his incapacity and perhaps outraged by his treason.

Yes! The chances were altogether against any show for border-State loyalty.

Those homes were as dear as ours. They were threatened;

ours were not. They had wives whom they held in their bosoms, and they pressed them closer, and they became *dearer*, at every signal of danger.

I need not say what these men have gone through; nor can I tell their number. That record is kept on high. Not half of their sufferings or endurance will be known till the revela-tions of "the last day." If heroism is to be measured by the amount of danger encountered and torture endured rather than sacrifice honor and principle, the men and the women of the border States will have the highest meed of praise awarded to them forever.

That no charge of partiality or unfairness may be brought against the statements I make, which could be proved from a thousand sources, of the atrocities perpetrated on Union men by the Confederates, I quote from the resolutions unanimously adopted by the "Union Democratic Convention" held in Louisville the past month (March, 1863), composed of dele-gates from every Congressional District in the State.

"*Resolved*, That the people of Kentucky have suffered every insult and injury at the hands of the so-called South-ern Confederacy, and are stimulated by every motive of in-terest and honor to oppose and overthrow it. This Confede-racy has sought and now seeks to break up the Union, forever dear and necessary to them the people of Kentucky; and when by their often-repeated decisions they refused to join in the work of treason, infamy, and ruin, it trampled down their State Constitution, put up a weak and usurping Government over them, and placed pretended Senators and Congressmen in its conclave at Richmond, assuming to speak their voice; it invaded their State with armies, and sought to conquer and carry them away from a Union they revered to one they de-tested. It ravaged by bands of marauders—not soldiers— their fields time and again; robbed them of their public re-venues and private property; destroyed their public records; burned their towns and houses; carried away their non-combatant citizens into long and loathsome imprisonment, where many still languish; murdered many of them, sometimes in their own homes and in the presence of their families, and sometimes by cruel and infamous deaths, extending their atrocities even to women and children, thus setting at defiance all the laws of civilized warfare; and these efforts have continued and increased with the increasing aversion of the people of Kentucky towards all its wicked designs, and now threaten to break with fresh force upon that State and people. That therefore the people of Kentucky can never cease their efforts for their own protection, and condign punishment of the authors of these wrongs, and the complete overthrow of the rebel Confederacy; and all citizens of Kentucky, if any there be, who refuse to support their State and fellow-citizens against such unprovoked wrongs and cruelties, or profess to sympathize with such enemies, are false to their allegiance, to friends, neighbors, State, and nation. That, nevertheless, of one thing the people of the revolted and the loyal States, and of the world, may rest assured: Kentucky will submit to such a despotism only when she has no power to resist it."

Yes, the people of Kentucky have had to pass through the fire; and fire educates men quick. So have hundreds of thousands in Tennessee, Missouri, Virginia, and North Carolina. Of what they have gone through we heard only a tithe, and comprehended still less.

But the hour of their emancipation is hastening. They alone can hereafter retard it. Their only salvation is to come in, heart and soul, with the cause of the Union, and give up *all* for that. *They must give up slavery: they must not try to save it.* Every effort to protract its life only hastens its doom, and prolongs the sufferings of its protectors.

Come forward, then, and rank yourselves with the friends of the Union, and the whole North and the whole world are with you.

The voice of God to the border States is sounding with

clarion notes:—"Come out from her, my people, that ye be
not partakers of her plagues."

"Is not this the fast that I have chosen? to loose the bands
of wickedness, to undo the heavy burdens, and to let the oppressed go free, and that ye break every yoke?"

"Then shall thy light break forth as the morning, and
thine health shall spring forth speedily; and thy righteousness
shall go before thee, and the glory of the Lord shall be thy
rearward."

"Violence shall no more be heard in thy land, wasting nor
destruction within thy borders: but thou shalt call thy walls
Salvation, and thy gates Praise. Thy sun shall no more go
down, neither shall thy moon withdraw itself: for the Lord
shall be thine everlasting light, and the days of thy mourning
shall be ended."

A most graphic illustration of this divine philosophy for
the government of nations is found in a speech delivered by
Cassius M. Clay before the law department of the University (Albany, Feb. 3, 1863). In closing he says,—

"When, long years ago, knowing the nature of slavery, we
desired by peaceable means to check its power and to subject
it to the civilizing influences of the age, North and South,
we were told to be quiet:—time would cure all things,—Providence would provide a remedy. In peace the time had not
come; and now in war the time has not come! In vain we
gave utterance to the 'voiceless woe' of the four millions of
men, women, and children in slavery, and implored the eight
millions of whites to let the oppressed go free. The prejudice
of color bound the non-slaveholding whites, alike with the
black, to the masters' chariot-wheels. See them now like
dumb cattle driven to the slaughter; they are thrown in heaps
into their last resting-places: no stone marks their dishonored
graves. See now 'the desolator desolate!' Within the shattered hovel, by the broken hearth-stone, the wan, expectant
wife gathers her ragged, starving children. Alas! the husband,

the father, and the brother will return no more! Yes, Providence at last speaks! By the wasted fields, the blighted industries, the exhausted treasures, the desolated hearth-stones, the tears of the widow and the orphan, and the shedding of blood, Deity calls upon us to execute justice. The madness of the parricides has broken the shield of the Constitution. Men of the North, having now the legal equitable power over slavery, I warn you too that God decrees liberty to all or to none! The hopes and fears of a life-struggle are with me crowded into a day. I would that you could feel as I do the urgency of the crisis, which determines the destiny of so many millions now living, and the vastly more millions yet to be born. Then would you be persuaded that as much as the liberation of the slaves is a '*war measure*,' yet far more is it a '*peace measure.*' If you would have peace, be just; for *justice is the only peace.*"

XXXIV.

The Commissariat of the Army.

Soon after the news of the bombardment of Fort Sumter reached New York, I had the pleasure of meeting one evening several accomplished military men (Europeans and Americans) at the Astor House, when the military situation of the country was thoroughly discussed. At their request, I drew up a brief presentation of their views for the public press. I extract here a paragraph or two, as it appeared in the New York "Daily Times," from that portion which concerned the commissariat, this being the chief subject of their solicitude in view of the rising emergency of setting an immense army of new men in the field.

Although the entire plan proposed was not adopted, it was gratifying to know that, with the full approval of that mature and gallant soldier, Major-General Wool,* it received

---

* I can scarcely withhold from the reader a very characteristic and noble letter from this great and loyal-hearted man, written in the beginning of the rebellion. It was through strange councils that this accomplished soldier was so long kept from active service in the field, while his eye was not yet dimmed nor his natural force abated.

"Troy, 12th May, 1861.

"Dear Sir:—I thank you for your kind favor of the 7th instant. Absence from head-quarters has prevented me from acknowledging it before the present moment.

"I am much gratified to find you—as well as all my friends—ready and determined to defend the right and our country in this moment of great peril. After thirty years of incessant efforts, treason has done its worst. I had hoped Virginia, having before her the examples of her great men, among whom stood Washington, the Father of his Country, would have

the best consideration of the Government, and perhaps all
the advantages contemplated were secured by the energy of
the Administration.

NECESSITY OF ESTABLISHING A DISTINCT DEPARTMENT IN
THE GOVERNMENT TO SUPERINTEND THE COMMISSARIAT.

The commissariat of an army has never yet been complete
in the organized military power of any nation. It is the last
one that is provided for, and the first one that should be
thought of. No nation in history ever lacked fighting-men.
No nation ever has sent a *perfectly equipped army* into a campaign,—equipment meaning every thing needed to eat, and
drink, and wear, and sleep with, and fight in any emergency.
Starvation has reduced the strongest garrisons. Men cannot
fight on empty stomachs. Demoralization in armies grows up
in most instances from incompleteness in the commissariat.
Men cannot fight in a campaign without the *means* of fighting,

---

remained steadfast in support of the Union. But, alas! she too has turned
traitor, and disgraced herself for all future time.

"It appears to me a greater opportunity could not be presented for you
to instruct the rising generation, by laying bare the villany and treasonable conduct of the demagogues of the Southern States. I know of no
one more capable of doing justice to those whose object has been to rule
or ruin our prosperous country. They preferred to rule in hell rather
than serve in heaven.

"But yesterday we were a great nation, and commanded the admiration
of the world, with an empire extending from the frozen regions of the
North to the burning sands of the South, containing a population of more
than thirty-one millions, and enjoying a prosperity unparalleled in the
history of nations. Every city, town, and hamlet throughout the land
was growing rich as if by magic, and no part more prosperous than the
South. How is it to-day? I must leave it to you to describe its condition
and the causes. Those who sow the wind must expect to reap the whirlwind. Employ your pen, and lash the traitors naked through the world.
No one can do it better than yourself.

"If I could wield the pen as well as yourself, I would make it more
powerful than the sword.
                    "Your friend,
                                        "JOHN E. WOOL.
    "To Hon. C. EDWARDS LESTER, New York."

any better than a mechanic can work without tools and materials.

It has been proved all through human experience that no army, while it was well supplied with the absolute necessaries for the business in hand, ever became ineffective, unless from political or social causes. An obnoxious general, or a sudden change of events from any other cause, may produce some defection; but demoralization has seldom come from any other cause than an incomplete commissariat. The bitterness that takes hold of the soldier's heart when he is not well fed, well clothed, well armed, well encamped, is so great, that in a thousand conflicts for the cause of justice, country, and truth, mutiny has broken out, demoralization has come, and defeat has been the fruit of this state of things.

In the Commissary Department of our hastily organized Union army, there is no lack of men or money, and, unless political or personal favoritism and nepotism prevail to a great extent, our national army will be well manned and well officered. The only danger will be that the men will not be taken care of. There is money enough to take care of them all, and that money will be spent as free as water. There is already rolling over the great North a *Pactolus* of gold for this purpose. But there are some things that must be looked after now, since we have more men than we can equip and more money than we can spend, which, well considered, will not only secure our triumph in the vindication of our Government against all its enemies, but do it cheaper, better, and more effectually than it ever can be done if these prudential considerations are left out of sight.

Although we are in spirit the most martial nation on the earth (hardly excepting the French), and although we are the most liberal, we have a set of people in America always looking at the main chance,—always keeping the eye upon practical results. We have such unquenchable and irrepressible confidence in our resources, and ability to *improvise* them, we are very likely now to be "caught napping" in providing "the tools" for working out this great business we have taken in hand. Cæsar himself was stabbed by a few assassins because he was taken unawares; and yet Cæsar had left a million of corpses of the enemies of Rome in the rear of his legions. England suffered deeply in her exchequer and her soldiers—more deeply still in their privations—in the Crimea, because the English commissariat was so incomplete. This was not owing to any lack of money, or men, or means; but political *red tape* had swayed England so long that her army cost more to feed and clothe than any army that ever went on a campaign, and they were fed worse. Lord Raglan himself had no good dinner for thirty days, until a French officer gave it to him. The appropriations for army rations were considerably larger than for the French. But their food was badly cooked, their provisions were in bad condition, and they were badly fed throughout. At the same time Soyer, the immortal French cook, having been sent by the Emperor to take charge of the kitchens and the stomachs of over one hundred thousand Frenchmen, gave every soldier and officer a fine meal twice a day, fit for any gentleman of taste, even an epicure, to eat and enjoy, at precisely three-fifths of the expense that it cost the British empire to feed badly the same number of men. The English soldier's camp cost more and was less comfortable than the Frenchman's. More Englishmen died from bad diet and unnecessary exposure than Frenchmen. Englishmen fight well always; but the French took the Malakoff. In fact, the French were in such a physical and moral condition through that campaign that they nearly ran away with the glory of it. There is no danger that our men will not be supplied with arms and accessories, equipments and munitions; but on the very start we learn that some of our Northern regiments had nothing to eat but bad bread and raw pork, for thirty, or forty, or fifty hours. And even in the city of New York our troops have lain down on the wet ground with empty stomachs, and, when called upon to reconstruct bridges and relay railroad-tracks and lift locomotives from ditches, have worked in a hot sun, with no protection for the head except dark-colored caps, inviting sun-strokes, with nothing but uncooked provisions or musty crackers to eat, and, for a wonder of all the ages, not enough fresh water to drink,—and kept this up for forty hours, making it a matter of heroism for soldiers to divide small rations of decent food between each other from regiment to regiment! Here is the danger; for this all comes from almost total neglect of a commissariat system,—a system which we have not got, and which we must have, or we shall have de-moralization in our army, following exhaustion of strength, bad treatment, cheating and robbing by speculators from the stomachs, the backs, the hands of brave men, all means of enabling them to fight those great battles which are to make this Government eternal. Soldiers can endure a great deal; they expect it when they start; but they cannot suffer un-necessarily, either by robbery or neglect, without becoming demoralized. The better your men are on the start, the worse they become as you go on, if they are not looked after. When a free citizen offers himself, he means all there is in the uni-verse that he has any interest in, his own life being the last thing he thinks of. His family, his possessions, all fade into nothing. He only goes to protect his flag, which alone makes all his other treasures worth any thing.

It has been the concurrent testimony of officers who have seen much military service in Europe, that no Government makes such generous provision for its soldiers on the march, in the camp, and in the field. The rations are not only far more abundant, but they are of better quality. This has been true from the beginning, barring those exceptional cases which only confirm the rule. No army is paid so high, and in none is so efficient a sanitary *régime* enforced.

And it must not be forgotten that all this has been a work of *improvization*, and that the history of war through all ages furnishes no parallel to the military preparations this country had to make. It has amazed the world, and revealed inexhaustible resources in the soil, the machinery, the labor, the energy, the genius and determination of the people, to which even they themselves were utter strangers. It has been a herculean work; but the giant has grown strong in the midst of his labors.

*   *   *   *   *   *

Since these considerations were first presented, two years have gone by; and it will not be said that our million of men in the field have been neglected one hour, when it was in the power of the Government to administer to their necessities and comfort in the field.

XXXV.

A Summer Morning's Ride to the Country-Seat of the old Patriot and Poet, Joel Barlow.—A Hospital.

It was one of those heated, pulseless mornings which are often felt in Washington in midsummer. The still air burned on the cheek; even the insects which bask in noonday sultriness had fled to their night-homes among the drooping leaves. The air could not move: every breeze was dead. The Potomac seemed to have stopped; for in its long and broad sweep to Alexandria it showed not a ripple or shimmer. Not a cloud moved over its bosom, which lay all unfolded, reflecting nothing but the great dome of the Capitol, as the sun rising behind it painted it, in all its grandeur and beauty, on the deep blue of the river.

Looking out from my window, I was glad enough to see that my friend W—— had come up with his mettled grays.

"I've called to take you in for a drive out among the hills, where we can get at least one mouthful of fresh air."

Rising over the heights of Georgetown, a cool breeze came down the river from the northwest, and in making the circuit around Fort Gaines the magnificent panorama of the Upper Potomac opened upon us, with its thousand hills, many of them crowned with tented encampments and waving flags, all threaded by the great river as it came down cool and sparkling from its picturesque mountain home.

Leaving the public road, we entered a gate-way, by the side of which stood the lodge that in olden time had guarded the entrance to the magnificent estate of JOEL BARLOW,—the soldier, traveller, ambassador, poet, patriot, scholar, friend of science, and patron of arts.

On his return from Europe, after an absence of seventeen years, he resolved to settle down and devote the rest of his life to his favorite pursuits,—letters, art, and society. His ample fortune enabled him to gratify all his highest tastes. He purchased an estate of two thousand acres near George-town, more varied and entrancing in its scenery, and more commanding in the wide sweep of its surroundings, than any other spot in the immediate neighborhood of the then youth-ful capital of his country. A fairer spot could hardly have been found. The estate was nearly all one park of fine old oaks of primitive growth, interspersed with many other kinds of the finest forest-trees, and the variety and magical effects of artistic culture of species that were lacking imparted higher embellishment to what nature had already made so beautiful. Abrupt hills, covered by gnarled oaks and lofty evergreens, still cast their shadows down into deep tangled dells and gorges, through which crystal brooks find their mur-muring, tinkling way.

A winding road of a quarter of a mile brought us out on a high, commanding tableau of several acres, in the centre of which Barlow erected his substantial, massive, brick-and-stone mansion, and where he intended to pass his life and end his days. It is a spacious, grand, and cheerful edifice. A wide hall divides the main body of the house. The suite of large rooms on the east was devoted to the *grand salon* and the gallery of sculpture, painting, and rare objects of *vertu;* on the west side was his great library and the dining-room. A circular carriage-road swept by the entrance; while on all other sides a vast and splendid garden extended, ornamented and enriched by every native and exotic tree, shrub, fruit, and flower that could live in the climate. Birds of all varieties of plumage and song filled this paradise-scene with music, and sparkling fountains scattered their cooling spray on the summer air. Through ample vistas among the monarch trees, the most captivating landscapes opened in all directions.

The city of Georgetown—even then gray as an old French town perched on an eminence—lay below; the rising capital was clearly seen in the distance; the wild scenery of the Upper Potomac mountains was unfolded on the north; while on the south the broad Potomac itself, with its majestic tide, went sweeping by, in its long and tranquil reaches, to the sea..

Here Barlow clustered around him every thing which wealth need purchase, or a chastened fancy invent. But Kalorama (as he called his estate) had one charm besides, without which it would have been a desert to its master. His house was the scene of princely hospitality and elegant society. All the great, the learned, the accomplished, and the beautiful men and women of that wonderful age were, sooner or later, his guests. His old friend and companion George Washington, alone, was not there. But there was Adams, and Jefferson, and Madison, and Monroe, all the fathers of the republic, all foreigners of rank and learning, artists and poets; and these circles were embellished by the most gifted and brilliant women of the age.

The spirits of the great departed seemed still to haunt those stately halls; and I confess that when I was aroused from my revery by the tap of my friend's hand on my shoulder, saying, "Now, Charley, shall we look through the wards first?" a cold shudder went through me; for it had only just occurred to me that I was standing in the very centre of

"*The Small-Pox Hospital of the Army of the Potomac.*"

I somewhat suddenly withdrew for a ramble in the garden, remarking to my friend I thought I would see *that* first.

Under the shade of a broad-spread clump of flowering shrubs I sat down on a marble seat, to contemplate the strange contrast. The garden, evidently, preserved the main outlines of the original plan. The walks, the trees, the grass-plats, were still there. But they showed no sign of the pruning hand. The fruit-trees were dying; the box had outgrown its borders; tall and noxious weeds were growing in wild luxuriance over the genial soil. The out-buildings were going to decay. The fences were falling down, and the whole place looked forsaken and desolate. One spot alone was blooming, and it was the oasis in the desert. The surgeon and his attend-dants had taken care of it, and it was one mazy labyrinth of flowers. How changed all this from other days, when travel-lers from a distance came to see what could be likened only to the gardens of Armida !

In those days Barlow was in the very noontide of his in-tellectual vigor. Born in the village of Reading, Connecticut, in 1754, he was now in his fiftieth year. His learning was vast in its range, and his devotion to science and literature had become the ruling passion of his life. Long familiarity with the great men, the languages, and the society of Europe had specially fitted him for the work he proposed to do. He resolved to write a great epic poem; and in ten years the "Columbiad" appeared, in what would even in our times be termed splendid style. During this decade he alternated his labors by making a careful and exceedingly valuable collection of materials for an elaborate history of the country. It will always be a fruitful source of regret to historians that this work was never executed. The scholars and statesmen of his time who knew Barlow's plan, and had seen chapters of the work already written, did not doubt that the writer would leave in his history an imperishable monument to his fame.

Another enterprise also received his most earnest efforts. Feeling and knowing, with all statesmen, how much strength and glory are imparted to republics and empires by insti-tutions for the promotion of science and art, he labored un-ceasingly to persuade Congress to establish a national Insti-tute, modelled after the Institute of France. Washington, Adams, Jefferson, Hamilton, Burr, and all the illuminated men of the time, were his coadjutors; and the whole plan was ready for adoption, when two events occurred which arrested its progress,—the second war with England, and the departure of Barlow for Europe.

One evening President Madison drove out to Kalorama for a private conversation with Barlow. They sat for several hours in the library undisturbed, engaged in an earnest conversation on the condition of Europe, our relations with the great Powers,—particularly with Napoleon, then in the zenith of his splendor, and England, with whom it had now (1811) become plain enough we must have a second contest.

No American—not excepting Jefferson, who had so recently retired to Monticello—understood the politics of Europe better than Barlow. He was popular in France, and was sure of a cordial greeting at the court of Napoleon.

Barlow was requested by the President to accept the mission to the Emperor; but it would involve the interruption and perhaps the final failure of his plans for the rest of his life. For several hours Madison was unable to shake his decision. But by persuading him that he would be able to negotiate a treaty of commerce and indemnity for former spoliations, and thus not only secure justice for many of our citizen, but fortify our Government with France in anticipation of an approaching war with our common foe, this appeal to Barlow's patriotism turned the scale. He consented to go. Alas! when he turned to take a final look at the enchanted home he was leaving, he was looking on it for the last time.

He sailed for France. He made no progress for several months, being, as he said, "continually baffled by the intrigues of the Minister of Foreign Affairs,—the Duke of Bassano."

It was only in October, 1812, that he was promised an opportunity of cutting the Gordian knot. He was invited to a personal conference with the Emperor at Wilna, in Poland, where the restless genius of conquest and glory had halted on his way to Moscow.

Barlow set out at once, and plunged into a Polar winter.

Over long tracts of his journey he encountered all the horrors of hunger and cold. But his lion-heart never gave way; and he pressed on.

He reached the little Polish town Zarnavi, and lay down to die. He was resting in a Jewish cottage, where he experienced the time-honored hospitality of that ancient and venerable race. All the tenderness which the daughters of Israel are taught to show to the friendless "stranger within their gates" was shown to the dying ambassador.

His last intellectual effort was a poem he dictated a day or two before he died. It was a withering satire of resentment on Napoleon for having so cruelly betrayed the hopes of the world. He was buried at Zarnavi, near Cracow; and his remains rest there to this day.

*   *   *   *   *   *

"We have been very fortunate in our hospital," said the surgeon. "We have had a good many difficult cases; but we have lost very few. The air is pure, we have every thing we could desire, and we are almost as much out of the world as though we were on top of the Blue Ridge: so we have got along finely."

I was glad to hear it of course; and although I have never felt much afraid of disease in going through hospitals in any part of the world, still I did not feel any special *hankering* for a more minute inspection of the sanitary condition of this private party who had gone out to pass the heated term at the country-seat of Joel Barlow.

I breathed a little freer as the carriage rolled down the gravelled road. We stopped a few moments at the tomb of the Barlow family, which stands at the foot of the great lawn of sixty acres which slopes gracefully down from the southern front of the venerable mansion.

The breeze had freshened; fleecy clouds were drifting under the far-off mazarine-blue sky. One touch, and the grays snuffed the fresh air and left the road and the dust behind them. We were all glad enough to go fast,—horses, passengers, and particularly the coachman, who declared that "if he had just known what a dreadful place he was going to, he would as soon have driven down to Tophet."

"That's nice in you, my man, with that face of yours so pitted up that one would suppose you had had the small-pox all your life."

"Yes, your honor. But I might carry it away in my clothes and give it to the babies."

21*

XXXVI.

The Law of Empire in the Western Hemisphere.

LORD BACON somewhere says, " Men *discover* laws; God makes them." Philosophers interrogate Nature, and as fast as they find out her laws they mark the progress of science. The steam-engine, the printing-press, the cotton-gin, the daguerreotype, the magnetic telegraph, each has to be invented or discovered but once. One Columbus is enough for one hemisphere.

It were well if statesmen should act on the same law as applied to the political world; for both systems—the physical and the moral—came from the same source and are swayed by the same Master. The brain of Shakspeare sprung from the same moulding hand that chiselled the gothic peaks of the Alps and painted the last evening's sunset. Certainty of results, the conditions all being complied with, is the physical law of the universe. A thousand Galileos could not make the peasant of the Apennines believe that the sun will not rise to-morrow. Experience has taught him the un-varying order of nature. Why should we stop here and press along our bewildered track through the moral and political world, heedless of laws of action and of states, which just as inevitably control the fortunes of men and the fates of empires ?

Let us trace these analogies into the political world, and see if we cannot find just the same certainty and precision in results there that Galileo and Newton discovered in physics, or Shakspeare and Alfieri demonstrated in the drama, or Cooper and Scott in romance.

The question, then, meets us, *What is the law of empire in this new world?* There is a law of existence for all beings and all things,—from the mote that floats in the sunbeam to the Bengal tiger in his jungle. Historians have been busy with the *general* problem of empire from the earliest nations; and Tacitus, Gibbon, and Sismondi have helped us to a better interpretation of the law which has controlled the growth and decay of the panoramic commonwealths that have gone by in their solemn movement over the broad fields of history. From such sources we learn that the frequent captivities of the Jews, and the repeated destruction of their gorgeous capital, followed by the carrying away of the whole nation into slavery, did by no means effect their extermination; nor was that work brought about even by the remorseless persecutions to which they have been subjected by every nation under heaven except our own. The sons of Abraham are still a nation, and they are more numerous to-day than they were when they turned their farewell gaze upon the falling towers of Jerusalem. England has at last been compelled to acknowledge the Jews as citizens; and the scattered children of Jacob could to-day send a million of armed men to recover their own land, which has been cruelly robbed from them by Pagans, Othmans, and Christians. Whence sprang this vitality,—this power of endurance,—which makes them above all the people of the earth THE ETERNAL NATION? *They have always been believers in the only true God, and they have never lost their nationality.*

We glance at Switzerland, and we learn that she has always been free. The hunted spirit of liberty has always found a home there. The reason is plain. Among those everlasting mountains a race of men have been nurtured, amidst the sublimest scenes of the physical creation, where the hardiest characters have been formed, the sternest wills educated, and the deepest love of liberty inspired. *Despotism never flourishes among mountains.*

Another illustration. France has learned that, although she may conquer, she can never hold in subjection the nations which lie beyond her present boundaries. Those bounds are the Rhine and Alps on the east, the Mediterranean on the south, the Pyrenees on the southwest, and the ocean-waters on her western and northern shores. She has often swept over them with her chivalric legions, and, sooner or later, her colors have waved from almost every capital in Europe. But she has generally lost her conquests as rapidly as they were made, and she has always been compelled to retire within her natural boundaries as soon as the tempest of revolution subsided and Europe settled back to its repose.

England may seem to be an exception to this rule; but she only confirms it. She has till recently been long the greatest of the commercial Powers, and Providence gave to her the mission of spreading civilization. This she has done through the four quarters of the globe. But the time came for her to fall under the operation of the same law which fixed the fate of Rome. Like that mighty empire, she started from small beginnings. Nineteen hundred years ago, the Roman standard first floated on the shores of Britain. Then a race of barbarians, clothed in the skins of wild beasts, roamed over the uncultivated island. The tread of the Roman legions was then heard on the plains of Africa and Asia, and the name of Rome was written on the front of the world. Nearly two thousand years have rolled by, and Julius Cæsar, and all the Cæsars, the Senate, the people, and the empire of Rome, have passed away like a dream. Her population now numbers less than that of the State of New York, while that island of barbarians has emulated Rome in her conquests, and not only planted and unfurled her standard in the three quarters of the globe which owned the Roman sway, but laid her all-grasping hand on two new continents. Possessing the

energy and valor of her Saxon and Norman ancestors, she
has remained unconquered and unbroken amid the changes
that have ended the history of other nations. Like her own
island, that sits firm and tranquil in the ocean that rolls round
it, she has stood among the ages of man and the overthrow
of empires.

A nation thus steadily advancing over every obstacle that
checks the progress or breaks the strength of other Governments, making every world-wide tumult wheel in to swell its
triumphal march, must possess not only great resources, but
great skill to manage them. Looking out from her sea-home,
she has made her fleets and her arms her voice. Strength
and energy of character, skill, daring, and an indomitable
valor, exerted through these engines of power, have raised
her to her present proud elevation. Salutes in honor of the
birth of the present Prince of Wales were fired in AMERICA,
on the shores of Hudson's Bay, along the whole line of
the great lakes to Vancouver's Island, and their echoes reverberated over the undiscovered gold-fields of Frazer's
River,—in New Brunswick, Nova Scotia, Newfoundland, in
the Bermudas, at one hundred points in the West Indies, in
the forests of Guiana, and in the distant Falkland Islands,
near Cape Horn; in EUROPE, throughout the British islands,
from the Rock of Gibraltar, from the impregnable fortifications of Malta, and in the Ionian Islands; in AFRICA, on the
Guinea coast, from St. Helena and Ascension, from the Cape
to the Orange River, and at the Mauritius; in ASIA, from
the fortress of Aden, in Arabia, at Karak, in the Persian
Gulf, by the British army in Afghanistan, along the Hima-
laya Mountains, the banks of the Indus and the Ganges, to
the southern point of India, in the island of Ceylon, beyond the Ganges, in Assam and Arracan, at Prince of
Wales's Island, and Singapore, on the shores of China; at
Hong-Kong and Chusan, and throughout the settlements
which had begun to open that new continental world of Aus-

tralia to the breaking of a day of civilization. No prince
had ever been born whose birth was hailed with rejoicings so
universal among civilized and barbarous nations. It was
the welcome to a new prince from

> "That Power whose flag is never furl'd,
> Whose morning drum beats round the world."

But she has long ago learned that her provinces are held by
a frail tenure; that the branches of her power are already
grown too large for the parent tree; that the heart of an empire may go to decay, while a distant dependency continues
to flourish. Nor do her statesmen, in all the pride and pomp
of empire, always forget that a power greater than her own
has left only feeble traces of its existence in Italy, and that
"the barbarian's steed long ago made his manger in the
golden house of Nero."

England is to-day, however, the mightiest Power in America except our own. She is, in fact, the only European nation that ever stepped on this soil which had *all* the elements
of endurance for governmental control under propitious circumstances to perpetuate it.

This will be apparent as we come to the main point in our
argument, which is to show THE LAW OF EMPIRE IN THE
WESTERN HEMISPHERE. It is safe to say that monarchy is
the law of government in Europe; and it is quite as safe
to say that democracy is the law of the cis-Atlantic world.
The fact speaks for itself. With Europe the case is settled.
Republicanism cannot flourish there. Hierarchy, rank, class
legislation, unequal taxation, unjust laws, with centuries of
time and thousands of precedents to sanctify the system,—
such are the obstacles to democracy in Europe. When it is
born in the throes of a wide-spread revolution,—as in 1848,—
it dies in its cradle, it is stifled. All Europe knows this.
This accounts for the great fact of the peopling of this continent. *The masses* of Europe feel this in every pulsation.

They pluck up the ancestral tree and bring it to grow in a more congenial soil. They have tears to shed, when they leave the homes of their fathers, which are nearly unknown to us nomadic Americans. We are always on the wing. Europeans cling to the hearth-stone closely until they leave it forever. The millions of men and women now in this land, who were born in Europe, bespeak the confidence which the great body of the people of the Old World feel in our political system, and show how little hope they had in the establishment or resurrection of liberty in those countries where their fathers are buried. A few gifted minds in Europe foresaw this actual state of things at the period of our War of Independence. Of such was Edmund Burke, whose words to the Prime Minister when he was attempting to force *the Stamp Act* through Parliament are known to every reader. Nor can we ever forget, in this connection, the prophetic lines of Bishop Berkeley, fifty years before 1776, where, in speaking of the Anglo-Saxon race here, he says,—

> "Westward the star of empire takes its way;
> The first four acts already past,
> The fifth shall close the drama with the day:
> Time's noblest offspring is the last."

But to be more specific in our illustrations. The New World was discovered by Italian navigators in the employment of Spain, Portugal, and England; and it was taken possession of in the name of Rome. *Neither Spain nor Portugal owns to-day a rood of ground on the continent of America.* There is but one kingdom on this continent,—Brazil; and that is entirely independent of the mother-country. Spain has lost all her vast possessions on this side of the Atlantic, except Cuba; and this island she has held through no strength of her own, but solely through the jealousies of other European states, none of whom would allow it to change hands, or through the forbearance of this republic.

In attempting to hold these American colonies, Spain and

Portugal attempted an impossibility,—and for the simple reason that they tried to force upon them the political system of the old monarchies of Europe. That system would not do here; it was not suited to the New World: it would have been easier to reconcile them to the temporal reign of the Pope over them. They were good Catholics enough, and bigoted withal, as they are to this day. But they protested as vehemently against the monarchical pretensions of the Prince of Rome as ever Protestants did themselves. Monarchy would not do in America, even when imposed by the Vicar of God. The only apparent exception to this rule is Brazil. But her people voluntarily chose an imperial form of government, and with it *the sovereign of their own choice.*

Thus the mighty empires of Spain and Portugal in the New World have thrown off the political system of Europe, and with it went all the ligaments of race, all the prejudices of a bigoted faith, all the allurements of rank, all the associations of home, and all the *souvenirs* of history.

France comes in here. Once, as we have shown in another place, she held much the larger portion of the continent which is now held by us. Her sway was undisputed from the mouth of the Mississippi to the roots of the Rocky Mountains, and from the mouth of the St. Lawrence to the cliffs of Lake Superior. Her missionary scholars, her cavaliers, her soldiers, explored the continent, erected fortifications, and gave a civilized language to a hundred barbarous tribes. The traces of her science still surprise us in our wilderness explorations: her fortresses are still standing; the names she gave to lakes, mountains, rivers, prairies, and stations still remain; and she has made her own court language of the world the only medium of interpretation between millions of civilized and savage men along our northern borders, even up to the present hour.

But when her strifes with England at home were transferred to America, she lost her New World possessions. To found colonies and foster them through growth into independence is the prerogative of England. France never founded a successful colony. She is a brilliant, heroic, and scientific nation; but she has few adventures to recount in foreign lands. Of such adventures England's history is chiefly· made up. Although far ahead in civilization of her great rival in the times of the Crusades, she achieved far less in Palestine with her Godfrey de Bouillons than England did with her Cœur de Lions.

In attempting to hold her colonies in America, she found herself unequal to the terrible struggle with England; and thus, with the surrender of Montreal, in 1760, *the French empire on this continent passed away.*

Next came England herself. Her statesmen who were in power from the beginning of the Revolution made a series of fatal mistakes in their American policy. Worse blunders than they were guilty of are not recorded in the whole history of politics. That England lost her Thirteen Colonies *through sheer blunder* is now too plain to require illustration or to admit of argument. She made a broad distinction between the natural and political rights of Englishmen abroad and Englishmen at home. In claiming the imperial right to tax the colonies while they had no representation in Parliament, she laid down a principle utterly repugnant to the whole history of English liberty and utterly subversive of the British Constitution. This was the rock on which her statesmen split her empire. Burke, Fox, Chatham, and Barré gave timely warning of the result; but it was unheeded until the bolt had fallen.

Here we can advantageously pause a moment, to trace out the early workings of *that great principle which lies at the bottom of the whole political system of the American world,* and to vindicate which this domestic war is raging. Every citizen of a republic should comprehend his own Govern-

ment,—the causes which gave it birth, the spirit of its
Constitution, and the spirit of its founders. Without this
clear comprehension of causes and results, he can never
be prepared to serve the state with ability, nor even to go
intelligently to the ballot-box. In this respect the present
generation are far behind their fathers. *Those* men studied
Government *as a science*; we study party politics to *win*.
The difference is infinite.

*Why, then, did England lose the United States, and why
must she lose every one of her colonies in the New World?*
The Thirteen Colonies were forced into independence. They
had no alternative but to be absolutely free or absolutely
enslaved. The idea of a Declaration of Independence
dawned slowly on the American mind; and it was with the
deepest reluctance that they at last took arms against the throne
of England, by whose immovable base they were so fastly
moored. The proofs of the loyalty of the colonists are scattered thick all through their history. There was not an
American home in which the brilliant records of England's
achievements were not read with pride.

Up to the time of the embarkation of our fathers, England
was their country; and our ancestral history is the history
of Britain. The great writers of England, till the period of
the Commonwealth, wrote and thought for our fathers as
much as for the fathers of any Englishman. Besides, around
English history there is a charm which can be found in no
other. The recent and the remote,—the plain and the obscure,—novelty sprung up by the gray remains of antiquity,—
all the elements of the touching, the beautiful, the gloomy,
and the grand, mingle with the chronicles of the fatherland. With us all is familiar and modern. It is true, we
read with pride and emotion our fathers' struggles, when the
story leads off through the toils of the Revolution back to the
gloom of the green old forests, and the desolation of Plymouth
Landing, or the inhospitable banks of James River; but

there the story ceases in America, and we must cross the water for an account of our antecedent national existence. We personally, then, have an interest in England, and we can betimes forget America, as it slumbered on, unwaked by the sea-gun of Columbus, while we retrace the glory of our ancestors, through successive generations, to the time when the Roman conqueror first planted the eagle of Italy on the rocks of Britain and returned to tell of a stormy island in the ocean, and of the rugged barbarians who dwelt in its glens and hunted on its cliffs.

Yes, all this feeling in America was in favor of the supremacy of England here. But there was a stronger feeling still in the hearts of the colonists. It was an instinctive love of liberty; and although not a man in America could forecast the result, yet the great body of the American people were impelled by a political law, then not understood even by themselves,—a law which *has* shaped and *is* shaping every institution on this side of the ocean.

It is as necessary to have the history of nations before us when we try to deduce the laws of empire, as it is to have the phenomena of the natural world for determining the laws of nature. In this glance we are making at the empires that have come and gone over this continent, we shall infallibly arise at a clear understanding of the law of government by which events are decided in our Western hemisphere.

France first lost her American possessions altogether, and then England lost all her colonies here worth the struggle of keeping. Those that were left have never paid the trouble or cost of governing. *They have been too poor to govern themselves;* for self-government is, after all, an expensive affair. Free states almost invariably tax themselves more than despots venture to impose. In proof we adduce our American cities, which are the most expensively governed municipalities in the world,—also our voluntarily sustained clergy, who, taken as a body, are the best-paid priesthood in

Christendom,—last of all, the tremendous self-imposed exactions for raising the Internal Revenue.

France held on to Louisiana for a long period after the fall of her empire at the north. But, at the first suggestion of Jefferson for the purchase, Napoleon asked, "What will they give for it?" "It is a vast territory, and it should be worth more than fifteen millions to the United States." "That is not the question. Fifteen millions is far more than it is worth to us. If we keep it a little longer, we shall get nothing for it. Take the money." This purchase of Louisiana blotted out French power from North America.

It was soon after this event that the period of revolution came for the old colonies of Spain and Portugal. Hardly had Napoleon been driven from the scenes of his great achievements, when the tocsin of independence sounded from one end of the Spanish New World to the other. And we, cannot omit an allusion to a coincidence which we have never seen noticed. It was during the last days of Napoleon, and even while that terrific storm of May 4, 1821, was sweeping over St. Helena, tearing up most of the trees about Longwood, and shaking the humble dwelling where the hero of Austerlitz lay, that the last Spanish colony on this continent wrenched itself away forever from the greedy and remorseless grasp of the throne of Aragon and Castile. Her sale of Florida to our republic blotted her power from the continent.

And, now, how stands the question of empire in the New World? For all practical purposes, there is but one empire in North America at this hour; and we need not add that it is the dominion of this republic. Russia, indeed, holds nominal sway over a vast territory north of the British possessions, up to the Pole. But it very slightly concerns civilization to inquire what sceptre pretends to sway those ice-bound, inhospitable regions. England claims and professes to rule a broad, intervening belt, stretching across the continent next to our frontier. But she scarcely interferes with these colonies, and allows them to govern themselves. She knows that to assert such rights over them as she tried to vindicate over us in 1776 would rend those colonies from her, as she would be equally sure to lose them by a collision with the United States. A reciprocity treaty has already effected a practical annexation of those colonies to this republic. English statesmen have at last learned something of the law of empire in the New World. They do not venture to interfere materially with the wants or the wishes of their colonies. Indeed, the thing has been carried so far to the other extreme that Canada, Nova Scotia, and New Brunswick complain that in the withdrawal of the usual body of English troops, business grows dull in their chief towns, and that the Queen's Government in other respects seems to treat the colonies too much as independent states and too little as loyal subjects. Thus the lesson has been taught that men in America must be free, and thus the lesson has been learned.

Such considerations show very plainly the irresistible tendency to national consolidation on this continent, and demonstrate the absurdity of any attempt to dissever or break up this Republic. All the tendencies are in the other direction; and if Jefferson Davis were a statesman he never would have made so stupendous a mistake. His blunder, if possible, was more gigantic than his crime.

22*

XXXVII.

The Quakers on the War-Path.

This insurrection has disturbed the deepest fountains of the life of our people,—both the good and the bad. It has agitated the serenest waters. Even the members of the Society of Friends have been among the bravest and best contributors to the war. In the field their gallant sons have done all the duties of citizens as nobly as their fathers have performed them in the calmer scenes of domestic and civil life.

At one of the regular meetings of the Society of Friends (Orthodox) a committee was proposed to be raised to inquire into and attend to the cases of young men, sons of members, who it was supposed had, in clear violation of all the standard rules of the Society, enlisted for military service in this dreadful war. It was notorious that a large number of this class had actually shouldered the musket and marched with their regiments; and it was strongly suspected that many of these boys had actually received the warmest blessings of their demure but none the less heroic mothers, and the inspiring encouragement of gentle sisters, on their departure.

But, as the case had been brought up before the meeting by some of the strictest Friends, it became necessary to give it the most serious consideration; and the members of the committee were duly proposed.

The first rose, with great dignity, and, with that inimitable serenity which always characterizes the proceedings of the Orthodox Quakers, requested to be excused, on the ground that he could not conscientiously serve in that capacity, since, very much to his pain and sorrow, among the young members who had enlisted for the war he *had a son!*

Another member desired to be excused on the ground that, without his knowledge, *two* of his sons had not only joined the army, but were already in the field.

Finally, the third member rose, and stood some moments without speaking. He was a venerable man : he looked like the patriarch of the solemn assembly. His hair was white, but his cheek looked " like a rose in the snow." " Friends, we in our weakness cannot foresee the purposes of the great Father of all things; nor should we attempt to scrutinize his almighty designs. It becomes my duty to inform you all that my youngest *son, two* of my *grandsons*, and several of my *nephews*, have also taken up arms in the defence of our beloved country; and I am very much afraid that I could not serve on the committee with any good to our cause."

A reverent silence brooded over the assembly, and for a protracted interval the silence remained unbroken. At last the " mover of the motion" rose, and proposed that " the whole matter should be temporarily postponed."

A very large number of the brave young men of the Society of Friends (Orthodox) have gone to the field, and they have fought with a heroism, and a faith in the endurance of the republic, worthy of the loyalty of their Society to the great principles of humanity and religion. I can make no estimate of their numerical force.

But by far the larger number of the Society of Friends who have joined our army belong to what is popularly known as " Hicksites." *They* embraced the great cause on the start. From Pennsylvania, New Jersey, Indiana, and other States, it is quite probable that not less than five thousand Quakers have enlisted and fought in our armies. Call them " Orthodox" or " Hicksites," it matters little to us : so long as our fellow-citizens are ready to fight and die for the country, they are our best-beloved brothers.

XXXVIII.

The Nation Taxes itself to Redeem its Pledges and Sustain its Honor.

NEVER, perhaps, was such a sight witnessed as was seen when the Congress of the United States last year enacted the Tax Bill. All direct taxes are odious. Men do not like to have the tax-gatherer come round and unceremoniously thrust his hand into the pockets of his neighbors.

Sir Robert Peel said,—

"We have taxed the dependent classes into extreme poverty. Now, to raise money to relieve the Exchequer, we must reverse the order of our financial policy, and tax the rich! *Tax incomes.* People who have revenue can pay. Remove the duties on bread, and I will take care of the rest. The corn-laws must be abolished. Cobden is right."

On this system our tax was laid for internal revenue.

We saw and knew that great and unforeseen emergencies were impending. A country was to be saved,—*not lost.* We let our representatives in Congress know *that we were all in earnest,*—that we must have all the money we needed—no matter how large the sum—to defend from sacrilege the old shrines where we had always worshipped. So Congress had to pass a bill to tax all our people to pay the interest on any amount of money we might borrow from each other to carry on the war.

Not a decent member of Congress dared to go home and confront his constituents until he had voted for one of the extremest and most intolerable measures of taxation ever heard of on the earth!

But this was the act of the people. They meant all they said.

"The Union! It must and shall be preserved." "We will foot the bill." It was the grandest mortgage-deed in history!

"We will pay"—whom? Each other. "My lands and tenements, my household goods,—whatever I have or may have—come, take all; and, if this fail, come and take me, and I leave my all for my share, and go with the flag."

Here was a basis for making a national debt much greater than the debt of England, and due and timely provision made, not only for the payment of its interest, but with the dead certainty of leaving a balance every year, by which the sinking fund should absorb the principal at an early period.

Who ever heard before that the people of a nation asked to be taxed? Who ever before heard that a nation commanded its representatives to tax them? Was it pianos, silver plate, billiard-tables, alone! No! the people came rushing up to the financial altar, eager to pay their quota to sustain a common government erected for the common good, and sustained by the universal will.

This income tax went into operation. It touched every house and home and heart in the country. It spoke its own language.

It said, "I come for money to carry on the war."

We gave; and we will give, till the last shot has left the locker.

In this great crisis, a good man was wanted to put this law into execution. That man was found.

Mr. Chase chose Governor Boutwell, of Massachusetts. He accepted the post. It was a hard and a thankless task to fulfil his mission. But he went at it with the firm resolution and the crystal head with which such men always undertake public duties. He entered on chaos; he evolved light. He saw confusion; he brought out order. He had a difficult task. For the second time in the United States, a direct tax had to be laid on the income and the real and personal property of our people to sustain the national Government.

Every thing now depended on the way of carrying this statute out.

Governor Boutwell took the work in hand as a matter of business; and he went through his course of duty so well, that few or no men had occasion to complain against him, although he had to make over one hundred decisions, to determine the meaning and application of the Internal Revenue Law.

This is extraordinary; for such a case never had existed, and perhaps never will again.

The excise law was passed July 1, 1862, and the country had two months' notice of the time when it would take effect. During these two months, the factories, distilleries, and breweries were in operation constantly. When the 1st of September came, the productions not only fell off, but many establishments were shut, and in others the business was materially diminished. The excessive production of July and August filled the warehouses, consumed the raw material, especially cotton, and left the country without the means or the inducement to continue business upon an extended scale. Consequently, the revenue was for a while moderate, inasmuch as the people had been consuming the stock of free goods. Almost the entire product of whiskey and tobacco for the months previous to February was exported.

The receipts are now about $1,300,000 per week, and increasing each month.

One of the most gratifying facts in the whole matter is the readiness of the people to meet the unusual demands made upon them by the provisions of the excise law; and in none of the States are taxes more readily paid than in Maryland, Kentucky, and Missouri.

Should the war be closed during the present year, our war-debt will be less than $1,500,000,000, the interest on which, when funded, will be about $80,000,000, while the revenue from the excise law alone will reach one hundred and fifty millions, for the year 1863-64.

The law was put into operation on the 1st of September last; but there were many delays, and many circumstances calculated to keep the income at a point below the probable average in future. The stamp law was not understood; we were not able to obtain the engravings until December; and the supply of stamps was not adequate till the first of the year. The use of stamps is, in fact, optional with the people, and continues so till the first of this month,—June, 1863. The first arrival in California was since the 15th of February; and the entire receipts for stamps from the country west of the Mississippi River do not amount to one hundred thousand dollars. The receipts from stamps previous to March 1, from the whole country, were $3,603,934 85, and the total revenue to that date is $20,598,336 62.

With the return of peace in the South, our revenue would exceed $225,000,000. Should a tax be levied upon cotton of two to four cents per pound, the income could be increased $20,000,000 at least over the largest sum named. If the war is carried over into the year 1864, our chief additional resource for a time will be to levy a tax upon cotton, without drawback upon exports. This will be a necessary burden upon our manufacturers and upon the manufacturers of Europe. Had England and France disclaimed any sympathy with the rebels, the rebellion would have been suppressed long ago. Were England and France to disavow all sympathy with the Confederacy, and compel their subjects to observe an honest neutrality, the days of the rebellion would soon be numbered. If, however, the rebellion is encouraged, England and France will share the loss and suffering.

Thus manfully and in straightforward style did the American people show the earnestness with which they entered into the serious business of taking care of their country.

They pledged their lives in the field, their fortunes at home, and, above all, their sacred honor.

That debt of gratitude will be paid.

XXXIX.

What Our Republic Needs Now.

ALL nations that have made any mark on the world, or left any record in history, have had a strong nationality. A Swede never was taken for a Russian; a Spaniard never was mistaken for an Englishman; a Turk never was supposed to be a Frenchman; a Scotchman never was taken for a man born on another soil. So we might go through all the nations of modern time; the same thing would hold everywhere true. It was so with the ancient nations. Wherever an Egyptian went, he was at once recognized as having come from the banks of the Nile. Wherever the Greek went, men looked upon him as a traveller from the land of Pericles and Homer. So, too, no matter how far he wandered from the Eternal City, the Roman was always looked upon as a man just from the protecting shadow of that great empire.

But how is it with Americans? And yet we have a wonderful history. We have crowded more memorable deeds within a narrow space, during the brief period of our existence, than any other nation that ever flourished. We have crowded more illustrious names into our annals, and our record in after-ages will be read with more astonishment than we now read the record of the most romantic achievements of the nations that have gone before us. But there is no people where so few of the population are swayed so little by the sentiment of nationality. True, when Americans meet abroad, they at once recognize in each other a common senti-ment; but at home they seem to have little in common with each other. There is more sectionalism in America than in any other great nation. Take the British empire, on which the sun never sets; no British subject can be found in the circuit of the globe who does not represent the national sentiment of his empire. No Englishman will be heard any-where to decry or disclaim his queen. There is no sectional-ism in the British empire; there is no sectionalism in France; there is no sectionalism in Russia, nor in Prussia, nor in Spain, nor even in dilapidated Portugal; and yet none of these nations have inherited so great a treasure in the form of guaranteed civil rights, nor so great a treasure in all the aggregate forms of good which we denominate civilization.

The existence of sectionalism in America explains the otherwise incomprehensible fact of the lack of a spirit of nationality. Within sight of the dome of our Capitol can be seen Mount Vernon, the home of the Father of this republic. It is allowed to be put up at auction by its unworthy and sordid proprietor,—in whose veins, *thank* God, no drop of Wash-ington's blood flows,—and when, forsooth, it does not bring as much money as his avarice greeds for, an appeal is made to the women of America, and they come forward to purchase this home of the great patriot, to rescue it from its present hands. If there had been a national sentiment in America, that spirit of nationality would have proclaimed itself long ago, in an act which would have been everywhere applauded, and the tomb at least with the home of Washington would have been purchased by the nation and guarded in safety and veneration, as the Mecca of liberty in the Western world. Again, every dollar that is expended for the construction of ships-of-war for our navy is begrudged. We are unwilling even to maintain a line of steamers between New York and Liver-pool; and much less do we seem disposed to hold any steam communication with South America. It is next to an im-possibility to convince our people that any administration is willing to vindicate our international rights on the Isthmus,

23

although it is the natural and necessary highway to the western borders of our empire. Again, while the nation is clamoring for a railroad across the continent to the Pacific Ocean, no administration seems to have the will to press it upon Congress. It is recommended session after session, but it remains a dead letter. These are only a few illustrations that we could bring to show that the leading men of America —those who govern us, who sit in our legislatures, State and national—are insensible to the claims of a sentiment of nationality. There is a spirit of jealousy between the representatives in Congress from one section of the nation, which shows itself in opposition to any benefit or advantage to be gained by any or all other sections. New York, the commercial metropolis of the Western world, has been trying for a quarter of a century to have a mint established there, even if it were only a branch mint. But we have been obliged to send one thousand million dollars to Philadelphia to be coined, at great expense and still greater inconvenience and protracted delay. In all our public debates this spirit of sectional jealousy arises, and it mixes itself up with all our legislation, and we perceive the spirit everywhere. All these things indicate a lack of national spirit. Now, this can be accounted for, it is true, in part, by the fact that we have not had time to become a complete nation. John C. Calhoun said, shortly before he died, "*that we were not a nation, but only a confederation of nations.*" This would not be true if everybody at the North had a national sentiment, or if everybody at the South had a national sentiment. But it happens that there are so many diversities of opinion, and so great a lack of national sentiment, in every part of the country, —almost as much in one part as in another,—that it is only when some great national event transpires that we call out and create for the moment a common sentiment of nationality. It is then participated in by the great masses.

We have had a few national men in America, and they

have helped to preserve among our people all the nationality we have. The fathers of the Revolution and the early statesmen of the republic agreed so well in every crisis that they left us an example of nationality. But it was chiefly because they were great men, lived in moulding times, and were compelled by the necessities of the case to aggregate opinions and principles as well as to combine their action upon common points of effort.

After their time, however, the nation was obliged to pass through convulsions such as the war of 1812 on the question of fighting England, or in 1820 on the question of compromising the slavery matter, or in 1830 on the question of the Union as against nullification, or in 1850 on the question of the Union as against the negro " business," and more recently on the Lecompton difficulty.

The instances we have adduced show the prevailing lack of a national sentiment. This has arisen chiefly from three causes :—1st, Tranquillity in our republic, and peace with foreign nations; 2d, The immense influx of foreigners, who did not comprehend the institutions of our country well enough to act as they would have acted in their own nations; and, 3d, This general mixing up of all the nations of the earth in the eager strife for gain, which has demoralized this country to a greater extent than all other causes put together.

One of these causes, although it may not be primary in its character, should not be lightly passed over. We had hitherto lived in such tranquillity, and were so exempt from foreign wars, that we have not had our own domestic troubles blotted out by greater causes of anxiety in our conflicts with other nations. It was a maxim of statesmanship in Rome, and it has since been made so in Paris, to divert public attention from local and domestic interests to the more engrossing anxieties of foreign struggles. All Roman statesmen, however much they might differ in other things, agreed that the

safest way to insure tranquillity in Rome was to send its
legions into foreign nations to battle. Rome was always
tranquil while a great foreign war was going on; and that
stupendous republic had been in existence seven hundred
years before the officers of peace had an opportunity to shut
the gates of the temple of Janus.

They remained shut for twenty-five years; but historians
agree that during that period many of the seeds were sown
for the decline which ended finally in the fall of the Roman
empire.

In our own history we find some faint illustration of the
truth of this philosophy. When one generation had died
after the Revolution, and the question of the *complete assertion of our independence came up*, there was a strong dis-
inclination on the part of many of our people to another
conflict with England. True, the memory of the terrible
struggle of the War of Independence was yet fresh in the
recollections of many of our countrymen, and could they
have decided the national councils they would have voted
against another war. But a new generation had come on,
and, although young men were disposed to go forward in a
further and final vindication of the rights of the country
against the oppressive measures and the galling insults of
Great Britain, it was with the greatest difficulty that the
Congress of the United States could be persuaded to make
the war of 1812. But when the war had once been proclaimed, the national sentiment of the nation was aroused,
and it launched itself forward into the contest with heroism
which ended in victory. At the close of that war the nation
was so much occupied in the serious business of gaining a
livelihood, that we went on quietly for many years, so much
occupied in our own affairs that we allowed many an insult
from a foreign Power to pass by without retribution. Mexico
at last assumed such ground as could not be admitted, and
that war began. The President called for fifty thousand

volunteers, and in thirty days he had three hundred thousand. Young America launched itself on the plains of Mexico, and the spirit of nationality became the guiding spirit of the hour. There was, a few years ago, some nationality inspired by the spectacle of ten or twenty war-steamers sent off to battle with some half-barbarian despot in. Paraguay. But we shall not witness either the resurrection of the nationality we have hitherto inspired, nor, much less, the creation of a universal sentiment of nationality, except in some decisive conflict between the United States and a great foreign nation.

We are not pleading in behalf of war. But there are misfortunes that fall on nations infinitely greater than those which are entailed by war. Wars do not cause the extermination of nations, nor inflict half the trouble that comes from the decay of a national sentiment. No nation was ever yet exterminated by battle until it had already lost the spirit of its nationality. A nation is nothing more in the aggregate of states without this sentiment than is a man in the midst of his fellows if he loses all control of his own will. Switzerland has maintained her nationality, and she has remained unbroken and unconquered for ages. So has Hungary, who showed a few years ago how strong she was in sentiment when she levelled that brave blow on the breast of her spoiler. France is always fired by nationality, and in all her pride she exults in the glory which a Napoleon dynasty sheds over her. So, too, with England. All Britons rejoice in the supremacy of the home Government. We do not, of course, embrace Irishmen, because England has never been able, during the five hundred years of her despotism, to blot out the national sentiment of that brave people.

The result of all this is, that any American statesman who is afraid of a collision with one of the first Powers of Europe is not fit to have any voice in the national councils. We are very proud of our Washingtons and Jeffersons and Jacksons

23*

and Constitutions and Capitols; and we brag of the whole thing every 4th of July.

But foreigners have much less respect for us as a people than we suppose. They respect our history, because it is filled with the achievements of our fathers. They all look upon us with a kind of wonder, because the country is so big, and they innocently suppose big people must live here. They respect our steamers, because they outstrip in speed those of other nations. They respect our telegraphs, because we have fifty thousand miles of them. They respect our clippers, because they are the fastest sailers in the world. They admire our daguerreotypes, because they are the best. But, after all, Americans make a great mistake if they suppose that Europeans do not curl up the lip with some scorn when we talk about coming in collision with the Old World.

It is plain enough that we shall never be recognized heartily, socially, and respectfully as the First Power, or even among the very first, until the pride of foreign monarchs, so often displayed, shall be humbled in a terrific and, if need be, a long struggle for the vindication of the right of men to self-government.

In the Old World it is prescriptive right, hereditary privilege, ecclesiastic power, with all the retinue of titles and powers, and all other things, which command popular admiration. Here we have none of these questions or things, nor do we need them. But we must have something to supply their places; and this something can be had only by the display of that national power which shall prove great enough to protect all weak nations, and strong enough to defy strong ones, even if they melt all their decrepit carcasses into one body.   •

In this direction it is plain to see that the fates of America are being drifted by events.

Our newspapers agitate a few of their readers every morning by long and tedious despatches from Washington, or

Halifax, or Mobile, or some other place, about what Lord Napier has been saying, or what Lord Lyons is about to say, when by a little pluck in our statesmanship this telegraphic business would all be snuffed out.

Has it come to this, that England will attempt to establish a police over American waters, and make an arrangement with Nicaragua, or Costa Rica, or Guatemala, or San Salvador, or New Grenada, pledging her imperial power and her irresistible arms to keep American pirates off their coasts? We do not believe that England is foolish enough to offer her services in that business, where it is perfectly certain that it would be considered an insulting interference that would sweep one or the other of our Powers from the ocean. But British statesmen understand very well that our politicians have more faith in gas than they have in gunpowder, or firmness, or dignity, or, above all, in a national sentiment.

The Peace Society preaches to us about not going to war, precisely as good nurses talk to children about not eating sweetmeats and sugar-candy; but it unfortunately happens that as long as confectioners make these things children will eat them, and their fathers and mothers will give them to them besides, although it may just as inevitably follow that the services of the family doctor cannot be dispensed with when the colic comes.

Young nations are young children, and old nations are in their second childhood.

Our nation must be consolidated; and nothing can do it but to create a common interest, either for attack or defence. The heroism of every nation has been the only sentiment out of which nationality has been created. Without appealing to this, no great Government would have become what it has been; without this, no nation would achieve any thing. It is all vain to wait "for the good time coming,"—that political millennium when all nations will lie down together and kiss and smother one another to death with kindness and fraternal love. This is all nonsense. This is stuff to throw to cats and pups. It means nothing; for while humanity lasts it will be made up of men and women, and men and women are made up of will, of power, of heroism, of truth, of laws, of insults, of passions, of every thing human or divine. These qualities exist in human nature itself.

They are eternally in conflict, even in the individual man, or woman, or child, and they will remain there, unless by eternal duration virtue at last achieves a complete triumph over vice, and judgment and reason assume undisputed empire over all the prostrate passions. But even under God's own immediate sway, where inspiration teaches us that he has had immediate control over spirits without flesh and blood, and, consequently, without those types of passion that belong to the human race, he has had angels and devils,—on the one side of him a heaven filled with the choral music of uncounted seraphs, and on the other a hell filled with the howlings of damned spirits. People who suppose they are to pass through this universe in easy-chairs, never feeling one of the blasts of misfortune nor having their cheek visited by any rude wind of adversity,—people who are sighing forever for "that good time" will have a precious long time in getting it. The universe is a living, flaming, passionate, active thing. It is no place for people to go to sleep; for, even if they go to their graves, the day of resurrection will bring them out.

XL.

Mr. Lincoln:—What Kind of a Man—What Kind of a President—he is.

WHEN Mr. Lincoln entered the Presidential mansion, he could not have answered either of these questions. It is a matter of serious doubt if he could do it even now.

It was once a post for the retirement of a statesman of well-earned fame, for his coronation when he had earned the supreme honors of the state. In times of peace our great public men found their legitimate way to the Home of the Presidents (as Washington wished to have the White House called). Those honors then were always worthily won, and the laurel wreath kept green on the brows of all their wearers,—at least till the last of the primitive chieftains went to his untroubled rest under the shades of the "Hermitage."

Yes, those men lived to reap the rich rewards of peace after their battles, of repose after their toils.

But it was no pillow of down on which Abraham Lincoln was invited to lay his head. He thought he understood something of what had been committed to him; and when he stood on the eastern portico of the Capitol, all blanched before the surging sea of anxious men and women who were waiting to learn "What of the night?" would bring from the new sentinel, he uttered words to which the events of the future were to give an astounding and unforeseen significance.

Lincoln's Presidency was a heritage of trouble from the start. No good man in his senses would have taken the honor, if he could have foreseen a tithe of its bewildering heart-achings,—the treason, the blood, the agony it would cost the noble nation, betrayed by its own children, immolated before his own eyes,—or the home-troubles it would bring to his fireside.

But the men who voluntarily assume the direction of public, or even private, affairs, must be ready for any emergency. Nobody has any right to assume that everything will go right. Nor is there any ground to suppose that Mr. Lincoln did. On the contrary, his inaugural address clearly proved that his eye had pierced the probable future,—not, indeed, all that future which has since become history, for human ken could not reach so far. But that he has had to confront more surprises and grapple with more difficulties than could have been known to or anticipated by any human intelligence, will hardly be denied.

Some peculiar and fortunate qualities in his character have enabled him not only to save the country from ruin, but also to inspire and sustain a most healthy state of the body politic, in the midst of the avalanches and whirlwinds which have struck and shaken our whole system of civic life.

His first characteristic is *self-control.* He seldom, if ever, loses his equanimity. This gives room for the constant exercise of his judgment.

His second characteristic is his *good, plain, home-made, common sense.* "This is a quality," Southey said, "rarer than genius." So far as all the real business of life is concerned for men or nations, strong common sense is the surest and safest guide. Through this alembic all the unfriendly and dangerous elements of this terrible conflict have had to pass.

Another quality has mingled itself, by the laws of affinity in moral chemistry, with Mr. Lincoln's executive acts,—*humor, bonhommie, good nature.* Men have complained of him on this ground. They have charged him with *levity.* But these critics should remember one of the fine sayings of Malsherbes, the great Frenchman, "A fortunate dash of pleasantry

has often saved the peace of families,—sometimes an empire."
It is fully believed that Mr. Lincoln's cheerfulness has dissi-
pated many a cloud that lowered around the " Home of the
Presidents," and left its fragments " in the deep ocean buried."
And, last of all, *his firm faith in the durability of the republic
is unbroken.* All these qualities, united, make him what he is.

XLI.

Our New States.—The Founding of Wilderness Commonwealths.
They must be protected.—How,

By the statesmen and philosophers of antiquity the highest honors were awarded to the founders of free states. The
highest honors America has won have sprung from this same
source.

Would to God we had never reversed this principle of
eternal justice in the building of empires and the distribution of honors !

If we had always stood fast by the spirit and integrity of
the political maxims of Seventy-Six, what man or angel
could measure the strength and prosperity of our nation now ?
Who could tell how far humanity itself would by this hour
have travelled on its endless road of happiness and grandeur ?

But the Constitution of 1789 found slavery a part of the
social system of every one of the thirteen States, except Massachusetts. These States, however, while colonies, had always
regarded African slavery as a burden, and a curse on the achievement of their independence. They held "involuntary service,
except for crime," as a disgrace to a people who had fought
seven years for their own liberty. Hence a portion of them
took early measures for its abolition.

It is unnecessary to show the order in which the States
made provision for the abolition of slavery. But we may
glance at the manner and time in which slavery advanced or
receded in the legislation which has marked the progress of
our State and national politics.

FREE STATES.		SLAVE STATES.	
	Sq. miles.		Sq. miles.
Vermont	10,212	Delaware	2,120
New Hampshire	9,280	Maryland	9,356
Massachusetts	7,800	Virginia	61,352
Maine	31,766	North Carolina	50,704
Rhode Island	1,306	South Carolina	29,385
Connecticut	4,674	Georgia	58,000
New York	47,000	Alabama	50,722
New Jersey	8,320	Mississippi	47,156
Pennsylvania	46,000	Louisiana	41,225
Ohio	40,000	Texas	237,504
Michigan	56,243	Arkansas	52,198
Illinois	55,409	Missouri	67,380
Indiana	33,809	Kentucky	37,680
Iowa	50,914	Tennessee	45,600
Wisconsin	54,000	Florida	59,268
Oregon	185,000		
California	189,000		
Minnesota	83,531		
Kansas	78,418		
	992,692		849,650

Whole area of United States 2,936,160

Slave States taken out.. 849,650

Freedom owns...2,086,510

Thus we find that the area of freedom and slavery in the States recently stood nearly equal. But the process of extending slavery over free soil has for some time been effectually arrested, and all the rest of our national territory has been solemnly and forever dedicated to freedom.

Slavery has hitherto reposed its chief confidence in adducing the specious argument that since the North and the South had always, by virtue of the Constitution, held a partnership between slavery and freedom, the area of each should be very equally preserved and augmented. Hence the precedent had been established, that when one free State was to be admitted to the Union, another State should be admitted with slavery.

But the exactions of the slave party at last became so great that the free States were compelled to "shut the gate down" on any further extension of slavery. *This issue brought on the war.* Slavery must rule or ruin.

Forever afterwards the strife was limited to a single point, as I have said before :—*slavery or liberty must fall.*

This issue gave birth at once to the great act of Congress which declared that "hereafter no Territory shall be admitted to the Union with slavery."

This law has been accepted as a federal statute, and is being vigorously carried out.

THE NEW TERRITORIES, *New Mexico, Utah, Nebraska, Colorado, Dakota, Arizona, Idaho,* covering so vast a portion of the surface of the republic, are consecrated eternally to civilization. The black shadow of slavery has not polluted and cannot pollute those virgin soils. There labor will forever grow proud in the midst of its toil ; for the blighting mildew of human servitude will never fall upon those blushing plains or their rock-ribbed mountains of silver and gold.

What now must be the policy which enlightened statesmanship would dictate for the civil and military government of these budding republics ?

There was some danger that, in the immediate presence of stupendous perils pressing upon the eastern side of our empire, we might forget the hazards that menaced our western borders. That our Territories should not be forgotten is shown by the Indian massacres of Minnesota, and the murder of our citizens farther west. Other like scenes may occur at any day. It is the wrong moment for us to withdraw our protection from the scattered families and communities of the Far West. They braved every danger that confronts the pioneers who become the vanguard of our civilization. They knew how strong was the Government they were born under, and they did not feel one apprehension that in leaving the peaceful scenes of their early manhood's or childhood's home they would ever go where the shield of Washington would not still defend them. They all felt as adventurous Roman citizens did when, in the better days of the Empire, they left the banks of the Tiber to found colonies on the banks of the Thames, the Seine, the Guadalquivir, or the Danube. On the last hill-top they halted long enough to point out to the eye of their children the dome of the Campidoglio, on which they might never look again. They knew that, however far they wandered, they could not go beyond the protection of the Roman eagle. And it was only in the days of "the Decline and Fall" that this ceased to be true. Then Rome learned that terrible lesson,—that the heart of an empire may go to decay, while a distant dependency continues to flourish.

Let us avoid this danger. Our branches have not yet grown too large for the parent tree, nor must the fruit be shaken untimely to the ground. We know this is the doom which monarchy and its twin-brother despotism have written for us in the book of Fate. But our fathers held a better faith. They believed that the pen which wrote the doomsday book of nations inscribed one page for the successful and permanent establishment of liberty and self-government here, and its vindication against all domestic and foreign foes.

We have only just come to the test. The war of Independence was only the struggle of infancy to breathe free; the war of 1812, only the assertion of our rights of majority; the war with Mexico, only a brief but brilliant episode in the march of our civilization. But now a whirlwind has struck the half-grown oak, and it is struggling with the forces of the tempest in all directions. Secession is wasting its most malignant furies on the tree under whose broad branches it has breathed healthful air and beneficent protection. It has invoked to its aid every engine of destruction and every agency of malignity; it has hurled the firebrand and poisoned the arrows; it has tried to put out our national life; it has tried to wind up our history, and turn the fruit of all the heroism of our fathers, and the hopes of desponding nations, to ashes.

In the West and Southwest it has tried to make all the

Indian tribes as fiendish as itself. Every frontiersman and trapper has been tempted; every borderer's home is in danger to-day unless its master will become a traitor to the flag under which he was born.

There is but one remedy for all this, so far as our distant Territories are concerned. Our Governors and Indian Superintendents must be clothed with full military authority to vindicate the sovereignty of the Government and the absolute supremacy of the flag. They must be to us what the Proconsuls were to Rome. They can (if they are the right men) enrol for defence all our loyal citizens within their jurisdictions. And thus a wall of fire will be put along all our western and southwestern borders, which will give to those distant inhabitants a blessed feeling of security, and show to friends and foes that wherever our eagles fly, their young brood are just as safe as they would be if they were nestled under the arches of our Capitol.

The inauguration of this policy of consolidating our national system of pure and vigorous civil life throughout the whole West has received the best thoughts of the Administration, and a well-considered plan has been adopted and is being carried into effect. Freedom and the republic are growing stronger every hour.

XLII.

The Impossibility of the Final Division or Partition of the American Union.

This Union may seem to be dissolved. But it looks so only to the shallow, the doubting, or the untrue. To the innumerable host of the thinking, the believing, the loyal, and the brave, it stands stronger than ever. It is every day growing conscious of its strength. It corrects its mistakes as soon as they are detected. It recovers from adverses as fast as they come. It prepares for the future as the moments fly.

That it is impossible to produce a *permanent* division or *partition* of the Union of these States, it is only necessary to look at facts. The Union has never been *broken*. It has been threatened, barked at, hawked at, and wounded. But, like the national flag, torn and riddled though it may be in conflict, and even captured, it is the Stars and Stripes still.

To gain any difficult point, the chief obstacles must first be overcome. In order to break up this Union, certain obstructions must be got out of the way. Some of these *chevaux-de-frise* were interposed by the Almighty, who made the continent. Some were the work of the founders of the Union, who made the Constitution. Some we owe to their great and worthy successors,—the immortal post-Revolutionary statesmen, who cast over the Constitution and the Union all the light of their genius and patriotism. The *first* obstacle to remove would be *the geography of the continent.* A single river alone can and will hold these States together. The Mississippi is the eternal sentinel of the Union. Its waters spring from the cool fountains of the North, among its everlasting fountains of life-giving power. These waters, as they flow on through a score of States, mingling with each other, carry the language of empire with them, saying, *" This river is national ; it belongs to the whole country! God made it !"*

The complete exemplification of this fact and sentiment is so clearly stated in the note* below that I need not say any

---

* In the " National Intelligencer" for April 2, 1862, this whole geographical question is treated with a calm and dispassionate judgment which for half a century has distinguished that pre-eminently national and historic journal. It says :—

" We do but reproduce geographical data, often cited by others, and familiar to every intelligent American reader (but the bearings of which do not seem to be sufficiently understood abroad), when we say that whoever looks at a map of the United States will observe that the State of Louisiana lies on both sides of the Mississippi River, and that the States of Arkansas and Mississippi lie on the right and left banks of this great stream, eight hundred miles of whose lower course is thus controlled by these three States, unitedly inhabited by hardly as many white people as inhabit the city of New York. If we observe, then, the country drained by this river and its affluents, commencing with Missouri on its west bank and Kentucky on its east bank, we find that it includes nine or ten powerful States, large portions of three or four others, and several large Territories,—in all a country as large as Europe, as fine as any under the sun, already holding many more people than all the revolted States, and destined to be one of the most populous and powerful regions of the earth. Does any one suppose that these powerful States—this great and energetic population—will ever 'consent' to a peace that shall put the lower course of this single and mighty national outlet to the sea in the hands of a foreign Government far weaker than themselves? If there is any such person, he knows little of the past history of mankind, and will need to be reminded that the people of Kentucky alone, before they were constituted a State, gave formal notice to the Federal Government, when General Washington was President, that if the United States did not acquire Louisiana they would themselves conquer it. In the words of a distinguished citizen of that martial State, 'the mouths of the Mississippi belong, by the gift of God, to the inhabit-

thing further on this point. Whatever argument is presented by William II. Collins, Esq., of Baltimore, will be gladly listened to by any right-minded American.

---

ants of its great valley. Nothing but irresistible force can disinherit them.'

"If such is the interdependence of the country lying in the valley of the Mississippi that it must ever remain subject to one Government and share in one destiny, it remains to say that it seems equally impossible to draw a line of separation on the Atlantic slope east of the Alleghany Mountains and south of the Potomac. The geographical considerations which govern the decision of this question have been so clearly stated by an intelligent citizen of Maryland that we have but to recite them for the purposes of this argument. We quote from an able pamphlet addressed to the people of Maryland by William II. Collins, Esq., of Baltimore :—

"'If a line of separation is to be drawn on the Atlantic slant, where shall it run? The Chesapeake Bay and the streams emptying into it, together with the lands which they pierce and fertilize, will, for reasons stronger than human power, remain with the northern part of our country. If I read the map aright, Nature has so willed it.

"'It is deemed conclusive that, in the event of a separation, the northern part of the country will be the maritime Power. He who doubts this would scarcely be trusted by the strong common sense of the American people. If any thing in the future can be foretold, this would seem to be certain. Let the men of business, the thinkers, the statesmen, of our country, ponder this proposition well. Much depends on it.

"'Some twenty miles from the mouth of the Chesapeake lies the Hampton Roads, one of the noblest harbors of the world. Large enough to float in security the navies of the earth, its mouth is narrow, though of easy access. Fortress Monroe completely guards its entrance, and renders the harbor safe in war from an enemy. To the maritime power of our country that harbor, as a refuge from the tempest or the enemy, is of untold value. From the port of New York, and along the southern coast around the peninsula of Florida, no such harbor exists for the thousands of Northern ships engaged in commerce with the Gulf of Mexico, or with South America, or around Cape Horn, or with the West Indies. In peace and in war, Fortress Monroe is to the northern part of our country more precious than Gibraltar is to England. When England agrees to give up Gibraltar, then, and not till then, will the United States agree to surrender Fortress Monroe and the Hampton Roads.

"'But the possession of the Hampton Roads involves absolute control over the commerce of Norfolk and Portsmouth, as also of the James River, which empties into those roads south of Fortress Monroe. Will Virginia

Such is the decree of God as we read it in geography. It speaks from his own great emblems of power,—from his own visible creation.

---

ever agree that the great harbor at the mouth of her noblest river, commanding the commerce of Richmond and Petersburg, as also of her great commercial emporium, Norfolk, shall belong to a foreign Power? She cannot. She will not. It would be her utter ruin. Will the North ever agree to part with this noble harbor, so necessary to her commerce, and with the fortress which commands it? Never! Never!

"'The question, then, is, Can Virginia, with the aid of her Southern allies, take Fortress Monroe? If the South had a navy stronger than that of the North, she might take it. But so long as the North is the maritime Power, I suppose this fortress to be impregnable. Its garrison, if need be, can be relieved by fresh troops daily, its sick and wounded removed, its wants supplied even to the most minute, without any possible interference by any troops on the land. I say nothing of the Rip Raps; though that fort, if finished, as it easily can be, would add greatly to the command of the harbor, as also to the security of Fortress Monroe.

"'Here, then, is the state of the question. Virginia must have the control of the mouth of the Hampton Roads. It is indispensable to her. Under our Union, it has been guarded and defended by the General Government, for the uses of Virginia, as also of all the States of the Union. The North cannot part with it. Virginia cannot part with it. The result is of necessity. Virginia and the Northern States must belong to one Government, as they have done from the early colonial days.

"'I have spoken of the Hampton Roads as they concern the country at large, and the State of Virginia in particular. As a citizen of Maryland, I have also a word to say. The State of Maryland, and especially the city of Baltimore, has an interest in the Hampton Roads scarcely inferior to the State of Virginia herself. It is our outlying harbor on our way to and from the sea. Its sheltering bosom floats annually millions of our commerce and thousands of our sailors. Maryland can never agree, under any circumstances, that her right to use this harbor shall depend on any other tenure than its ownership by the country to which she belongs. The right to use this harbor in peace and war is one of the noble blessings conferred by the Union on the State of Maryland. This right she can never surrender.'

"The proposed line of separation, then, must run south of Maryland and Virginia. Can any one, with a map of the United States before him, draw any such line so as to meet the requirements of a possible political geography, and at the same time leave south of that line a territory and population sufficient to maintain and defend an independent Government

Second. An insurmountable barrier to the fiend of disunion exists *in a community of commerce, social and home
relations, with all their fireside souvenirs, and* A COMMON
LANGUAGE.*

---

against the will and interests of the United States? Can the 'cotton'
States' hope to form a confederacy which shall defy the Constitution and
laws of the Union? The desperate expedient of civil war, by which the
political leaders in these States sought to embroil the border slaveholding
States in their struggle, in order to consolidate their power, sufficiently
proclaimed the consciousness of their inability to erect a Government on
such a narrow basis.

"It seems, then, to result from a comprehensive view of the geographical
relations of the territory embraced in the Union, that a permanent separation of these States is a physical impossibility. At least this 'impossibility' deserves to be more thoughtfully weighed than it seems to have
hitherto been by such European statesmen as have been most impressed
by the conceived 'impossibility' of 'subjugating' the insurgents."

* Noah Webster has had more to do with the perpetuation of the Union
than any other man. His dictionary is, without question, the best lexi-
con of the English language ever made; and there is every reason to
suppose that it will hereafter constitute the chief authority for that
tongue wherever it is known throughout the world. The name of its
author is already regarded with veneration by the scholars of Europe,
while it is uttered with reverence in every district school-house on this
continent. As it appears from Merriam's press, it will stand for the
future: no considerable changes will be likely to be made in it for centuries to come. New scholars may make new discoveries, and future in-
vestigations will reward their toil in the progressive science of language;
but no accident or change, no future studies or discoveries, will be likely
to affect the fortunes of this book. Other lexicographers, starting in
early life, with the fruit of Webster's enormous labors in their hands,
may become illustrious in different departments of this illimitable science;
but the fame of their great leader will outlive them all. There may and
there will be, perhaps, as great statesmen in future times to serve the
country as Jefferson, Hamilton, and their colleagues, and in some coming
national trial men may be found who will fill responsible trusts as faithfully as our first President. But their fame will grow dim when their
contemporaries are dead, while the names of Washington and his companions will grow brighter with the progress of ages. It seems to be
one of the laws of Providence that the founders of nations shall never
divide their glory with those who come after them. Moses and Lycurgus,

From the best facts I can draw from the various censuses of the United States since 1790, I come to the conclusion that very few families exist in the South into which some Northern blood has not been infused by marriage. It is not a clearly-determined fact, but it is fair to suppose, that this

---

Romulus and Alfred, have left none to dispute their fame. Of such men history will tolerate no rivals. It is nearly as well-established a law with the founders and fathers of learning. The name of Cadmus inspires as much veneration in the Greek scholar to-day as it did in the bosom of Plato, and it will be dear to the scholars of all coming time. No future dramatic poet will ever, even in his hours of madness, dream of usurping the throne of Shakspeare; no future astronomer will lay his profaning hand on the crown of blind Galileo; a second " Paradise Lost" has never been written; the world never will look for another "Iliad;" Gibbon has made a second "Decline and Fall of the Roman Empire" impossible; Blackstone will be authority on the bench while society holds together; another "*Génie du Christianisme*" will never be called for; Edwards has written his Essay on the Will, Cooper revised his "Leather-Stocking Tales" for the far future; Halleck has done for his "Ode to Marco Bozzaris" what Gray did to his Elegy; Webster is dead, and the last ornament has been added to his colossal system by the hand of the great builder. There are many provinces in the illimitable field of empire, but the mightiest of all is in the intellectual world. He who controls the thoughts of men is their real master. If this be true in a general sense, it becomes doubly so in a special one. The maker of words is master of the thinker, who only uses them. Here is the field of the lexicographer. In this domain he reigns supreme. He stands at the fountain-head of thought, science, and civilization. He is controller of all minds; to him all beings who talk, think, write, or print, pay ceaseless, involuntary, eternal tribute. In this sense, Webster is the all-shaping, all-controlling mind and guide of this hemisphere. But he is so in a still more special sense. He grew up with the nation, he was coeval with its early intellectual origin, and he will perpetuate himself with its most distant progress. Not a man has grown out of our soil who has not drank at this parent spring. There is not a man on the continent on whom Webster has not laid his all-forming hand. His principles of language have shaped every word that is now, or ever will be, uttered, here or elsewhere, by an American tongue. His genius has presided over every scene in the nation. It is universal, omnipresent. No man can breathe the air of the hemisphere and escape it. And the sceptre he wields so unquestionably has been worthily won. It was not inherited, it was achieved; it cost a

process of intermingling has been going on so long that from
it all will be evolved a nationality which will, in spite of

---

struggle of more than half a century,—the struggle of a strong, clear
head, an honest, brave, untiring heart. No propitious accidents favored
his progress; no decisive casualties awarded the goal. The victory was
gained after a steady trial of sixty years.

Look at a few of the indices of his progress; for in the advancement of
mind there are certain reliable signs. Science, as well as machinery,
measures its revolutions. After the wheels of our new ocean-steamers
have made a million of revolutions, the hand of the dial marks one. It
was so with Bacon, Galileo, and Franklin: their books marked their progress through the unexplored ocean of learning. It was so with Webster.

America, then, the only free and, in the future, the inevitably great
nation of the earth, was just beginning her career; and Webster became
her schoolmaster. There had never been a great or powerful country
with a common, a universal language, without dialects, a unity in idiom
and pronunciation. In our own times we have striking illustrations of
this. The Yorkshireman cannot talk with the man from Cornwall. The
peasant of the Ligurian Apennines drives his goats home at evening over
hills that look down on six provinces, neither of whose dialects he can
speak or comprehend. The European *Malle-Poste*, in a day's drive, takes
the traveller where he hears a score of dialects.

This is the only country which has but one language. Three thousand
miles change not the pronunciation of a word nor the orthography of a
letter. These nearly forty republics are without a dialect or an idiom.
Everywhere, from the forests of Maine to the glowing savannahs of the
Great Gulf, and far to the Pacific coast, there are a hundred races, but
there is only one language. Around every fireside, at every desk, and
from every tribune, in every field of labor and every factory of toil, is
heard the same tongue. To Webster, more than to any or all other causes,
this nation owes its unity of language. He has been to us greater than
Alfred was to England. He has done for America what Cadmus did for
Greece.

In 1783, Mr. Webster published his first part of a grammatical institute
of the English language,—in other words, his "English Spelling-Book."
More than fifty million copies of this work have been used in this country.
During the long period he was maturing the dictionary, his entire revenue
was derived from the profits of the Spelling-Book, at a premium for copy-
right of less than a cent a copy. It has been the guide of every American:
—more than a million of copies were sold last year.

His herculean labors had begun. This little book, which is manufac-
tured for three cents, and costs the Oregon farmer twelve and a half for his

every thing, result in a national sentiment. The national sentiment springing from this source will, in any event, become too mighty to be resisted. If it be interrupted for a time by the din of war or the clamor of sectionalism, it will assert its rights to be heard at the bar of justice and before the jury of the world.

Not less than a quarter of a million of marriages between the men and women of the North and the South have been sanctified and ratified since Washington died. Besides, our citizens from every State have had and held confidential or open commercial communications with their friends in and through all the other States. So that we find a web and woof of commercial relations embracing and enfolding the great majority of our Northern and Southern people. Life on the one side is life on the other. So it is with death.

Woman! her great and all-controlling power is omnipotent here. Wherever this gentle and gifted Caucasian angel dwells, she instinctively clings to the sacred altars of home. In her supreme devotion to those she loves, reason

---

boy, ended with the work we are now speaking of, which glitters through the plate-glass doors of the library of the Queen of England, and which always lay open on the table of Hallam, the patriarch of history and the chieftain of British literature. We know of no man now living or who flourished in the last age, with whom he can be compared. He was a far more learned lexicographer than Johnson, and his dictionary has superseded his altogether. His fame is settled on an eternal foundation: he enters into the every-day thoughts of millions of men. He has educated thirty million living men,—not one of whom can ever forget his teacher,—each of whom, in his wanderings through the world, goes as the herald of his master, thus diffusing his fame around the globe and multiplying the army of thinkers and speakers who are to transmit it from age to age. Only two other men have stood on the soil of the New World who are so sure of immortality,—its discoverer, COLUMBUS, and its savior, WASHINGTON. Webster is its great and perpetual Teacher; and the three make up our trinity of fame. All careful readers of history know that nations speaking a common language are not long divided by political events.

has no place; it is love; and love blots out argument. It will die before it will argue. How, then, can Southern women be expected to divorce themselves from all they have to live for on earth? Even if they wear "the white, red, and blue" in their very hearts, must they not flutter the kerchief when the "rattlesnake flag" floats by? Then who can count the disappointments and troubles of so many homes, where hearts are half or whole broken, and all the blessed hopes that fed youthful visions withered, dead? All these elements of union have existed before; and, although these heart-strings may now seem to be paralyzed, they will again wake to the touch of friendship and tremble with the passions of love.

Commerce makes her own rules. She regulates all the oceans; she digs all the canals; she builds all the ships; she is the handmaid of human want and human luxury. She is already impatient to unfold her dove-wings for a new flight when this deluge is passed.

Again: before we destroy this Union we must overcome still another obstacle. We must enter every house and home and heart in America, and tear away the images of Washington, Jackson, Webster, Clay, and all their heroic peers.

No American believes this can be done. The traitor is not born who can rail at these names. They have passed into history. They belong to *the world* now,—not to America alone. They have been solemnly transferred to humanity,—that great keeper of all earth's hopes and treasures. There they are safe.

What said Jackson in December (10), 1832, when by one bold act he sent Nullification howling back to its South Carolina home?

In closing that memorable proclamation, he thus speaks:—

" FELLOW-CITIZENS :—The momentous case is before you. On your undivided support of your Government depends the decision of the great question it involves, whether your sacred

Union will be preserved, and the blessings it secures to us as one people shall be perpetuated. No one can doubt that the unanimity with which that decision will be expressed will be such as to inspire new confidence in republican institutions, and that the prudence, the wisdom, and the courage which it will bring to their defence will transmit them unimpaired and invigorated to our children.

" May the great Ruler of nations grant that the signal blessings with which he has favored ours may not, by the madness of party or personal ambition, be disregarded and lost; and may his wise providence bring those who have produced this crisis to see their folly before they feel the misery of civil strife, and inspire a returning veneration for that Union which, if we may dare to penetrate his designs, he has chosen as the only means of attaining the high destinies to which we may reasonably aspire.

" In testimony whereof, I have caused the seal of the United States to be hereunto affixed, having signed the same with my hand.

"Done at the city of Washington, this 10th day of December, in the year of our Lord one thousand eight hundred and thirty-two, and of the independence of the United States the fifty-seventh. ANDREW JACKSON."

What was the language Webster held at the same crisis, and on the most august occasion the Senate-Chamber had ever witnessed?

Familiar as these wonderful words may be to many readers, I cannot let these sheets leave my pen till I inscribe them here; and the man who does not respect me the more for doing it may have what comfort he can in loving his country less heartily than I do.

In reply to Senator Hayne, of South Carolina, Webster said,—

"I profess, sir, in my career hitherto, to have kept steadily in view the prosperity and honor of the whole country and the preservation of our Federal Union. It is to that Union we owe our safety at home and our consideration and dignity abroad. It is to that Union that we are chiefly indebted for whatever makes us most proud of our country. That Union we reached only by the discipline of our virtues in the severe school of adversity. It had its origin in the necessities of disordered finance, prostrate commerce, and ruined credit. Under its benign influences, these great interests immediately awoke, as from the dead, and sprang forth with newness of life. Every year of its duration has teemed with fresh proofs of its utility and its blessings; and although our territory has stretched out wider and wider, and our population spread further and further, they have not outrun its protection or its benefits. It has been to us all a copious fountain of national, social, and personal happiness.

" I have not allowed myself, sir, to look beyond the Union, to see what might lie hidden in the dark recess behind. I have not coolly weighed the chances of preserving liberty when the bonds that unite us together shall be broken asunder. I have not accustomed myself to hang over the precipice of disunion, to see whether, with my short sight, I can fathom the depth of the abyss below; nor could I regard him as a safe counsellor in the affairs of this Government whose thoughts should be mainly bent on considering, not how the Union should be best preserved, but how tolerable might be the condition of the people when it shall be broken up and destroyed.

" While the Union lasts, we have high, exciting, gratifying prospects spread out before us for us and our children. Beyond that I seek not to penetrate the veil. God grant that in my day, at least, that curtain may not rise! God grant that on my vision never may be opened what lies behind! When my eyes shall be turned to behold, for the last time, the sun in heaven, may I not see him shining on the broken and dis-

honored fragments of a once glorious Union, on States dissevered, discordant, belligerent, on a land rent with civil
feuds or drenched, it may be, in fraternal blood! Let their
last feeble and lingering glance, rather, behold the gorgeous
ensign of the Republic, now known and honored throughout
the earth, still full high advanced, its arms and trophies
streaming in their original lustre, not a stripe erased or polluted, nor a single star obscured,—bearing for its motto no
such miserable interrogatory as, 'What is all this worth?' nor
those other words of delusion and folly, 'Liberty first, and
union afterwards;' but everywhere, spread all over in characters of living light, blazing on all its ample folds, as they
float over the sea and over the land and in every wind under
the whole heavens, that other sentiment, dear to every true
American heart, 'Liberty and union, now and forever, one
and inseparable!'"

The spirit of sectionalism was rebuked; Nullification
hung its head; the majesty of the Constitution was asserted.
The glorious Union of these States became a new source of
pride and exultation, and ever afterwards Daniel Webster was
called THE DEFENDER OF THE CONSTITUTION.

But, foiled, defeated, and rebuked as the spirit of Nullification was, the leaders of that party had succeeded in gaining
a majority in South Carolina; and a convention was held at
Columbia, which declared that Congress, in laying protective
duties, had exceeded its just powers, and that its acts from
that period should be regarded as utterly null and void,—that
after February 1, 1833, the validity of that national statute
should be denied by the courts of the State, and that every
man in that Commonwealth who held an office should take
an oath to disregard it. And, finally, the convention declared
that if any attempts were made by the National Government
to enforce obedience to its statutes, they should be repelled,
and from that time "the State of South Carolina would throw
off all allegiance whatever to the Federal Constitution, and

assert and maintain her independence as a sovereign and independent State." The convention also put forth an address to the people of the United States, avowing the doctrines of Nullification, and calling upon all other Southern States to join with her in "a dissolution of the Union."

On the 27th of the following November, the Legislature of South Carolina met at Columbia. The Governor, in his message, approved of what the convention had done. He recommended the Legislature to request the President of the United States to withdraw the military forces of the Federal Government from the arsenal at Charleston, that the militia should be organized, that the services of twelve thousand volunteers should be accepted, and that appropriations should be made for carrying on a war with the United States.

It was fortunate for this republic that General Jackson then stood at the helm. Regardless of every consideration except those pure and lofty motives which sway the action of great and patriotic minds, he decided at once upon his course. He determined to crush the "Monster of Disunion;" and on the 10th of December, but a few days after the message of the Governor of South Carolina had been received, he published his memorable proclamation.

25*

XLIII.

The Great Republic still moves on in the Consciousness of its own Security.

THERE is no better way to test the integrity and power of a man or a commonwealth than to watch them in periods of trouble.* At those times only does true character come out.

---

* In the excitements of a great civil war and the struggle for national existence, our Government still shows a sublime faith in its perpetuity, and perfects its plans for the agricultural progress of the nation. The sword and the ploughshare, the spear and the pruning-hook, have worked together upon the problem of civil liberty.

No appeal has been made by the Government for the planting of extra crops to supply its soldiers in the field, or to gain by exchanges with foreign nations the means of carrying on the war. The Government has looked calmly and confidently to the future. This faith has been strikingly manifested in the organization of the Department of Agriculture during the darkest period of the war, and in appropriations for carrying it on, small, to be sure, compared with the magnitude of the interest, but increased from $60,000 (usually given to the Agricultural Division of the Patent Office) to $105,000 for the enlarged operations of the Department. No longer an appendage to a mere bureau, it has assumed the full dignity of a Department, and its establishment constitutes, on the part of our national legislators, a graceful recognition of the importance of *agriculture*, the first and most extended of our national labors. Its object is, to get and diffuse practical information upon agriculture; to perfect and put in operation a reliable system of statistics; to procure, propagate, and disseminate new and promising varieties of seeds and plants; to experiment in the acclimatizing of exotics of probable value to our rural industry; and to maintain a watchful guardianship over the interests of agriculture.

Nor is this the only benefit to the tillers of the soil, who furnish the sinews of war. The same Congress, in the same session, passed an act donating public lands to the several States and Territories, which provides

In this respect the order of nature seems to be reversed. The darkness of misfortune lights up the object, while the full noonday conceals it.

Neither men nor nations ever develop their native characteristics in times of florid prosperity. It is only when the storm comes that the individual, the oak, the ship, or the community show their real strength. Then there is and can be no concealment of weakness or defects. It seems to be a law of nature that every thing must pass through the crucible before its qualities can be determined. There is a Mint for Governments as well as for the precious metals. Governments pass through this Mint in civil revolutions, which either save or destroy them. What, then, is the surest test to apply to nations while they are going through foreign or civil wars? I would answer, *How strong is their consciousness of security, and how do they prove it?* By prosecuting their public works as in times of peace!

----

for colleges for the benefit of agriculture and the mechanic arts. It gives thirty thousand acres of land for every Representative and Senator in Congress, or *more than ten millions of acres* in all, for the establishment *of an Agricultural College in each State which may accept the generous provision.*

This initial step in aid of practical education is not the work of an old Government.

Thirty-five years ago, the annual average of our agricultural exports was fifty million dollars; when the war of the rebellion broke out, these exports were increased to nearly three hundred millions; and the astonishing fact is now manifested that, while the ports of the South are closed, and a million of laborers are withdrawn from the North, a vastly larger export has since been made of the products of loyal agriculture than ever before. The following exhibit of exports is illustrative of this remarkable increase:—

	1860.	1861.	1862.
Indian Corn	$2,399,808	$6,890,865	$10,387,383
Wheat	4,076,704	38,313,624	42,573,295
Flour	15,448,507	24,615,849	27,534,677
	$21,925,019	$69,850,338	$80,495,355

This rule we learn from all the great nations of antiquity. The public edifices of the Asiatic empires, those of Egypt, Greece, and Rome, went on uninterrupted, their enduring structures were uninterrupted, in the midst of all their foreign wars and home convulsions.

It has been so with great modern nations. The Escurial of Madrid, St. Peter's at Rome, St. Paul's at London, the Duomo at Milan, the palaces of Paris, the wonderful edifices of Russia,—all were founded, carried on, and completed in the midst of constant convulsions at home and abroad; and yet all these nations have either filled the full measure of civic greatness, or are now in the meridian of their power.

What corresponding signs do we discover in the United States during this terrible rebellion? *Every sign of conscious strength.** No public work has been suspended, except

---

* On the 22d of April, 1863, in the chapel of the University of the City of New York, Hon. and General Henry Wilson, of Massachusetts (Chairman of the Military Committee of the Senate of the United States), who has procured the passage of the act incorporating a National Academy of Sciences, said,—

" GENTLEMEN:—I hold in my hand the Act, passed in the closing hours of the Thirty-Seventh Congress, 'To incorporate the National Academy of Sciences.' In compliance with many kind requests, I am here to call the corporators to order. In rising to perform this agreeable task, I crave for a moment your indulgence.

" This Act, under which you have met to organize, incorporates in America, and for America, a national institution, whose objects, ranging over the illimitable fields of science, are limited only by the wondrous capacities of the human intellect. Such an institution has been for years in the thought and on the tongue of the devotees of science; but its attainment seemed far in the future. Now it is an achieved fact. Our country has spoken it into being in this ' dark and troubled night' of its history, and commissioned you, gentlemen, to mould and fashion its organization, to infuse into it that vital and animating spirit that shall win in the boundless domains of science the glittering prizes of achievement that will gleam forever upon the brow of the nation.

" When, a few months ago, a gentleman whose name is known and honored in both hemispheres expressed to me the desire that an academy of physical sciences should be founded in America, and that I would at least

from the exhaustion of appropriations through the villany or prodigality of that Administration which, through treason or imbecility, ushered in the rebellion.

On Mr. Lincoln's accession, the necessity of resuming these labors received early attention, and, the means being at once provided, they all went on. Among them were the *Capitol*, the *Treasury Building*, the *Aqueduct*, and other works of vast public utility, all of which were continued, and are going on now, day by day, with the steadiness of sun-

make the effort to obtain such an act of incorporation for the scientific men of the United States, I replied that it would seem more fitting that some statesman of ripe scholarship should take the lead in securing such a measure, but that I felt confident that I could prepare, introduce, and carry through Congress a measure so eminently calculated to advance the cause of science and to reflect honor upon our country. I promptly assumed the responsibility, and, with such aid and suggestions as I could obtain, I prepared, introduced, and by personal effort with members of both Houses of Congress, carried through this Act of Incorporation, without even a division in either House.

* * * * *

"The suggestion was sometimes made that the nation is engaged in a fearful struggle for existence, and that the moment was not well chosen for such a measure. But I thought otherwise. I thought it just the fitting time to act. I wanted the *savans* of the Old World, as they turn their eyes hitherward, to see that, amid the fire and blood of the most gigantic civil war in the annals of nations, the statesmen and people of the United States, in the calm confidence of assured power, are fostering the elevating, purifying, and consolidating institutions of religion and benevolence, literature, art, and science. I wanted the men of Europe, who profess to see in America the failure of republican institutions, to realize that the people of the United States, while eliminating from their system that ever-disturbing element of discord bequeathed to them by the colonial and commercial policy of England, are cherishing institutions that elevate man and ennoble nations. The land resounds with the tread of armies, its bright waters are crimsoned and its fields reddened with fraternal blood.

"Patriotism surely demands that we strive to make this now discordant, torn, and bleeding nation one and indivisible. This National Academy of Sciences will, I feel sure, be now and hereafter another element of power to keep in their orbits, around the great central sun of the Union, this constellation of sovereign commonwealths."

rising.   The matter will admit of some illustrations of the philosophy of the subject.

None but a few timid people have ever been afraid of this rebellion.   Every just and good man has wept over it in bitter sorrow.   But it has inspired no deep or lasting alarm among men of firmness, patriotism, and common sense.   The calmness of the surface of our public and private life has been disturbed, but the deep fountain has still been sending forth unceasingly its crystal waters, speaking the language of the heart of the nation, which proclaims its unbroken faith in the eternity of the Republic.

The country came up to a level with its institutions,—to a level with its great historic acts.   For some time our institutions had been superior to the acts of the people and their Administrations; but the all-engrossing cares and selfish interests of life had left the fortunes of the United States at the mercy of intriguing politicians.

But when the alarm-bell sounded, all true men sprung to their feet, and came to the rescue.   Even Indians fight for our Government.*

   *   *   *   *   *   *

---

* While the descendants of the Anglo-Saxon are engaged in a heinous rebellion against a Government which stands a monument of human liberty and civilization, what a beautiful and undying tribute to that Government, and an endearing and imperishable memento of the fidelity of the sons of nature,—the red man,—is the page of history recorded below!   Driven from his native hunting-grounds, to which he held an indisputable birthright, and compelled to seek new fields and new games, hunted and persecuted by the white man, cheated by false promises, his brain maddened and blood poisoned by the "fire-water," and almost beggared, depending upon the scanty allowance afforded by his trespassers, still his Indian instinct is not dead to his allegiance, and he now girds on the armor of the warrior and sheds his life-blood in defence of the Constitution and Government.

For some months preceding active hostilities between the North and the South, the loyal and true Cherokee and Creek Indians—appreciating the danger that was menacing our free institutions, which, while it had deprived them of their hunting-grounds, had placed in their hands the

The spring mornings in Washington are as fine as they are in Italy,—finer, if possible. The other morning (June 3,

---

appliances of more civilized modes of living, particularly in the culture of the ground—formed secret Union societies, for the purpose of strengthening the bonds of union in their midst and rendering efficient service to the Government. These Spartan bands held private meetings, in order the more effectually to mislead the rebel commissioners, then in their midst, from Georgia. Each member wore in the lappel of his coat a common pin, ingeniously inserted in such a manner as not to be mistaken; and so well was their secret kept that even those who had noticed the badge were induced to believe that it was a tribal insignia, and they were consequently given the *sobriquet* of "Pin Indians." In the early part of 1862, General Ben McCulloch completely surrounded their nation with a force of some fifteen thousand rebels, and endeavored by every art to enlist them in the Southern cause. But, while manfully spurning their bribes and scorning their threats, though temporarily restrained from espousing the cause of the Union, the disastrous defeat of the rebel McCulloch at Pea Ridge freed them from the restraint, and enlistments were immediately commenced, which resulted in raising a regiment of loyal Indians in a few days, and two more regiments in some six weeks,—the first composed of Creeks, and the two last of Cherokees. They were immediately placed under command of General Blunt; and their first engagement was at a point about eight miles east of Port Gibson, in which Lieutenant-Colonel Taylor, a rebel Cherokee, and one hundred others were killed, twenty-seven prisoners taken, and the rest routed. After this followed the battles of Newtonia, Mo., Maysville, Cane Hill, Prairie Grove, Van Buren, and Fort Davis, Arkansas, in all of which their prowess as soldiers was not only displayed,— crowning our arms with success,—but a singularly high degree of humanity and civilization, which renders them peculiarly prominent, when compared with the Indians in the rebel service, for their Christian advancement, and from which, we regret to say, some of our own soldiers might draw a profitable lesson.

Nor did this beautiful devotion arise from any mercenary motives. On the contrary, they were surrounded on all sides by the rebels, as also hostile tribes, and to have thrown themselves against the Union would have been a great advantage pecuniarily. In fact, their great temporary interest was with the rebellion; and only the loftiest promptings of duty, and an enlarged Christianized idea of the old Union and its mission in the benefits resulting from its preservation to the Old as well as the New World, could have impelled these noble sons of nature to pursue the course they did. And, although their homes have been desolated, a grateful *nation* will not withhold its reward.

1863), just as the languishing foliage, all covered with dust and wilting with heat, seemed to be doomed to another day of drought, a glorious shower came up and baptized the whole scenery of Washington and its environs with the distilled waters of heaven.

Every living thing rejoiced. The birds began to twitter from every tree, and just before sunrise their choral anthem was warbled up into the deep-blue sky.

The scene from the east steps of the Capitol was beautiful beyond description, and strange as it was beautiful.

The contrast was grander than art and historic associations alone could make; for it grouped into one picture all that art, history, and nature can cluster.

Above rose the gorgeous Capitol, crowned with its superb dome, slowly but securely rising to its completion,—the finest if not the largest dome yet swung in the heavens by the hand of man.

Opposite, in the Capitol Park, stood, in pure bronze, the sublime statue of the Goddess of Liberty, solemnly contemplating the great Temple of Freedom erected to her honor. The calmness of her look and the serenity of her attitude bespoke *consciousness of security* for the approaching triumph of the Republic and its worshippers.

Just beyond sat Washington, in Greenough's marble, surrounded by all the symbols of patriotism and statesmanship.

Still farther on, nearly hidden by the glistening foliage, stood the old Capitol,—once occupied by sages, now crowded with traitors.

Contrast all this with any scene at the South, where the arts of peace are going to decay, that the infernal art of war may work its desolations!

At no one moment since the insurrection began has any act of the Government in any of its departments displayed the least consciousness of weakness or danger. It did not in the beginning foresee how vast the outbreak would grow to be, nor did anybody else. But it has marched with the rebellion and shown itself fully competent to suppress it.

With this object in view, Congress displayed no hesitation in clothing the President with all the authority he needed to meet the great emergency; and although, as events have since proved, broader and sterner measures could advantageously have been adopted, yet it is exceedingly doubtful if Congress or the people would readily have acquiesced in the raising of more men or more money *at the time*. It required new developments to prepare the nation for the unparalleled expenditures and legislation which were afterwards adopted with unanimity and hailed with applause. But in no act of Congress or the people has any sign of weakness or hesitation been shown.

With officers in the civil and military service the case has certainly been far different; for blunders without number, cowardice in the face of the enemy, secret treason, and foul intrigue have been far more formidable obstacles to the vigorous prosecution of the war than all the ferocious hordes of the armed rebellion, with the acknowledged courage of the rank and file and the admirable military genius of their desperate leaders. Before such fearful elements of discomfiture and trouble, all the mystery of the protraction of the war and of many of its repeated reverses melts away.

This, however, by no means argues any conscious weakness on the part of the Administration, or the people, or the cause; nor does it lessen the certainty of final success. It only causes delay. But this delay brings with it incalculable sacrifices of life, happiness, and treasure,—a terrible holocaust, indeed, to be offered up on the altar of incapacity, cowardice, intrigue, and treason.

How unlike all this among *mere* politicians* and place-

---

* Any attempt at compromise with rebels in arms would sound the tocsin of revolution. There is no danger that Mr. Lincoln will attempt it. There is no evidence that he has ever thought of it since the rebellion be-

seekers, to the higher and better spirit of the masses of our people, who have no aspirations in politics except for the safety, the honor, and the endurance of the Republic! On more than one occasion since the first battle of Bull Run have I stood on the Capitol, or the Treasury building, listen-

---

gan. If he should hesitate, he is lost. If the politicians should vote it down, *the army will carry it through.* The army have made the sacrifice, —not the politicians; and they will have their reward. A million bayonets are lifted, and those who carry them have sworn vengeance for the blood of their brothers unrighteously shed. It cometh up from the ground!

Politicians, beware, and do not provoke the wrath of that patriotic host; for if they turn to wreak their vengeance on you, not a copperhead will be left above ground. You have heard some mutterings of half-suppressed indignation—some notes of warning—from the army. You can intrigue in secret conclaves, bully in lobbies, corrupt the press, buy votes in ale-houses, and live in luxury while the army is bleeding! But that army will be on your track. Secession and rebellion at the North, as at the South, must die.

The citizens of all the free and border States now in the army have spoken on this subject. Appended are two, selected from the proceedings of regiments and brigades :—

" They tell us, as they did at the outset, ' You are knaves and cowards,— mudsills; and five of you are not equal to one of us in battle;' and, in their incomprehensible arrogance and self-conceit, they still expect to beat the reveille and have roll-call at the base of Bunker Hill Monument!

" Under these circumstances, we are more than ever for the war. We are now, henceforth and forever, in favor of carrying on the war in dead earnest; we are opposed to all at home who oppose the war, and cry ' peace, when there is no peace,' and can be no peace except at the expense of our nationality, of our honor and manhood; we admonish all such as counsel peace and offer their sympathies to our enemies, that they are making a damning record for themselves and their descendants for all time to come; and we furthermore suggest most respectfully to all who feel competent to criticize the war and tell us how ' battles should be fought and victories won,' to shoulder the musket and come down to the front and give practical evidence of their ability in the science of arms and the duties of the soldier."—*2d Brigade, Indiana.*

" There will come a day when we shall return as citizens; and then will come a day of retribution to the wretches who have taken advantage of our absence to seize a power which does not belong to them,—since we have rights as citizens, although we are soldiers. Let the traitors tremble at the day of our return."—*109th N. Y. Vols.*

ing to the heavy boom of artillery that came rolling over the Potomac from a neighboring battle-field, mingled with the sharp clicks of a hundred hammers and chisels of honest mechanics, who were unconcerned for the safety of the country, believing with the firmest faith in its strength and lastingness, and wielding strong muscles in the citizen work of gaining their bread by the sweat of their brows.

Such faith and such works were characterizing at the same hour every field of labor, thought, and achievement throughout the free States,—all their workshops, all their arsenals, all their district school-houses, colleges, and higher seats of science and learning. From the lowest to the highest scenes of social life, the great heart, the clear brain, and the strong arms of all true Americans were earnestly directed to the duties before them, firm, hoping, cheerful, and brave. Never did a nation before pass through any great civil war with so little shock to society, with so little disturbance to the every-day occupations, responsibilities, and prosperity of life. Civil wars have generally been unmitigated curses while they lasted, however beneficent may have been their results. With us all this is changed. We are marching through a conflict grand beyond historic parallel, but we are marching in the sunshine. All the light beams on us. The passing shadows may sometimes fall on our pathway, but the dark side is always turned on our enemies. The Red Sea of blood will soon be passed. AND THE REPUBLIC IS THE PEOPLE. THE PEOPLE OF THE COUNTRY TRUST THE REPUBLIC.

THE END.

STEREOTYPED BY L. JOHNSON & CO.
PHILADELPHIA.